I0691573

The

Four

Samaritans

A Son Series

Novel

By

Doug Dahlgren

RH
Publishing

ISBN : 978-0-9833767-6-7

LCCN : Pending

Printed in the United States of America

Ridge House Publishing

Decatur, Georgia

Cover Concept and Design by :

Linda Stephens Dahlgren
Memory Magic

memorymagic@mindspring.com

Dedication

To:

Ruth Seay England Donald

My Mother-in-law and friend.

A strong supporter of my efforts, in this and in all I have done in the years I knew her....

Acknowledgments

Ruth Donald, Don Brooks, Dot York, Blane Woodfin
Patty Duke and Donna Dahlgren

Cover Design, *making the most of my wishes...*
Linda Stephens Dahlgren

The

Four

Samaritans

Book Four

of

The SON

Prologue

Humanity extended back... nearly to the entrance. Disgust rapidly overwhelmed the smile he came in with, but little choice in the matter led him to his place in line.

Checking the date on his watch didn't help his attitude or change anything. The line remained what it was. Leaning out, none too subtlety, he looked forward and counted twenty-three ahead of him.

It's not the first of the month, he quietly deduced, *but too damned close to it.*

First of the month always meant long lines, but this was the sixth and still the place was full. It appeared that all of humankind was represented in this small post office. The line was a cross-section of today's society. Each one there had their own personal and singular agenda that would take time... precious time. The non-smiling attendant appeared to move slower as the line increased.

Another deep breath followed another quick look at his watch.

"Why do I do this to myself?"

To him it was only a thought. But it came out... and fairly loud. So loud, the woman in front of him turned to offer her own look of contempt.

Tipping his large hat, he smiled and shifted weight from one boot to the other.

It's my fault. He said internally this time. The package had to go today. It was a birthday gift for his mom and he had all but forgotten.

Thank God, Sis called, his mind remembered. *Things could be worse.*

He probably should have planned a trip to see her. But with all he had going on, that seemed impossible. This package was his only hope.

The post office had four windows, but only one was open. The line, now extending behind him, was a virtual eclectic salad mix. This cross-section favored no particular race, nationality or anything else. None was represented more than any other. From appearances and actions at the window, this was the first trip to a post office for most. The slow moving clerk had to explain everything in detail... twice if not more, to each customer.

Through it all his awareness of the surroundings remained keen. Those senses were suddenly kicked to a higher level.

He had noticed the man in the denim jacket and blue shirt with the red bandana more than once. This man wasn't in the line. He stood beyond the string of humanity staring at the wall. His attention seemed focused on a row of closed post office boxes. The big problem was that this guy had been doing it far too long.

The line itself moved forward and the impatient cowboy checked the time again.

Ten minutes...not so bad really, he told himself. But his real concern and concentration was now more on the man in the blue shirt with the red bandana.

After several more minutes, which seemed an eternity, the lady in front of him was finally called to the counter. Her head down, she dug deep into a large purse while shuffling her feet forward. In what seemed like a continuous motion, she pulled out a massive wad of bills and raised the money nearly head high. Then, in a loud and clear voice, she proclaimed, "I need a $500.00 money order."

That's when everything got weird.

The man in the blue jacket with the red bandana quickly slid over to the lady at the counter. He grabbed her by the neck and reached for her handful of cash.

Screams filled the post office as the man next in line dropped his package and moved a step closer to the bandit. The blue shirted bad guy kept his hold on the woman's neck. With his other hand he laid the money on the counter and pulled a .44 Caliber handgun. It was leveled at the approaching man's face.

"No hero-crap today, bud," he growled. "Got it?"

Freezing in place, the cowboy managed to keep a steel eye on the bad guy who retrieved the money with his gun hand and moved toward the door. He dragged his victim with him and threatening her all the way. "Anybody moves before I'm gone..." he swore, "and she's dead."

Once outside, he climbed on a large, older model motorcycle and stuffed the cash into his blue shirt. The thief then shoved his victim to the ground and fired up the bike. As the machine wobbled and roared away, the cowboy rushed through the door holding out his cell phone, clicking away at the escaping motorcycle.

After helping the dazed woman to her feet, he stepped back toward the building and pushed a programmed number on his phone. It was soon answered, many miles away.

"Hey... you got time to do me a favor?" the cowboy asked calmly.

"Absolutely," the voice responded.

"I'm gonna send you some pictures. See if you can make out a license number on this bike for me, quick."

"I suppose you'll want a name and address to go with it?"

"You would be correct, my young friend. I'd appreciate that."

"Okay, I'll be back to you in a few minutes."

The cowboy had yet another question. "I don't suppose my friend has gotten tired of playing dead, has he?"

There was a pause on the other end. Then Ben Shaw responded in an odd tone of voice, "I don't really know what you're talking about."

"Okay," Murray Bilstock accepted, "Just thought I'd ask."

Ben tried to reroute the conversation.

"Let me get on these pictures for you," he proposed. "I'll try to have answers for you in about an hour."

The cowboy listened. He considered taking another shot at his pointed question, but decided to let it go for now.

"Thanks my friend," he conceded. Looking around to the now gathering crowd and the mall cop approaching, he added, "I'll be right here."

1

"Is life so dear or peace so sweet as to be purchased at the price of chains and slavery? Forbid it, Almighty God. I know not what course others may take, but as for me, give me liberty or give me death!"

Patrick Henry

His paper cup was less than half full. The lunch hour was winding down at the sandwich shop and he had consumed all the coffee he could stand.

Silas glanced toward the counter. A young woman in an apron was staring at him again. The first time he caught her, Silas looked away and rubbed at the mark on his face. That simple ploy worked for a while, she was embarrassed to be caught staring at his wounded face, or seemed to be. That gambit had worn off over the hours. It was time to go.

This effort had been unsuccessful and Silas didn't care for that. He had not overheard the conversation he came to hear. The hours spent there resulted in little more than the suspicious waitress. He stood and placed a ten-dollar bill on the small table.

That should ease her curiosity, he told himself and smiled at her as he walked toward the door. This sandwich shop was on Sunset Drive in Grenada, Mississippi. Not far from the large farm owned by Congressman Clyde Kinkaid. Many of his employees were known to grab their lunch at this shop. *Just not today,* Silas thought in frustration.

Farm employees did not wear uniforms or tags to identify themselves, but Silas' information indicated they did drive vehicles marked "CK Acres." All the cars or trucks he'd noticed today were privately owned. That seemed odd in itself.

Silas climbed into the van he'd purchased for this use and began to remove his disguise. The blond wig and moustache, the black horn-rimmed glasses and the overstuffed shirt that added thirty pounds to his appearance came off. These "tools" were placed into the same bag from which he retrieved a worn tee shirt and a cap. Rubbing the top of his head to pull his real hair back, he put on the baseball cap with the letter "M" boldly showing on its front. Other than the still obvious scar on his face, his appearance was completely different. Silas glared and glanced around while sliding into the driver's seat. He turned the ignition key and the van jerked forward.

His room at the Best Value Inn was less than a mile to the south, but Silas went the long way around. Rules that had always worked before were being revived.

Parking in front of the Inn, the foiled hunter walked through the lobby making sure he was noticed, and then walked down a hall towards his room. Just past that door was a side exit to the rear of the complex. He paused momentarily at his room, then sidestepped to the exit door and out to the back lot.

His Mercury sat near the end of the building, under an oak tree. It took less than a minute to switch out bags.

Back in his room, Silas laid out a new disguise and studied his notes again. His reason for being here was to verify Kinkaid's selection for "removal." This afternoon had proven fruitless and the scheduled time was winding down. What else could he do to verify this man's guilt? The heinous crimes were not tied to him as the rules required.

CK Acres had almost doubled its size in the past six months. The additional land was primarily undeveloped and came from three former owners. The last to sell had been a vigorous and vocal holdout.

Charles Callum had refused to sell at any price, until the untimely death of one of his sons. An accidental electrocution by a downed power line took the boy suddenly. Eyebrows were raised, but little else came of it. From that point Mr. Callum was a changed man. The papers were signed mere days after the funeral and Charles Callum would take his own life a few weeks later.

Kinkaid had been on the "watch list" for nearly a year already. This latest incident moved him to the top of that list.

Stan Parker worked for Mississippi Power as a line crew chief. His connection to Kinkaid was vague, but they did know each other. Ben had already verified a deposit made into Parker's bank account, $15,000.00 within a week of Callum's son's accident. Parker's alibi on the day of the accident was ironclad for him personally. But word had come through the Internet that one of the crewmen was having trouble dealing with his role in the plot. That lineman often ate at the lunch shop with members of the CK Acres crew. One young woman in particular would share a special table with him and they would talk. But neither was there today.

As Silas studied his notes, the local TV news played in the background. An alert caught his attention. The story was of little interest except to the families and the local community, but Silas leaned back and took it all in.

The power company lineman and the young female employee of CK Acres had been found dead. A murder-suicide it was called, a lover's spat gone out of control.

Silas laid down his papers and crossed his arms high on his chest. The report was over as quickly as it had appeared, but the hunter's quest was now satisfied.

All neat and tidy, ran through Silas' mind. The rumored conversations at the lunch shop were verified and clearly had been overheard by more than Silas' informant.

In the local Grenada area that would be that. The leak had been sealed, the tie to Kinkaid seemingly broken with no harm to the congressman. But Kinkaid and CK Acres were not aware of the guest in town, one who took this news in an entirely different way. It was the confirmation he had sought.

That guest, who now began to pack, had his proof. It was time to return to Georgia where he would finalize plans for the removal.

~

"I've got good news and no news," Ben said when Murray answered his call.

"Okay, what's the good news?"

"That bike tag is registered to a Montgomery Thompson in Dallas."

8

"And?" Murray puzzled.

"It was stolen from him over a year ago."

Murray shook his head in disgust. "That would be the 'no news,' huh?"

"Afraid so," Ben told him. "There weren't any leads at last check. The insurance company wrote it off."

"You got that from the tag?" Murray asked.

"Well, yeah...and the registration."

"What kind of bike is it?"

"Kawasaki 650," Ben reported from the stat sheet.

"This bike wasn't a rice burner," Murray told him. "It was an older model Harley with a fat tank. I saw it from the side before he took off."

"That makes sense in a way," Ben thought out loud. "He just replaced or swapped the tags."

"Yeah," Murray scratched his head. "Looks like I need to go at this from another angle."

"Something I can do from here?"

"Naw," the cowboy replied. "I need to do some old fashioned leg work."

"What did the local cops say?" Ben asked him.

"Ha," the laugh wasn't from enjoyment. "They told her they would file a report and to expect the feds to call. Being it happened in a post office, it's a federal crime."

"A high priority, huh?" Ben joked.

"You know it. They'll have her fill out a pile of forms to keep her busy, and that'll be it."

"This guy on the bike...he was a stereotypical biker type?"

"Classic," Murray answered. "Denim jacket, red bandana, big boots, and a huge chain at his waist."

"Tats?"

Murray had to think about that one for a second. "Tattoos? No," he finally replied, "Not that I could see, but it was cool out. They could have been under his jacket."

"Let me try something," Ben offered. "I have an idea."

The cowboy waited quietly for the follow-up.

"I've still got access to the satellite hook-up from Fernbank. Dr. Webster gave me code numbers to log on with. I'll check out some biker bars from the air, see what I can find."

"You can see a tag from that?"

"Many things are possible," Ben chuckled.

A revelation came to Murray and he blurted it out...

"That guy ain't from around here, Ben."

"What do you think? Dallas?"

"That... would be more likely," Murray assured him.

"Easy enough," Ben said while typing on his system. "I'll pull up a list of known biker hangouts in that area. Couldn't be more than two or three hundred, right?" he chuckled.

"Hopefully...not that many," the cowboy's voice was serious. "But quite a few I'll bet."

"Let me get to work then, see if I can locate that license plate."

"Okay, Ben. Oh...thanks, man. I'll get busy myself. I want this jerk."

~

Cheryl Duray woke up that morning with a shiver. She lay on the bare ground with a covering of branches and leaves. Of all the

10

troubles she had in her young life, at that moment her thoughts were of the odd weather. *This cold doesn't fit*, she told herself.

Cheryl had been missing for months and the search was all but exhausted. The upper Michigan girl had gone to Dominica, in the Caribbean, last April. The trip was her school's spring break party that she had saved up for.

Everything went fine and the group was having a wonderful time. Then, two nights before the trip was to end, Cheryl disappeared completely. Officials from the small island and the U.S. united in the search, but to no avail. She had simply vanished. There were no photos or surveillance videos. No sightings of her with anyone, no rumors of her going swimming late that night; there was nothing to go on.

Cheryl herself could only remember returning from the bathroom at a nightclub. She had been sitting at the bar and when she thought of it, even now, she would run her tongue across her lips. Her drink had become slightly bitter, not bad... just different. Her next recollection was of being held captive in a small cabin structure with opened cracks in the wood floor. She was kept there for weeks or maybe months. She had lost track of exactly how long.

She had spent many days and nights in the forest before, so that part of her peril didn't unsettle her. Cheryl had been raised an outdoors type by her father in the Upper Peninsula of Michigan. Her hometown of Kinross was near the Hiawatha National Forest.

Early on, she noticed an odd plant growing between the floorboards of her cabin.

Must have been dropped here as seedlings, she told herself.

The plant was Anise and it was not natural to the islands or anywhere with this type of warm climate. Her hunting and fishing background allowed her to know the value of this plant. The seeds

11

could be crushed into an oily mush that smelled like liquorice or tarragon, but mainly it could hide the human scent.

Through her time at the cabin, Cheryl had cultivated a double handful of the seeds. She kept them wrapped in a scrap of paper and hidden in her pants.

They had moved her again last night. The trip didn't take long at all, several minutes, but not as much as an hour. She did not drink the liquid they brought her before the move, yet pretended to be unconscious when loaded into the truck. The bag of seeds she had in the crotch of her pants went unnoticed.

Once at the new location, her captors had laid Cheryl beside four other girls outside another structure. This one appeared to be concrete block. It was new, very new. The smell of fresh mortar filled the air, even outside where they lay.

The men discussed supplies still in the rear of the truck. As they walked back to it, Cheryl saw her opportunity. She jumped up and ran.

Knowing they would have to get dogs to hunt her down, she had some time before they would start the search. Running a jig-jag pattern through the jungle to a point several hundred yards from the truck, Cheryl found a shallow creek bed. She crushed the anise seeds between two stones and made a mush, enough to coat her arms, legs, and neck. With her fingertips, she smeared traces of it over her clothes before standing and stepping into the softly running water. Walking carefully against the flow, Cheryl held a handful of the remaining mush tightly in her hand.

The surrounding vegetation was strange to her, but her mind dismissed it. The cogongrass and low growth, indigo bush trees obscured the huge pines that were everywhere. A thick abundance of vines and weeds wrapped itself around the trunk of a large river birch tree. It did not resemble anything in upper Michigan, but to her the tangled mess of bulging undergrowth looked like a sanctuary.

She stepped from the water, one foot at a time and rubbed the remaining mush on each foot before putting in on the ground. Crawling into the twisted brush under the big tree, she then covered herself with leaves, broken vines, and sticks.

The girl hid there as the men and dogs went by, returned and passed her again. The dogs were confused at the water line where they lost her scent. She could hear their yelps change in tone. Cheryl grew up around hunting dogs. She'd hunted with her Dad since she was eight years old. Their cries told her they were off the trail.

The Anise oil mush had worked. The water had also helped her "disappear," and the searchers went to a more remote section of the new property.

Fearful to move further with nightfall coming, Cheryl had slept where she hid. Now she was awake. Daybreak was quiet and calm. But it was cold.

The Caribbean doesn't get cold, her mind tried to alert her. But pure survival mode had kicked in. Her instincts did not listen to reason or logic. Cheryl picked a direction... and ran.

Scurrying for several minutes brought her to a large hedge of bushes. The vegetation was unlike any hedge she'd ever seen. But there wasn't time to worry about that now. They were tall. Some eight feet at least, so her first reaction was to go low. She crawled down to get through them and realized there was a fence. A chain link fence covered in heavy vines.

Chain link in the jungle? Common sense fought through the confusion. Silent thoughts cautioned her, *something is not right.*

But there was no time for rationalization. Without pause, Cheryl stood and grabbed at the vines with all her strength. She pulled looking for growth that would support her weight. Climbing the vegetation while getting footholds in the fence, she finally reached the top and half fell over to the other side.

What she saw there only added to her bewilderment. Just beyond the deep drainage ditch covered in well-mowed grass, lay ribbons of concrete. Four lanes of highway, with a median of still more well-manicured grass down the middle.

Cheryl Duray staggered to the edge of the road with eyes wide and her mouth agape in bewilderment. Her body covered in dirt and mash from the berries presented as much confusion to the passers-by as she was experiencing herself. Cars in both directions slowed and some stopped. She looked around with a blank stare as people cautiously approached to help her.

Cheryl reflexively stepped back from those coming to her aid. With her arms half raised, she continued the retreat until bumping into a flat, steel post. Turning away from those coming to help her, Cheryl saw the bright, shining metal of the piling. Her frightened gaze traced upward to the sign it displayed.

The sight sent her to her knees and she tried to steady herself with her arms. People gathered around, one wrapping her in a blanket.

Cheryl looked up again. It was still there, she wasn't dreaming. The sign, shaped like a shield, declared itself to be marking Interstate 55.

In smaller letters above that, there was one word...

"Mississippi."

2

Silas' chosen route to Mississippi had been through Nashville, Memphis and then south on I-55. The rules were clear about "never taking the same route twice," so he had left Grenada the prior afternoon going through Jackson and finally stopping in Meridian for the night.

He had been thinking about the mission while driving so did not have the radio on. His mid-morning stop at a fast food joint in Tuscaloosa, Alabama, brought him up to date on the news.

The big, flat-screen TV was talking about Mississippi as he stood in line for his breakfast sandwich, but he paid it little attention at first. He already knew of the murder-suicide, but then it occurred to him, *this was national news coverage.*

Why would that local case be national news? He listened intently as he took a seat.

The girl's name, Cheryl Duray, struck a cord and the film footage shown was of I-55 near Grenada. Silas picked up his food and moved closer to the screen.

"Missing for over five months," the report continued, "Cheryl does not know how she came to be in Mississippi and at the farm of a United States Congressman."

Silas leaned back and reached for his cell phone. He pushed number one on the speed dial.

"Hey..." Ben's voice came through. "I was wondering when I would hear from you."

"I take it you've heard the news?" Silas asked.

"Oh yeah...it's a pretty big story."

"What about Kinkaid? Where is he?"

"He tried to get out of Washington this morning, but they stopped him at Reagan Airport."

Ben waited for a response that did not come, so he continued, "looks like this mission is aborted, huh?"

Silas muttered to himself and then answered Ben, "I guess so... karma got to him first."

"Are you coming in?" Ben asked.

"How did she get to Mississippi... and not know it?" Silas queried in response.

"I'm not sure." Ben expected the question. "You want me to look into it more?"

"I do," Silas responded bluntly. Then standing from his seat, he stared at the T.V. "I'm on my way, but I have a weird feeling about this. Find out all you can, I'm about four hours out, maybe more."

"Okay...I'll start a new file on her." Ben confirmed. "I can reach out to folks from her area and see what I come up with."

"Have they said where she's from?"

"Yeah, that was in the original story...back when she went missing." Ben searched for a note he had made with that information on it. "She's from a town called Kinross. It's in the upper peninsula of Michigan...they call it the 'U-P'."

"Okay," Silas said with an unconscious nod. "Get everything you can." Then he hung up abruptly.

Picking up his egg sandwich and coffee, Silas headed for the Mercury. The target and focus had changed, but his intensity was now even higher.

~

Light snow floated down in Duluth, Minnesota. They called it "lake effects" this time of year, but it was still snow. The office of RP Pest Control had been quiet this morning. So serene, the owner had allowed his coffee to grow cold while looking out a window. The phone on his desk jarred the silence and the noise through it was like three rocks rattling in a soup can.

"How long till we can replace the 'link'?" the garbled voice asked through a distortion device. "Our chain is completely broken. I already heard from Tabuk. They're not happy."

The voice alteration was so prominent the man in Minnesota had to think about what he had heard. But he knew of the events in the news and was expecting this call.

"It could take a while, boss. CK had our biggest warehousing operation."

"He doesn't get the chance to say anything... to anybody... you understand?"

The meaning of those words rang true, even through the mangled connection.

"That's already being handled, sir."

"It better be...this is just unbelievable. How could this freakin' happen?" Frustration came through the masked voice.

"That damned new area on the farm," Minnesota replied. "He told me it had been checked out... we just don't know what happened."

The line went dead with no further response. None was really needed.

Reino Petteri leaned back in his office chair and stared at the ceiling. His concentration turned back to the window as the falling snow picked up intensity.

Much like home, he thought quietly.

Petteri often thought of Finland lately. He had been here for two years and frankly was tired of it. Now this added trouble, trouble that could mean death if he didn't handle it right.

Closing his eyes, the fingers from one hand found the bridge of his nose. It was a reflex, a move that came naturally when he was frustrated and needed to think.

~

Ben Shaw was deep in his research, running news reports of the girl's initial disappearance through a filter to sort out any special details. Problem was... there wasn't much in the way of details. She had simply vanished.

Her turning up was not a big surprise to those back home. They, those who knew her, basically expected it.

"Cheryl knows how to take care of herself," was the singular comment heard most often. Everyone noted that she was an outdoors type, trained by her father in survival skills in extreme conditions. She had been through trials most girls that age never thought of. They hunted and fished together since Cheryl was seven years old. She was also known for her tenacity and perseverance.

"A female Jonathan Crane," Ben smiled as he commented to himself. When his cell phone rang, it was lucky he heard it. Buried under a pile of newspaper printouts, Ben found it on the tenth ring.

"Hey...I'm here," he answered without listening.

"Ben?" Murray said from the other end. "Catch you at a bad time?"

"Naw...no," the boy apologized, "Just got caught up in something else."

"You find that bike, yet?"

"Oh, man," Ben sighed. "I'm sorry. This other thing sidetracked me. I'll get on that in just a bit, I promise."

"It's okay, Ben. Just don't forget me, okay?"

"No...I won't."

"Other thing, huh?" Murray quizzed.

The color drained from Ben's face. He knew he had slipped up, but he stayed quiet.

"You almost sound like you're on a case for our old friend." Murray's voice was probing and a bit sarcastic.

"Murray, I'll get on this motorcycle thing right now, I promise."

"Is it Mississippi?" Murray pushed a bit more.

"What?"

"Mississippi. You know...that girl that got loose. The congressman's ranch?"

"Yeah, right... I heard about that...last night." Ben tried to evade.

"I'm sure you did, Ben." Murray thought to himself and decided not to push it any further. "I'll look to hear something chop-chop, okay?" he followed up.

"Right away, Murray."

"Talk to you later, Ben."

Murray Bilstock wasn't really upset with the situation anymore. He knew how Jon was, how Jon thought, and why. Murray didn't like being excluded, but something told him that wouldn't be forever.

Mississippi, he thought. *Need to keep an eye on that situation.*

3

The turbo prop, Beech 1900 landed at Columbus Air Force Base in Mississippi from Andrews at 1845 hours. The main cargo was recently deposed congressman, Clyde Kinkaid.

Having arrogantly waived extradition, Kinkaid was being brought home to Mississippi for trial. The irony is that Kinkaid's initial arrest at the airport was brought on by his dismissive attitude when approached about the girl found at his farm. That, and the fact that a loaded gun was in his briefcase, allowed local authorities to detain him. It was determined, with permission of the Speaker of the House, that Kinkaid should be returned to Mississippi to respond to questions there.

He was to be held at the infamous Starkville Correctional Facility, for his own protection, until formal charges were either drawn or he was vindicated.

Kinkaid's transfer from the plane to a prison bus was uneventful, as the twenty-four mile drive to Starkville was expected to be. A special holding cell had been set up at the downtown Starkville location on Lafayette Street. The now ex-congressman would be kept in solitary confinement for his own protection.

With Mississippi State Patrol vehicles front and rear, the bus driver's route to Starkville was through low traffic areas including Old West Point Road. It was along that stretch of two-lane, just beyond the Osborne turnoff, that the attack was carried out.

A rocket-propelled grenade struck the trailing patrol car just above its front axle. The hood flew away in one piece as the engine and the interior compartment erupted in a blast of metal fragments and fire. The two patrolmen inside were killed instantly.

The flash from that blast, through the dimming twilight, caught the attention of the bus driver and the leading car of the caravan. They were distracted long enough for the car's driver not to notice the logging trailer lying flat across the road.

Standing on the brakes through the collision did not slow the car enough. Metal standards from the trailer ripped into the patrol vehicle's windshield. The impact there was fatal to one officer and trapped the other. The bus glanced off the rear of the patrol car and slid sideways, ricocheting violently from the trailer's front rack. Then spinning and rocking to nearly forty-degrees off its left side tires, it came to a stop with the rear wheels off the pavement.

Two teams of four each approached the bus from either side of the highway. Checking the front car, there was no movement. The injured patrolman lay still and quiet, which may have saved his life. The heavily armed men then quickly overpowered the shaken bus driver and the two guards on board.

Kinkaid was whisked away and as the bus driver later recalled, "he did not look too pleased about who had him."

~

The Mercury pulled into the third level basement quietly. There was no greeting party. Silas grabbed his bag from the trunk and rode the elevator to the next level where Ben was working.

"Anymore news?" he asked the young man.

Without looking up, Ben replied in a sullen tone. "Oh, yeah...but you're not gonna like it."

Silas turned his head toward Ben and stared in silence.

"My source, closest to the scene," Ben began, "tells me there was a hit on the caravan taking Kinkaid to Starkville."

Silas moved closer while he considered what he had heard. "Is he dead?" he asked.

"Nobody knows." Ben leaned back and looked at his mentor. "Whoever it was, killed three state troopers and took him away. The bus driver says Kinkaid was alive when they left with him."

"These people killed state police and left the bus driver alive?"

"Yeah, I know," Ben agreed. "Makes no sense that they'd leave a witness."

"No word of any kind since?" Silas pried.

"No...but I have ears on it." Ben assured him.

Setting his bag down against a table, Silas looked toward the elevator again. "I'm going upstairs for a while. Call me if anything breaks, okay?"

Ben nodded and Silas headed for the elevator. He made it two steps when he stopped as though hit by a board.

"What about the girl?" he asked as he turned back. "Do those with her know about this?"

"Yes." Ben moved to another computer screen and pulled up some information. "They were taking her home, but now she's in Chicago somewhere...in a safe house."

"And how are you doing looking into her?"

"Stuff is pouring in. I've got filters looking for any unique story or tidbit that's different." Ben shrugged and followed with, "It's gonna be awhile on that."

Silas once again moved to the elevator. As the door started to close, he caught it with his hand and spoke in a loud voice, "That's good work, Ben," he said. "Thanks."

~

One North Wacker Drive overlooked the river in downtown Chicago. The building's main client was a large legal firm, but one suite of offices was secretly owned by the Federal Bureau of Investigation. Converted into a secured apartment, with outer rooms for protection details, the suite sat some forty-six stories above the city.

Cheryl Durant and her mother, Rita, settled in to what would be their new home until the fugitive ex-congressman was found. The threats to Cheryl were unknown but assumed to be severe.

"What about Dad?" she asked her mother. "Where is he?"

"Cheryl, stay calm. He's locking down the house and the out buildings. There's a team of agents with him and a dozen neighbors. He will be fine."

Rita kept a close eye on her daughter. The doctors had barely any time with her before the news of Kinkaid's escape. The FBI felt a hospital setting would be too dangerous.

Stepping to a window, Cheryl opened the blinds to stare out at the river and the lights of the city. The lights were so different from what she was accustomed to. Even before her capture, her world was on a smaller scale. Land, trees and sky, lit up by stars, not street lights.

"We came to this city when I was little," she remembered. "I never thought about coming here again."

"What?" her mother was confused by that statement.

"I love the country, the woods, this isn't for me. I don't like it here."

"It's just for a short while, honey." Rita Duray smiled and reached out to hug her daughter. "I thought I'd lost you for good. We can make it through anything... after these last few months."

"I wish Dad was here." Cheryl said again.

"I told you, he'll be fine. He's a strong man," Rita reminded her. She wasn't convincing herself, she didn't need to. Her confidence in Weston was complete. And, he had raised Cheryl to be the same.

"I know, that's why I'm worried," Cheryl responded, turning from the window to look her mother in the eye. "He'll go after that creep himself. I know him, I know he will."

Rita said nothing. She pulled her daughter to her and looked out the open blinds with her own worried stare. Cheryl had amazed the doctors in her short time with them. Her ordeal had not left her traumatized as they expected. Within hours she was her confident, old self again. The inner strength instilled by years of watching and learning had allowed Cheryl to snap back almost instantly.

Just like Westy, she thought silently, *just like her Dad.*

Not only was the girl like her father, Cheryl understood him. She knew him very well. Rita knew her husband would go after those who had tried to hurt his daughter.

Rita Duray looked out at the lights along the river, hugged her child even tighter, and tried not to let her worry show. Clyde Kinkaid had a new, worst enemy. Cheryl was right.

~

By quarter past twelve that night, Ben Shaw felt as though he knew more about Cheryl Duray than her closest friend back home. She was accomplished, unassuming and liked by many. No different than thousands of other young girls around the country, except that she had vanished. Her disappearance had gained attention primarily because it had happened out of the country.

Other girls went missing, most near their homes or school. But Cheryl's case stirred memories of Aruba and an unsolved crime in that Caribbean paradise.

Big news for a while, Ben thought to himself as he threw a stack of printed materials back on the desk. *The public's attention span didn't last very long.*

That was true. It had been big news for a short time, maybe a few weeks. But then other issues took over and the media put Cheryl to the side, until now.

A beeping noise from across the room finally caught Ben's notice.

"You're kidding me!" he shouted as he pushed his rolling chair to that position. Ben had set up a program to run through the satellite telescope. It was to search biker bars and hangouts from Dallas back towards Caddo Mills looking for one specific tag number. The program had a hit.

A pub on Texas Highway 78 between Garland and Wylie appeared on the monitor. Ben zoomed in on a group of motorcycles and there it was. The nearly seventy-year-old Harley Davidson panhead clearly displayed the tag Murray was looking for.

"That's a 'fat tank' alright," Ben smiled while reaching for his phone. He hit speed dial and sat back with a confident smile.

"Murray?" he asked when it was answered. "You awake?"

"I can be... What's up?"

"I found your Harley with the stolen tag."

"Seriously?"

"Yes, sir. It's at a pub outside Wylie...on the way to Garland. The place is called Monkey Dust."

"It's there now?" the cowboy asked.

"I'm looking at it on the satellite feed."

"Thank you Mr. Ben. I'm heading that way...should he leave before I get there, can you tail him?"

"Some...I think." Ben thought about it and added, "I'm not real sure about that, to be perfectly honest."

"Alright," Murray responded. "I'll get there quick as I can."

4

Clyde Kinkaid sat in a van parked outside the Home Café in Bruce, Mississippi. The restaurant was closed, but he could pick up Internet service and news from inside the building.

"I need to get out of the country," he told the man with him.

"Boss...I think you should lay low for at least a week...maybe more."

The ex-congressman gave the man a hard look. "Lay low?" he snapped. "I can't just 'lay low'. I have business to conduct."

"Boss, there's a 'hit' out on you, man."

Kinkaid stopped and took a deep breath. "You know this?" he asked sheepishly.

"There was another team coming for your bus tonight."

"What?" Kinkaid looked confused. "What...where are they now?"

"They're in a ditch near West Point. We took 'em out. They'll be found at first light and the questions will start."

"Who sent them?" the startled man asked. "Do you know?"

"Petteri," the man answered. "We got that much out of one of them."

Kinkaid lowered his head. "So much for loyalty," he muttered softly. Then looking at his friend, he asked him, "where do I go...to lay low?"

"I've got a place over in Arkansas. You can hide there till this blows over."

"Blows over?"

"Well...I mean till Petteri's people give up."

"Where's the girl?"

"The Feds have her. I hear in Chicago... somewhere."

"What about the others? There were still four others at the farm when it was busted."

"No...we got them out of there that night," the aide told him. "When we couldn't find the Duray girl, we knew it was trouble. Two were processed and two were shipped."

Kinkaid nodded approval and muttered, "Good."

"Can that Duray girl identify you?" the aide asked him.

"No....well," Kinkaid paused to think it through. "I'm not sure. She was there when I visited two months ago." He looked at his friend as he recalled the event further. "She may have seen me...they brought several girls out from the cabin while I was in the area."

The aide pulled a cell phone from his pocket, "So she can identify you?"

"I just don't know." Kinkaid relented.

"We can't risk it."

"It was my farm, Marv. They got me anyway."

"Not if no one saw you there, Clyde." The aide seldom used his boss's first name. "We could have denial and doubt... without a witness," he said as he dialed the phone.

"So what are you going to do?"

"We've got to eliminate that witness."

Kinkaid's eyes lit up as his aide's cell call began to make sense to him. "The mayor..." he cried out. " That SOB owes me big!"

"He knows his city," Marv stated flatly. "He should know where they have her."

"But what about now?" Kinkaid asked. "The Feds and Petteri' men are after me. What do I do in the mean time?"

Putting his hand on the phone, Marv responded, "Like I said, you lay low."

"Don't toy with me, Marv." Kinkaid lashed out. "If you have an idea, spill it."

"They have to believe you're already gone...out of here."

Looking toward the closed business, the ex-official muttered, "I should be."

"Mayor Rigby, please." The aide spoke into his phone, "This is Marvin Acree. That's right, Acree." He placed his hand back over the unit to address his boss.

"I've leased a plane," Acree explained. "There's a dummy manifest and the names of three dead guys as passengers. When the FAA figures that out, it'll be flagged. Petteri will hear about it and figure that was you slipping away. All you have to do is go to Arkansas and stay out of sight for a while."

Kinkaid closed his laptop. "This thing isn't much good now, is it?"

"No, sir," his friend told him. "Not if you don't want to be found."

~

Lucy touched down just off County Road 78 about two hundred yards north of Wylie, Texas. The newer, faster Lucy Too would've taken longer to prepare for flight and this was a short trip, so the Bell 407 got some exercise.

Murray Bilstock climbed out and adjusted his black, Kevlar suit. It was no longer an exact copy of Jon's original, but the basics were the same. Two layers of Kevlar material, sewn in a quilt style with energy absorbing gel tucked into the squares, made the uniform nearly impenetrable. The hydraulic powered arm and legs gave the wearer the strength of two dozen men.

The gloves were new, as was the hood and hockey style mask Ben had fitted him with. Jon would never have approved of the mask, but Murray saw the suit as not merely defensive, but an awesome offensive weapon.

Checking his Glock, he holstered it. Murray carried his trusty chrome plated Colt 45 revolver in his left hand and walked toward the bar.

The building sat on a stone foundation with heavy timber pillars supporting the front porch area. Raw wooden slats covered the exterior and the metal windows looked oddly undersized.

The huge main door stood partly open, allowing music, loud profanities, and neon light to float through the air from within. With no other structures visible for miles, there was no one to complain.

Patron's vehicles were left at all angles in the dust and dirt around the building. There was no organized "parking area" except for the motorcycles. They were lined up neatly, perhaps for protection from cars and trucks as much as anything else.

Murray had not heard anything further from Ben and indeed, the bike he sought was still parked as he was told it would be.

Reaching into the engine, Murray felt around for a fuel line.

This thing is cold, he thought. *He's been here a while.*

Finding several sections of tubing, he pulled with the powered arm and ripped them out. The smell of gas told him he had been successful.

The armored cowboy stepped to the front door and carefully peeked inside to make sure no one was standing at the door. Then unceremoniously, he stood back, raised his powered right leg, and kicked it back through the opening and off its hinges.

Every sound except the music stopped. All eyes landed on Murray as he moved into the bar. A quick glance around the room located his prey.

At a poker table sat the man with the blue shirt, jacket, and red bandana. Before Murray could utter a word, gunfire erupted from all angles. Rounds struck and bounded off him in different directions. Some hit hard, and he could feel the slight sting as they flattened and fell to the floor. Others ricocheted into the walls, nearly hitting people at the bar and smaller tables. He'd had enough within a few seconds.

Murray raised his arm with the Colt and fired one round into the ceiling. The loud bark of the revolver brought silence to the room.

"The next one of you morons that shoots at me...dies." Murray bellowed. "Am I understood?"

The room remained quiet.

Lowering his gun hand, Murray moved toward the one he sought. As he came closer, the man in the red bandana became nervous and started to get up.

"You're coming with me." Murray commanded him.

But the man stood abruptly, tipped the table over, and ran out a rear door.

Murray calmly turned and walked back through the bar. No one stood or got in his way. As he reached the front porch area, the man in the red bandana was on his bike desperately trying to start it. Finally reaching down, the biker felt the liquid escaping from his engine. Anger flashed in his eyes. He glared at his pursuer in the black uniform and leaned back toward his saddlebags.

Murray changed the Colt to his right hand, took a step forward, and extended his arm. "Don't!" he barked loudly at the biker.

There was a slight hesitation by the man with the red bandana, but only slight. Pulling a long barrel .357 pistol from the side carrier, he tried to level it at Murray.

The Colt .45 roared again. Sparks danced from the .357 and the man flew off the motorcycle like a rag doll, landing on a bike next to his. He and the machine lay flat on the ground, a small red spot slowly growing on the man's upper chest.

Standing over him now, Murray spoke slowly and clearly, "You owe a lady $500." He reached down, flipping open the blue jacket and pulled out a hand full of bills from one pocket.

The man spit blood and tried to move, he could not. "What lady?" he demanded. "You're crazy as hell."

"You and I...we know." Murray chided him. "Don't you now?" He stepped back and ordered the gathering crowd to return inside. Then looking back at the biker, he quoted the man himself. "No Hero stuff today, right?" he reminded him.

The injured man's eyes grew to the size of dinner plates. "Who... the hell... are you?" he stammered. "Some damned Good Samaritan?"

Murray laughed to himself and stared down at the man. "I'm just a cowboy, friend," he told him. With his Colt tucked under his arm, Murray counted out $500 and threw the rest down on the injured biker. "Don't mind the comparison though," he added. "Not at all."

The man in the black suit then checked the crowd again.

"You do not want to mess with me," he warned and pointed in their direction. Then stepping over the biker, he walked into the darkness... toward the unseen Bell helicopter, Lucy.

As his friends came to try to help him, the biker thought he heard the sound of a copter in the distance, but the noise of his friends confused him.

"The shot went clean through your upper chest, man." One man pulled at him and asked, "Can't you get up?"

"I can't move my damned legs," he responded. "Hell, I can't move at all."

Another man picked up the .357 and commented, "I'll be damned! His shot sheered the hammer clean off this gun."

They opened the injured man's shirt.

"Steve, that's a tiny hole you got there, man. That bullet fragged into pieces."

Others gathered to gawk and stare. They tried to help him stand.

"Aaaagh!" the man screamed. "I can't move anything...I can't move!"

"Leave him be!" a woman hollered from the back of the crowd. She pushed her way through them and knelt down, her white uniform showing under her coat. She took a closer look at the wound. Her face went pale as she stood and ordered everyone back.

"That fragment must have clipped his spine," she explained. "Call an ambulance...now!"

5

Kinross, Michigan, has a prison, an airport and in late August every year they have a County Fair. Thirty miles below Sault Ste. Marie, the Chippewa County town was home to nearly 6,000 residents. Perhaps the most famous of whom was Cheryl Duray.

Cheryl's family lived some six miles west of the main town area. Far enough out to need a dog sled in winter to go for groceries. The family loved it there. The eight to nine months of isolation that could occur was offset by the warmth and beauty of the summer months, or weeks in many cases. Weston Duray came here for that reason.

His folks were part Swede and part French. He was raised in the Dakotas, North and South, so his always-present cowboy hat and attitude was accepted by the other Kinross inhabitants. Many had come to mimic the farmer-cowboy out of pure respect.

Weston met Rita there when she was just finished with high school and he was working in the Hiawatha National Forest as a ranger. His service in the first Gulf War had made him even quieter than he had been before, but Rita felt "at ease" with this man. Though he was eight years her senior, Rita made most household decisions. She was the boss unless there was a real emergency. In those times, Weston would step forward without question from anyone, even Rita.

They had one child, a girl. Raised with grace and beauty by her mother, while her father taught her self-reliance and survival skills. Little did he know how valuable they would be to her.

Kinross was today covered in Federal agents. Cheryl's kidnapping and escape brought not only attention to the tiny town, but with the ex-congressman's get-away, there was now also danger.

Special Agent Tom Bruster was in charge. His detail was to keep tabs on Mr. Duray, for his protection. He had gone to town that morning for an hour, tops. On his return, a quick walk around the property gave Agent Bruster cause for concern.

"Where's Westy?" he asked a neighbor who had been helping his friend gather supplies.

"Hummm?" the man lifted his hat to scratch his balding head. "He was here a minute ago."

"Come on, man." the agent pleaded. "Don't do this to me."

"Tom...I'll tell you." The neighbor walked the agent into the barn and pointed to an empty stall. "That horse needed some exercise. Westy said he did, too."

Bruster yanked a baseball cap off with one hand and rubbed his forehead with the other. "Will you tell me which way he went?"

"Into the forest...you won't find him. He's after that bastard who's threatening his daughter...again. I wouldn't want to be him, I'll tell you that much."

"He's gonna ride a horse... to Chicago?" the agent asked sarcastically.

"Naw...if I know Westy, he's got a car, a truck or hell, maybe even a bi-plane hid out in there someplace," the man pointed into the woods. "You don't understand, yet."

"Understand? What is it you believe I don't understand?" Bruster demanded.

"You don't come up here and mess with a man's family... not more than once."

Bruster stepped toward his own truck and pulled a radio receiver from the cab. "Boss...we've got a situation out here," he sheepishly reported. "Duray's gone."

~

"Gerardo, I have disturbing news from the states."

That announcement awoke a man who hardly made a bump under the silk sheets. It wasn't about his size. It was the bed... the bed was huge.

It was round and measured twenty-two feet in diameter. The room was also round with a wall of windows that faced the ocean. The entire house was opulent. It seemed to face the water from every room.

This bedroom belonged to the owner. He owned the house and the group of killers known as the Palm Cartel. They controlled Acapulco's drug traffic and afforded their leader with his luxuries.

That leader, Gerardo Palmero, managed the takeover of the area through patience.

For almost a decade, two other cartels had fought a bloody battle for the once picturesque resort city. Murder rates were counted in dozens and the violence drove out citizens and tourists alike. When the fortunes and numbers of those gangs were all but depleted, Palmero sent in his men to kill the survivors. It didn't take long.

They turned the area into a money machine. The southern coast of Mexico now provided drugs to the other provinces and several southern states. The shadow of the Palm was quieter, but no less deadly to any opposition.

"Ugggh...." Palmero groaned as he rolled over. "What is it...why do you wake me like this?"

"It is Stefan, Sir," the scantily clad female spoke clearly. "He has been injured."

That information didn't make sense at first. Stefan was Gerardo's half-brother by a different mother. Stefan was trouble. He didn't follow rules or orders well. Gerardo finally sent him away, for good...he thought.

Stefan had gone to Texas where he called himself Steve Palmer. His light complexion gave him cover from his Mexican roots. Steve became a thief, a small time hood, and a biker wannabe. Gerardo had heard little of him in the past several years.

"What happened?" Gerardo asked and crawled to the edge of his bed.

"He is in a hospital... in...Garsland...Texas," she reported.

"You mean Garland?" he rubbed his eyes, "Near Dallas?"

"Si," she agreed. "Garlands."

"He fall off his bike...or what?" the aggravated cartel leader guessed as his feet hit the floor.

"Shot...someone shoot him." The woman paused then added, "he cannot move."

Gerardo stared at the floor while that soaked in. He groomed his hair with his fingers and rubbed his face. "Cannot move...what?" he asked in low tones.

"Nothing... below his neck," she responded bluntly.

The mob leader raised his head forward and turned it to look at her. "What do we know? Who did this to my brother?"

"Someone there heard Stefan call him the Good Samaritan."

"Get dressed," he snapped at her. "You are going to Texas. Go to Stefan and find out who did this." Gerardo's fingers gripped the edge of the bed tightly, pulling hard enough to rock the entire mattress. "This Samaritan...he is finished with his good work."

6

Ben came down later than usual that morning. The smell of coffee drew him to the kitchen where Silas and Marsha sat in silence.

"Something... wrong?" Ben inquired at the scene.

"You were up pretty late, huh?" Silas asked him. There was a touch of Jon in his voice.

"About two o'clock, I guess," he replied and took a quick look over at Marsha. She sipped her coffee and kept her eyes on the table.

Silas' voice, even more tempered by Jon's influence, spoke again. "I don't pry into your business, Ben. I don't snoop," he said.

The young man stood quietly in complete confusion.

"I went down to the work area this morning," Silas continued. "To see what you'd found out about that girl's situation."

"Sure...yeah," Ben answered through creased eyebrows.

"You had a message from our friend, the cowboy."

"Murray?" Ben didn't realize at that point what it could be.

"He was thanking you...said the suit and the new equipment worked...great."

Ben was supposed to keep Silas informed of any new "toys" he came up with. The hood and mask for Murray had been kept just between them.

"Oh...those things," he tried to recover. "He wanted to add a hood... and a mask to the suit. He said it made a complete outfit."

"It sounds like he's used it already."

"Yeah...he had a thing he was working on." Ben admitted.

"Is he messing with my case?" Silas asked sharply.

"No...no," Ben started.

"Is he in Mississippi?"

"No, Jon..." he realized his mistake, but kept going. "He has his own issue he's working on."

"Do you know what he's into?" Silas asked.

"He was going after some smalltime hood," Ben recalled. "The guy stole money from a lady at the post office over there."

Silas nodded and stood. He walked to the counter and poured more coffee.

"I need you to keep me informed...of everything," he said turning back to Ben.

"I know," Ben apologized. "I know."

Marsha stood and gave Ben a hug for support. "He just feels responsible for Murray," she whispered to him. "You understand, right?"

Ben silently acknowledged that he did.

Silas spoke again, this time it was all business. "Could you see if anything new has happened overnight on our case?" He put his cup down and headed toward the stairs.

"Sure," Ben said, following him.

The two climbed the stairs to the master suite and the elevator.

~

Duluth was covered in white. It never really snowed hard, just steady all night. Reino Petteri had gone beyond being anxious waiting for a call that never came.

The news was covering the hit on the ex-congressman's prison bus, but it wasn't conclusive. *There should be a body*, he thought. *Why was Kinkaid missing?*

Lutz always calls, Petteri kept running the thought through his mind. The team leader had come to the states specifically for this job. *I'm lucky he was so close*, Petteri tried to calm himself. *If he hadn't been in Ontario for that other job, he'd never have gotten here in time.* The concern in Petteri's mind was compounded by the fact that Lutz had left his own "crew" in Canada. He took the bulk of Petteri's men for this job. Three may not seem like a lot, but it left the Finlander with only one other man he could trust.

The Finish mobster walked to his coffee maker. What was still in it was nasty. He set about making another pot. *Maybe by then I'll hear something*, he told himself.

~

Westy Duray had ridden his horse into the forest for nearly two hours. Having practically "lived" in that forest for over twenty years, Duray knew every tree and trail.

At a spot he had set up for a hunting emergency, he pulled back the covering over an in-ground dugout. It held blankets, rope and keys among other survival gear, including a 9mm, Kahr CM9, short barrel pistol. He checked the four, 6 cartridge magazines plus the one already onboard. He strapped the ACE holster on and pulled a bottle of water and some beef jerky from the hiding spot. From a sealed box, he pulled an old, flip type cell phone. Carefully wrapped batteries were checked and then installed. When it powered up for him, he turned it off and slipped it in a coat pocket.

Duray knew he was about as far out as his horse could return from, so he undid the bridle and saddle, slapped the quarter horse toward home, and put the tack equipment into the hole.

After restoring the covering and camouflage to the spot, he hiked another half-hour to where an old truck was buried in tree branches. It took a few minutes to uncover, prime the carburetor, and check it out, but it fired on the first try.

The rough terrain led to an old logging trail with deep ruts. He turned onto the trail heading south.

~

The two-way radio sounded off loudly on Captain Everett Cummins' shoulder.

"Sir, this is Stewart at the command center. Over."

Captain Cummins walked away from the group he was with at Starkville's main prison. Speculation about Kinkaid was already too thick. He didn't know what this was about, but he wasn't taking any chances.

"Go ahead, Stewart," he answered while pushing the button.

"Sir, a detail searching the area has found four dead bodies in a ditch. Over"

"Say again," Cummins ordered.

"Four, that's four dead bodies in a ditch, about three miles from the attack site."

The captain covered his radio with his hand for a second. He wanted to ask if Kinkaid was among the dead. But that would be apparent, if it were true. The Lieutenant would have said so already. He released the radio and formed his question in another way.

"Any idea who they are...over?" Cummins asked.

"No ID's, no nothing. But they're full of holes. Over."

"I'm on the way, Lieutenant." Then he added, "Keep that area secured, nobody gets in until I get there."

Lieutenant Stewart quietly nodded and then realized there was no one to see. He keyed his radio, answering sharply,

"Roger that, sir. Over and out."

7

Chicago's mayor did indeed know Marvin Acree. It was Acree who had run the mayor's campaign several years ago. That was before the operative moved to Mississippi for a more lucrative position with a U.S. congressman. An influential congressman, who had skillfully guided millions to the mayor's election bid.

"Marv," the mayor answered his phone. "How are you, my friend?"

"I'll be direct, Mr. Mayor. You have a special guest in your city. We'd like to send our regards."

"That's pretty hush-hush, Marv. Your boss has bad 'mojo' around him right now."

"It's really important to us, Mr. Mayor...and I mean really important."

The mayor rubbed his forehead before he spoke again. "Marv, call me back in an hour. I'll get the name of a good florist that's in that area for you."

"Thank you, Mr. Mayor," Marv told him. "One hour."

Silas leaned back from the table full of papers. He and Ben had been going over every detail, looking for something about Cheryl Duray that could help them.

"Ben," he asked while staring up at the ceiling. "Do you know where her father is?"

"He's supposed to be at the family farm with a protection detail."

"See what you can find out right now...I'd be willing to bet you he's not there."

Ben spun around to a computer and began typing. "Did you find something?" he asked.

"Cheryl and her dad have a plan for most contingencies." Silas picked up the document and rolled his chair toward Ben. "If there was an emergency and they were separated...tornado, fire, terrorist attack...whatever, she knew she could get hold of him within 24 hours."

"How do you know this?"

"She wrote about it several times on social media sites before her abduction."

"Then why didn't he find her for five months?"

"It was for her to find him...she wasn't able to activate their system." Silas pointed to a paragraph on the page.

Ben read the words and smiled. "Not a bad idea, actually," he agreed.

The Durays had a secret number Cheryl was to call should anything odd ever separate them, a cell number that would only be used in such a situation.

"After the given amount of time had passed, she was to call that number from wherever she was," Silas explained. "If that didn't work, they would meet two days after whatever happened...at a certain location."

Ben read on. "I don't see any location listed."

"That was just between them. The cell number and the meeting place were not written down."

The computer behind Ben began to beep as the requested information came through. He turned back to the machine and read the latest report from Michigan.

"Jon, you were right," he declared and then realized what he had said. "Sorry... Silas."

There was no change in his blank expression. "What does it say, Ben?" Silas asked flatly.

"Well...you were right for one thing," Ben answered and continued to read. "He got away from the protection detail. It says he rode off into some big national forest up there."

"When?"

"Early this morning."

Silas stood and looked at Ben. "Get in touch with our friend at the FBI. Shuck, I think his name is...tell him you need to know the location in Chicago...where they have the girl."

"You think he'll tell me?"

"Explain to him who you are...don't give anything away about me, just explain that you are trying to help. He's smart enough to put it together."

"Okay," Ben nodded. "But how is just the location going to help?"

"When she hears her Dad has left the farm...she'll try to call him 24 hours later."

"We don't know what that number is."

"Ben," Silas almost looked disappointed. "If you know where she is, you can get her number. She'll call from that room."

Ben's face dropped. "Okay, that's one for you," he smiled sheepishly.

"Get busy will you?" Silas was moving toward the elevator. "I'm going upstairs to pack some stuff. I need to go."

"What?" Ben shouted after him. "Go where?"

"Mississippi," Silas announced. "It says Kinkaid's private office is in Jackson.

"He won't be there," Ben surmised.

"Right, but I need to look around while I have the opportunity."

~

The scene was horrific. Yet through the morning mist, the bodies piled on each other in the ditch appeared peaceful, almost tranquil.

"Still no identification on any of them?" Captain Cummins asked.

"No, Sir," Lieutenant Stewart spoke up. "We took pictures for the facial recognition software. Nothing's come back yet."

"They won't be from around here."

"I believe you're right, Sir. Do you see those shoes?" he pointed at one of the bodies. "Those are European made. The soles have a distinctive pattern."

The captain stood back and smiled at his subordinate. "You picked up on that?"

"Actually, one of my men was in the service in Germany till last year. He recognized them from his time there."

Cummins nodded and walked around the ditch. "When can we get them out of there?"

"The coroner just got here. He needs to do COD and TOD and record the scene. Should be about two hours."

"Cause is pretty obvious," the captain quipped. "The time, I'll bet, was about a half-hour before that bus was hit last night."

The lieutenant acknowledged him with a head nod, but said nothing further.

"Tell your man that was a good catch." Cummins said while leaving. He pointed back to the ditch and added, "The shoes."

"Yes, Sir," Stewart replied. "I'll do that."

8

"I'm your sister...from Lubbock."

The soft whisper of her voice seemed more a dream than reality to Steve Palmer. The drugs were controlling his state of consciousness as he lay in the hospital bed. But he still struggled to open his eyes.

"Maria?" he muttered at the face hovering over him. "What are you doing here?"

"Did you hear me, brother?" she spoke a little louder. "I am your sister. Here from Lubbock. I'm here to check on you."

It began to make more sense to Palmer now. Slowly, but increasingly, it came to him. Gerardo had sent his number one girlfriend to check on his injured brother.

"Si, Maria." he told her. "How is everyone in Lubbock?" His eyebrows climbed high on his forehead as he played along. He could move little else.

Maria looked around and back toward the door. To insure they were alone.

"Who did this to you?" she asked.

"I don't know who it was." Steve said quickly. Then added, "do they still have me tied down? I can't move at all."

She stared hard at him questioningly, and then pinched him on the forearm. There was no reaction, none at all.

"You don't know what happened?" she asked.

"Look," he admitted. "I rolled a woman who was flashing a wad of cash. Some dude remembered it and he found me, somehow. I don't even know..." his voice trailed off.

"Who was the woman?" Maria inquired.

"I don't know her either. Just some broad at the post office...up in Caddo Mills."

"When was this, do you remember that?"

"Tuesday," he thought out loud. "Last Tuesday. Yeah, that was it."

Maria nodded and stood back away from the bed.

"Hey, sister," he hollered at her sarcastically. "What did the doc say? How long are they gonna keep me tied down like this?"

"It may be a while Stefan." she replied as she walked toward the door. "And you're not tied down."

"What!" he screamed as she left the room. "What are you talking about? Come back. I'm must be tied down. I can't move...I can't move, damn it."

~

Weston Duray drove across nature trails and low brush till he found Hwy 123 going south. It was paved...somewhat. Still showing centerline markings in a few places, but most of that was worn away. Few even knew this old road was here, but Duray had put it in his plan. The tattered pavement would take him to another, better maintained road just above Lake Brevort. The small, arrow shaped sign pointed right and declared, Worth Road. He was there.

One mile on Worth Road, he remembered. The old truck picked up speed as it clearly enjoyed the smooth, flat surface. Duray watched carefully through the White Birch and bright red leaf Sugar Maples lining the road. And then he saw it. An old Jeep parked to the right flashed its lights. It was Waylon Steggers.

The Steggers owned and operated Wild Trees Cabins on Lake Brevort. Waylon would take guests and tourists on sightseeing excursions in his Dehavilland Beaver seaplane. Mackinac Island was the main attraction on most trips. Today he would fly a friend well beyond that area, south along the edge of Lake Michigan to the airfield at Ludington.

Ludington and then home was about as far as he could go without refueling. Refueling would leave a paper trail. His friend did not want one of those today.

"I've got a hamburger and some fries in that bag," Waylon told Westy. "Figured you might be hungry."

"Thanks...is there anything on the news about me?"

"You mean, anything but?" his friend responded with a smile.

"I wish they'd just leave me be," Duray said in frustration. "I can handle this."

Steggers turned off the Worth Road toward Lake Brevort. The Jeep bounced and rocked, but neither man seemed concerned.

"You sure you can deal with these A-holes on your own?" the driver asked.

"They're like any other bad guys," Duray countered. "They all think the same."

"I hope you know what you're doing. I've rented a car at Ludington in my brother-in-law's name. There's an envelope under your seat with all you'll need."

"Waylon, I don't know how to thank you."

"You're still ahead of me...it'll take a few more adventures for me to catch up and besides...it's my pleasure."

Duray nodded and reached for the envelope. There was also cash in it.

51

"Waylon..." he started.

"Oh shut up," his friend cut him off. "You might need a few extra bucks on the road. Just be damned careful.

The Jeep pulled up along the lake and there sat NF 61WTS floating on her pontoons. They loaded Westy and his bag into the plane and were off in minutes.

~

Murray Bilstock stuck five hundred dollar bills in an envelope and put it in Yvonne Barkley's mailbox. A note said, "Please be more careful next time." He signed the note, "a friend."

Yvonne would contact the police to report the money had been returned. Again, they asked her to come in and fill out a few forms. She declined.

~

Silas had been in the air that day as well. He flew to Jackson to save time. The G5 pilot was glad to see him, but asked no questions other than his standard, "Should I wait here for you, Sir?" as they landed.

Silas looked at his watch. "It's 1 o'clock now," he answered. "You can either stay or come back around 7 P.M."

"I'll drop down to Shreveport for the afternoon," the pilot suggested as he reached over to a storage pouch behind the right seat, "I need to install these updates on the co-pilot software."

With Jon looking on, he opened the package containing eight small discs and a manual.

"Two hours to load, it says," reading from the instructions Foster confirmed his decision. "Then about an hour to shake it down, that should work."

"You can do this by yourself?" Jon asked with no idea what he was talking about.

"Oh...Those guys down at Shreveport PD airport are a great help...and the FAA is right next door. They can inspect it while I wait."

Silas smiled. "That stuff is your territory," he started and then it hit him, "you mean you're supposed to have another pilot with you?"

"Until this software package came out...yeah. I've had it a couple of years now, right before I met you actually."

Nodding as though he understood, Silas said the first thing that came into his head, "That's good thinking...you shouldn't just sit here anyway, that could be noticed."

"Good luck, Sir..." Foster grinned. "Great to see you again."

Silas nodded and stepped off the plane, equipment bag in hand.

Ace Rental Cars had a Crown Victoria available.

"That'll have to do." He told them.

The drive to Kinkaid's office building took less than thirty minutes. The Regions South Building was the tallest in Jackson. Home to lawyers, real estate companies and one engineering corporation, it also housed the catering division of a major chicken sandwich fast food company. Ben's research provided Silas with the perfect cover to be wandering around inside.

Complete with insulated bag, Silas stopped at several floors of the twenty-four story building, pretending to be delivering lunch, as he worked his way to floor number nineteen. The southern side of nineteen was Clyde Kinkaid's personal office.

Stepping off the elevator, a sign on the wall pointed left to "K. Kinkaid." Silas instinctively turned the opposite way in the event anyone might be there. The entire floor appeared to be empty. The offices to the north side were not occupied and Kinkaid's area showed only darkness through the glass outer walls.

Silas pulled a small electronic box from his bag. He held down a side button and slid the box along the door jam. As he suspected, a red light came on.

Alarm system, Silas said to himself.

Holding the box in place, he keyed in several numbers on its keypad and then tapped a set spike, securing the unit to the door jam. Slowly, he picked the lock and opened the door without the system realizing the door was open.

The outer area was mostly empty. The desk and chair were obviously for show. Some people liked the appearance of a receptionist, but Silas could tell there wasn't one.

The inner, private office was much more cluttered. The desk, piled high with papers, had no organization to it. Many stacks were of pending bills from Congress with staff member's notes scribbled across sections.

Silas sat in the man's chair and looked around, scanning the room. At first, it almost went by without notice. Then he turned quickly back to his left and a picture hanging on that wall. He took out a cell phone and snapped a picture before dialing.

"Yeah," Ben answered. "How's it going?"

"I'm sending you a picture of a picture. Take a look."

Ben stared in disbelief at the image. "Where did you find that?" he asked.

"I'm in the man's office. It's hanging right here on his wall."

"It's the same, Silas." Ben was digging through a drawer and pulled out a copy he had of the picture from Shanahan's office. Sheri Shanahan was the Atlanta attorney who headed up the coup attempt last year. She had two of the star pictures in her offices.

Ben held up his copy and said again, "It's the same thing. I'm looking at the other one right now."

The numbers shaped into a star were in the same order on both pictures.

"Did you ever decipher the code?" Silas asked.

"No...if there is one, it's deep."

Silas had been looking through drawers at the desk as they spoke. A note taped to the inside of one caught his eye, RP P 218-555-9209 written by hand on a small piece of paper.

"Ben," he changed gears suddenly. "Make a note of this phone number, see what you can find out about it for me." Silas called out the number and the letters with them.

"Sure, anything else look interesting in there?"

"This guy's not a housekeeper. Doesn't look like he has any secretary or anyone to do filing for him." Silas scattered a few papers and continued, "I think I'll just photograph what I've found and we'll let the computers sort it all out."

"Remember, I kinda need to know what I'm looking for to write a program."

"Yeah," Silas smiled to himself. "I'll have to think about that...say...did you find out what room the girl is in?"

"Sure did." Ben's voice was proud of himself. "They have an entire floor sealed off for her in the Wacker Building."

"Can you tie into the phones there?"

"Already done. There are six hardline phones on that floor and four cell phones. Three are all right together in one area," Ben explained. "That has to be the security team. The other is off by itself. I figure that's her or her mom."

"She'll likely use the cell phone, don't ya think?" Silas asked.

"I'll watch 'em all. When she calls, we'll have her number and get his."

"Ok, that should be in the morning sometime..." Silas paused again. He had been feeling under the drawers and found a paper taped to the bottom of one.

"Ben, I found something you need to put at the top of your list. This is definitely a code of some kind. I'll send a picture of it now." He clicked the camera on the phone and pushed the send button. The picture now on Ben's screen seemed almost simplistic. Without lines, the information was organized in neat columns and rows. The listings included: H18-25 275K and L1 110K followed by L2 250K. The 275K and 250K were lined out by hand and 312K and 290K written in their place. Not knowing what they were made the entries quite complex.

Ben's eyes scanned the page rapidly. The listings for LV 500-750 g 35K and then LV 1.5Kg up 95K caused him to think out loud.

"There's a word that was erased under one of the notes," he pointed out. Using the computer to enhance and clarify the smudge, Ben sat back startled by his own discovery.

"It says 'Liver,'" he blurted out. "Could this note be something from a grocery store or a butcher shop, maybe?"

"What makes you say that?" Silas injected.

Ben was checking his thought on the Internet. "Here it is," he interjected. "The weight of a human liver is 1.5 to 2.7 kilograms." He took a breath as his thoughts continued, "L1 or L2...lungs maybe?"

56

Silas didn't care for the image that gave him. He grimaced quietly and put the paper back under the drawer.

"Ben, stay on that. Look for anything else it could be, okay?"

"Yeah...I shouldn't have jumped to that conclusion...I'll keep looking."

"I need to move around some and see what else is here," Silas told him. "Talk to you later." But he sat where he was... in deep thought. *This doesn't look good at all.*

Silas stood and moved to the star picture on the wall. "Ben doesn't jump to conclusions," he muttered audibly. "I don't like this. Not even one little bit."

He turned and stepped toward the desk again, but something made him look back at the star picture. "If this is even close to what I'm thinking, they won't leave that girl alive to testify," he thought out loud.

Silas had wanted to learn more about this man Kinkaid before leaving Jackson, Mississippi. Things do not always go according to the first plan. He took out his cell phone and punched the button labeled, G5.

"Harold," he said as the phone was answered. "I should get to Chicago...and fast."

"Be to you in an hour, sir," the pilot told him.

~

Captain Cummins sat at his desk. Papers stacked in front of him could not keep his attention. *What is going on with all this?* His mind kept wandering back to the dead men in the ditch and the missing prisoner. Even the phone ringing failed to break through to him at first. When he did grab at it, the force nearly knocked it off onto the floor.

"Cummins," he announced, sounding almost out of breath.

"Sir, some of the reports have come back. I thought you should know about this right away." It was Lieutenant Stewart.

"Go ahead... please." The captain implored him.

"Facial recognition matched up one of the guys as Kaspar Lutz. He is listed on Interpol as a gun for hire."

"Is he the one with the shoes?" the captain asked.

"No...different guy. But Lutz had a note inside a coat pocket. Handwritten, it said 'RP – 225K – 4M – Miss,' all on different lines. The things that add up quick are the last three."

"I'm with you," the captain stared down at the note he had just made. "$225,000 for four men in Mississippi. That's pretty clear."

"Exactly, Sir. But who or what is RP?"

9

Maria Chavero sat in the public library in Caddo Mills, Texas. The local newspaper was still in the dark ages as far as archives of their paper. They used the old microfiche system with a scanning reader.

Knowing the date of the incident at the post office, she searched for the report in the next day's edition.

"Here we go," she said out loud while focusing in on the story. It identified the victim, gave her address, and then at the bottom listed a material witness who had tried to help her, Murray Bilstock of Highway 6, Caddo Mills.

Mr. Bilstock, she thought more quietly this time. *I'd hate to be you right now.*

Taking a notebook from her bag, Maria dialed the number Gerardo had given her.

"Do you know who this is?" she asked the man who answered.

"Si." The reply was short but adequate.

"Bilstock Ranch, Highway 6, Caddo Mills. Murray Bilstock."

"Just the one man?" he asked.

"Just that one."

The line went dead and Maria pushed for a new dial tone and then called home to report her success. The phone rang for several minutes. Palmero was not there or not answering. She knew she wasn't his only, but tried not to think about it.

I'll call again, later, she told herself.

~

Lake Ouachita had a new guest that no one knew about. The lake lay within a National Forest of the same name in Arkansas. The small cabin was owned by Marvin Acree, though title to the property listed Buckville Holdings as owners.

Marv had been very careful about privacy at the lake house. He knew this day would come, but he always thought he would be the one who needed to disappear for a while.

"The satellite TV works, but don't use the phone," he warned his boss. "And for God's sakes, stay off that computer."

"I know," Kinkaid acknowledged with reluctance. He walked to a window overlooking the water. "You got a boat?"

"It's put away for the season." Acree thought a minute and added, "There's a couple of poles out in the shed. You can fish off the dock."

Looking like a disappointed twelve year old, Kinkaid nodded and walked toward the main bedroom.

"Where do I sleep?" he asked looking into the room.

"You can have that room. I won't be here all the time."

"Where are you going?..." Kinkaid started but was interrupted by Acree's cell phone.

"Yeah, go ahead," Marv answered.

He listened in silence for what seemed too long for Kinkaid.

"What?" he demanded. "Is that the mayor?"

Acree waved him off and responded to the caller. "Thanks. Tell him we appreciate it."

Acree looked at his boss with a stern expression. "They found her. A team will hit in the morning," he explained. "It should look like a robbery gone bad."

Kinkaid sat down on a sofa and rubbed his hands together. "I'm glad you're with me, Marv. I like the way you work."

"You'll still need to stay here a while." Acree told him. "I'll get with the lawyers and see how they want to proceed."

"No witnesses, right?" Kinkaid smiled. "What's the problem?"

"We still need to have you turn yourself in... and how we claim you knew nothing will be important. Not just saying it, how you say it."

"I can't stay cooped up like this forever."

Acree winced and answered sarcastically, "Hell...you're welcome."

"I don't mean that...like that," Kinkaid snapped back. "I just need to get back to my business. I need to take care of Mr. Petteri too, you know?"

Acree sat down across from his boss, "One step at a time...okay?"

Clyde Kinkaid stared at him for over a minute then replied, "You're right."

~

Weston Duray knew where he was going. His wife had shared the location with him through their good-bye hug. He drove the rental car from Ludington to Chicago, hugging the big lake's shoreline the best he could.

It was nearly dark. A quick trip to a fast food drive through and he found a spot to park along North Wacker Drive. The building's lights offered a clear view of anyone coming or going. Weston checked his weapons and cell phones. He ate his food. Another half-warm burger, but it was sustenance.

If they come for her, it will be soon, he told himself. *They might surprise Cheryl and Rita...but they won't surprise me.*

Darkness brought with it the cold. The building was only a few blocks from the big lake and the wind could be fierce. He looked at the thermos bottle he had filled with hot coffee from the restaurant. *I'll need that later,* he reminded himself.

The lights from the building and the thinning traffic changed the entire scene. Duray checked his watch. It was nearly 7:30P.M.

If they come, he thought again. *It will be in the early morning hours. Most covert attacks come at 0300 when the prey is most vulnerable.*

Setting the alarm on his regular cell phone for 0215 he eased back and slumped down in the seat. *I should sleep for a bit,* he yawned. It had been a full day.

The blanket from his bag felt good pulled up around his neck. The cowboy hat stayed on the back seat for now, but he did have a thick sock cap.

"Under six hours now," he sighed and breathed in deep. He would wait.

10

Traffic at this time of night was light, especially for a big city. The drive from Midway Airport took less than fifteen minutes and the rented Mercury rolled up Wacker Drive toward the Number One building. Mercurys were becoming harder to find. It occurred to him that they could become a novelty, drawing attention he didn't need.

Putting those thoughts aside, Silas noticed the parked car right away. It had a Michigan tag which wasn't too unusual for Chicago, but it registered with him. The man slumped over in the front seat could just be a homeless drifter, though he doubted that. Another trip around the block and he stopped about a hundred yards behind the Michigan car.

Deep in his bag, which he had in the trunk, Silas found an old, tattered overcoat and a fedora with a broken hatband. Choosing the smallest of three cameras with him, he checked its battery and laid the lens cap on the bag.

He pulled the trunk lid down quietly and pushed until it clicked, then moved toward the car with the Michigan tag. Walking slowly and deliberately, he faked a limp. His movement appeared almost like rocking as he passed the car.

The lens of his digital camera peeked through a hole under the arm of the big coat. The apparent street person took over 50 shots as he walked by the vehicle, never looking at anything other than the sidewalk straight ahead of him. Three car lengths up, Silas crossed the empty street, turned left again, and headed back to the Mercury.

The pictures served to confirm what he already thought. This had to be the father, Weston Duray, come to watch over his little girl. The big hat on the back seat caught Silas' eye right away.

"Another cowboy," he heard himself say as he smiled.

He studied the man's face the best he could. Without seeing his hair or even the ears, the features were still strong enough he felt he would recognize him again. And that would more than likely be in a tough situation, with no time to spare.

Back to the trunk, Silas picked out weapons to go with his suit. He could change in the car. *I should do that now*, he thought.

When he was satisfied that he was ready, the Mercury moved into a closer position. He pulled ahead of the other car, into a small driveway on the same side of the street. He knew he wouldn't be allowed to stay there after daylight, but his thought process once again became audible. "It'll happen before dawn," he said.

Silas' watch said 12:15, but that was Eastern Time. He leaned back but stayed upright. Neither Jon nor Silas required sleep while on a mission. It was another strict discipline of the Rules.

~

Gerardo Palmero looked out over the bay, a glass of wine dangling in his right hand.

Maria should have called already, he said to the lights and the water lying before him. *What is the problem?*

He finished off the Vinho do Porto and threw the glass high toward the water. The sound of it breaking on the patio below was covered by the cell phone's ring. Gerardo stood and wobbled back to a small table holding both the phone and a half full bottle.

"Si," he answered in more a demand than a question.

"It is done, my Gerry."

"Done?" he challenged. "What is done? I haven't heard what you found out yet. How can it be done?"

"You already told me who to call, my love," she purred back at him.

Gerardo realized the table he was looking at was rocking. In fact, the entire room was moving. He carefully stepped back out to his chair. The wine was working on him.

"What of my brother? How is he?"

"Stefan will not walk again, I fear."

"How...what did this?"

"The shot or a piece of what the shot hit, broke off and bounced from his collar bone, internally."

"Bounced?"

"Si, my Gerry," Maria continued. "It bounced into Stefan's spine and lodged there."

"Then they can take it out!" Palmero shouted.

"No...no my love...they cannot take it out."

Gerardo said nothing. Maria listened for him, but he remained quiet nearly a full minute. Finally, Maria softly asked, "Gerry...are you still there?"

"Why can they not fix him?"

"The surgery would kill him. Besides...the damage is done."

"You found who did this thing?"

"Si," Maria said with pride. "And he is being dealt with."

What is this person's name?"

"Bilstock, my Gerry," she answered. "He is Murray Bilstock."

The words she spoke, the sudden cool breeze, or both shook Palmero into near sobriety. "Bilstock?" he repeated. "You say Bilstock?"

"Si, Gerry. Murray Bilstock."

Gerardo's mind whirled. That name was familiar to him. The senator who was killed by that assassin, his name was Bilstock. Many believed that assassin was now dead. Others thought this Bilstock person, the senator's son, worked with the assassin and not long ago. *This could be useful to me*, he thought and then spoke firmly.

"Have they killed him yet?"

"I don't think they are here yet...no." Maria responded in confusion. "What is it?"

"Stop them," Gerardo commanded loudly. His thoughts had conjured a plan that could bring him favor with high-ranking U.S. officials. Officials who could help him spread his drugs through their country. Officials who would love to know for sure that this assassin was dead. "Have them bring him to me."

"Si," Maria answered. "As you wish, Gerry."

Gerardo hung up and turned to look back out over the bay, his bay. He had conquered it through patience and intellect. He would now conquer the U.S. by the same means. This Bilstock would be his bait.

"If this assassin is still alive," he said to no one. "He will come for his friend."

Gerardo laughed and walked back to the small table. He picked up the bottle and turned it up to his lips. After two large gulps, he lowered it and wiped his mouth with his arm. Walking back out on the patio, he puffed out his chest at the night.

"My brother has finally brought me something I can use," he smiled.

Raising the bottle high, he proclaimed aloud, "To Stefan! You will make me even richer than I am today!"

Reaching back as far as he could, Gerardo then launched the bottle out into the dark.

~

It was 0215, in Chicago. Weston Duray's alarm watch began to buzz. He sat up with a slight start and then realized where he was. A shiver ran through him and he reached down for the thermos bottle. Drinking straight from it, the coffee helped.

He leaned backward and grabbed his hat from the backseat. The sock hat came off and it went on in one smooth motion. Duray looked around. All was quiet.

He took another large hit from the thermos and blinked his eyes several times. Checking his watch it was 0220. Westy was fully awake now and the vigil would continue.

If he noticed the nose of the Mercury sticking from that driveway ahead of him, it did not register. He kept his attention on the building's entrance. Another turn of the thermos and it was empty, but he was ready.

11

His head was in Lucy's engine compartment when the phone rang. The noise reverberated in the hanger anyway, but given the late hour and Murray's position, it gave him a start. The phone lay on a workbench and had rung several times before he got to it.

"Yeah," Murray answered. "What's up?"

"Mr. Bilstock, this is Deputy Charles." William Charles and Brownville's acting sheriff, Irv Stallings were in the Dallas area for a training session. They had stopped by Murray's place earlier in the day and were now in Caddo Mills meeting with the local authorities. It was just a social, get to know you visit. Drinking was involved.

"Yeah, sure Bill," the cowboy recognized William Charles' voice.

"I can't locate Irv...I mean acting-Sheriff Stallings."

Murray's instinct of "why call me?" was overridden by his ego.

"What's going on, Deputy?" he asked. "Can't locate Irv? I don't understand."

"He went to get us some coffee, about two hours ago. I haven't heard from him since."

"Where are you, Deputy?"

"We've been at the local sheriff's office since dinner. You know...knockin' a few back. Irv went to get some coffee so we could..."

"Alright," Murray interrupted him with assurance. "I'll be there in thirty minutes."

He wiped the grease from his hands and grabbed his hat. Lucy wasn't ready to fly and the Sikorski was tied down so he jumped into his pickup. He tried to call Irv himself while on the way to Caddo Mills, with no response.

Irv Stallings had been the perfect choice to be acting Sheriff after the death of Horace Wilbury. Elections wouldn't be until next fall, but Irv was a sure thing when that time came.

Murray pulled up to the Caddo Mills Sheriff's office. All the building's lights were on. It was nearly midnight, *why all the lights*, he thought. Slamming the door on the pickup, Murray walked double-time to the door and all but threw it open. What he saw stopped him in his tracks. Stallings and Charles along with the local sheriff and his two deputies were all tied up in chairs. They were gagged and obviously beaten nearly to a pulp.

"What the..." came out before something hit him over the head.

By his watch, thirty minutes had passed when Murray regained consciousness. Bound and lying in the back of a large sedan, he tried not to let them know. The car was moving, but not too fast. The surroundings were still dark, no streetlights, very few stars were visible. The ceiling liner of the car displayed the glow of another vehicle's headlights. It wasn't a chase...they were together.

A Hispanic man in the front passenger seat was on a cell phone. He spoke in Spanish, but that wasn't a problem for Murray.

"Si," the man said. "I need to confirm a message received earlier."

The man listened and then answered, "Understood." And he closed the phone. Looking at the driver, he then announced, "Change of plans was correct. We don't kill him now. We take him to Palmero."

~

Silas had relied strongly on Jon's persistence to stay awake into the early morning. Vehicles had driven by through the night, but mainly city trucks and delivery vans. The two black SUVs caught his eye right away. When they stopped in front of the One Wacker building, Silas straightened up. It was 2:53 A.M.

In all, five men exited the SUVs. Heavy overcoats covered whatever it was they carried. As they entered the building, Silas reached for his door handle, but a small light to his left made him pause. It was the dome light of the car from Michigan.

The other man, the cowboy father, had opened his door and climbed out. He crossed the street in a hunched over fast walk, his right hand clearly holding a handgun.

Silas waited for him to follow the others inside.

~

"Ladies," the voice at the door said. "We need to move...now." The voice was followed by a gentle knock.

Rita Duray jumped up and ran to the door. She started to open it, but stepped back.

"What's wrong?" she asked.

"Mrs. Duray, this is Agent Hascker. We picked up some activity down in the lobby."

He didn't tell her the entire story. The agent charged with the overnight watch viewed the men coming in through a monitor. The camera was hidden high on a crown molding on the main floor. As they entered the lobby, they opened their coats to take hold of the Mac 10s with both hands. He wasn't sure if they were .45 caliber or 9mm, but he did note the suppressors. This was a professional hit-team.

The agent went into action, alerting his team and didn't see the man who had followed the others in. Nor had he noticed Silas.

Using the leg strength of his black suit, Silas had jumped up onto the side fire escape. He scaled the metal stairs to the fifth floor and then accessed the building near the rear corner. Finding the service elevators Ben had pointed out in his emailed diagram, Silas rode to the forty-fifth floor. He stepped quietly from the lift, looking and listening.

Opening the door to the stairwell offered no clue. All was quiet, no faint echoes, nothing.

They knew exactly where they were going, he thought. *They're setting up, probably right outside the door.*

Still a floor below, he carefully stepped into the main floor area. The four passenger elevators stood across from each other, two on each side. He watched floor indicators above them. One read steady at "46," the other next to it was counting up. Currently on "35."

*The father...*Silas said to himself. *He's going to walk right into it.*

As he watched, the elevator stopped on "37." Silas stepped to where he could see those across the hall. Both were moving, one going down, and one moving up.

That one stopped on "47." Silas headed for the stairwell.

~

Westy Duray had started two elevators from the lobby. Both set for floor thirty-seven. Then running back across the lobby, he followed those to the same floor.

Once there, he quickly ran across to the two units now standing open. Sending one down, Duray jumped into the other and continued up. He stood beside the control buttons as the doors opened. Carefully, the father looked out on the floor above his daughter's sanctuary. He was alone.

He listened for any commotion below him. There was none. Duray found the stairs and slowly, quietly crept down to the next floor. He did not hear the man who stood below him in that same stairwell.

Opening the stairwell door, he could hear the sound of muffled voices. Weston Duray flattened out against the wall and moved forward toward the corner. The voices became whispers. He heard the sound of a door opening.

Then all hell broke loose.

12

The agent asked Rita and Cheryl to stay in their room while they checked the hallway.

"Keep this door locked, it's bullet proof. Just stay back from it, okay?"

"Please, be careful." Rita begged him.

Hascker nodded and pulled the door closed. He looked at his agent standing at the suite's main door. "Go," he ordered.

Five men stood outside the door. Three within four feet and the others back several yards. The men on either side of the door opened fire towards each other.

The agent at the door hit one gunman before the spray from the Mac 10s knocked him backwards. Two FBI agents were killed immediately and Hascker dove to his left, returning fire as he moved.

Westy Duray surveyed his surroundings. The floor had been staged as a construction area, all part of the subterfuge for his daughter's protection. A large tool cart stood sideways in the main hallway, just past the corner. Duray leapt into the hall near the cart, blasting away with a military style Colt 45 and the Kahr 9mm.

The two gunmen closest to him were hit. Both fell. One spun wildly from his knees, returning fire at Westy in a frantic wave of the machine gun. The two others dove into the suite through its open door. A short shoot-out with Hascker ended with his death.

Westy jumped behind the large steel cart supposedly full of tools. It stood on heavy six-inch wheels that held it above the floor. The rounds coming at him screamed as they ricocheted in different directions.

The Mac 10 wielding assailant slowly climbed back to his feet, looking for Duray behind the box. Westy took his .45 in both hands and took a defensive posture against the cart. He noticed a figure come from his right and step into the hall.

All in black, this other man stood straight up with an outstretched right arm pointing at the machine gunner. Startled at first, Duray bounced off the wall and lay flat on the floor behind the cart. He looked under it, back to the gunman. He could tell from his feet, the machine gunner had turned toward the man in black.

Duray heard two shots come from his right and the machine gun wielding assailant spun again and fell face first toward the cart. Westy reached under the cart. His arm lay flat on the floor with the .45 pointed forward. As the man fell, his face landed three feet from the cart. He half-grinned at Duray and struggled to pull his weapon around toward the girl's father. Duray fired twice. Both rounds struck their target.

Westy jumped to his feet and looked for the man in black. He was nowhere in sight. When gunfire erupted from within the suite again, Duray ran to the door, but it was over. The man in black stood inside, near the protective room's door. The other gunmen were on the floor face up, their eyes fixed in blank stares.

Duray raised his weapon, but the man in black extended only his empty left hand.

"Wait," Silas barked out. "I'm on your side."

The frantic father tilted his barrel upward and studied the man before him. Despite the menacing outfit, something about this man eased his mind. Lowering the handgun to his side, Duray demanded, "Where's my family?"

Silas knocked gently on the door. "In here, I'm hoping," he said.

A woman's voice sounded from behind the door, "Weston...is that you?"

Silas stepped back as the other cowboy grabbed the door with both hands.

"Rita?" he called out. "Are you okay?"

The door opened and Westy was reunited with his wife and daughter.

The sound of sirens interrupted them. Though still blocks away, they could be heard echoing and getting louder on the street below.

"You need to come with me," Silas ordered.

"Who are you?" Westy demanded.

"Look...I'll explain what I can, but we need to get your family away from here, now. This place is compromised. You understand that, don't you?"

Duray looked around briefly. "But those are cops coming."

"Are you sure who's paying them?" Silas asked bluntly. He pointed to the dead men in the heavy coats, "I'd almost bet you these guys are cops, or took their orders from one."

Weston Duray glanced at his wife and daughter. He took a chest filling breath and nodded his agreement. "Where do we go?" he asked the man in black.

"This way." Silas pointed to the stairs.

"Our stuff..." Rita turned to back into the room.

"Leave it," Silas called out sharply. "Please," he added in a more moderate tone.

They followed him down the stairs to the thirty-sixth floor. There, Silas listened carefully to the commotion headed up.

"Come with me," he motioned and they left the stairwell, scurrying into the service elevator. At the third floor they checked the fire escape and the alley below, it was clear.

They climbed down to the street and circled around, the wrong direction at first, till they found the Mercury.

"My car is over there," Duray pointed.

"Forget about it." Silas told him.

"But a friend will have to pay for that," Duray tried to explain.

Silas stiffened and looked him right in the eye, " I'm not just saying this. I'll cover it. Okay?"

Duray relented and the four of them rode toward Midway Airport while the Chicago authorities engulfed the building. The ride was short and quiet, but when the destination was clear, the silence was broken.

"Why are we here?" Westy asked as Silas pulled into Midway.

"You guys still need to hide. My pilot will take you to my home. You'll be safe there...I promise."

"Pilot?" Duray's ire was building. "Just who are you, friend?"

"You can call me Silas. Ben will meet you at the house. You'll be fine there."

"What...where are you going?"

"I need to go back. One or two of those hit men were still alive. I have questions for them."

"Ha!" Westy laughed. "If you could get to them, they wouldn't say a word."

Silas pointed to the G5 and the pilot waved that he understood. Then looking back to Westy Duray, Silas added, "I can be amazingly persuasive."

"Why should I even trust you? I don't know you, not one bit."

"You saw what happened back there. That was the government trying to protect your family." Silas waited for a response that didn't come, and then added, "You've got little choice right now."

Duray's head tilted and he took another angle. "I'll go with you, then."

"I knew you would," Silas said sincerely. "But you need to protect your family right now. You need to stay with them."

The two men stared at one another until Weston Duray finally mumbled under his breath, "thank you."

"We'll talk again," Silas promised and slid behind the wheel of the Mercury. He looked back to the man from Michigan. A man he found he had great respect for. "Enjoy Georgia," he offered and drove away.

"Georgia?" Duray repeated, but Silas was already on the phone to the pilot.

"Get them to Dalton Airport, will ya?" he asked. "I'll have Ben see if George and Doris can meet them there with an escort to the house."

"Where are you going, Sir?" the pilot was concerned.

"I'll be in touch," he answered. "Just take care of them right now."

The pilot started to reply but could hear the line was already dead. "Will do, Sir," he said anyway as he went to greet his passengers.

13

The news was not received well in Arkansas.

"What do mean, 'they're gone,' Frank?" Marvin Acree bellowed into the phone.

The man on the other end of the call stood outside the forty-sixth floor suite in Chicago, blood and bodies all around him. The gold shield on his coat declared him a Captain.

"Look," he shot back in anger. "I can't talk right now, Marv. I've got FBI crawling all over me and this whole place. Do you understand me?"

"Frank..." Acree tried again. "People don't vanish, not even in Chicago."

The captain walked to the end of the hallway. "We found a rental car down on the street. It's not in his name, but from the look of it... that father was here."

"Duray?" Acree challenged. "He was there?"

"We don't know for sure...not yet anyway." The captain looked around to be sure he was alone. "If he was here...he left his car. You tell me what's going on, huh?"

Clyde Kinkaid walked up on Acree in the cabin. "What's up Marv?" he asked. "Everything okay?"

Acree covered the phone and looked at his boss. "I don't know yet, I'm working on it."

"Did they get her?" Kinkaid pestered.

"There may be a hiccup...that's what I'm trying to sort out."

Kinkaid's expression froze.

"Who did you use?" Acree asked into the phone.

"That's another big problem, Marv," the Captain told him. "They were on the job from the Hoffman area. Thing is, they were supposed to come in, do their thing and get out."

"And?" Acree pushed him.

"The whole crew is dead...except one and he doesn't look like he's going to make it." The captain checked around him again nervously. "Them and the FBI team that was guarding the girl."

"Frank, that just doesn't make sense." Acree tried to rationalize what he was hearing. "You mean the girl's father came in... killed everybody and then disappeared with his daughter?"

"And his wife," Frank added wryly. "She's gone, too."

Acree sat down and rubbed his forehead. "Contain everything the best you can, do you understand? Lock it all down if possible."

"I've got three dead FBI agents here, Marv. That's gonna be tough to do."

"Get the mayor involved if you have to." Acree snapped. "It's his ass, too."

~

Ben Shaw saw only one dilemma with Silas' request to send his mom and George to meet the Durays.

"You're supposed to be dead, remember?" he candidly threw in.

Silas' chest heaved. "You have to tell 'em, Ben. No big details, but they need to keep it to themselves."

"Mom knows," Ben revealed. He couldn't keep it from him much longer. "She figured it out right away. George took a couple of weeks."

Silas was not shocked, but the news did come as a small blow to his ego. "They told you this?" he appealed.

"Not in a major discussion, no...I could tell by the way they acted."

"And you're sure they aren't talking to anyone about it?"

"Mom confided in Marsha, Marsha told me. Mom has never said a word to me about it."

Silas pulled the Mercury to the curb. He was one block from the Wacker Building, perpendicular to the street itself. The activity there was furious. Three ambulances were parked, lights out and engines off. Another, still fully lit, suddenly left the scene with sirens wailing.

"What's that?" Ben asked of the noise.

"I'm back at the building. An ambulance just left."

Silas watched the emergency vehicle make a right turn at the corner. He drove straight ahead to intersect with it on the next street. The road he was on took him over the river.

"One of them is still alive, then?" Ben had figured.

"Yeah," Silas barely muttered. "I thought one of 'em in the hall was still breathing." The emergency vehicle had turned left, rushing south along Canal Street.

"Good guy or bad guy?" The young man asked over the phone.

"One I want to talk to."

Ben's eyebrows rose. "Bad guy," he surmised.

Silas' mind went back to the other subject as he drove, following the ambulance. They turned west on Harrison, running parallel to I-290.

"So...you're sure they aren't talking to anyone about it?"

"Jon," the boy wasn't worried about "names" at that point. "They respect you. They don't understand this...well, George does some, but it's what you want."

The high speed tracking pursuit went under the Kennedy interchange.

"Who else knows?"

"Nobody's talking..." Ben started.

"Who else?" Silas cut in on him.

"Daniel has indicated he thinks something's up."

The ambulance slowed and turned into a hospital at the corner of Ashland Ave.

"And Murray?" Silas asked as he looked for a spot to park the Mercury.

"He keeps badgering me about it, I mean really pushing." Ben voice changed an octave. "He hasn't said he knows, but I think he does."

"I knew I couldn't keep it up forever." Silas lamented. "But I thought maybe longer than this." He pulled into a short term parking area near the Emergency Room and watched as attendants rushed to unload the cargo.

"You're still in charge, Jon." Ben tried to assure him. "It's all up to you."

Silas changed the subject yet again. "You need to set up the house for our guests."

"We'll figure it out," the boy assured him. "Marsha is already moving stuff around in the guest room." Ben paused a second and then quipped, "I guess the girl can just bunk with me."

Silas smiled and shot back, "What are you, ten?" he laughed slightly. "Thanks though, I guess I needed a grin."

"Just checking... to see if you were listening."

"You're lucky your mom isn't listening." Jon's voice emerged.

Ben froze for a second. It was almost like talking to two different people. He chose not to make a big deal of that.

"She can have my room," he tried to sound disappointed. "I stay down here most of time now anyway."

Before Silas could get away, Ben remembered more important news. "Oh...there's something else you need to know," he nearly shouted.

"Yeah, make it quick."

"I told you I was zeroed in on the phones for that floor of the building."

"She never needed to make the call." Silas was confused.

"Well, but others have," Ben explained. "I picked up a cell phone call between two guys, a Captain named Frank and another guy named Marv...interesting stuff."

"Did you trace the other end?"

"Close as I could get," Ben explained. "The number is registered in Mississippi, but the call came off an antenna in Arkansas."

Halfway out of the Mercury, Silas stopped to ask, "Can you replay the call for me?"

"Coming at you now."

14

Murray had been transferred into a truck while it was still dark. He saw that before the hood was applied. Still pretending to be out, that was about all he knew. He figured he was being taken south, but couldn't be sure.

At some point, the ride got rough. "Off-road for sure," he muttered under his breath. And indeed they were. The rugged portion of the trip lasted about an hour. The next phase he was confident in. He was placed into a helicopter that flew low, very low from his knowledge of air pressure.

Once over the Rio Grande, the copter went to a more suitable altitude. Time was difficult to measure, but Murray felt the sun breaking in on him before they landed. He could also hear the sound of the ocean as he was dragged from the copter.

When the hood was finally removed, he was in a room with a high window and bright sun lighting the entire area. Murray rolled himself into a position he could stand from. Through the window he saw the huge bay and the high-rise buildings lining it. Having been there several times before, he sat back down and leaned against the wall.

"Acapulco," he said. "What the hell?"

Ben had barely gotten off the phone with Silas when another line rang out in the second sublevel basement of the mansion.

"Hey, Daniel," Ben could tell by the incoming number that it was Daniel Seay calling from Pittsburgh.

"Ben, I just had a distressing call from Irv Stallings in Texas."

"Distressing?" Ben asked. "How so?"

"Murray has been kidnapped."

The younger man heard him, but it didn't make sense. "What?" he fired back.

"Last night," the business manager of Jon's company spoke in short, concise sentences. "Irv and his deputy were in Caddo Mills. They were used to lure Murray into town. There were five of them in all."

"Well...what...where did they take him?"

"Don't know and haven't heard from the kidnappers, yet."

"Was Murray alive?"

"Yeah, Irv was pretty sure he was still alive when they left with him."

"I need to...." Ben started but then caught himself.

"Look, Ben," Daniel's voice was strict and serious. "If this is some device to draw Jon out, make sure he thinks about that before he does anything."

"Jon?" Ben attempted to play dumb.

"You heard me. I said 'if'... and what I think I know doesn't matter. It's what you know that does... right now."

"Okay, Daniel." Ben tried to think of something slick to say, but his concern for Murray was growing. "Thanks...I'll see what I can do."

"Do you need me down there?" Daniel asked.

"I appreciate the offer, but I won't know till I find out what's going on."

"Alright," Daniel conceded. "I'm here if you need anything."

"Thank you, sir."

~

From his bag, Silas had dug out an old blond wig and a fake beard. The scar was too identifiable to let show this time. He wore the beard and a cap into the hospital's emergency area, and then found a storage closet.

There were white coats and nametags in the closet. Silas quickly donned the wig and some dark glasses. With the help of some other items he found his appearance became that of a doctor. The cracked clipboard from the trashcan completed the look.

It wasn't hard to find the room the gunman was in. A police guard was stationed outside. Silas walked up, checked the information printout on the door casing while the officer looked on, and then went straight into the room.

The gunman was not only alive, he was awake and talkative.

"This damned shoulder hurts bad, Doc. I need some oxy."

Silas raised a finger to his lips, muttered, "hush", and then turned back to the door.

He motioned for the guard to come to him.

"I've got to stabilize that wound," he told the officer. "It could get loud in here, just keep everybody out for a few minutes."

The officer nodded his head and Silas closed the door and pushed the lock button. Again, the gunman called out for some painkillers. His left hand was shackled to the gurney, but his right hand was free. Silas reached for the button at his own waist and the powered arm came to life.

"So, you guys came over from Hoffman Estates to do this job, huh?" he asked.

The gunman's face wrinkled and he glared at Silas. "Who the hell are you?"

"I'm here to ask you a few questions. That's who I am."

"Well, you can go straight to..." the man began, but Silas interrupted him.

"I only have a few questions and I have very little time...but that's okay."

He picked up the man's right hand with the powered arm. Try as he did, the gunman could not pull away. Fear crossed over his face and he swore, "It don't matter how little time you have, you're not getting nothing from me."

"Oh, but I will," Silas explained. "You see," and he bent the man's index finger in on itself at the first knuckle, "I only have a few minutes...but you only have ten fingers." With that he applied pressure that broke the knuckle with a "pop." The gunman screamed in agony.

"Hurts a bunch, don't it?" Silas asked him. "Bet that took the other pain away too, didn't it."

What color had been on the gunman's face was now gone and he was trying to breathe. Silas maintained his grip on the man's hand.

"Who sent you to Wacker Street?"

"Go to hell," the man exclaimed with spit and trembling lips.

Silas bent the man's middle finger in and broke it also at the first knuckle. As the man screamed again, Silas leaned into him.

"I asked you a question," he warned.

"Frank..." the man managed to get out. "Frank Borton."

"Captain Borton?" Silas asked.

"Yeah."

"Who does he work for?"

"I don't know," the gunman said defiantly.

His ring finger was next to go. Silas partly covered the man's mouth this time to muffle the scream.

"Some guy on the mayor's staff...I don't know his name."

As Silas reached for the man's little finger, he cried out, "Walt! He called him Walt one time...God sake's man. That's all I know."

"I believe you," Silas told him. "Last question, did you go there, knowing the job was to kill that little girl?"

The man looked at him as though he did not understand what he meant.

Silas repeated himself, "Did you know that was the job when you went there?"

"Yeah... we knew," the man answered with disdain for the question. "It is what it is, ya know? It's a crappy world sometimes."

Silas leaned away and then took a small step back. He filled his lungs slowly as he considered what this man had said.

"It made no difference to you?" he restated his question.

"It was just a job, you know?" The man in the bed stared at Silas as though there should be understanding between them. "You do what you gotta do," he added.

Silas stepped further back and rubbed his own jaw. The coldness of the man's response wasn't as shocking as it was definitive. To Silas, it left little choice in his answer to it. The calm gaze with which he stared down at this man became a glare. Reaching into his pocket, Silas took out a small white pill. In one fast, smooth motion he stepped back to the bed, forcing the pill into the man's mouth and covered the opening with his other hand.

"We can't have that, now...can we?" he said as the pill quickly dissolved. The gunman's eyes squinted and then rolled back as he went limp.

Silas walked to the door and opened it. "Code blue," he called out. "Crash cart in here STAT. This man is having a heart attack."

As the emergency staff began to spring into action, Silas stood in the hall pretending to make notes on a clipboard. The attention level grew more and more around the room and the now dead gunman. Silas turned; he laid the clipboard down and walked to the corner of the hallway. After one last look to be sure he was being ignored, he pulled the wig and beard from his head, stuffing them into his shirt. In a nearby restroom he left the white coat and combed his real hair before casually walking to the exit.

He was back at the Mercury before the "thirty-minute" time limit for parking was up.

15

Gerardo Palmero entered the concrete room alone. He looked more an everyday businessman than the drug lord he was. He brought a wooden chair with him and came within four feet of Murray before spinning the chair backwards and sitting down.

"Why am I here?" Murray looked up from his position on the floor. "What's going on, man?"

Palmero's gaze seemed to go through his captive.

The cowboy refused to show concern, about his own safety or anything else. "I asked you a question," he asserted calmly. His chin rising even higher than it had been.

The drug lord's eyes went to the ground and back up rapidly. His face was now a grimace, tight with anger. "He will not walk again, you know," he blurted out.

"Who?" Murray asked. "What in blazes are you talking about?"

Palmero stood to avoid the sun's glare as it moved higher through the small window. He gathered himself from his outburst. "That doesn't matter now," he said almost softly. "Will he come to save you?"

Murray pushed his hand against the wall, near the floor he sat on. His legs were cramped from the sitting position he'd been in, but he managed to stand. "If we're gonna communicate at all, Mister..." he declared. "You need to start making more sense."

"My brother," Palmero spit out with renewed aggression. He stepped forward, right into Murray's face. "I don't know why he thought you were a Samaritan," he continued. "You're just a dirt kicker."

Now Murray's eyes widened. "That thief...that biker?" he asked. "That's your brother?"

Palmero did not answer. He turned away and went back to his chair. Turning it around, he sat before speaking again.

"Will your friend come for you?"

"What friend?" Murray asked again.

"The one who kills. The one your congress fears."

Murray concentrated more on his expression than what he would say next. He hoped not to give himself away through a look. "Man, you are confused," he laughed. "That ain't me."

Palmero paused. His expression did not change either. He was stone faced. "I know this. You are not him." He did twist his head slightly to the left as he continued, "That one killed your own father." He watched for a reaction that didn't happen and then went on. "Now you work with him."

"He's dead," Murray advised coldly. "Haven't you read the papers?"

"You are fortunate I don't believe you."

"Why is that?"

"If I thought what you say were true...you would already be dead yourself." The drug lord smiled a thoroughly sinister smile that lasted only for a second. "If he does not come for you...you will be soon enough."

As Palmero walked toward the door, Murray shouted, "How's a dead man going to come for me?"

Palmero opened the door and stepped through it. He looked back inside the room, now adorned with a chair and his prisoner. "Pray for his resurrection, Mr. Samaritan. That's the only hope you have."

~

Ben was still on the phone with Daniel as the flashing blue light let him know the guests had arrived. Marsha was upstairs to greet them so he didn't feel rushed. Once upstairs, he went through the kitchen to the big garage area.

The reaction from the Durays was not unlike others, when first brought to the mansion.

"You kidding me?" Westy asked George. Mrs. Duray had nothing to say, her eyes spoke for her.

"It really is quite a house," George confirmed. "You will soon see why I know you'll be safe here."

Rita, Doris, and Marsha had stepped to the elm tree. The guest from Michigan put her hand up to her mouth.

"I've read about this place," she said turning to look for her husband. "The owner is that Son person. The man who everyone thinks killed those congressmen."

"He's also the man who saved the president," Doris retorted. "Don't forget that."

"Much of what has been written about him isn't true." Marsha's expression overwhelmed the words she had used. "You've met him," she continued. "You've seen the man he is."

"They said he was killed," Rita was asking what was true.

"We thought he was," Marsha explained. "It's best that we treat things as though he were. It's for the safety of everyone concerned. Now that includes you and your family."

Rita seemed to understand. "Until Cheryl went missing...I was very naïve."

Marsha reached out and took her hand for support. "I was to a point also," she offered. "And I was a cop."

"I can't judge anything right now," Rita said frankly. "He saved us, all of us up in Chicago. That outweighs everything else."

"Come," Doris told Marsha. "Let's show her the house."

Cheryl was busy looking around the landscape, "It's built into the mountain," she said out loud. No one heard her other than Ben. He had just stepped into the main garage area. As much reading her lips as hearing, he knew exactly what she said. His eyes were locked on the young woman.

The pictures didn't tell the story, he thought... remembering all the study he had done on this girl. *She's amazing.*

Having unconsciously leaned on the door button, the huge fold-up door with the one way glass lifted leaving the two young people only a couple of feet apart.

"Oh," Cheryl smiled at him. "You must be Ben."

"I...I must... what?" repeating part of what he'd heard was the best he could do.

"You must be Ben, silly." she smiled even bigger. . "Hi, I'm Cheryl."

The boy gathered himself as he saw Marsha coming toward him. "Marsha, we need to talk..." he said grabbing her arm.

"Ben...this is Mr. & Mrs. Duray," she introduced them.

"Hi, nice to meet you guys," Ben reached out to shake Weston's hand. He looked back at Marsha, "I need a minute...really."

Stepping in the direction of the house, away from the others, Marsha's face took on a worried look. "What's going on, Ben?"

"Murray has been kidnapped."

She just stared at him in silence.

"I heard from Daniel," Ben went on. "He'd had a call from Irv Stallings. It happened last night."

"Can you reach Jon?"

"He doesn't want me to call him. It could blow a cover or something. I just have to wait."

"Do you know who took Murray?" She asked.

"No details at all," Ben shook his head. "No call yet from the kidnappers either."

Marsha rubbed her forehead. "Let me get these people settled in." She took two steps and looked back at Ben, "If you hear anything, come get me."

Ben nodded and then noticed a presence off to his left. It was Cheryl.

"Something wrong?" she asked.

"Nothing to do with y'all," he said seriously. "One of our friends is in trouble."

"Oh...I'm sorry," Cheryl responded and then couldn't help but smile.

"What?" Ben wanted to know why.

"You talk cute," Cheryl told him. "I never talked to a southern boy before."

"Well, you sound pretty different yourself...aye?" Ben teased.

The girl smiled again and tilted her head just a bit. "I hope your friend will be okay."

"Yeah..." he tried his best to contain himself. "Me, too."

16

Petteri had become caught up in pest control business calls. Business people supposedly can compartmentalize and focus on the matters at hand. Though his mind still swayed into concern about the hit team, the owner of RP Pest Control did his best to focus.

When the "line-two" light began to blink, Petteri lost that focus on pest control.

"Sir, I have to go," he rushed his customer. "I'll need to call you back." And with that he punched the second-line button expecting to hear the team leader on the other end.

"They're all dead, you fool!" the garbled voice cut through him.

"What do mean?" Petteri leaned forward in disbelief.

"Your people and Lutz were found in a ditch this morning," the voice continued. "They never got to the bus. Where the hell is Kinkaid?"

The man in Duluth slowly stood and turned to his window. Somehow the glare from the sun hitting the fresh snow helped settle his thoughts. Kinkaid was their employee, to a degree. But he was an established force on his own. He had his own organization and that fact had never been an issue, until now.

"Acree is behind this," Petteri said as the notion came to him. "He's the forward thinker. Marvin did this to protect his boss."

"Who's going to protect you, Reino?" The voice, distorted by design, would never use names, but it did this time. The threat was clear. Anger now joined the emotions in Petteri's mind.

"I hear you," the Finlander said calmly. "Threats are dangerous things, you know. If you scare me, and I mean actually scare me, I will take action to protect myself."

The voice remained quiet.

Petteri gave it a minute. The line was still open so he went on. "We both have a problem, we need to work together, or this could be fatal to us... equally."

Another moment of silence went by. Then the voice came back, much subdued. "Get busy," it said and the line went dead.

~

Silas had left the hospital a couple of hours earlier. A round about trip back to the Wacker building and waiting for the majority of the investigative team to leave took most of that time.

There would be a small contingent left to guard the site, but they would be foot patrolmen. They would be easier to deceive than a hardened detective, but in this case that did not matter so much.

With a fake ID from the Chicago Tribune, Silas entered the forty-sixth floor from the side stairs. He noticed right away that the huge tool gurney was gone. The carpet was ripped up and men were already repairing holes in the wall sections. No blood anywhere.

They must have taken lessons from Argus, he thought. Somebody *doesn't want this story told.*

The Argus drug cartel had taught him much about covering up at any cost. They too left no evidence, ever.

A young officer approached him, puffed out with authority. "Hold it right there," he commanded. "How did you get in here?"

Over the man's shoulder, Silas could see the apartment door wide open. Several men were at work inside, pulling down walls and gathering furniture.

"I heard there was some trouble here," Silas grinned. "Trouble might be a good story."

"No story here, bub." The officer started to reach for his radio. "Just a party that got out of control. The contractors took advantage of their access, that's all."

Putting his hands up, Silas backed off. "My bad," he pleaded. "My information was vague to start with. I was just hoping for a good lead, you know?"

The young officer took his hand from the radio, his ego having been stroked. "Okay then," he replied sternly. "You need to leave here, now."

With hands still raised Silas nodded and stepped away, back to the stairs for one level and then the elevator. At the Mercury, he pulled out a phone and dialed Ben.

It rang seven times before the boy answered.

"Jon," the muffled voice said. "Hang on, please...I need to talk to you."

Clyde Kinkaid was restless. He didn't care for sitting and waiting. His empire had been built on action, quick decisive action. He trusted Marvin Acree, but did not agree with all the man's tactics.

"What is Frank doing about this?" he demanded from the bedroom doorway.

"Calm down, will ya?" Acree was concerned to the point his normal subordinate attitude was set aside. "I'm trying to think."

"He's a liability now." Kinkaid threw out at him.

"Who?"

"Frank... Your police captain."

"He's getting the place cleaned...completely. The mayor's office is on board with it. He's not a liability...so forget that."

"The FBI knows what's going on," the boss insisted. "Get your blinders off. The whole connection is compromised."

Acree's face contorted. "Whole connection?" he asked. "This is the mayor of Chicago you're talking about."

"You want to die or go to jail?" Kinkaid walked to the sofa and sat down. "Marv, you're a good man, but you need to think bigger. Much bigger."

Acree looked at his boss with disbelief in his eyes. "We don't have that kind of juice, Clyde."

"We have to act like we do." The man on the sofa instructed. "Be the big dog or get treated like a bitch." His eyes were now taut and fixed. "Are you a bitch, Marv?"

Acree felt weak suddenly. He reached for a chair and sat trying to gather himself. He had been caught up in being "in-charge" and he had liked it. But he was seeing now why the boss was the boss. He always told himself he could make tough decisions, but what Kinkaid was talking about was both crazy and correct at the same time. It boiled down to survival. No matter how crazy it sounded.

"What is it you want me to do, boss?" he asked.

~

After hanging on for over four minutes, Silas heard Ben come on the line.

"I'm sorry, man," Ben's breathless voice explained. "I was on the line with a call from kidnappers."

"I'm listening."

"It's Murray, Jon. They took Murray."

Silas tried to rationalize how Murray could be involved in this mess. It made no sense at all. "What did they say?" he asked the boy.

"They want to talk to you."

"Me?" Silas was stunned. "Who are they?"

"The Palm Cartel, Mexican drugs."

"I'm supposed to be dead...what do they want with me?"

"Their leader is betting you're still alive. He wants to talk to you or he'll kill Murray."

"What did you tell him?"

"It was a woman...she was in Texas. I was able to track her phone to Austin."

"The Palm is run by that Palmero dude, isn't it?"

"Yes...he's in Acapulco. I'm sure that's where they have Murray, but the woman didn't say. She gave me a number for you to call."

"Did she threaten with a time line?" Silas asked.

"No...no mention of a deadline or anything. She just said to call that number."

The plane is on the way to get me," Silas was thinking as he spoke. "Bring up your satellite and get what you can on their compound. Pictures... the whole deal."

"All right," Ben confirmed. "Then what?"

"Don't know yet," he said frankly. "We'll make it up as we go... See you soon."

17

Murray was on tiptoes at the window when he heard the door open behind him.

"Now we wait," announced Palmero.

"Wait for what?"

"Your friend to call."

Murray slid along the wall into a sitting position, shaking his head. "I thought I told you... he's not with us anymore." The sarcasm in his voice was thick.

The drug lord ignored him. "Your friend will be a value to me," he said in now broken English. "Many American politicians will pay great sums for what I shall do."

"Okay...so you think he's alive, regardless of what I tell you. And...he's going to come way down here and rescue me... Is that about right?"

The smile disappeared from Palmero as he came closer to his prisoner. "For a gringo Samaritan you lie a lot."

Murray had been thinking about that term, Samaritan. He remembered the biker calling him that. "That biker guy," he stood back up. "The one who stole a woman's money, you telling me he's your brother?"

"Si," Geraldo nodded. "You should be more careful who you mess with."

Murray found those last words to be amusing, but kept a straight face. "Words to live by, for sure." He responded. "I don't understand though. That ugly dude was American."

"His mother was from Tucson, an Air Force brat she called herself." Palmero seemed to enjoy relaying his family history. "Our father had a strange taste in women."

"You said he wouldn't walk again," Murray wanted some clarification. "I shot a gun from his hand," he stressed. "And he fell over a bike. How does that add up?"

"Something got into his spine. They cannot take it out." Geraldo leaned into Murray's face with anger.

They stood silently, staring eye to eye for several seconds. Then the drug lord smiled again. "Your friend will come," he said in defiant tones. "If he is half the do-gooder Samaritan you are...he will come." Palmero glanced down at the floor. His tongue rubbed the inside of his cheek in a reflex motion as he pictured getting his hands on the assassin from America. "And then you both will learn..." he smiled and looked back up at his captive. "Samaritans do not last so long... outside the Bible."

Murray Bilstock again tried to remain stoic. He knew Jon was alive and he knew this Mexican madman was right. *Jon will come*, he thought quietly. *I just hope he plans it out first.*

~

The search for Clyde Kinkaid was on. Reino Petteri had closed the business early to concentrate on survival. The walk to the coffee shop on East Superior turned out to be colder than he planned for. His first cup was used primarily to warm his fingers. He looked down at the ceramic mug that normally would be taken for granted and smiled.

How quickly I have become soft, he thought.

This shop offered free Wi-Fi service, which also meant a certain amount of anonymity. When Petteri felt he could trust his fingers, he pulled an electronic tablet from the backpack he had worn and began searching files. The code was not high-level security. Yet it was effective, especially for a man in the pest control business.

Under "larger rodents" he listed several contractors and contact numbers. The area codes would be the most encoded part of the list. Not wanting to draw attention to their location, those numerals were converted into letters at the end of their name and certification references. "404" for instance, would become DJD. J, the tenth letter, offered the first zero, so that's how it was used. Email addresses would list the letters before "@" in reverse. Again, not a super sophisticated code, but effective in most cases.

Petteri sent out a "call to arms" to seven independent thugs. Used only on rare occasions, their ranking had moved up recently without their knowledge. The incidents in Mississippi had left Petteri with virtually no crew. The enforcers were asked to call him on a special number at given times that day. The first call back came as he sipped his third cup of coffee.

No names were used, other than the target's. Petteri answered silently and waited for the caller to ID himself with a number.

"Two, here," the voice said.

"Kinkaid. Find and terminate. ASAP."

"The congress guy?" the voice asked.

"Can you handle this or not?"

"Sure...I'm on it," the thug replied.

"There will be others to work with you," Petteri assured him and the call ended.

Soon, the fourth call ended and that was that. He had lined up the team, though one acted a bit odd about others being involved. The man from Chicago had the strongest credentials so allowances were made. He maintained his own crew of secretive killers and didn't work well with others.

He didn't say "no," Renio assured himself. *I'll take it at that.*

It was time to go back to his shop. Petteri packed up and looked outside. Remembering the cold, he retrieved a different phone and called for cab. The short ride would cost $7.00, but he didn't care about that.

He would think to wear gloves next time, he told himself.

Of his new top seven, four were located in the northern midwest. One was from Pennsylvania, but two were in the south. One was in Georgia, and the other in Arkansas. The three who were not chosen would surely hear about the job.

That could be awkward, he thought. *But seven is just too many.*

~

Acree and Kinkaid now sat at a table in the cabin's kitchen. The roles having swapped again, Acree was all ears.

"Who do you think Petteri will use now?" Marvin asked. "Lutz is in Canada."

Kinkaid looked up at Acree in near disgust. "Lutz would have been his first pick. Coming after me... he'd use his best." After giving that a second to soak in, he followed with, "Lutz was in that ditch...I'll bet your life on it."

Acree thought it through and his expression showed he agreed. "Do we have his list anywhere?" he asked next.

"No..." Kinkaid admitted. "I knew Lutz was his main guy. After that it would be the independents, Pilfoy in Chicago and Eubanks, the contractor down in Georgia. They might be loyal to him." The ex-congressman bounced his pencil on the table as he thought. "Reach out to Pilfoy. See how he acts toward you."

"I'm already working there through Borton...you know that, right?"

"Borton is too hot by now, I already told you that. They'll tie him to the Wacker mess by tonight," Kinkaid declared. "Go around him."

Frank Borton was indeed "hot." His department had not caught up with him, but a stranger in town was now looking for him.

18

It would take another two hours for the G5 to reach Midway Airport. Silas didn't care to waste time so he headed for the 83rd precinct building of the Chicago Police.

Parking a block down, when he lowered the trunk lid, a grey haired man with a dark moustache and a suit coat over blue jeans stepped from behind the Mercury. His ID said "Henry Jacobs, Parole Officer 5th District of Northern Illinois."

"Where's Borton's office?" he asked at the sergeant's desk, flashing his ID.

"Third door on the left...down that hall," the young officer pointed.

He knocked once but didn't wait for an invitation. Borton was on his phone. The man glared up at him and pointed, "Get back out there till I call you in."

"I think you'd best hang up, Captain," Silas ordered as he stepped forward.

"I'll call you back," Borton said abruptly into the phone and immediately punched another button to call for help.

"Before you do that," Silas cautioned him with a small recorder in his outstretched hand. "You might want to listen to this." The intruder pushed "play" on the machine and it began with "Marv, I've got FBI crawling all over me and this whole place." Silas stopped it at that point and looked for Borton's reaction.

"Where the hell did you get that?" the captain demanded.

"That's not important, believe me," Silas warned him. Stepping closer he went on, "I know who Marv is." Then he continued, "and I know who you are. Who is Walt?"

"No one mentioned any Walt," Borton challenged, his eyes widening.

"Your man from Hoffman Estates mentioned him at the hospital."

"He's... he's dead," the captain spit as the words left him. "I just heard."

"He is now," Silas said calmly. "It happens."

"What do you want? And better yet...what are you gonna do...kill me here in my office?" Borton stood and watched the man touch a small button at his waist.

"No...I don't see you being any use to me dead," Silas explained. "One of two things is going to happen. The second can happen at any time...remember that."

"Yeah?" Borton asked. "What's the first?"

"You're going to tell me who Walt is and you're going to help me with information about this attack on that girl... every time I call on you."

"Ha!" the captain grinned. "Sure...and if I don't?"

"This recording...and you only heard a small bit of it... will go to your commissioner and the local newspapers." Silas smiled a bit, "I'm aware," he said. "A couple of those folks might be as corrupt as you. But I'll find someone that isn't... trust me."

"I might just take my chances, smart-ass." The captain sat back down and smirked at his guest. "I know too many people in this town. You can't get to me like this."

"I wasn't quite finished," Silas announced sternly. "You interrupted me."

"Oh...yeah, sorry," Borton almost joked. "What else you gonna do?"

"Then... I will kill you." The tone of Silas' words drained the color from Borton's face. He'd been threatened before, many times actually, but this chilled him to the bone.

"I don't like people who hurt children," Silas finished.

"Walter Greer," the officer started slowly. "He's in the commissioner's officer." Borton swallowed hard and added, "The Chief answers to him."

Silas nodded and turned for the door. "I'll be in touch," he told the man.

~

Three computers were running searches Ben had designed and a fourth was connected to the satellite feed from Fernbank in Atlanta. Basic information put the cartel in Acapulco, but details were slim.

He found out that the Palm had taken over the area about two years ago. One of his search programs was looking for new construction since that time.

"Wow," Ben exclaimed as the system spit out what he sought. "He's built himself a fortress... right on the water."

The ringing of the intercom almost went unnoticed to him as he dug deeper into the construction that had taken place in Acapulco. Ben pushed himself away from his position and rolled across the floor to his main desk. Slapping the intercom, he hollered out, "What?"

"Ben," it was Marsha. "I'm going to bring Cheryl down to your work area, okay."

106

That was not a normal thing to do...guests did not come into the second and third level unless Jon said so. Before he could formulate an objection to it, he heard himself say, "Sure."

The smile that came over him brought with it a new thought, *Cheryl, huh? Okay.*

He suddenly became aware of his appearance and mess surrounding him. Ben jumped up and tried to straighten papers and pick up stuff from the floor.

~

The corners of the room, near the floor, were cooler. The bright sunlight filled the room and raised the temperature considerably. Murray had moved his chair to a corner. He had left his watch on the workbench in the hanger, so guessing at the time was the best he could do. The sun wasn't in direct sight through the little window. It wasn't glaring off either side so, *it must be straight up noon in Acapulco,* he thought.

His captor had not returned since earlier this morning.

How long would he wait for Jon's call? he asked himself. *Heck...the bigger question was would Jon call?*

Other than the chair left for him, this room was completely empty, not even dust on the floor. He considered breaking out the glass in the window to make a weapon, but it proved to be thick. *Must be some of Jon's bullet proof glass*, he laughed. There was little else to do but laugh, and wait.

~

"Let me talk to Greer, quick." Marvin Acree commanded when the phone was answered. "This is Acree.

It took a minute, but Walter Greer was soon on the line. "Marv, things are a bit messy right now, you shouldn't be calling here."

"Messy... my ass they're messy." Acree took charge of the conversation. "You let her get away...an 18 year old girl got away!"

"Why don't you just take an ad out in the damned paper, Marv? For Christ sake man...stop with all the names and details will ya?"

"I want Pilfoy's number or how to reach him."

"I already let you to talk directly to Borton. You want to be totally in charge now?"

"Borton screwed this up." Acree complained. "I want Pilfoy."

"How 'bout I have him call you?" Greer suggested.

"Make it fast," he demanded. "My boss is getting nervous...and when that happens people get hurt."

"Threatening me won't help any, okay?" Greer got snippy. "I'll get hold of him as quick as I can. Like I said...we have a situation around here. I've got three...now they tell me four dead area cops and the FBI wants answers."

"Borton handled this screw up for you?" Acree asserted. "Didn't he?"

"He does the details."

"Well he messed this up, big time. Take care of him."

"Marvin...that's my call, not yours."

"I'm telling you..." Acree tried again.

"Yeah...well you're way over the line right now." Greer warned him. "Back off while you can. I'm telling you."

Acree took a breath. "I'll be at this number till tomorrow. I'm waiting to hear from him."

"I'll see what I can do." Greer said and hung up.

Marvin rubbed his face trying to bring his color back before he talked to Kinkaid. *This whole thing has swung way out of control*, he thought to himself.

19

The ride back to Dalton was uneventful for Silas. There was much to do, but sleep was also a necessity. Harold Foster rolled the G5 to its hanger before waking his boss. The man's eyes looked that tired to him when he boarded at Midway.

"Did anyone call for me?" the groggy Silas asked.

"Naw, it was quiet for a change."

"Thanks, Hal." He stood and grabbed his bag. "Go get some rest yourself."

The pilot nodded and pointed to the starboard side of the aircraft. "The car is right out there, Sir. We're in the hanger."

Silas smiled... nodded back and stepped off the plane.

The man reacted with a jerk when the third line on his desk phone rang. Before answering, he pushed a button under his desk. It activated the distortion device for that line.

"What is it?" he started without a greeting.

"I've been contacted twice," the caller said. "Petteri called... and now Greer calls to say Acree wants me to get in touch with him."

"I'm not surprised," the warbled voice responded.

"Okay...what do want me to do?"

"I don't need any more killing within our ranks. Kinkaid must understand his new position. He simply can't be the player he had been."

"So...we take him out? That'll stop it.""

"No," the voice answered quickly. "Not yet. I have plans that included his knowledge. I've got to get the distribution system back up. Without that, we could get too far behind in our deliveries."

"Neither one knows I work directly for you, do they?"

"And we keep it like that. You're one of our best men...that's all. The trouble is... you've been bumped up the rankings by Lutz getting killed."

"How did that happen, anyway?"

"Kinkaid and Acree went off the grid way too quick. I tried to reach out and stop it, but Acree was way ahead of me. That mess in Chicago is going to be a problem, too."

"The cops?"

"Yeah," the voice agreed. "I didn't expect them to go through the mayor... to get at the girl. Now he's involved and he ain't happy."

"Who took them out?"

"Could be the girl's father got there. They found evidence to that fact."

"You really think one man did all that?"

"Do I?" the voice asked. "No. Not for a moment. But that's all we have right now. I've got my own mess to deal with."

"One other thing I don't understand..."

"Go ahead," the voice allowed his question.

"Petteri said you wanted Kinkaid silenced."

The line was quiet for several seconds. Then the garbled voice started again. "When that girl escaped, everything started happening really fast... I underestimated my own people."

The voice became heavy breathing, which had an odd sound through the device. The man in Chicago waited. It was extremely unusual for the boss to open up like this.

"I have parts orders I can't fill," the voice finally went on. "Tabuk is really on my ass about it. They called before I even knew all the details of how she got away. When I called Petteri I wasn't sure what I should do. I needed to know what he knew and what he planned to do. I was pissed at Kinkaid... and said a few things."

"She was missing overnight, boss," the other man added. "Somebody should have notified you right away."

"Now you're just kissing up," the voice chided him. "They searched for her all night...look," he tried to sound convincing. "What happened is done, even the Lutz thing."

"But Petteri sent his own team in with Lutz."

"I already knew about Lutz," the voice was bragging now. "He called me to verify. Petteri told him I wanted them to kill Kinkaid." There was a rasping, deep breath and then, "That had been true, but I changed the orders. I never called Petteri back, he didn't know about it then, and he still doesn't." Pausing again for a second, the mysterious voice then added, "Neither did Acree, unfortunately."

The man in Chicago did not like what he was hearing. Rubbing his forehead he spoke with near impertinence, "So Lutz was killed for nothing?"

"I didn't know Acree would react that fast... I'll deal with him later," the voice promised. "Right now, I need to smooth this over and get the network back up before they send someone for me."

"Call 'em then...call Kinkaid and Petteri. Tell 'em it's over."

"Would you believe that?" the voice asked. There was no answer. The distorted voice then issued his orders. "Contact Acree, tell him you'll work on it if... there is no interference from anyone else. They are both reaching out all over and I need that controlled. Make them both believe you're working for them alone."

112

20

Silas pulled into the third level basement to no greeting party whatsoever. He grabbed his bag and took the elevator up one floor to Ben's workshop level.

The young man and the girl were in deep study of something on the table.

"What going on?" Silas asked.

"Hey," Ben turned holding up a picture. His voice was pitched high and he spoke faster than normal. "I was mapping out the Acapulco drug fortress when Cheryl noticed this picture on the table." It was the star made of numerals.

"Yeah, does she know what it is?" Silas asked flatly.

Cheryl spoke up, "No Sir. But I saw one like it on a field trip last year."

Silas said nothing. He looked at her and waited for the explanation.

"It was hanging in the Governor's office in Lansing," she went on.

"Think it has anything to do with this case?" Ben threw in.

"Which one?" Silas sat his bag down and pulled up a chair. He pointed toward Cheryl, "this girl's kidnapping, or Murray's?"

"First things first, right?" Ben had gotten the message.

"I need to see what you've learned about Acapulco," Silas started. "How long has she been down here?"

Cheryl looked shocked but spoke right away. "I'm sorry. Should I leave?"

"She's already seen everything I can show you," Ben said sheepishly.

Silas reached for a fresh notebook and pulled his chair closer. "Go ahead...what have you got?"

"The place is definitely here," he said, pointing to a map on his screen. "It's been added on to quite a bit in last couple of years. Mainly these six towers and the walls between them."

"That's pretty obvious," Silas commented while leaning in. "A fort... for goodness sakes."

"Exactly," Ben went on. "This guy is anything but subtle. These two buildings, here and here," he pointed to structures within the compound. "Barracks of some type. I figure they can hold twenty or thirty guys each."

Silas put his finger on a main building near the center of the compound at the rear. "Is that where Murray is?" he asked.

"That's the main house...the original building for the property and yes, I bet that's where they have Murray."

"Can you focus in on that building to find phones, like you did in Chicago?"

"Way ahead of you," Ben bragged. "It's already set up."

"I need to call this guy, do we have a name?"

"Yeah, the leader is Geraldo Palmero, but he didn't give a name when he called. I just found it out."

Silas looked over at Cheryl. "Whatever you hear... or whatever happens next...please stay quiet." And he put his finger in front of his lips, "Can you do that for us?"

The girl nodded without a sound.

Silas picked up the phone Ben had laid out for him and a piece of paper with the number to call. It rang five rings before the man answered.

"Well, my friend," the voice in Mexico reverberated like an echo. "You did call."

"I understand you have a friend of mine there." Silas said sternly.

"Perhaps," Palmero countered. "Are you the man I seek?"

"I'm the one you'll deal with."

"Ah... Si. Very nice... a tough guy."

Silas gave that comment a few seconds to lie there and then went on. "Look Geraldo, I need to speak to him. Proof of life... you understand?"

"Ah, you don't trust me, Mr. Crane?"

"Nothing to do with trust... I just don't know you yet. And call me Silas."

He could hear the drug lord walking and going down a flight of stairs. Ben was working feverously at his computer.

"What do you want from me?" Silas asked the man.

"Now you're getting serious," Geraldo mocked. "I want you of course, Mr. Crane." His voice tried awkwardly to mimic a scene from an old James Bond movie.

"You should be careful what you ask for..." Silas taunted back, "You might get it."

"Ah...I like you, senor!" Geraldo laughed. "More tough guy, eh?"

"Why do you think you want me?"

The sound of a door opening delayed the next words.

"You would make me very popular with many American businessmen. Congress type businessmen, you know?" Geraldo puffed. "Many of them think you are dead."

Silas could hear Murray from a distance ask, "Who are you talking to?"

"Your friend wants to know if you are alive, I think." Geraldo handed the phone to Murray.

"Who is this?" Murray demanded.

"Lucy says she misses you." Silas quipped at him.

"Yeah...well, I miss her and her sister. How are we going to deal with this?"

At that, Geraldo grabbed the phone back. "So...you believe me, now?"

"I'm going to ask you, just one time... let him go, and I'll forget all about this." Silas warned.

"Still the tough guy?" the drug lord laughed again. "You come see me and we'll discuss it, yes?"

"Oh...I'm coming." Silas said and he looked at Ben who nodded. Silas then hung up.

Geraldo smiled at Murray. "He's very rude for a dead man," he said.

"We still have pretty good doctors in the U.S.," Murray smiled back at him. "You're gonna need one before too long."

"You, him...my brother, all you Americans think you are tough guys. John Wayne is dead you know?"

"Don't count on it," Murray warned. He did his best to conceal his smile. *It was Jon...and he is coming,* he beamed silently. *What can I do...other than just wait?*

116

~

Back at the mansion in Dalton, Ben was telling Silas what he'd hoped to hear.

"That's definitely the place. The call was coming from that building," he said.

"I heard the man going down some stairs and unlocking a door." Silas added.

"There is a basement style level on the backside of that house, facing the water. It's about twelve by fourteen and has one small window on the rear."

"That's where he is." Silas nodded confidently. "That's where I'll find him." He stood and walked toward the elevator, turning back with a puzzled look on his face.

"That phone number I gave you...the RP thing," he asked Ben. "Did you check into that?"

"It's some pest control company in Duluth... to be honest," Ben admitted. "This Murray stuff kinda took over. That's all I've got so far."

Silas nodded. "Understood... you did great, Ben... finding our friend." Then he looked at the girl sitting at the table with Ben. "I'll need to talk with you in detail soon. We're not forgetting what happened to you...I promise you that."

Cheryl smiled. "You already saved my life," she said.

Silas paused and just continued to look at her. He then turned but spoke as he walked on. "Your father was there, too."

Cheryl nodded, but Silas didn't see it.

21

The call Marvin Acree had waited for finally came.

"Where are you now?" he asked the caller.

"I'm in Chicago."

"I need to know who screwed up that Wacker mess, and where the girl went."

"You want a bunch, don't you?"

"I don't have time for cute talk, okay? If you can't help me I'll find someone who can." Acree's temper was on a short fuse.

"Yeah...that worked out really well for you last time, didn't it? If you want me to handle this then you need to back off and let me work. No interference...from anybody."

Acree was confused. "What's that supposed to mean?"

"I've already heard from Peaches down in Georgia. You called him too, didn't ya?"

"I need this done."

"Well, anyone else you've called...call 'em off." Pilfoy's tone was firm. "If they get in my way...I walk. Is that clear?"

Acree didn't like being told what to do, but this was an exception. He also knew Pilfoy was the next best thing to Lutz. He appeared to be nothing more than an accountant, but he was a cold-blooded killer. Pilfoy had a team of ghosts. Nobody knew who they were except him. Marvin Acree made his decision.

"Okay," he told Pilfoy. "It's your job. When can I expect completion?"

"When I'm done," the man said and hung up.

Acree's face flushed with color and he almost crushed the phone in his hand. As Kinkaid walked up behind him, he did his best to calm down.

"You got it handled?" Kinkaid asked.

"It's done," Acree responded. "I've got the right people on it."

~

The three flights of stairs down to the Mayor's office was his preferred path and Walter Greer walked every chance he could. He claimed it was good exercise, but the truth be told, he feared the elevators.

He strolled down the hallway on the fourth floor like he owned the building, passing guards and security personnel with a smile and a nod. He was the Special Deputy Commissioner of Police assigned directly to the Mayor. It was that suite he went into, waved at the secretary, and preceded on to the large double doors entering the Mayor's private office. Two quick raps with his knuckle and he let himself in.

"Oh...I'm sorry, Sir. I didn't realize you were in a meeting," he said immediately.

"That's fine Walt." the mayor smiled. "Charles was just leaving."

The assistant DA had been briefing the Mayor on the attack last evening downtown.

"Charles," the mayor stood and raised his finger. "Be sure to make those Hoffman people our priority. We need to know who killed them and those FBI agents."

"I'll do that, Sir," the man answered. He then dipped his head toward Greer and left the room. Greer pushed the large door closed and turned to the man behind the big desk.

"What the hell went wrong?" he demanded.

The mayor sat down and looked up at his guest. "You have some nerve, Walter."

"I have some nerve?" Greer nearly shouted. "This could bring us all down and you talk about nerve?"

"Don't yell at me," the mayor leaned forward with both hands on his desk. He stood again and bowed forward towards the man across from him. "Your people screwed this up."

"Hoffman Estates?" Greer complained. "You had to use men from Hoffman Estates?"

"Now you sit down and listen for a damned minute." The mayor's voice was up two octaves till he gathered himself and continued. "I was just going over what happened last night... with the DA's office. Would you care to hear it?" he added with sarcasm.

Greer's chest heaved. He did not speak through his clinched jaw, but nodded that he would listen.

"Our office...no...your office actually," the mayor explained, "received a call that there would be an assault on the girl's safe house by a person or persons unknown. Without time to locate the correct numbers to call for the FBI in charge of her protection, your office sent in an extra detail to help the FBI."

Greer felt himself relax as he listened. *The old man didn't get where he is by accident,* he thought quietly.

The mayor went on with his story. "The detail, volunteers from Hoffman, apparently ran into the perpetrators as they arrived on the scene. In the gun battle that ensued, they, along with the brave FBI agents...were all shot. Three of our men died at the scene and one died later at the hospital." The mayor then leaned back in his chair and glared at Greer in defiance.

The visitor rubbed his face with both hands. "That could hold up," he said softly.

"I couldn't hear you," the mayor almost shouted. "What was that?"

"I said...that's pretty good. It should work."

"Now...with that 'heat' turned down," the mayor's tone changed as he spoke. "I want you to find out who did this. Is that clear...Walter?"

"And find the girl, right?"

"The girl is Kinkaid's problem now," he waved as if swatting at a fly. "She can't hurt me. But whoever came in here and messed with my business...in my city...I want 'em dead."

Greer stood and nodded. The cover was a good one and the logic made sense. He looked up at the mayor again and the expression on the man's face gave him pause.

"What is it?" Greer asked him.

"That mess wasn't some coincidence," the mayor muttered. "Have you heard any reports about the 'Son' fella, lately?"

"He's dead, isn't he?"

The mayor tried to smile as he looked back. "Yeah...so they say."

Greer stood quietly for a minute then turned to go. As he got almost to the door he remembered a detail from the first report.

"Where is that car we found outside the building?" he asked.

The mayor raised his eyebrows at him wryly. "I was beginning to think you'd forgot about that. It's in the motor pool lockdown area, behind this building."

"Here?" Greer questioned.

"Where would you put it? In public view?"

"You're right again," Greer acknowledged. "I'll start with the car."

22

Ben found Silas sitting in his library...Jon's library, outside the master bedroom.

"Something wrong?" he asked.

Silas looked up at him and laid a book down beside his chair. "I'm trying to plan how to get into that compound. It's got to be a surprise," he said as his eyes panned down. "But that compound, Palmero's fortress, is heavily guarded and has its back to the water."

Ben stared at the book lying on the floor. "I see you're reading about General Washington."

His mentor cracked a slight smile. "Yeah," the man half muttered under his breath. Then looking back up at Ben, he continued.

"My mind keeps going to the Delaware crossing of 1776," he explained. "I know this has to be a surprise, like that attack was." Pounding his fist into the chair, Silas complained, "I just can't figure why the thought of that river crossing won't leave me alone."

Ben leaned down and as he picked up the book he had a revelation around what Silas was saying.

"It wasn't just the surprise that was important. It was the danger involved," the boy offered.

Ben opened the book to a famous painting of the revolutionary General's crossing of the Delaware River in freezing temperatures. "It was so dangerous, the enemy never expected it," he said to his friend and mentor.

Silas' head turned to him with a nearly blank stare. The man's eyes finally focused on his young assistant and a grin appeared.

"That's it, Ben," sprang from him. "The surprise has to be something Palmero would never imagine." He stood and walked over to a table. A large map of Acapulco was spread across it.

"Attacking from the sea or anywhere from the land would be walking right into his traps," Silas thought as he spoke. He picked up a pen and raised it arm's length above the map. "I have to drop in," he said as he released the pen. It bounced off the map when it hit. "From high enough he'll never see me coming."

Ben stayed quiet and listened to the man work.

"Find Tim Spiegel's number," Silas directed. "Call and tell him you want to make an ultra-high altitude free-fall jump. Ask for some instructions on what precautions to take."

Ben was reluctant to mention it now, but an idea had formulated while he studied the compound's towers. The thought of dropping in from above filled in the missing detail of his scheme.

"Jon," he said mistakenly. "I mean...Silas... Do you remember those laser guided munitions we got from the surplus vendor?"

"Those short nosed, 55 mm rounds?"

"That's them," Ben smiled. "What if I could rig six of them that you could fire on your way down? You know...to take out those towers."

Silas actually froze in place for a second. "That might just work, Ben." He smiled at his assistant, "I like it." Making a note for himself, the man continued, "Call Tim first, let's see if this is doable."

~

Geraldo Palmero sat in his expansive office on the main level of the house. He called a meeting of his main Lieutenants, the head goons of his army. Drinking directly from a bottle of Jack Daniels Old

No.7 to ply his speaking skills, the drug lord waited until everyone he had called for was there.

"Bring in the protective patrols from outside the city," he began with a huge swing of his arm. "I want all my men here, till I say otherwise."

The men looked at each other slightly but none spoke, not even a word.

"Bring the heavy guns in from the hilltops," he commanded. The gang had recovered four M101 howitzers from the police in Acapulco two years ago. They were used to guard the entrances to the city. He now wanted that firepower inside his compound. "Set them up between the towers."

That order stirred some alarm among the men. "Is the government coming again?" one asked in Spanish.

"No," Palmero snapped back. "A great prize will walk right into our hands...but we must be ready to catch it when it does."

"Will this prize have an army?" the man continued.

"If he does...he will not have it for long," the leader declared boastfully. "Now go, this needs to be done by tomorrow."

The men disbursed. Several were concerned by the lack of details but too afraid to push the madman for answers. Palmero was known to kill captured police officers for sport and had ordered entire towns destroyed to make a point. That was when he was sober. A drunken Palmero was like a ticking bomb. No one wanted to play with it.

~

Jordan Sterns was a bit surprised by the call that afternoon. It was the Chicago crime lab on the line. A Lieutenant Vaughn wanted to know about a rental car in Sterns' name.

"It appears to have been used in a violent crime here last night," the officer explained. "What can you tell me about this vehicle?"

"Not much," Sterns told him. He had to think fast. "I had reserved a car with my credit card, but then ran into someone I knew and didn't need the car."

"You didn't drive this car, sir?"

"Nope," the man told him. "Didn't need to. Guess I forgot to cancel the reservation."

"I see," the Lieutenant replied. "Let me ask you...do you know a Weston Duray?"

Now things were beginning to make sense to Jordan. "I've never met him, but I've heard of him...sure." Sterns knew his brother-in-law was a close friend of Duray's. He quickly accessed his credit card records on his laptop computer.

"Just how do you know of him, Mr. Sterns?"

"Why...wasn't that his kid who got kidnapped last spring? Heck, everybody around here knows about him."

"Just for the record, Mr. Sterns," the officer asked. "What city did you rent this car from?"

Scrolling down the list of charges, Sterns found the answer. "Ah... I was in Ludington and Scottville on business," he stalled. "I rented it by phone from a company in Ludington. I'll need to go get my notes to tell you the company."

"That's alright, sir." The Lieutenant rubbed his forehead in frustration. "Thank you. I'm sure you'll be hearing from the rental company as well. We've notified them that the car is down here."

"Thank you officer," the man said and hung up. He then walked into the kitchen at his home. "Carol," he asked his wife. "Where's your credit card?"

"I let Waylon use it a couple of days ago. He's good for it, whatever he bought."

"Yeah...I'm sure he is." the man said as a concern came over him. "He's not down in Chicago, is he?"

"Waylon?" his wife laughed. "No. He's up at the lodge. I talked with Sue this morning."

Jordan Sterns left the kitchen but hollered back, "If I get a call from a rental car company...come get me, will you?"

"Rental car?" his wife asked.

"Yeah...it seems we rented a car yesterday."

23

NCIS Agent Timothy Spiegel was entertained by Ben's phone call for several minutes. He finally stopped the young man and asked straight out, "let me talk to Jon."

"What do you mean?" Ben faked the best he could.

"I mean Phil Stone called this morning. I know about Murray, okay? It was just a matter of time till Jon resurfaced, we all knew that."

"I ah...I just want to try skydiving, Agent Spiegel." Ben gave it one last attempt.

"Sure you do," the agent half laughed. "Are you jumping HALO or HAHO?" he asked abruptly. "And... your suit is rated to thirty below, right?"

"Thirty below?" Ben didn't understand.

"Are you going to free fall and for how long? HALO is High Altitude Low Opening, That's one minute...maybe two near terminal velocity, or are you going chutes away, we call it HAHO, from the jump?"

"I don't have any idea, sir," the youth finally admitted.

"Let me talk to Jon."

Ben handed the phone over and after a short, deep breath Silas spoke.

"Hello, Tim."

"So...you're going after Murray and you need to jump in. Is that about it?"

"Can you teach me what I need to know?"

"In about six months...yeah," the agent said smugly.

"I don't have six months, Tim. I realize there's more to it from that height, but it's nothing I can't learn. I need to do this now."

"Jon...it's good to know you're okay by the way," his voice clearly jubilant. "But how high did you jump as a Ranger?"

"Eight to nine thousand feet," Silas replied. "We popped chutes at 1250 feet."

"Thirty to forty thousand feet is a bunch different, my friend."

"You guys came in from forty when you got me, right?"

"Yeah...it was around there. But we trained for months to be able to do that." He became very serious in his tone, "its fifty-five below zero at 35,000 feet. You need supplemental oxygen, pressurized suits...it ain't for amateurs."

"I can't let them know I'm coming in. It has to be from above ground radar detection. The incursion must be a complete surprise...even after I'm down."

"Where is Murray?" Spiegel asked coldly.

"Acapulco."

"Damn," the former Seal exclaimed. Scratching his head, he continued, "those winds are tough down there."

"You'd need to drop by GPS coordinates down to 10,000. Those controlled mini-chutes that are hard to ride. It's a bitch of an entrance, man."

"I'm not leaving Murray down there."

"Okay...calm down, didn't really expect you to," the agent clarified. "There's only one thing to do."

"So...you'll teach me?"

"Well, the best I can," the retired Navy Seal responded. "And ...I'll just need to go with you."

~

There was a message for Petteri when he returned to his office. The note, left by an employee who was on the inside of the operation, said only, "3:30 today."

"Finally," the area chief said out loud. "I was beginning to wonder if they got out of Mississippi at all."

The reference was to a refrigerated truck that was overdue by six hours. Its destination was the docks at Duluth and a freighter named "Cordova Queen" flying the flag of Panama. The "CQ" carried dozens of sealand containers, some plain, and some with coolant compartments.

Petteri checked his watch. It was 2:10 in the afternoon. The ship would leave port at 1640 hours or 4:40 PM.

"This will be close," he said again...out loud. But there was no one to hear.

Petteri pushed on the intercom button. "Shari," he called into the box. "Can you close up today?"

"Sure, boss," the young woman answered back.

"I'll be back in the morning. Just take any messages that come in...okay?"

"Got it," she said and her boss grabbed his heavy coat and went out the back door of his private office. He needed to contact the boat captain, to make sure he would wait or stall if necessary. He couldn't do that from his office.

~

Marvin Acree had spent the morning calling back his other resources to conform to Pilfoy's demands. Larry "Peaches" Eubanks claimed he already had expenses in the four hours of work he'd invested.

"Expenses?" Acree scolded him. "Searching 'Google' on the internet? You sure you want to push me... over that?"

Eubanks backed off with a minor huff in his voice, but he did remember his place in the pecking order.

"Who are you going with then?" Peaches couldn't help himself.

"I can't tell you that, man." Acree's temper was growing short. "If they knew I talked, they'd kill both of us."

Eubanks grunted and gave up. As he put down his phone he mumbled under his breath, "Pilfoy."

~

Petteri found the ship's captain at a bar on Canal Park Drive. Sitting alone in a high backed booth, the man nursed a beer with the appearance of being in deep thought.

"Jurgon," Petteri called to him as he approached the booth. "May I join you?"

The captain took on a look of concern. He knew full well who had just walked up on him, and it wasn't a usual occurrence. Petteri slid into the seat opposite Jurgon Walcovitz and waited for the waitress... who was coming their way.

"Just a beer," he told her. "Lite beer, please." And the woman spun on her heels, back toward the bar.

"What causes your visit?" Walcovitz asked without looking up.

"The shipment will be here. I just wanted you to know that."

"The freight crane has already been pulled back," the captain informed him. "It's too late."

Petteri held his tongue at first. He tilted his head back and in doing, saw his beer being walked across the room. Laying a ten-dollar bill on the table, he motioned toward both bottles while sliding the bill to the waitress. Without a word, she picked it up and was gone.

"Jurgon," Petteri said in a low and steady voice. "I will remind you who makes a call like that...and it's not you."

The captain raised his head. "That'll be $4,500 added to the invoice for the crane to come back," he stated.

"Just have it there," the Finlander mob boss was now red in the face. "The truck gets in at 1530." He slid up and out from the seat, pushed his untouched beer toward the captain. "This is yours too, my friend... And drift high near Marathon tonight."

Marathon, Ontario, is one of the northern most points along Lake Superior. The Cordova Queen would normally turn starboard, south by southeast toward the Soo Locks, at least twenty-five miles from the shoreline near there.

Walcovitz seemed to snap into consciousness.

"A helio pick-up?" he asked.

Petteri stared at him, but didn't answer with words. He slid from the booth and after a short silent pause, left the captain to his dinner.

24

The second level basement area was well lit, but still cool. Ben kept the temperature at sixty-eight, or close to it, most of the time. The computers and monitors put off volumes of heat, and heat could be deadly to the machines.

Cheryl Duray had borrowed a sweater from Ben and was sitting in a pile of printouts and articles about herself when he returned to his work area.

"I can't believe all this," she said almost sounding disgusted. "You know more about me than I do."

"Possibly," Ben laughed. "Anything you need a refresher on?"

The girl threw a handful of papers at him, half pretending to be mad and half teasing.

"Under normal conditions," Ben confessed. "This could be considered kinda creepy, I know."

"Why all this about me?" she asked.

"That's the big question. Jon wanted to learn why you were chosen, why you were taken." He took hold of a rolling chair and pulled it toward him. "We know there are others, many not identified or even listed as missing, but your case was big news...for a while."

"I have no idea why they took me," she confided to Ben. The thoughts about all that stuff made her shiver. She snuggled herself down into the big sweater and looked directly at Ben. "You must have been on this from the time I got away, how is that possible?"

Ben sat down and took on a more serious tone. "Jon was already looking into that guy, Kinkaid...before you got away from him..., and we thought we knew what he was up to."

"Why was he after him, then?"

"The land deal," Ben stopped suddenly. He realized she probably had no idea about that. "Kinkaid had forced some people to sell their land to him," he explained. "He caused a young man to die in the process."

Cheryl's eyes grew large. "That's why they moved us," she figured out.

"Moved you from where?" Silas asked as he walked up from behind them.

The two young people turned toward him. "We were just talking about all this intelligence I gathered about her," Ben responded.

"Yeah...I understand that," Silas said coming closer. He looked straight at Cheryl and asked again, "Do you know where they moved you from?"

"No...I really don't," she answered.

Silas grabbed another rolling office chair and took a seat. Pulling up closer to them, his face took on a serious expression. Again, he looked directly at the girl.

"Cheryl," he started. "I need to ask you some questions if you'll let me... and I need them to be away from your folks."

Her face twisted slightly like she didn't understand.

"I don't want your answers influenced by their presence," he disclosed. Then pointing at Ben, he added, "His either."

Ben stood and asked her, "Do you want me to leave?"

"No, no...it's okay," she waved for him to sit.

Silas could tell there was closeness growing between the two, he wasn't sure how Ben would react to the questions, but decided to allow it. As the youth sat back down and inched his chair closer to hers, Silas gave it a few seconds and then began, "Were you drinking the night you were taken?"

"Yes," she said without any hesitation. "I had a local drink, something with rum in it...but just the one."

"You told the authorities that you remembered it tasting different when you came back from the restroom...is that accurate?"

"It was bitter...kind of salty," she told him as her face displayed the signs of a new revelation coming to her. "It smelled a little like the paint shop back at the farm," she blurted out and then added, "funny...that just came to me."

She paused as if reconsidering, then added, "But it did smell like brush cleaner... in a way."

Silas spoke again, with Jon's knowledge and tact, "That's GHB," he said calmly. "Did you ingest much?"

"Huh?" she complained. "What is that...the date rape stuff?"

"Gamma-Hydroxybutyric acid," he explained. "It's what made you sleepy."

"And I don't know... even now, I can't remember how long I was asleep."

"Did you finish the whole drink after it tasted funny?"

"I don't think so..." she thought. "Maybe a couple more swallows. I can't remember."

"That's okay," Silas was ready to move on. "This one you need to think about," he said coldly. "Were you molested at any time?"

The girl's face looked to the floor while Ben's flushed with a combination of embarrassment and anger. Silas gave her a couple of minutes and then tried another angle.

"Did you recall being 'hurt' or 'sore'..."

"I know what you're asking about," she cut him off and looked up sternly.

The girl took a deep breath and paused. Her now steel gaze caught Silas straight in the eye. "I remember a doctor...at least he looked like a doctor," she rambled some as she told the tale. "He was examining several of us one day." She finally blushed and said right out, "I don't think I was raped. I don't know about the others."

Silas had more questions. "The doctor's exam, was it listening to your chest and stuff like that?"

"Eyes, ears, nose...throat, the whole works," she began to shake slightly and Ben unconsciously reached out for her hand. "He used a stethoscope and took x-rays. It was spooky."

"How many other girls do you remember?" Silas asked.

"They kept us apart most of the time...the exam day there were four of us and the day I got away there were four, but they were different." Her eyes showed that the thoughts coming to her were things she had not considered before. "A couple were anyway."

"Do you know any names?"

"No..." she nearly sobbed. " We weren't allowed to talk to each other."

"Okay, "Silas slapped his knee to indicate it was over for now. "I'm sorry to make you go back through all that."

"It's... alright," she stuttered softly.

"No...young lady," he answered firmly. "It's not alright. Not one little bit." And he got up and walked to the elevator. He needed to get away from them now, before his growing anger showed and drew questions he didn't care to discuss. Not until he was sure it all added up... the way it appeared right now.

But Ben, he considered. *Ben will put it together soon enough. He's just caught up in other feelings right now.*

When the doors to the elevator had closed, Ben pulled her chair around to face him.

"I've only seen him that upset... twice before," he told her.

"He's worried about his friend, I know," she reasoned.

"No...he can handle that. That stuff he understands." Now it was Ben who stared at the floor. "When my Mom got hurt... and then Marsha...he had that look."

"What's he going to do?" Cheryl asked.

Ben stood straight up from his chair. His eyebrows climbed high on his forehead.

"I'd hate to be the guys who did this to you," he responded with an expression reflecting Silas' resolve. He then looked away from her, trying in vain to conceal his own anger.

"And he will find 'em," he declared. "All of them."

25

The Lake Superior Maritime Center was trying to close down for the day. Business wasn't what it had been, back in the height of the iron ore trade. Steel mills were closed or closing and the cost to haul the ore to Europe was an obstruction in itself. They loaded goods of other kinds here as well, all going to the northeast or even further.

The Cordova Queen was one of five ships the group used, depending on the schedule and timing of the shipment. Sea Box containers would arrive by truck at the dock. The truck/train container boxes carried manufactured products that normally could take the slower, but less costly route to the east coast.

The unit coming in late this day was a cold storage box. Not unheard of, but usually one that would travel by rail for expediency. This container was special.

Captain Walcovitz had to promise the dock master a case of Irish whiskey to get the huge crane rolled back out. The truck being late would add expenses all around, yet it had to be done. The fees for the service were about what Walcovitz had guessed. The whiskey was simply to make it happen.

"I'll need the top units lined up flat," he explained to the man in charge.

"You're not asking too much there... are you?" the dock master laughed. "You think wind drag is that bad?"

"Just do it," Walcovitz ordered. His voice wasn't joking and the man could tell.

The tops of the containers would serve as the landing pad for the helicopter from Marathon, Ontario.

~

The ladies had occupied the kitchen at the Dalton mansion, getting to know each other while simply trying to ignore the situation. Coffee had become a pot of tea once Weston and George quit coming in for refills.

Weston sat with George in the living room. It hadn't taken him long to notice the window glass.

"How thick is that stuff?" he asked.

"I don't even know," George admitted. "Thick enough so far."

"So," the guest's eyebrows rose, "it's been tested, huh?"

"We've had some excitement here, but it usually tapers off pretty quick." George gave him a sideways glance. "This place is tighter than a tick."

Duray grinned. "I love the way you people talk," he finally smiled, something that had not happened since they got there.

"It was mostly for your consumption, sir, I assure you." The DA knew he had broken the chill.

His guest smiled and asked innocently, "So...when is our host getting back here?"

"He's been back for several hours already."

"Oh...really?"

"No offense on his part, I assure you. There's a couple of irons in the fire right now, as we say down here." George tried to make light of it. "More than just your situation, unfortunately."

"So...he's been here...moving around and I couldn't tell?"

"He'll show you how...I'm pretty confident of that, but yes, to answer your question...quite easily."

"Who is this man?" Duray asked suddenly. "Is he really an assassin?"

George Vincent leaned back in the huge leather wing chair. His looked changed to serious as he considered how to answer the man.

"You're gonna force me to face some facts I try to ignore...or at least rationalize my way through them."

Duray shifted in his chair. He understood the gravity of his question and allowed the man time to formulate a response.

"If he were anyone else...if I had not witnessed what I have... with my own eyes," the local lawman began like he was forcing himself. "I would say he was a killer." George then stood and walked directly to the bookcase across the room. He pulled down a copy of The Federalists Papers.

Weston was watching. "Are those all his books?" he asked.

"Yeah," George acknowledged and turned around. "You know, it seems foolish in my own mind...trying to justify what Jon does to someone else. At first, I just accepted it. Mainly because what he did benefited people I cared about."

"I can certainly relate to that." Duray threw in without hesitation.

George smiled and handed him the book. "I bet you can," he quipped and stepped back to his chair. "Jon sees certain things in this world... in pure black and white."

Duray listened intently.

"We all want the right things to be done," George continued. "But talking about it is as far as we go." He picked up his coffee cup but didn't drink from it. He had forgotten for the moment how long it had been sitting there. Offering a self-deprecating smile, he set it back down. The guest showed no reaction.

140

"When wrong doing is suspected at top levels... especially in our government, Jon proves it to himself...or tries to." George then looked Duray straight in the eye. "When he does prove it...he doesn't hold back."

"What if he doesn't," Duray asked. "Prove it, that is."

"Proof is a necessity to him. Without it he does nothing."

Weston glanced down at the book George had given him. The DA didn't let the opportunity go by. He sat back down with both hands over the ends of the chair's arms.

"The men in that book were patriots," he said. "But in their day, some saw what they did differently."

"I know," the visitor agreed. "History is written by the winners."

"That's one way to put it, for sure." George shifted again and went on. "Jon does what he believes is right...and he's satisfied to let history sort it out."

"The Silas business...is that Downer from the Sons of Liberty?"

Leaning back in a bit of a surprise George smiled broadly this time, "Exactly."

"I pride myself in the ability to size someone up quickly," Duray bragged rather boldly. "This guy is a test of all that, but I think he's genuine...I really do."

"That's why we try to protect him," George confided to him. "And that 'we' I speak of...includes the current President of the United States."

The Yankee cowboy grinned at his new friend, "I heard about that." There was a considerable pause till he added. "Now I believe it."

~

Clyde Kinkaid had spent the evening out on the front porch. The afternoon's comfort began to turn cooler and he stood, shaking his shoulders as in a shiver. He could see Marvin Acree nestled in a large chair inside the cabin, reading a hunting periodical. Kinkaid nearly threw the door open and came in making a grand announcement to his host and associate.

"We need to go to Kentucky," he blurted out.

Marvin Acree put down the magazine and stared at his boss in frustration. "Not again," he complained. "Look...I'm going along with you on most things, okay? But I thought we agreed, no moving around. It's just too dangerous."

"I know," Kinkaid brushed the objection off. "I'm not talking about moving around wily-nilly. The farm they'll use next is in Kentucky. Mine is over...kaput."

"So...they have to keep the process going, right?"

"Harkness doesn't know how to operate at that level...he just doesn't." Kinkaid sat down next to Acree. "They need me to run the place...it's what I do."

"Boss...you seem to forget. You're an ex-congressman on the run from the law. How the hell are you going to run anything?"

"I just need to see it. Get a feel for the layout, you know?" the egocentric hoodlum couldn't hold himself back. "Then I can operate it from anywhere! Hell, I could go to South America and run it from there."

Acree actually understood what his boss meant and on one point he agreed with him. But he couldn't allow it now.

"Look, boss. I swore to Pilfoy that there would be no interference while he worked. Us moving about, especially going to Kentucky, could appear to him to be just that."

"If I don't prove my worth, and soon...they won't feel they need me," Kinkaid said in a resolute voice. "It's my only chance to survive."

"Let's give Pilfoy three or four days," Acree pleaded, "maybe a week."

"Four days," Kinkaid said as though he'd won an argument. He raised an arm and forefinger into the air. "Then we go to Kentucky."

26

The light coming into Murray's window was now from the moon and those few tourist hotels that still operated in Acapulco. Sleep would overtake him soon, so the cowboy sat with his back to the door.

At least they won't catch me sleeping, he told himself.

He stared out wondering what the next day might bring. Jon was alive. He would be coming for him, but when, and how?

I need to be ready to help, his mind shouted. *But how do I do that? I can't see much and can't hear anything.*

Weariness, and the relaxation from knowing his friends were coming, finally got the better of him. His head bobbed two or three times and then Murray slept. The moon had climbed high and now lit only the base of the window ledge. Sitting on the floor with his back against the door, the cowboy rested with his chin on his chest.

Reino Petteri was restless through the night. He had returned to his office, to sleep on the leather sofa. The office was but six blocks from the docks. He heard the big ship leave the marina around 8:30 P.M. It had been scheduled to sail at 6:00 P.M.

The delay would mean the truck had arrived and the merchandise was loaded. That should have given him some ease, but it didn't. The entire business was in turmoil. Major leaders were literally at each other's throats, and there were questions of how they could move forward.

Reino's mind became engulfed with thoughts of home.

Finland would be frozen over by now, he dreamed. He would keep that thought till morning.

~

Those in the Dalton mansion had settled down hours ago, everyone except Ben.

Silas had come back down, after the girl went upstairs, to ask for another computer program. One that would search news and law enforcement files for any new missing girls, anywhere.

"These guys aren't through, Ben," he declared. "There are young women out there right now in serious danger."

"It's not just white slavery either, is it Jon?" the boy asked.

Silas allowed the error in his name. "I'm afraid not," he answered. "Those lists concern me even more than the thought of sex slavery."

Ben's face displayed contempt. He couldn't help but wonder what they had planned for Cheryl. Glancing from the floor back up to Silas, he tried his best not to concentrate on his growing feelings for the girl. Stepping to a computer terminal, he finally spoke.

"I'll have the program up in a couple hours," he promised.

Silas nodded and retired to a sofa across the room. It took two blankets to get comfortable, but he slept there. Ben would finish his work and lay his head on the table. He'd done that many times before.

~

Marvin Acree also had trouble sleeping that night. The sound of Kinkaid's snores didn't help but that wasn't the issue. His boss's concerns about staying viable to the syndicate were true. His own loyalty to Kinkaid meant that could also affect his value, or lack there-of.

~

Captain Walcovitz stayed at the wheel that night. He held more speed as the big ship went into her starboard turn and the Cordova Queen slid across the water to her left. Enough that her lookout called "land ho" as he spotted the lights of Marathon getting brighter.

Walcovitz held his course for several minutes and then reversed his engines to slow the ship down. This action further exaggerated the drift toward land, but the captain knew the area. He put the engines in forward again at five knots and maintained that slow pace.

The helicopter came in low with its lights out. The pilot made one pass over the Cordova Queen and then circled back, landing on top of the cargo carriers. He killed his engine and climbed out, moving directly to the refrigerated container.

Walcovitz watched from the command center as the man cut the security strip, and unlocked the padlock to open the container. He came out from the unit carrying a blue box with a cylinder attached. Setting the box down, the pilot closed the container door, reset the lock, and retrieved another seal from his coat. The numbers would prove to be an exact match to the seal he had cut.

After adjusting a valve on the small box's cylinder, he placed it in his helicopter and climbed back behind the controls. The rotors came to life and in a couple more minutes, he was gone into the night.

The Cordova Queen's engines roared into a higher gear and she lurched forward and away from the Canadian coastline. The entire dance lasted less than ten minutes.

27

The strong aroma of coffee led Weston Duray to the kitchen that next morning. Silas was already there. It was the first they'd seen of each other since Chicago.

"Morning," Silas greeted his guest. "I trust you slept well."

"As could be expected, I suppose." Duray answered. "I appreciate your hospitality," he said sincerely. "But much more of this... of being cooped up... will do me in."

"Nobody knows you're here," Silas replied and pointed to the coffee maker. "I understand how you feel, I'd be the same way, but this is the safest thing for all of you right now."

Duray poured a cup and stepped to the table. "I don't want to sound ungrateful, because I'm very much so," he explained. "I just need to be doing something."

"When my other friend gets here, we'll have some major planning to do. A man like you... might just be a help in that regard."

"Absolutely," Westy smiled "Anything I can do."

Ben Shaw staggered into the kitchen and mumbled something before getting his own coffee. As the morning progressed, others gathered around the table.

Tim Spiegel's chartered helicopter landed in Dalton around mid-morning. He called and Silas headed out alone, to go get him.

"I could have sent the plane for you," Silas complained to him over the phone.

"Well, I'm here, now," Spiegel reminded him.

Silas thought for a second before he answered. "And I'm damned glad that you are, my friend," he said.

148

He met the NCIS Agent at the Dalton airport with his Jeep Cherokee. Spiegel busily unloaded his gear and tossed it toward the utility vehicle. Silas thanked him again and Spiegel grinned.

"I know...hell, I'm charging all this to you anyway," he beamed at his old friend. "I had to make several stops along the way." Spiegel glanced down at his bags and added, "I hope I've got everything."

"What is all this?"

"Helmets, regulators, bailout bottles, masks and a couple of special suits and chutes I borrowed from the Golden Knights in Tennessee."

Silas appeared totally confused. "I didn't realize..." he started to say.

"Yeah, I know. HALO jumping is critical stuff." He threw the bags into the back of the Jeep. "There's serious planning and equipment involved."

Spiegel finally caught a full view of Silas' injured face.

"Damn, man!" he reacted. "What's the other guy look like?"

Silas hardly changed his expression. "The other guy was a tree...and he's fine, I guess."

"You came close to actually being dead, didn't you?"

"Most people still think I am," Silas straightened up to respond. "I'd like to keep it like that...as much as possible."

The discussion on the ride back quickly turned to the upcoming mission.

"The house sits right on the water," he offered. "So there are only three sides to deal with. We come in from above and take out the defenses on the way down. Ben has that figured out for us."

"How do we get out of there?" Spiegel asked.

"Still working on that."

Spiegel didn't comment. He just leaned back, looking none too surprised by the answer.

As they turned onto Highway 71, Tim's reaction to the mansion was the same as many other's had been.

"This is your house?" he asked as they drove up the front driveway.

"It's a starter home." Silas said dryly.

Ben, Cheryl, and Weston Duray came out to meet them. Silas began the introductions.

"Tim...this is Westy Duray and his daughter, Cheryl. Guys... Special Agent Tim Spiegel of the Navy Intelligence Service."

"NCIS, Jon." Tim corrected him. "Naval Criminal Investigative Service, it's different."

"Pleasure to meet you," Duray extended his hand.

~

The phone ringing at 11:30 A.M. was an ominous confirmation of his concern. It was "that" phone again, the one he dreaded to hear.

Petteri's eyes stretched wide and he rose from the couch. His neck wouldn't move. The position he'd slept in was the culprit.

Forcing himself to move toward the desk, he pulled open the drawer that held the phone.

"Yes," he answered it with apprehension.

"Everything for nothing," the voice began its rant. "The merchandise was not good. The subject died and our customer is pissed."

Petteri rubbed his head thinking of what to say. "It happens," came out of him. "You know it does, we can't panic over this one time."

"The new facility screwed up the packing container," the voice rattled through its encryption.

"Which container? The packing box or the big unit?"

"Does it matter? The cells were decomposing. The tissue was dead when it got there."

Petteri knew it did make a difference, but there was no use trying to get that from his boss right now. "I'll go down there and check the methods used."

"This should be Kinkaid's job," the voice lamented. "This is his fault, the SOB."

"I'll leave this afternoon," the Finlander promised. "I will call you when I know what's what."

"$678,000 invested and no payday for it," the voice continued. "Gone...it's gone." And then the line was quiet.

Reino put the phone down and went to the door leading to the outer office area. His receptionist was there. She had been running the morning's business and let him sleep. He wanted to thank her, but that would have to be later.

"I'm going to need a ticket to Lexington this afternoon," he ordered. "First flight out. Can you get that for me?"

"Yes, sir," the young woman answered while grabbing her phone.

"I'm going to run home to pack a couple things," he said pulling his coat on.

"I should have everything ready when you get back, sir."

Petteri nodded and went back out through his rear office to his truck.

~

Outside the modest home in Muskegon, Michigan, four men sat in a stake out. Two were in a van parked a half a block from the house and two were in the woods behind the residence. The grey skies and dirty snow slush made the temperatures feel worse than they were.

"No sign of Sterns," one reported from the woods by cell phone. "Looks like a car is gone."

"Any movement in the house?" the van replied.

"Yeah...there's a woman in there. She's got some project going on, keeps moving from room to room. No phone calls, though."

"Okay..." the leader of the group acknowledged from the vehicle. "I'll check in with the boss... See how he wants to handle it."

One of the men in the woods had an additional idea.

"Right...say... bring me a coffee, will ya?" he half joked.

"You're getting soft, Clegg," the man in the van laughed and redialed the phone. He reported what he could to their main boss back in Chicago.

"Keep an eye on the house for another day or two." Pilfoy told them. "If Duray is around there...or using that house for staging anything, I need to know."

"What if it's clean, boss?" the man in the van asked.

"I'll cross that bridge when we come to it. Just keep watch on everything that happens there...got it?"

"Yeah...we got it."

Putting the phone back in his pocket, the van driver looked to his partner.

"Damn Clegg anyway," he shivered. "Now I want some coffee."

"There's a donut shop around the corner." The man stuck his hand out for money. "Want I should go get us some?" he asked in broken English.

Staring the other man down, the driver reached for his wallet. "Don't be long," he warned.

Watching the man walk toward the corner, he then folded his arms across his chest and scrunched into the seat. "Damn Clegg anyways," he repeated himself.

Inside the house, a woman stood beside her front window. She eased the blinds out at their side, peeking toward the van. The men in the woods, beyond her backyard, had set off a silent motion sensor as they moved closer. The man walking away from the van looked at her home too many times. Easing her way to the bedroom, she found the note, the one with that special number.

28

Lunch at Dalton had been ham sandwiches and store bought potato salad. The men were excused to their planning and went upstairs to ride the elevator. Cheryl gave Ben a look and he quickly included her in the group.

Tim and Weston were briefed on the status and layout of the encampment at Acapulco and Ben added some facts concerning the surrounding streets and buildings. George Vincent stood to one side.

"Since Palmero took over the area," Ben began. "The tourists have stayed mainly on the other side of the cove." He pointed to an area on the map, which was west of the cartel's fortress.

Taking their silence as understanding, Ben moved his finger to the compound itself.

"The road out front is paved," he said looking up at them, "but traffic is light. Everyone gives the place a wide berth."

"How wide, exactly?" Duray asked.

"Two, maybe three blocks... from what I can pick up off the satellite."

The newest cowboy didn't follow up, but appeared to be storing that info for later.

"The towers are here," Ben pointed them out, "and here."

Then he zoomed in closer and directed their attention to spaces between the barracks buildings and the towers. "There has been considerable activity here since Jon... I mean Silas, spoke to Palmero." The objects in the photos were pretty clear.

"Cannon," Tim Spiegel declared. "He's bringing in artillery."

"They look like 105's," the youth went on. "But we can't be sure. That's close enough though...they're big guns, whatever they are."

"He's expecting a full frontal attack then." George added.

"Run through those pictures again," Duray asked. There were five shots with the cannons in different positions. Ben replayed the footage.

"See that?" the Michigan man pointed. "In that one the guns are pointed out to sea. He's got them where they can turn around easily. He has no idea where you will come from."

Spiegel smiled. "The drop makes better sense... now even more than before," he declared. "Those guns can't shoot straight up and at night... they'll never see us coming."

"Aren't the winds rough out over that water?" Duray asked.

Spiegel was impressed and his expression showed it. "Yes, sir," he replied quickly with a direct stare. "They can be extreme off the coast there."

"You'll need to free-fall towards a beacon of some kind," Duray went on. "Coordinates won't do much good till you get lower."

"You're a jumper?" Spiegel asked with a smile.

"It's been a while," the man acknowledged.

Cheryl Duray walked around behind her dad. She put a hand on his shoulder. Without looking, Duray covered her hand with his own.

"It's okay, baby," he assured her. "Your mom will understand this." He then looked back at Spiegel. The room was deadly silent.

"It's like riding a bike, so they say anyway." He then looked at Silas. "You'll need a third man...on the ground...in town."

Silas gave the man a serious stare and spoke for the first time. "I can't ask you to..."

"You didn't," the girl's father broke in. "I'm saying I'll go."

"Look...this is a dangerous..."

Again, the new cowboy wouldn't allow him to finish. "And coming to Chicago to save my daughter wasn't?" he said with heavy sarcasm. "I won't say 'I owe you' but we both know I do." Duray took a slow, deep breath and stepped into Silas' face, nose to nose. "That has nothing to do with this," he declared. "Samaritans do what's right...and only for the right reasons." He now stared a look that went through Silas and challenged, "You want to argue that with me?"

Silas' expression changed ever so slightly. Turning to the map, he lowered his eyebrows and leaned over the table to make a note in his pad. Still he said nothing.

Duray sharply glanced over at Spiegel.

"C Company, 509" he told the man with great pride in his words. "I may be a little older than you...but I can still cut it."

"A Pathfinder huh?" Spiegel leaned back in respect. "How high did you jump?"

"Thirty-six thousand feet...there about," Duray retorted, "three times."

Silas remained quiet. He knew full well what a Pathfinder was. The Army's specialized parachute team would clear the way for other units. At the beginning of the first Gulf War, they were used to open a path for the Delta Force. They knew all about unannounced entrances.

Silas also knew what question would come up next.

"Jon," Spiegel looked right at him. "You need to be the guy on the ground." He waited for some disagreement or even a look that never happened. Then continued, "We'll jump in, stir the pot and cause all hell and confusion...you walk in and get Murray."

Silas' blank gaze didn't change. He slowly looked toward Ben.

"How many extra suits do we have on hand?" he asked him.

"Enough," the boy smiled.

"Tim is a bit taller than me...or Murray. Can you make one work for him?"

"No problem," Ben responded. "The material is workable." He looked at Duray and quickly assessed him. "He won't be a problem to fit either."

Silas nodded without a word.

Spiegel appeared confused by that conversation. "I've got two jump suits...I borrowed from the Knights."

"Wing suits?" Duray lit up as he asked.

"Yeah," Spiegel beamed. "Solid black."

"They won't get 'em back, you know," Silas twisted his head and smirked.

"Yeah...they know too," Spiegel agreed. "They cost over $900 each. But they'll fit over the flight suits or whatever you're talking about."

"These are a bit more than flight suits." Ben smiled.

Petteri left Lexington, Kentucky's Blue Grass airport driving south on I-75. He turned the rental car east at Richmond and then south again near Irvine.

The community of Drip Rock, Kentucky, sat in the low hills of the Daniel Boone National Forest. Population records for the area are vague at best, but it is believed that four to five hundred residents call the area home.

Red Lick Ranch had been operating as a cattle farm for thirty years with little notice or fanfare. In recent times, the employees seemed to come from outside the area and were not well known to anyone.

The gates at the ranch were like many others, always standing open from the road, but there was one major exception here, the two men with shotguns sitting twenty yards inside the property.

One walked up to the rental car with his weapon resting on his shoulder. The car's window came down and a voice from within it called out, "Where's Harkness?"

The man lowered his gun and leaned over to see who had spoken.

"Mr. Petteri?" he asked tentatively. "What are you doing here, sir?"

"Is Harkness here?"

"Yes, sir," the man pointed toward a roofline that could be seen in the distance. "He's at the office."

The window rolled up and the car spun its tires moving forward. The armed man stepped back, waving his left hand to disperse the dirt cloud.

29

"So," Special Agent Spiegel looked straight at Ben. "Jon tells me you have some fancy munitions we can use on this fortress."

The others watched intensely as the youth walked to a storage cabinet and came back with a prototype he had been working on.

"It's a miniaturized, laser guided rocket," he said handing the model to Spiegel.

"What's the payload?" he asked.

"Twenty—four ounces of C4 with an impact blasting cap."

"And the guidance?"

"The same as from the F-4 fighter and the C-130 gunship really. You lock on with the laser and then fire when ready."

Duray spoke up at that comment. "It stays on target once you lock on?" he asked.

"Yes, sir. For up to three minutes."

Spiegel leaned in toward the monitor. "Bring that shot of the compound up again, please."

Ben focused the display on the interior grounds. "Is that what you wanted?" he asked as the NCIS agent stared into the screen.

"That's great," Spiegel commented as he reached out. "We could each target three towers and then set them off at about the same time, right?"

Ben's eyes flickered as he thought about that. He positioned his hands in a "v" shape and spoke as he thought. "A mounting bracket...with the two outside units at about thirty-five degrees," he said. "It will take about sixty seconds to target three. Is that doable?"

"I like it," Duray smiled. "Ninety seconds would give us time to go after those cannons as well."

"How about the barracks?" Spiegel remembered.

"I can handle the barracks," the voice said from the far end of the table. Silas was making notes as he spoke, but could feel all eyes landing on him. He looked up, stone-faced. "This could work," he declared. "Shock and awe...the right way."

"There's just one thing I haven't heard discussed," Duray started.

"I pulled a few strings through Washington," Spiegel stepped in. "My old boss schedules training flights out of Lackland AFB." He looked at the older cowboy and asked, "Is this what you were wondering about?"

"I think so," he leaned back and grinned. "You're talking about our ride, right?"

"There's a C-130 that will pass over Acapulco tomorrow night...not this night," he tried to emphasize. "Two nights from now would be a better explanation I guess, at 0320 hours."

"At what altitude?"

"Thirty-seven thousand, four hundred."

"How can we get the door open at that height?"

"We'll be the only human cargo," Spiegel explained. "They can depressurize the bay ahead of time. That means we'll be exposed for ten minutes before we jump."

"Exposure" meant to the temperature. It could be as low as fifty below at that altitude. The jump suits were made of polypropylene and were highly insulated. Their protection would make the temperatures tolerable.

"You said you have oxygen, right?" Duray inquired.

"I have jump bottles and a large tank on board the plane," he answered. "This will let us go 100% oxygen for at least 45 minutes ahead of the jump."

"We did pre-breathing before we went into Afghanistan in '01," Duray told him.

Spiegel noticed the others appearing to have been lost in the discussion. "You have to clear all the nitrogen from your blood at that height, or you get the bends like a deep diver coming up." They still weren't with him. "The pure oxygen flushes all the nitro out...it takes about 30 minutes or so to do that."

Finally the faces showed understanding and Spiegel looked back at Duray who was nodding. Jon was up and walking away.

"I'll be back in a few," he hollered over his shoulder. "Just need to check on some things."

Ben Shaw jumped up and followed him. "Silas," he called out.

The man stopped and waited.

"I didn't want to say anything in front of everybody," Ben started.

"What is it, Ben?"

"That program about the missing girls you ask me to set up," he began.

Silas remained quiet but his look demanded more information.

"I had to filter it down. It's amazing how many kids go missing every day."

"Filter it down, how?" Silas asked.

"No repeated runaways or drug problems. I set it to only uncharacteristic disappearances of girls above eighteen years old."

Silas nodded approval but said nothing.

"That narrowed it down to three since I started. Two out on the west coast and one in North Carolina...from a bar on the beach in Wilmington."

"A bit late in the year for the beach, isn't it?"

"Never too late for a bar, though," Ben retorted.

The logic made sense. Ben's reasoning fit the pattern or what little they had of one. Silas' head bobbed ever so slightly in agreement.

"Stay on that," he said. "Find out what you can about her." With that Silas turned and reached for the elevator call button. Before he could touch it, the door opened and Marsha leaned to step out. She caught herself and first stared at Silas for a second, then looked right past him to Ben.

"Daniel is on the phone," she announced. "He wants to know what's going on about Murray."

"Crap," Ben clenched his fists. "I meant to have called him already."

"What does he know?" Silas threw in. "About me?"

"Confirmed...nothing," Ben tried to explain. "I think he suspects, but we haven't told him about you... no."

"I'll talk to him," Silas declared. "Which phone is it?"

Marsha nodded and showed the slightest of smiles. "The one on the kitchen counter," she answered. "He's on hold."

Jordan Sterns' meeting was interrupted by a buzzing sound. He didn't recognize it at first, though he had been the one to set it up. When the noise did register in his mind, he stood abruptly and asked that everyone in the room leave.

162

Clipped to his belt was an item he put on every day, for so long he had all but forgotten its purpose. The buzzer was a communication from his wife. It meant something was wrong and he needed to come home...quickly and carefully.

Twenty minutes later, Sterns car pulled into the driveway of his home. The garage door lifted and the vehicle disappeared inside.

The two men in the van, parked down the street, checked their weapons and called to others in the woods.

"Go," the leader ordered sharply. "Go now."

The four converged on the home from front and rear entrances. Guns in hand, they kicked in the both doors and at nearly the same moment. Before they could say a word, the entire scenario changed.

Sound of sirens and the glare of blue lights flashing caught their awareness first. All four intruders froze for a second, wondering how that could be. The next moment was filled with voices yelling at them.

"Drop the weapons and get on your knees...now!"

One of the invaders, close to the back door, turned toward his right and fired into the kitchen. That act was met with overwhelming force. The shooter quickly slumped and fell with three shots in his chest. The man with him dropped his gun and raised his shaking arms high.

Their leader dove behind a sofa for cover. He stuck his handgun over the top and lifted his head to see. A red dot appeared on his forehead and the sound of another shot rang through the house.

"Clear...clear...clear," a voice shouted loudly as several men stepped into the main room. They took the other two into custody and checked the dead men just to be sure.

Sterns' car had delivered more than just him to the home. Hiding low up front, and in the backseat, were four armed officers of the Michigan State Police.

Had Pilfoy done a bit more homework on the renter of the car found in Chicago, he might have discovered that Sterns was an undercover drug enforcement officer for the MSP.

"Who the hell are these guys," Sterns asked. He didn't recognize any of them as local drug mobsters. He pushed one of the survivors against a wall demanding, "What's this all about?" Checking the prisoner's hands he found the fingers smooth. Any prints had been removed chemically. "I asked you a damned question," he pushed again.

The man looked back at him with a blank expression.

Another officer grabbed Sterns, "You can't do that, Jordan. Back off, man."

Sterns stepped back and glared at the silent intruder. Reaching into the man's coat, he pulled out a wallet. The license said "Illinois...Chicago, Illinois."

His face became pale and he turned to his wife, showing her the ID.

"You see this?" he almost roared in anger. "Where is your brother? They could all be in danger right now." He grabbed for his phone, still talking as he dialed, "This is about Duray. Waylon gave Duray that car." The veteran cop showed fear his wife had not seen before. "These aren't ordinary bad guys," he stared at his phone, waiting for an answer.

30

The roofline seen from the entrance was of a large log structure sitting on stone pilings about four feet high. The large wrap-around porch revealed that it had once been a residence. Three men stepped from the front door as Petteri's car reached the parking area. Two carried weapons.

"Mr. Petteri," the man without visible firepower began. "What brings you here?"

"Are you serious?" Petteri almost screamed as he slammed the car door. "You haven't been told?"

"Told what, Reino?"

"Don't try that overly friendly crap with me...Wilbur."

Wilbur "Deacon" Harkness hated his first name being used in front of others.

"Alright then," the embarrassed man came down from the porch and got right into Petteri's face. "What's your damned problem?"

The Finlander turned his head to his right and nearly whispered, "You have two seconds to step back away from me." Harkness' anger was building, yet he knew who he was dealing with. Shaking with rage, the man moved back but continued to glare at his guest.

"How did you process that last order?" Petteri demanded.

Concern replaced some of the anger on Harkness' face. "Why?" he asked.

"You used that veterinarian, didn't you?"

"Look...we were pressed for time, Reino. What's wrong?"

"The tissue was degraded," Petteri said in a more calm voice. "Kinkaid's out...you get a shot... and this is what happens."

"It wasn't all our fault, man."

"What do mean? It was your job."

"She'd been dead too long by the time she got here. There wasn't even any Viaspan used. It still had blood in the tissue."

Petteri looked surprised, "Wait a minute...you're supposed to get sections. Packed in freezer containers."

"Well yeah..." Harkness explained. "'Supposed to' is right. We received a body wrapped in a sheet."

"You're not serious...no liquid nitrogen?"

"Maybe two blocks of dry ice in the box with the body, but that was it."

Petteri stood in silence. Then it hit him, "There were two subjects for parts."

"We got the one, that's all."

"None of this is right," Petteri spit as he spoke. "It's all been handled wrong."

"You didn't know?" Harkness asked in disbelief. "I thought it was because of the urgent situation." The man began to turn pale. "We did what we could."

"What about the rest of her?"

"The liver was all we thought we had saved," the man answered. "Doc said he thought it would do."

"Where is the body?"

"The incinerator, man. We don't leave stuff to be found."

Petteri climbed back into his car. He closed the door and lowered the window.

"What else do you have here?"

166

"Two live subjects for shipment," Harkness responded. "Came in two days ago."

"You may have to keep them here for a while. It's too hot to try to move 'em again."

"Yeah," Harkness complained. "I got a call this morning that another one is coming in."

"Hands off," Petteri reminded him. "None of them get touched."

"They all know that, Reino. How long till we can move them?"

"I wish I knew," he said as the car pulled away.

~

She started to stay in the taxi. Maria Chaperon's route home from Texas was less than direct. She had stayed and shopped, spending Palmero's money on food, drink, and clothing. Anything she could bring back into Mexico.

The commotion around the compound was familiar to her.

"Gerry is preparing for war," she shook her head and muttered to herself. The driver turned to ask if she needed help with her bags, but by then four men had appeared from inside the compound. They took her luggage and packages and one took her arm. The choice was no longer hers.

~

"Daniel..." he started. "How are you my friend?"

The other end of the phone was silent for a bit, then the part-time reporter, now COO of Crane Industries answered.

"Jon?" he started... with relief nearly breaking his composure. "I always knew you had to be alright."

"Sorry for the subterfuge," Silas now took over the conversation. "I hope you understand."

"I think I know you well enough," he laughed. "Working with you, understanding is a relative thing." Daniel paused but only for a second. "Can I assume this revelation is still close knit?"

"Please, if you would...I'd appreciate it. I thank you for telling Ben about Murray."

"Yeah...I guess that's why I called." His tone went to serious. "I know you're on it, do you have an idea?"

"Yeah, we're working on a plan to go into Mexico to get him. You'll be seeing some fairly large expenses on different accounts about this." Silas realized as he spoke, "You needed to know about that in advance anyway."

"Well, our friend from New Orleans has already spent a pile," Daniel told him. "Just who all is in on this?"

"Murray," Silas listed off, "now Tim Spiegel and that kidnapped girl and her family, George, Doris, Ben, Marsha and you."

"Kidnapped girl?" Daniel was lost. "The Michigan girl?"

"Yeah...we're working on what happened to her, too."

"You know..." Daniel's voice was in a near laugh. "When I heard about what happened in Chicago...the thought crossed my mind."

"Listen, friend," Silas explained. "We'll talk more later, I promise... I need to go now. Murray is in real trouble."

"Go..." Daniel directed him, "and be safe."

~

Murray Bilstock sat, back against the door, thinking, *He's coming...He won't be alone... or will he? And how does he get in here?*

The cowboy had been over every inch of the walls and floor in his cell. Nothing he could break loose or get a hold of. The door was thick with resins and the hinges were solid casings that couldn't be pried open.

When Jon's assault begins...the bad guys will likely come for me, he realized. *I need to slow them down somehow, but with what?*

He had looked over it, at it and through it. It was so simple it didn't register with him till just then. *The chair!* He almost shouted out loud.

Wooden, with a cane seat, the chair was solid and sturdy. He left it where it was. The worse thing now would be for his captors to remove it before Jon got there.

He sat back against the door, staring at the chair. Relieved that he was now a part of the plan, in his mind if nowhere else.

~

"I just heard from Harkness," Marvin Acree announced as he walked into the room.

"Harkness called you?"

"He'd had a visitor...Petteri came...in person."

Kinkaid stood. His face began to turn red. "What was he doing there?"

"That last shipment got messed up. The brides are okay, but the donor bodies weren't handled right."

169

"They sent Petteri in?" Kinkaid couldn't believe it.

"Harkness said he didn't know what had happened, but the man showed up there, and he wasn't happy."

Kinkaid reached out with both arms to his sides and suddenly became calm yet still very serious. "We can't overreact...not yet."

"Harkness said it was our people that screwed up...and there's a body missing," Acree carefully shared what he knew.

"Missing?" the boss asked, still in control of himself. "How is that possible?"

"We probably won't ever know," Acree added. "Four of our guys were killed in the shootout... when the raid came down. The others aren't ones who would know about the girls."

"There's a body somewhere on my land, Marv." Kinkaid rubbed his head with two hands trying to maintain his cool. "This can't be much worse. You have to find that body and get rid of it."

"Boss..." Acree pleaded. "I can't get anyone near the place right now. Cops are everywhere." Reason set in for a second and he added, "There may not be any body...they could have just lost count."

"They better not find any dead girl, Marv. Your big plan on how we get out from under this blows up if they do."

Acree didn't necessarily agree with that, but he didn't argue. "I'll see what I can do."

31

Silas carried a bag from the elevator that appeared heavier than it was. Whatever he held under his arm looked more like a toy than anything else.

Inside the bag were a mini Rocket Propelled Grenade launcher and four 40mm rounds. The firing unit weighed five pounds and was just under 28 inches in length. The missiles weighed three pounds each. Rolled up neatly beside the RPG were two black Kevlar suits. Several handguns with magazines surrounded the other items.

"What is that?" Duray asked of the metal object Silas carried. As the man pulled it out, all could see the object with its four spokes and circular center.

The spokes had mini turbines at each end and the entire unit sat on rails, like a tiny helicopter, for landing gear.

The center, round section was about five inches in diameter and housed the controls and electronics.

"It's supposed to be a camera mount for surveillance," Silas raised it so the others could see. "I had it modified somewhat."

"Is that the control box, like an RC aircraft?" Ben asked. Even he had not seen this thing before.

"Should be," Silas answered. "But it's now more of a homing device."

At that point, there weren't any more questions. The group remained mum as everyone basically waited for more information.

"It's rated to lift and carry sixty-five pounds. I weighed this bag at forty-three pounds so it should handle it fine."

"Okay..." Spiegel finally broke down. "What does all this mean?"

"First of all, I'm flying into Acapulco commercial, as a regular tourist." He waited for everyone to catch up. "I can't carry my gear on a commercial flight, so you'll need to drop it to me."

"Drop it from the plane?"

"That's where this wheelie-gig comes in," Silas beamed. "You shove it out the door on my first signal. I've set the altimeter to start the engines at two thousand feet. The homing beacon should do the rest."

"You figured out a signal?" Duray had that question on his list.

Silas pulled an oversized pen from his pocket and pointed it at the far wall. A red light streamed into the wall that changed to blue for five seconds and back to red.

"You should see this from forty thousand with no trouble," Silas put it back in his pocket. "It's a plain pointer by appearance. They won't know what it is at customs."

"How does all this work?" Spiegel asked. "The timing sounds impossible. You have to signal us where to drop."

"Your plane gets to the area at 0320, right?"

"Yeah."

"Watch for my laser signal pointing to the northeast at 0317, kick the drone and the bag out the door the second you see it." Silas paused and looked at each man to see if they were with him. "You jump three minutes later and watch for the signal again."

"The bag should be to you by the time we jump." Duray was counting the seconds.

"Yeah..." Silas nodded. "You guys dive to fourteen thousand and pop chutes." He looked at them to see if his jargon was satisfactory. If it wasn't, they weren't saying.

"Then rig the missiles, fire away and still have a full minute to maneuver to the roof," he went on. "That time allows me to get ready on the ground."

"Awfully close," Spiegel finally muttered out loud. He rubbed his chin and looked up at Silas as he thought.

"Everything's close, Tim." Silas smiled while checking his watch. "Harold will take us all to San Antonio in the G5. I've got a flight to catch there at 6:00 P.M. He'll drop you guys at Lackland in plenty of time for your ride."

Everyone stood in silence. What they had heard could work, but it was risky.

"Ben," Silas pointed at him. "Can you have those brackets for the laser missiles ready by in the morning?" Before he got his answer he was moving to the elevator.

"Yeah," Ben motioned with both hands. "I don't see why not."

Stepping into the elevator, Silas looked back at them. "We all need to be ready to leave here by 11:00 A.M. tomorrow."

~

The survivors of the Muskegon home break-in attempt were in the "booking" process at the main police precinct. Jordan Sterns and his wife had locked their home, the best they could, and followed the patrol wagon to the station.

"Sterns," a voice came from down the hall on the main floor. "Can I see you in here a moment?" It was the precinct captain.

Leaving Carol on a side bench, the undercover cop walked to the captain's office and stepped inside.

"Close the door, will ya?" the captain asked courteously.

Stern did as he was asked and turned back to the superior officer, whose mood had changed dramatically.

"What's with you, Sterns?" he demanded. "Some old Confidential Informants pop your house and you're making a federal case out of it?"

"That's not what we've got, Cap," Sterns insisted.

"When they check those guy's IDs, you will find they come back as dead guys, probably dead for some time. The Social Security numbers will also be from dead folks."

"You know this, how?"

"It's a hunch right now, boss. But a damned good one." The officer leaned over the captain's desk. "Did you see their hands?"

"I haven't seen the men yet," came the reply. "I just heard about your actions at the scene."

"No prints, on any of them," Sterns straightened back up as he continued. "Their age... older than your regular hit man, yet young enough. They're known as 'ghosts,' boss."

"That's Chicago stuff," the captain had heard of this group. "What would they be doing up here?"

"If I'm right, it's got to do with that Duray family from up in the U.P."

"Sit down, detective," the captain pointed to a chair. "I need to hear this."

32

Tim Spiegel asked Marsha to show him how to get down to the workshop. She had informed him that Silas was gone to the little house for some supplies.

Walking up to the third floor to get to the basement seemed odd to him, but Spiegel followed along. When she opened the elevator for him, he all but laughed. "Very Jon Crane, huh?" he snipped.

"Like most everything else," Marsha smiled back. "It works."

The ride down was quick and the door sprung open at the workshop level.

"How's it going, Ben?" Spiegel asked while stepping from the elevator.

"Good..." Ben replied over his shoulder. "Your suit should be ready and..." Finishing a last adjustment, he laid down his torch. "These brackets are just about done."

Ben spun and held up the unit he had been welding. Looking somewhat like the tip of Poseidon's spear, it contained three housings for the miniature missiles with one simultaneous trigger. A large CO_2 cartridge would initially launch the missiles from the bracket in a spray pattern. Some fifty feet out, the rockets would fire and the laser guidance system would direct them to the pre-selected targets.

Tim came closer, "Yeah, the suit is really weird. I expected it to weigh much more than it does." He reached out and took the bracket from Ben. "Speaking of weight," he looked at the bracket, and commented, "About two pounds by itself, huh?"

"Yeah," Ben grimaced. "Light as I could make it."

175

"What's the total weight, loaded to fire?"

"Just under ten pounds for the whole thing."

Spiegel raised and lowered the bracket like a training weight. "That won't be too bad. We can handle that for as long as it takes to target the towers."

"I've got a couple of twelve pound weights you and Mr. Duray can practice with, if you like."

"Great idea, Ben." Tim set the unit down and changed the subject, "How many other mini-missiles do you have?"

"After these...eight."

"Could you rig a single holder for me, and four other missiles I can load and launch if need be?"

"Sure," Ben assured him. "Is four enough?"

"I hope. I don't really want to carry too much, but they could come in handy if things get weird."

Ben slid himself across the room to a different monitor.

"Have you heard of this before?" he asked as he brought the Mexican's artillery cannons on screen. "These things read as though they have GPS guidance to fire."

"You're kidding."

"No, my sensors picked up tests they were running. They can target from a cell phone."

"No..." Spiegel started and then quickly corrected himself. "I didn't mean I hadn't heard of it. The guidance device selects a target and downloads the GPS coordinates from a satellite. That info is sent to the gun."

"Yeah...it's all here. I can interact with it from right here," Ben bragged.

"Trouble was," Spiegel continued. "It didn't work most of the time." The NCIS agent picked up one of the laser guided missiles, "I prefer these, myself."

"I'll have them in your bag, sir."

"Young man...you can call me Tim."

~

The slight of stature man sat across the room from his desk. He stared at its flat surface, or more the cell phone that lay atop it. Tobias Pilfoy knew what the delay meant. He couldn't reach out and call them. The phone he wanted to hear from was likely in some cop's hands, just waiting to try to trace the call.

How could this have gone wrong? He wondered. *Everything about this mess seems to be jinxed.*

He wasn't concerned about any phone records. The last communication he'd had with the team was by phones they both discarded right after the call. He checked for news reports from that area. Nothing.

"They were there...sitting on this guy's house and now nothing," he muttered under his breath. "Who is this Sterns guy?" he asked himself.

~

Still upset by Petteri's trip to Kentucky, Kinkaid had made a decision.

"Get Franz on the phone," he ordered his associate, Marvin Acree.

Looking stunned by the request, Acree stumbled, "I can't do that...I mean...I don't have any way to contact him and he doesn't call me himself."

"You've talked to him since we've been here, haven't you?"

"I haven't talked to him at all."

Kinkaid nearly circled the room with his nervous walk, "Is he still in Caracas?"

"I have no idea," Acree tried to reply. "He doesn't tell me these things."

"He's doing this," Kinkaid spewed angrily. "Petteri didn't go to my territory on his own. Hell...even he knows better."

"You're supposed to be in hiding, boss...you keep forgetting that." Frustration was overcoming his respect for the man.

"He's toying with us, Marv." Kinkaid's eye's boiled with rage. "Franz is just playing games."

Marvin Acree didn't agree with his boss. He nodded as though he did, but inside he was worried about what to do next. *The man is really losing it*, he thought quietly.

~

Standing before a full-length mirror in the guest bedroom, Weston Duray pounded on his own arm and chest, which was protected by the black Kevlar suit.

"This thing is truly amazing," he proclaimed to his wife sitting near-by.

He touched a button on the belt and then picked up a quarter from the dresser.

"Check this out," he held it toward Rita and squeezed it between his thumb and two forefingers bending it nearly in half. His wife was not moved, nor did she appear impressed by the sight.

"Are you doing this out of a sense of gratitude?" she asked bluntly.

Her husband turned away, very slowly. He placed the bent coin back on the cabinet before replying, "How long have you known me?"

Rita did not respond, he really didn't expect her to.

"In some ways..." he began again. "I can understand that question." He turned the hydraulic power of the suit off and removed the black gloves. "You know I don't do things for that reason...and neither do these guys." Walking over to the bed where she sat staring at the floor, he stood beside her and gently touched her shoulder.

"The man they're going to rescue is important to them. That makes it important to me."

Rita looked up, "I know all that... and I understand that part. But how long has it been since you've jumped...especially from that high?"

"It's better equipment than I've ever been around, believe me. We're going to go on full oxygen way before the jump and decompress ahead of time."

"It's still been years, Weston. You're not as young as they are."

Duray stopped and turned away. "Fourteen years, three months since my last jump," he said solemnly. "You don't forget how, Rita."

"That wasn't from so high, Westy," she argued.

She had him there. His last HALO jump had been more than twenty years earlier, in the military. Scrambling for a rationalization, he spoke as he thought.

"I know more about it than this Silas guy does." That sounded pretty good to him and Rita was still listening so he went on. "If I let him do the jump, it could jeopardize the whole mission. I know what I'm doing," his tone became stronger as he realized he really just wanted to do this.

But Rita wasn't through. "How are you getting back from there?"

The question was one Duray was avoiding himself. That had not been concluded yet.

"I'm sure they have a plan," he tried to comfort her. "We've been busy working on how to get to this Bilstock guy." Though he wasn't convincing anyone, including himself, he said it again. "I'm sure they have a plan."

The worried wife nearly jumped to her feet.

"That's it!" she screamed in sarcasm. "They have a plan? What plan?"

"They're gonna help me find the men who took Cheryl...when we get back."

Rita's expression locked into a glare. She said not a word, but took several deep breaths.

"When we get back, Rita," Weston said again. "And we will get back."

33

Acapulco's southeast side was now a war zone. Or at least an area ready for war. The streets were blocked directly in front of the compound, only limited traffic was allowed through. The towers were manned twenty-four/seven with lookouts able to see eight to ten blocks in all directions.

The chance of an attack by sea was countered by the artillery, which sat pointed toward the bay. Pre-positioned boats had been calculated for their GPS to help target any vessel approaching from the south.

Amazingly, tourists were still in the city. International warnings of the dangers in the area dissuaded some, but Palmero's controls on the city were considered an improvement over recent years. Casinos and clubs were in full swing, especially across the bay. But even as close as two blocks from Palmero's fortress, bars and small clubs vibrated with music. The Alvarez Airport was watched by two groups of the drug kingpin's men. As they waited for darkness to settle in on the second night of the siege, business was a bit tense, but it continued.

Geraldo sat alone, on the second floor front porch. There he could view his compound and the surrounding area. The Paradise Hotel, four blocks away, had lost many of its guests during the defensive buildup. The resort remained open for the few leftover, valiant souls who sought excitement...or perhaps drugs.

It was quiet again this afternoon. *He said he would come,* Geraldo reminded himself silently. *I am ready for him.*

~

CWO Luke Diaz missed the first call for him from the states. He had been on a training run with several new pilots assigned to his squadron. The message simply said, "Silas will call back."

Is this a trick, he thought, *or a trap to find Jon Crane?*

Diaz had talked with Murray a couple of time since they were down in Panama. The story was Jon had been killed on a mission. The Blackhawk pilot could tell Murray didn't buy it, but the evidence pointed that way.

Sitting next to his desk, Diaz popped a beer and leaned back to wait. It didn't take long until the phone rang again.

"Hello?" he answered cautiously.

"Luke," the voice started. "Murray is in trouble."

The voice sounded familiar, but Diaz couldn't be sure.

"What does Robinson mean to you?" he challenged the voice.

"Your mini copter," Silas replied without hesitation. "You and it saved our asses."

"There are rumors of your death around, you know?"

"I do know. I started them." Silas remained very serious. "No time to explain now. Murray is in Acapulco. He's in big trouble and we're going in to get him."

"We?" Diaz asked. "How many is 'we?'"

"Three in...four out."

"What do you need from me?"

"I need an extraction. I can't have my jet land there. It can be in Guatemala waiting for us, but not close enough in Mexico."

"I've got a bird with external tanks. It can make 1250 miles in one hop, but that's it. I'll have to stagger the run."

"Can it be done?" Silas asked.

Diaz spoke as much from ego as anything else. "I'll make it happen," he said. "Where and when in Acapulco?"

"Around 0400, Thursday. Can you find the Campo de Golf Resort course?"

"Nighttime on a golf course?" Diaz was almost laughing. "If this wasn't you I wouldn't believe it."

"Anything else you need to know?"

"Where will the G5 be in Guatemala?"

"Retalhuleu, it's the closest long runway."

Looking at his flight maps, the pilot commented, "The miles look doable. I'll need to touch down at Retalhuleu on the way over to refuel."

"I'll have it arranged and paid for, plus whatever costs you incur."

"Just get Murray out of there, okay?"

"If I don't...I won't be at that golf course either."

Diaz knew that was sincere. "God's speed, my friend," he said solemnly.

"Same for you...and thanks, Luke."

~

Thinking about the situation in Kentucky had given Reino Petteri a sick headache. Conditions at the farm were not good. The live subjects needed to be moved, preferably on to the overseas shipping point. He checked in the rental car and walked to the terminal at Lexington. It would be too late to call by the time he got back to Duluth. What he was now thinking would break protocol but something had to be done and quickly.

183

His boarding pass stamped, Petteri found a quiet spot in the corner of the waiting lounge. He had forty minutes till his flight.

He hit "last call re-dial" and took a huge breath waiting for it to ring.

The distorted voice answered on the seventh ring, "What is it?"

"I left Kentucky a few hours ago, Franz. It's bad there."

"We do not use names," the voice warned.

Normally that threat would have rattled him. But to Petteri, his concerns far outweighed the chance a name might be overheard.

"I'm telling you," he reported firmly, "those 'brides' need to go overseas, now."

Franz let the insolence go without another warning. "It's complicated," he said calmly. "The escorts are nervous. They won't fly right now." The last part was a lie. Franz was the one nervous about discovery right now.

"That's silly. There's no way the TSA or anyone else is even close to being on to us."

"That damned girl escaping has everyone lying low right now," the Franz voice insisted.

~

"Ben?" Silas asked as his young wizard answered the phone. "Do you have this number captured?"

"Yeah, what's the deal?"

"You've altered phone locations before...I need this one done for me now."

"Sure," Ben assured him. "I can skip the signal off a few satellites and make it look like it's from anywhere."

"Okay...then, always from here. Georgia."

"Can do." Then Ben realized there must be more. "You want it traceable, too, right?"

"You got it," Silas responded. "Don't make it too easy. But let them trace it back to here."

"What else do you need?"

"Don't we still own that cane farm in Guatemala?"

"I believe we do, why?"

"Order some fuel fit for a Blackhawk helicopter, I don't know what that would be, but just find out, okay?"

"We have a source for all types of fuel," Ben told him. "How much?"

"Enough for 2500 miles, whatever that would be. Bill it to the farm and send it to the airport at Retalhuleu. Put under 'will call' for Luke Diaz."

"Luke, from Panama?" Ben remembered. "Murray's friend?"

"The same...Oh...here's the tough part," he explained. "It needs to be there in twenty-nine hours."

"Okay..." Ben knew that would be close, but he also knew saying it wouldn't change anything. "I'm on it."

34

The Captain of Homicide Division, Muskegon Police sat in silence for nearly a full minute, after Jordan Stern finished his story. Twenty years of investigating homicides in the area had made him an expert on domestic causes for murder. This wasn't a domestic case. It was much larger and more complicated. He needed more information.

Looking up at the undercover officer he calmly asked, "So... you know of this Pilfoy through one of your snitches?"

"Yes, sir. There're several who tried Chicago at one time or another," Sterns answered. "Most of them find the game too rough down there." He studied his superior for any insight as to what he was thinking.

The captain pulled a notebook from his shirt pocket and opened it on the table. "How is your brother-in-law?" he asked.

"We haven't talked to them in a day or two."

"What's his name?"

"Waylon Steggers."

"This is your sister's husband?"

"No, sir," Sterns corrected him. "He's my wife's brother."

"You said 'them.' He has other family with him?" the captain continued.

"The wife's folks live there, with her brother and his wife."

The senior officer looked up again. "Who called you from Chicago?"

"I didn't get the name..." Sterns admitted. "I had no idea what it was connected to at the time."

Closing his notebook, the captain spoke as though thinking out loud. "I don't need this mess in my little town," he said. "This Duray stuff is bad business. I feel bad for them, but Muskegon shouldn't be involved."

"My concern is the emphasis will move on to the U.P," Sterns interrupted him. His reference was to the area above Lakes Michigan and Huron that the locals call the "U.P."

"We've got two big time hoods dead. And two more in custody right here," the captain responded. "They won't let that go lightly." Growing concern now showed clearly on the man's face. "I know about these people," he added.

Down the hallway, Jordan's wife was ending a call on her cell phone. Carol Sterns stood from her chair as the call ended. She had located her brother and the rest of the family, now she needed to tell her husband.

The narrow hall was all frosted glass walls and doors. Carol knew Jordan and his boss had stepped into an office on the right side, but she wasn't sure which one. Half running and stopping to peer through the fuzzy glass made her cadence appear erratic, but she finally saw shadows through the glass and pushed that door open.

"Jordan," she blurted out. "I found them."

The undercover officer's expression froze as he responded. "Where?"

"They all went up to The Soo, the Ontario side to do some shopping." "The Soo" was local shorthand for Sault Ste. Marie, both the Michigan side and Canada.

"Did you tell them to stay there?" Jordan glanced toward his boss and quickly back to Carol.

"They're already on the way home, Jordan. They took Waylon's plane."

~

Silas came into the house from the lower level. He brought weapons with him, three MP5s, four Glock 23s and three XM8 Assault rifles. Two of those were standard 12.5 inch barrels but one was equipped with a heavy gauge 20 inch barrel and held a 100-round drum magazine.

"What does that do to the weight of your bag?" Spiegel asked.

"The two rifles add fourteen pounds with magazines," Silas answered. "It should still be fine."

"Why two in your bag?" Duray asked.

"Murray will need one as we leave, I'm guessing."

"I thought the suits had Glocks?" Spiegel threw in."

"Yeah...those are just for spares," Silas confirmed. "I love the Glocks, but they can jam. We don't need that this trip."

Heads nodded all around and the packing began in earnest. Silas looked over at Ben, changing the subject. "Anything new on that other situation?" he asked.

Ben took a quick look at Cheryl's father who had paused. He knew what that "situation" was as well as Ben did.

"There's activity all over," Ben advised him, "nothing but the bad guys moving around. It looks like they're after each other right now. It's quite a dance."

"I think you're right," Silas agreed. "If you find out who's the lead dog, we're in business. Until then, we monitor all of them."

"There is something going on at a farm in Kentucky."

"Really?" Silas raised his head. That state brought strange memories. "Have you let Swanson know?"

"She's all over it," Ben replied. "I like her...she's a lot like you."

Silas smiled and stood with his bag ready. He then pulled a smaller one from under the table.

"More, yet?" Duray teased him.

"This is for my flight to Acapulco," he explained with a grin. "You'll see."

~

The modest office of Assistant Police Commissioner Walter Greer had one main door. When Captain Frank Borton stuck his head in, Greer gazed up at him in near disbelief.

"What are you doing?" Greer angrily muttered at him.

"We need to talk...now," came the reply from the officer.

"Never...you know never... to come to this office."

Borton slid sideways inside the room and closed the door. "You hear me out," he warned. "This is serious."

Greer, now void of all color in his face, pushed back from his desk and tried to seem in charge. "Sit down then," he pointed toward a chair. "And lower your voice."

"A guy came to see me the other day," Borton started. "Actually, it was right before dawn... the night that girl and her mom went missing."

"The father?" Greer instinctively asked.

"No...no, I've seen pictures of him. It wasn't the father."

"Then who?" Greer leaned forward, his color suddenly returning in shades of red.

"He didn't give me his name." Borton took a deep sigh and went on, "but he knew about Hoffman, he knew about Acree and he knew about you."

"Me?" The assistant commissioner threw himself back in his chair. "How the hell does he know me?"

"He had your name, man. He wanted to know who you were."

"Wait a minute..." Greer was now confused. "He knew my name but didn't know who I was?"

"He knew about 'Walt.' He wanted to know who 'Walt' was."

"What did you say?"

Looking away, Borton searched his mind for an excuse rather than an answer. "He threatened me, boss," the man tried weakly.

"Threatened? Are you kidding me?"

"Naw," the cop started shaking visibly. "It was more than that. This guy was... spooky." Grimacing to hold back fear and shame, Borton made direct eye contact with Greer and added, "Something about him...I don't know, man. I've never seen anything like it."

Greer stopped cold and shrank even more into his chair. *This veteran officer and time-to-time killer was actually scared by one man,* he thought to himself. "I just don't understand, Borton," he explained, shaking his head. "Just one man?"

"He had a recording of Acree and me...talking from the building within an hour of the hit. The FBI was there and I was trying to keep things under wraps when Acree called."

"Because I hadn't called to tell him everything was okay." Greer spoke through his hands that were now cupping his head as he shook it. "What a mess."

"I ain't supposed to be talking to anyone...this guy said I would hear from him again."

Walter Greer slowly pulled his hands away from his face and looked calmly at Borton. "Go back to your office," he told the cop. "Let me handle this, I think I know who this might be."

"Who, Walt?"

"This is all Kinkaid's fault. That 'Son' guy is still around...and he must have been on to Kinkaid. That's how he got drawn into this girl's deal. She was on Kinkaid's farm."

"That assassin guy is dead... didn't you hear?" Borton contradicted him.

Greer's expression had become pensive. He inhaled deeply and turned to Borton in one smooth motion. "I'll handle this, Frank."

"What about me?" The cop wondered out loud. "What do I do?"

"Don't talk to anybody else...just stay calm. I'll handle it."

~

The decision was made silently. There was no discussion or consultation. None of the others at the meeting noticed the subtle change in expression registering the judgment made. The meeting had nothing to do with his thoughts and no one present had anything to do with this business.

Time to clean up and start over, he told himself. *This has gone too far already.*

35

The living room of the mansion served as the good-bye room for the Duray family. There was no discussion. The decision had been made and confirmed. This meeting was simply for hugs and good wishes.

The morning sun reflected off the thick glass and Tim Spiegel could tell he had walked in on a private moment.

"I'm sorry," he offered shyly.

"That's okay, really." Duray smiled and turned loose of his wife and child. Cheryl jumped into Spiegel's arms and hugged him. "Take care of my daddy," she ordered.

"I'm hoping he'll take care of me," the NCIS agent smiled.

Ben opened the door from the main garage. "He's here," he declared.

Silas had pulled the Jeep to the top of the driveway and stood with the back opened. Spiegel and Duray added their bags to what was already there and they closed the rear deck.

"Jon!" Ben called out.

Silas, who was now in full "mission" mode glared at him but said nothing.

The youth moved closer and lowered his voice. "I had a message from Major Swanson," he started.

Silas' expression eased and he nodded for Ben to go on.

"There's been a visitor to the farm in Kentucky. The name didn't mean anything until I ran him through the computers."

"Okay?" Silas was anxious to hear the payoff to this story.

"The guy owns that pest control company in Duluth. You know...the phone number you found in Kinkaid's office."

Silas looked over the top of his Jeep to where Rita and Cheryl Duray were standing. His fist softly pounded the seat back of the vehicle, and then he turned back to Ben.

"Good work," he spoke as if in a trance. "I've got to take care of this first."

Ben handed him a note with a phone number.

"Is this the one?" Silas asked. "For my call to originate from here?"

"Yup," Ben nodded. "No matter where you call from, it'll look like you're here."

"I'll be calling you first to be sure it's working. Then I need to know where Palmero is when he's talking to me."

"Good luck," Ben stuck out his hand. "Say 'hi' to Murray for me."

Jon's persona came forward at the gesture. He looked at Ben's hand, then grabbed it and shook it firmly. "I'll do just that," he smiled.

Silas turned the Jeep around and headed down the driveway. A glance in the rear-view mirror showed Marsha standing motionless in the doorway of the garage. He stopped.

"Something wrong?" Spiegel asked.

Putting the car in reverse, Jon's voice answered him. "I just forgot one thing."

He climbed out of the Jeep and walked up to Marsha. Gripping her arms above the elbows, he kissed her forehead and whispered, "It's going to be alright."

"Bring him back," she urged softly. "Bring 'em all back."

Jon winked, nodded, and stepped back to the Jeep. Then they were gone.

~

The change of climate from Kentucky to Duluth was harsh. Petteri shivered as he walked from the terminal building to the parking area. His heavy coat went from draped over his arm to "on" quickly.

"I'm getting weak living here," he muttered to himself. The snow had been light but relentless. Fortunately his truck was inside a multi-layered parking structure. Vehicles left outside were now covered in nearly a foot of frozen confection. His was affected only by the extreme cold.

But cold weather can leave more than snow on a cold metal surface. A handprint can leave oils that freeze and shine different from the car's finish. As he approached his truck, Petteri noticed several odd markings on the hood and side door panel. Despite the cold, he climbed under the truck to look.

"Damn," he muttered. "Who is this now?"

Standing back up, he called for a cab and then walked back into the terminal building. Dialing a second number, he spoke quickly when the man answered.

"Section twelve, row five, number 23 at the airport lot nearest the terminal," he stated calmly. "Looks like three, maybe four blocks of C4 wired to my ignition."

There were profanities in Finnish from the other end of the call followed by, "I'll get it taken care of boss."

"Bring the truck back to the office when it's clean," Petteri continued with his orders.

"Right," the voice responded. "Will do."

~

Captain Frank Borton looked up from his paperwork as his door opened.

"Knock before you come in here," he bellowed at the man holding a liter size soft drink bottle in his left hand. Not recognizing the man, Borton leaned back against his chair.

"You Borton?" the man asked as he fiddled with the soft drink container.

The police captain threw his hand forward, realizing the danger in front of him.

"What the..." was the last the officer got out.

The bottle had turned bottom towards him and exploded with little noise. The 9mm slug that came through it caught Borton in the forehead, knocking him backwards and out of his chair. Liquid flew in all directions. The man calmly removed the overcoat he had on, dropped it and the weapon from his gloved hand, and left the office. He casually pulled the door closed behind him. After checking both directions and finding no noticeable activity, he coolly walked down the hall and exited through the front door.

~

Marvin Acree came into the cabin's bedroom where Kinkaid was watching TV. It was obvious to the boss that Acree was worked up over something.

"Franz is sending a team to get us out of here," he announced.

"What?" Kinkaid wrinkled his face and swung his feet to the floor.

"He just called ...garbled voice and all," Acree went on. "Things have gotten worse so he's called a meeting."

"How did he get your number?" Kinkaid asked.

"Greer, I guess. He really didn't say."

"Did you tell him where we are?"

"Naw, he didn't ask. Greer knows I have a place in Arkansas, just not exactly where." He didn't notice the skepticism swelling on Kinkaid's face and continued, "We meet the team in Little Rock in two days."

Kinkaid stood from the bed. He walked toward a rear-facing window and spoke with his back to his friend. "How long were you on the phone with him?"

Acree froze as it finally came over him.

"I don't know...five...six minutes," he recalled.

"Marv," Kinkaid turned and now showed his alarm. "Leave that cell phone 'on,' but leave it here," he ordered. Kinkaid was visibly upset, more than Acree had ever seen him. Yet his words were fairly calm, "We need to get out of here...now."

36

Harold Foster had the G5 at 29,000 feet, heading west by southwest for San Antonio, Texas. At their cruising speed of just over 425 knots, they would be at Lackland AFB in around two hours.

"Are we all clear on the schedule?" Silas asked.

"Yeah," Spiegel's answer was almost dismissive. "But are you sure this hover-craft can stop that weight from a free fall?"

Silas didn't look up. He stared at the bag with the drone unit thoughtfully before he responded. "Kind of an odd time for that question, isn't it Tim?"

Weston Duray leaned back in his plush leather seat and smiled, silently.

"I'd just hate for you to be left outside, while we got all the fun," Spiegel teased.

"I trust that drone as much as I can right now. We'll see if I'm right," Silas was serious and deadpan. "I'm going in there for Murray... one way or the other."

The NCIS agent nodded. "I believe you would," he muttered out loud.

"What does it home-in on?" Duray piped in, changing the subject somewhat. "You never showed us that."

Silas pulled one of three cell phones he carried. "This serves as a phone and has the signal built-in." Holding it out, he continued, "It also has a GPS screen."

After a quiet period that seemed to last forever, Spiegel spoke up again. "I've added a couple of com-sets into that bag...they don't weigh but six ounces. They're short range but we can all communicate once we're on the ground."

Silas looked at him in agreement. "Are you both comfortable with those suits Ben gave you?"

Duray sat straight up and nodded. "A thing like that would be neat to have around... all the time," he surmised.

"When we're done...it's yours," Silas stated, as a matter of fact.

With raised eyebrows Duray smiled, nodded again, and rocked back.

Quiet again consumed the cabin. Each man had his own thoughts to go through. It stayed that way until about an hour out from San Antonio.

Silas stood and picked up the other odd bag he'd brought along.

"I'm going to change," he declared.

"Change?" Spiegel asked quizzically.

"You don't think I'm going into Acapulco looking like this, do you?" He grinned at them and disappeared behind the privacy curtain. Within twenty minutes, a slightly overweight, bearded tourist type came back to Silas' seat. The flowered shirt and shorts added to the package.

Spiegel laughed, asking him, "and just who might you be, Sir?"

"Winston Bagley of South Boston," Silas said as straight as he would at customs later. "Here to test your gambling machines at the casinos." The small bag he carried also contained a bright blue purse with over two hundred silver dollars inside. Along with that was a leather pouch full of folding money.

"You're looking to get hit over the head right away, aren't you?" Duray posed at him.

198

"On the contrary. Sir," Silas replied and still in character. "I should get an escorted cab ride... right to my hotel with all this."

~

Above Lake Michigan, NF 61 WTS rode softly for an amphibian seaplane of her age. The DeHavilland Beaver had been built in 1953, but Waylon Steggers kept her looking new. The only issue with it was communications. The beast was loud.

Speaking between the pilot and passengers was possible only through the headphones and microphone system on board. The headphones also served to block as much engine and air noise as they could.

Steggers and his family swept low off the big lake, immediately gliding over Lake Brevort and the Wild Trees Cabins. The pilot searched for anything that looked out of place. His sister's phone call concerned him, but natural instincts pulled at him to get home. Two loops around at 1200 feet showed nothing, all was quiet. Then it hit him. That in itself was wrong.

Where was Johnny Wages, the young dockhand who worked for him *or any of the guests for that matter?* He thought.

A flash of light from the dock house answered his question. A high caliber round ripped through the left wing material but fortunately hit nothing else.

Waylon pulled hard on the stick and the DeHavilland climbed higher.

"Hang on!" he yelled into his microphone and felt his cell phone fall out of a pocket and onto the floor. His wife retrieved it, looked at the screen, and frantically tapped Waylon on the shoulder.

"Look at this," she said trying to stay calm.

The screen of his phone showed four missed calls and two text messages. The first said, "don't go home." and the second simply, "don't land!"

"Is everyone alright?" the pilot asked into the intercom system. Everyone responded in the affirmative so he added, "I'm going in to take a closer look."

Climbing high with the dense forest under them, he circled out and dove in from the high west side. Coming out of the sun made them nearly invisible on the ground and allowed the plane to retreat back over the tall trees, east of the cabins.

One black SUV was seen leaving the area at a high rate of speed. Waylon turned the dial on his microphone and called out, "Wild Trees One this is Wild Trees Air, come in...over."

After two minutes and three other calls a young voice answered, "Air, this is WT One," he said. "They're gone...whoever they were...over."

"Anyone hurt?" Waylon asked. "Over."

"Negative, air," the voice responded. "They wanted to talk to you...then got a bit rough when one guest wanted to leave."

"Why are they leaving?" Steggers asked.

"One of 'em got a call...that's all I know," the youth responded with excitement still ringing in his voice. "Then they bugged out all at once."

Steggers looked at his wife and father. He put the microphone down acknowledging what they were thinking without saying a word. Then raised the microphone back to his lips. "One, I'm coming in...meet us at the dock...over."

~

The eighth floor at City Hall in Chicago held five offices. One blew up at 2:25 PM that afternoon. Debris flew out and fell on LaSalle Street and broke windows in surrounding buildings on its way down.

The office of Walter Greer was completely destroyed and for over an hour, there was no sign of him. He was presumed dead until searchers found him in the restroom around the corner from his office. He lay under two sheets of granite wall dividers that had been stalls in the restroom. The Special Assistant Police Commissioner was taken to the hospital by guarded ambulance.

The gaping hole in the building claimed one casualty, other than the injuries to Greer. A mailroom clerk received broken arms and cuts to the face as he was thrown down a hallway by the blast.

37

Another day was passing with little activity for Murray Bilstock.

"What is this...three now?" he asked himself out loud.

Push-ups and jogging in place passed the time. They brought him some food twice a day, *if you could call it that*, he thought. Murray had grown up eating Mexican food, but this was something else.

Mostly beans and not the refried kind, they were boiled and served with a flat cornbread thicker than a tortilla. The beer was cold. At least that was good and had some nutrition value to it.

"McDonald's for a solid month when I get out of here," he said doing sit-ups next to the chair.

It was nearly dark when he heard a passenger jet loop in overhead and bank left toward the airport. He leaned the wooden chair against the door and sat down.

It would be another long night, he told himself.

Alvarez International Airport was not particularly busy this evening. Tourist travel to the area had slowed over the past several years, but business and some well-heeled gamblers would still come through.

Silas approached the counter at customs in the persona of Winston Bagley. He placed his two bags on the counter and smiled at the uniformed clerk. The clerk unzipped the main bag and casually unloaded the stacks of twenty-dollar bills across the counter.

Occasionally he would glance up at the man in front of him, with no change in his expression. He looked at the plastic pocket protector in Silas' front shirt pocket. It read "Citizens Bank of Boston" and held three pens. One, looking no different than the others, was the laser pointer.

A smaller bag, within the one, contained the coins Bagley had brought to gamble with. The clerk left them where they were and looked at the man before him. He then deliberately laid his hand on one stack of twenties, tapping it with his fingers. His eyes never left contact with Silas's.

Glancing down at first, Silas grinned at the clerk and nodded ever so slightly. The stack of bills under the man's hand quickly disappeared beneath the counter. The others were piled back into the bag, also in rapid style.

The clerk opened Winston Bagley's papers and stamped both passport and clearance certificate. He then picked them up, closing them abruptly, and handed the documents to Silas. The whole process took less than three minutes.

"May I get a cab to my hotel?" Bagley's soft, whiney voice inquired.

The clerk pointed to the glass door about thirty feet away and then motioned for an assistant to help the tourist get to his cab. The drive took thirty minutes.

The Copacabana Beach Hotel sat directly across from the golf course and about a mile from the Palm Cartel's compound. Out his room's window, Silas could see heavy equipment on the golf course. But through the dark he could not tell what it was. Hoping that wouldn't prove to be an issue later, he pulled the special phone from his pocket and called Ben.

"I'm here," he said. "All is good...except the junk I see on the golf course."

"Junk?" Ben repeated.

"See what you can find out about what's going on there...let Diaz know what he needs to know, okay?"

"Will do."

"Is this thing working right?"

"You're sitting right next to me." Ben answered firmly. "The signal shows it's coming from Dalton."

"Good. We'll use this a bit later."

"Hey...before you go," Ben stopped him from hanging up.

"Yeah...what?"

"There are all kinds of weird activity going on back here. I don't have it figured out yet, but it looks like it's all to do with our friends from Chicago."

"The kidnappers?"

"Looks like it, yeah. I'll stay with it. There have been shootings and a bombing this afternoon at City Hall in Chicago...the office of some guy named Walter Greer."

"Really?" Silas wasn't too surprised. "Do stay on top of that, please."

"Why does that name sound familiar?" Ben asked.

"He's in my notes from the trip to Chicago," Silas explained. "Somebody is cleaning up. Almost confirms they know I'm on to him. Just stay with it, okay?"

"Alright, I will...oh...the C-130 will soon be in the air. I heard from them a few minutes ago."

"Better thaw out those steaks," Silas teased the youth. "Murray will probably be hungry."

"My pleasure! Good luck."

Checking his watch, it read 11:45 PM local time. Silas had a few hours before the C-130 would pass overhead. He pulled off his costume and began turning it inside out.

~

Walter Greer sat in his home, staring out at the dark and plotting his next move. He was now under 24/7, high security from the city of Chicago. Many considered that stronger than what the Secret Service offers. The mayor insisted and Greer took him up on it.

His new offices at 121 N. LaSalle would be on the same floor as the mayor, with much tighter security than before.

All in all, it was working out, he thought quietly.

~

In Duluth, Minnesota, Reino Petteri sat in the front window of a Dry Cleaning business directly across the street from RP Pest Control. He had keys and security codes for this building, as the owners of that business did for his. It was kind of a neighborhood watch situation for small business. With the earlier attempt on his life, Petteri used his access to this building as a spot to watch from, safely.

His truck had been delivered and parked around back of his offices. Disarmed from the explosives, that would have left a huge hole in the airport parking garage, the truck now sat under cameras from all angles. Petteri switched from one view to the next on his nine-inch tablet computer.

As he watched and tried to stay awake, Reino also ran through the possibilities of who was doing this?

Was it Kinkaid? He thought, *or perhaps even Franz?*

There had been no warning. *No real surprise there,* he laughed inside. But there wasn't any follow up, not yet anyway.

He looked at his watch. It was 2:35 AM.

~

The streets of Acapulco were nearly deserted. There had been a time when even this early morning hour would have been bustling with people and vehicles. Bright lights from the tall buildings shined more on each other than on the streets below. There was activity within some of them. Now mainly drug deals by low-level representatives of the Palm Cartel. Buyers would come to them these days. A dangerous trip if you weren't sincere in your intent. The tactic was effective. There had been little trouble from outsiders since Palmero took over the city.

Above the building's lights the sky was mostly clear. Numerous stars filled the dark space as the moon slid off to the west. While clear, the visibility was still limited. Air traffic, other than those destined for the area, would fly over at extreme altitude. They were invisible to the naked eye from the ground. The noise level was also quite low.

Few cars were out, at least at this end of town. A moped roared by, sounding like a 650cc bike cutting through the tranquil serenity. Nearing the gates of the drug lord's palace, the occasional service truck would crawl by, cautious of the guards in the compound. Only a homeless vagrant, pushing his shopping cart, occupied the sidewalk across from the Palmero Complex.

38

Ben monitored the situation from his workshop. Cheryl Duray sat nearby. She had started out watching everything with Ben, but as the hours grew she blinked her eyes, nodded some, and now slept head down on the worktable.

Through satellite radar, Ben knew the C-130's training mission had gone as planned. The zigzag path across Mexico was mostly at 25,000 feet, but now the plane began to climb. At 0305 they were at 39,250 feet, heading south by southwest.

Ben flipped open a cell phone and keyed in a text massage. "39plus and on schedule," it said. Pushing "send," he closed the phone and got into position.

The recipient of the message leaned into his rolling cart, laying that phone down where he could see it and took out another one. On this special unit, he dialed Geraldo Palmero's number. At that hour, it took the drug lord several minutes to answer.

"You keep strange hours, Mr. Tough guy," Palmero started.

"I think I know where you are," Silas responded coldly.

Pushing a button on the side table, Palmero continued his brash attitude. "I was beginning to think I would just have to dispose of your friend here and be done with this."

"Good to hear you haven't done that," Silas remained calm.

On the far side of the complex, a technician was tracing Silas' call for his boss.

"I'm getting tired of feeding this man, Mr. Hero. When are you coming to get him... huh?"

"Like I said," Silas continued. "I think I know where I'm going now." He checked his watch for the time. It was now 0312.

"When can I expect to see you, then?" Palmero asked jokingly.

Silas stuck the laser pointer into the ground, at a slight angle toward the northeast. He then turned back to the cell phone.

"Soon," he told the man. "I'm closer than you'd think."

Palmero received a text from his technician. It said, "Dalton, Georgia. USA."

"You better hurry, my friend," Geraldo warned. "I grow weary of this game."

"Time can fly when you're having fun," Silas reminded him and then turned serious again. "Just remember...I am coming."

"Aw...there's my tough guy friend once again, huh?" Palmero grimaced. His tone became harsh and extreme. "I will feed you your words, gringo."

"See you soon," Silas retorted calmly and hung up. Checking the time again, it was now 0316. A new text came in from Ben on his other phone. "He's in the mansion," it said.

Leaning over the pointer, Silas waited for the exact moment.

Spiegel and Duray were ready. They had been on full oxygen for 50 minutes and the rear ramp of the big transport aircraft was being lowered. What hit them both first... was the cold. Duray glanced over at Spiegel and grinned, flashing a "thumbs-up."

Spiegel checked the bag and the drone one more time. He had worked with it through most of the flight. All appeared to be in good shape.

Duray's voice echoed in his earpiece, "Is it ready?"

He looked across the open tail section and checked his microphone. "I sure hope so," he responded. "It's just about show time."

Straightening the lines between the bag and its drone, Spiegel pushed them closer to the exit. Both men craned their necks to search the ground for the signal from Silas. A red, then blue stream of light cut through the air on one side of the aircraft.

"There," Duray spoke through the intercom. He nodded toward the starboard side and looked back to Spiegel.

"I see it," the other man almost shouted.

~

The ridge on Blue Ouachita Mountain was remote, cold, and uncomfortable. But it overlooked the Acree cabin and was on the far side from the access road to it. New growth trees around them obscured their silhouettes against the sky, but it was cold.

"This is silly," Marvin Acree complained. "We're going to freeze to death up here."

"Just wait for it," Kinkaid was stoic in his response. "I believe it will happen and soon. But... I need to see it myself before we move on."

Acree grunted and pulled his blanket up around his chin. There was no fire for warmth. That would give them away. A small tent, more a lean-to set against the driving wind than a real tent, and the blankets, were all that separated them from the elements. Then he saw the lights.

Punching Kinkaid's arm, Marvin pointed toward the access road, several miles below them. Two vehicles stopped just short of the driveway to Acree's mountain getaway. What they were doing couldn't be seen through the distance and the dark, until they fired.

Three RPGs were launched simultaneously. Contrails streaked from the car's location in wavy arches of smoke and fire. When they impacted the cabin the explosives roared in rapid secession. The last ignited a huge propane tank sitting beside the structure. Balls of reddish fire rose while strains of white and yellow gas flew up and out, carrying pieces of the cabin with them. Mesmerized by the fireball, they didn't notice the vehicles turning around.

Acree stood straight up. Pushing a pine branch from his view, he caught a glimpse of the attackers leaving the way they had come. He grabbed at Kinkaid's coat with both hands.

"How did you know?" he demanded. "How could you know?"

"Franz doesn't call you directly...remember," the former congressman uttered, his voice unnaturally calm. "Now, we need to go to Kentucky. But we go in through the back door."

All that remained of the cabin and the explosion was a few small fires and tons of smoke billowing everywhere. The black and grey cloud climbed the mountain. It would soon be to their position.

"Let's get out of here," Acree sighed and started toward the car parked behind them. "I'm tired of freezing my ass off."

Silas' bag, with its drone escort, fell for two minutes and forty seconds traveling over six miles downward. At forty-nine hundred feet, an extra twenty-nine hundred courtesy of Agent Spiegel who reset the ignition altimeter, the four motors kicked in and the turbo-props began to turn.

Silas pulled his other cell phone and punched in "L3." A radar screen appeared and the silent homing beacon went out. From the blip on the screen, he could see the bag was still out over the bay, at nineteen hundred feet and closing. He turned back to the laser pointer, positioning it to the southwest and switching it back on.

Back at 39,250 feet above the Bay of Acapulco, the skydivers were suited and geared up. Their individual air tanks had been checked and the auxiliary bags strapped in place. Tim Spiegel saw the red and blue stream of light piercing the sky and looked over at Weston Duray.

"You ready?" he asked as both stood on the open tail of the C-130.

Thumbs up and a grin from Duray was his answer as the man stepped out and tumbled away from the aircraft. Spiegel dove out with his hand on his microphone key. Tumbling head over heels twice, he straightened out in a dead spider form to slow his fall. He quickly found Duray just off his right and the signal light still marking their path.

Keying the microphone, he declared, "Two clear."

The C-130 pilot responded sharply, "Roger, Angel One. God's speed."

Folding his arms in, he passed Duray pointing forty-five degrees head down toward the beam of light. Spiegel checked his altimeter. It read 34,240 and a fall rate nearing terminal velocity. Over his shoulder he saw Duray, coming on fast.

Spiegel studied his jump partner closely. He appeared to be doing just fine. They had been free falling for almost one minute at that point.

39

Ben reverently watched the proceedings from his workshop. A loud beep from across the room caught his attention. It also stirred Cheryl from her sleep.

"Did you hear that?" She popped up wide-eyed.

"Yeah..." Ben responded while rolling his chair to the other table. He pulled up a screen that was monitoring phones in other areas of the country. A red square on the screen flashed that one unit was out of service.

"That's interesting," he muttered.

"What?" Cheryl called out, still trying to regain her senses.

"The cell phone in Arkansas has gone out...completely."

"Maybe they turned it off," she offered and pushed her chair closer.

"Naw...even 'off' it would radiate a signal like a beacon."

Cheryl looked shocked at the answer. "I never knew that. So anybody can trace you when they know your cell number?"

"Through your SMS card, not just your number," he continued while trying to find the missing phone. "This one has to be under water or it's toast. It quit way too suddenly."

The falling bag was now at twelve hundred feet and crossing over land just beyond the Palmero complex. Silas did not yet have a visual of the payload. The sudden inclusion of headlights didn't help.

An old pick-up truck with wooden side risers extending the trucks cargo bed had turned slowly onto the road from a side street

Silas had not noticed. Its heavy load of crated mangos piled high and pressed the chassis down on its wheel wells and axle. The driver struggled to change gears, adding that grinding sound to the squeal of metal fenders rubbing on rubber tires.

The truck was still over a hundred yards down the street when the drone and its cargo came into view. Quietly drifting toward the homing signal on Silas' cell phone, it flashed briefly through the varying layers of light. The trajectory of the approach came obviously too close to the path of the truck. Silas tried to wave his arms at the driver, but the man was busy fighting his gearshift and checking mirrors.

The bag flew in and wrapped itself around one of the wooden standards on the back of the old pick-up. The driver did not notice.

In a controlled yet nearly frantic state, Silas searched for a diversion. He grabbed the small bag he had in his cart and shoved the metal shopping trolley out into the road. It wobbled, stuck on one of its wheel's flat spot, and flipped to its side in front of the truck.

The impact was minor but did get the driver's attention. Silas, still in vagrant garb, waved his arms at the man protesting in Spanish at what had happened. The driver climbed out, handgun in hand and an attitude to go with it. He moved toward the busted cart and Silas retreated to the rear of the old, overloaded vehicle. Quickly, he stepped onto the rear bumper and freed the bag and drone from the two-by four that had caught it.

Throwing the bag out of sight, Silas noticed another problem. The truck had stopped in the path of the signal laser. Its beam now hit the wooden bed extender and went no further.

~

Marvin Acree fumed as he drove off from the high spot above his former cabin. The sight of the old logging road gave him an idea. He turned down the narrow, treacherous path and drove with abandon through the tress.

"What are you doing?" Kinkaid asked.

"Settling the score," was the terse reply.

"With those guys?"

"They tried to kill us...and they destroyed my cabin."

"No...no...no," Kinkaid shook his head. "You need to think this through, Marv."

"This trail will cut across...I can get in front of them down there."

"And what then...kill 'em all...Right there?"

"That's the plan, yeah." Acree snarled as he concentrated on the rugged trail.

Kinkaid sat, still shaking his head "no." Acree drove a few minutes further and finally asked, "What's wrong?"

"I don't know about you sometimes, Marvin," he answered slowly. "They think we're dead right now. They will for a day or two."

"Yeah, but there's no bodies...they will find out we were gone, ya know?"

"In...a...day...or...two," Kinkaid spelled it out deliberately. "Right now we have the perfect cover to move around."

The main road was now seventy-five yards ahead. Acree stopped the car and turned off his headlights. Within minutes, the two SUVs went by unaware.

Kinkaid looked over at Acree. "We'll take care of all that later."

Acree grunted and slowly moved forward.

214

~

Weston Duray had pulled his arms up and spread his legs wide. The web design of the skydiving suit rapidly slowed his fall rate. Spiegel did the same maneuver and with some adjusting they were soon at the same altitude, now barely under 27,000 feet.

Duray motioned to where the light had been. Spiegel acknowledged the issue and flipped his body position to look in all directions while Duray stayed on point.

Rejoining his partner, Spiegel gave the "I don't know" signal with both hands as the divers spread-eagled as much as they could. Both tried to slow their descent as much as possible.

~

The truck driver had cleared the road of its obstruction and now moved back to look for the offending cart's owner. Silas jumped to the side under brush and tall grass, but had paused at the laser long enough to grab it and turn it off.

Without benefit of a flashlight, the driver had little chance to see anything in the shadow of his vehicle. He mouthed a few obscenities in Spanish while climbing back in his truck and re-cranked the engine. The gears complained loudly as the truck pulled away.

Silas flipped a switch and the laser came back on. At first he held it by hand, then after sticking it back into the ground, he pulled the zipper on the big bag and began to change out of his beggar costume.

40

"Is everything alright?" Cheryl asked. She stood behind him, leaning over Ben. Her hands rested on his shoulders as they both studied the satellite view of Acapulco.

"Can't really tell," he responded out loud while his mind was trying to concentrate. It kept repeating over and over, *damn...she smells good.*

"Can you see my dad and Agent Spiegel?"

"No, but that's good. We're not supposed to see them...yet."

Ben quickly changed screens, going through several views of the compound to see if any undue activity was happening. The lights of the old pick-up caught his attention and then he noticed the laser coming back on behind the truck.

"That's a bit odd," he mumbled too loud.

"What?" Cheryl shook him, demanding an answer.

"Calm down," Ben nearly shouted at her. He reached up and grabbed one of her hands. "Let me look around."

He tried to explain what he had just witnessed. "Could have been the angle of the view, but it looked like the laser was late or off for a while." He continued to search different views. "Everything else looks fine now. It's back on...must be no big deal."

Cheryl's hands slipped down into a hug around Ben's neck. She didn't say anything, but he could hear her breathing and thought he felt her heart beat against his back. He tried to think of something to say, something to capture the moment. What came out was an unconscious blurt.

"Have you seen anything about the golf course yet?" he asked.

Her hand pulled back to his shoulders as she straightened up.

"I'll go look again," she told him and stepped away.

She didn't notice Ben shake his head slightly as his mind screamed at him, *idiot!*

"There's still no mention of that golf course," Cheryl reported. "I don't know what Silas saw there. Can you see it through the satellite?"

Ben had slid down the table and was reading information from another screen.

"Naw, I tried earlier. It's too dark. Nothing but big shadows and those could be anything...or nothing."

"When will the chopper be there?" she asked.

"Diaz refueled in Guatemala and is back in the air," he said. "He should be there in twenty minutes."

~

Having slowed their fall rate by some thirty-five percent, the skydivers searched the ground for their missing signal. They were approaching 22,000 feet.

Weston Duray was first to see the blue light streaking toward them again. They were off course, but not by much. He waved at Spiegel who gave the thumbs-up indicating he had also found the beam of light. They were behind schedule now, only by seconds, but those could matter in the long run. Simultaneously they pulled in their extremities and angled toward the beam's origin. Hurricane force winds ripped at their suits and the little areas of exposed skin. The fall rate increased to 124 mph, terminal velocity. This jump was not for the timid or the inexperienced.

~

The suit felt good to Silas. He remembered arguing with Ben about even getting the first one, but he would admit now that he felt naked without it. The bag still had another suit and the weapons. He checked the Glocks and loaded an MP-5, slinging it over his shoulder. He pulled the rocket launcher from the carrier and slid an 80-meter shell into place. It was time for things to start happening.

Silas quietly moved down the road, still in the dense scrub brush and shadows, until he could see through the open gate of the compound. The barracks building sat some forty yards inside the gate, just as the satellite photos had shown. It was mainly dark, but the front doors stood open allowing some light to escape from within. He could see no movement there or at any of the windows. Any occupants seemed to be settled down, if not asleep.

The driveway to the main house ran past the barracks and then split. It circled around to the front door, which was a good hundred yards deep into the compound. That set of doors was closed. There were lights on in the house, but only a few.

Silas checked his watch. *They should be getting close to popping chutes*, he thought. He adjusted the straps on the bag and his weapons then stood silently in the dark, waiting.

~

Ben looked down at the small, digital counter in the corner of his main screen. He hadn't told Cheryl what it was, that would only serve to worry her. The five numbers were whirling rapidly at this point, even the first two digits changed quickly. Fourteen thousand became thirteen and then twelve. *They were supposed to slow down by now*, he thought silently. Realizing he was staring at the counter, Ben tried to alter the position of his head, but his eyes remained glued to the spinning numbers. He was monitoring the altimeter on Spiegel's belt and it was time for those numbers to slow down...way down.

When twelve slid into eleven he glanced over at Cheryl. Ben prayed silently for two things, that she would not notice his concern and that the numbers would slow down.

~

Spiegel stared at his altimeter and Duray, sensing it was about time, watched his partner closely. At 11,750 feet, Spiegel waved at Duray and pulled his main chute cord. A mere second later, Duray did the same. Their high-performance, squared wing chutes deployed perfectly. The snap and pull upward was dramatic as the rate of decline slowed. Spiegel had not loaded any "diaper" chutes, which normally would have slowed the fall rate before the main chutes deployed, because they might be seen from the ground.

Both men tucked into a fetal position and fought off the tendency to roll backward into their lines. The all black chutes took air and immediately began to fly. Not only down, but also in a forward direction at just over twenty miles per hour.

The swinging sensation eased up and Spiegel checked his altitude. The meter read 8600 feet and they were now falling at thirty-four feet per second. He glanced over at Duray who was visibly smiling and giving another thumbs-up. They had just over four minutes left to accomplish their goals before impact.

Both men pulled their bags around and unzipped them. This was no easy task. Though the wind speed had decreased significantly, it was still a force to be aware of. The mini rockets were already lined up on the mounts Ben had fabricated. The men each slipped the loop guards around their wrists before lifting and removing the brackets from the bags. Duray targeted the towers on the right while Spiegel set his for those on the left of the compound. Once all six rockets were set, they looked at each other and nodded.

The trigger on Spiegel's unit worked just fine. All three missiles charged and were propelled away from the bracket by the CO_2 cartridge. Splayed out in the three-prong "V" pattern, they gently arced downward. The ignited rockets would fire in a few seconds, sending the missiles into their targets at over 600 miles per hour.

Duray's unit did not work.

He pulled the trigger, again and again. On the third pull the ignition lights came on, but the missiles still would not release. Duray banged the bracket with his free hand, shaking the mounting hardware but still nothing. Quickly, he inverted the unit, checking for any loose wire. The wiring was all enclosed in the framing metal so if it had come apart, he couldn't see it.

With the ignition having activated the missiles, he had less than twenty seconds until the rockets fired. If that happened while he was still holding the bracket, he simply wouldn't survive the blasts.

~

Inside the Palmero compound, Murray sat in his chair against the door. He slept more than the other nights, but was still somewhat restless. At one point he thought he saw a glimpse of something floating past the window in a large arc. *Shadows from some boat*, he told himself and settled back down in his chair.

Geraldo Palmero had just slipped back into sleep. The phone call from Silas, at that early hour, disrupted him in more ways than one. He rolled to his side as his first snore and snort nearly took his breath from him.

On the main floor, Maria lay awake in a guest room, staring at the ceiling. Sleep would not come. Her heart beat as if it would jump from her and she knew not why. Something was wrong, she didn't know what, but her sixth sense was churning.

41

Silas looked skyward and thought he caught a glimpse of something. *It was about time,* he thought and it was. When he looked back toward the compound he noticed a guard had stopped and was gazing in his direction. Silas remained frozen in place staring back, but not moving a muscle.

The guard hunched down, bending forward at the waist, his head moving left then right, straining to verify what he was looking at. Straightening up, the guard stepped forward, slowly. Still moving his head from side to side, he came closer to the gate. The guard was now about sixty yards away from Silas. The man in the black suit moved only his thumb, releasing the safety on his assault rifle.

Weston Duray made a split second decision. He pulled the wrist strap from his arm and tossed the entire bracket, missiles still attached, off to his right. He then pulled the toggle cable on his left side, which steered his chute in that direction.

The bracket tumbled end over end toward the intended targets. The big question was which angle would they launch into when the rockets fired?

Spiegel had not noticed the problem. He was setting up one of the single missiles Ben had supplied him with. He planned yet another "hit" on the compound before he landed.

Duray's fast approach into his path finally caught his attention. He jockeyed his own chute out and away from his encroaching partner, nearly dropping the single missile in the process.

Before any communications could take place to explain, Spiegel's first three missiles fired and curled their way down. Seconds later, Duray's three went off, the ignition blasts freeing them from the bracket. At first they screamed upward and actually toward the parachutists. Spiegel steered hard left and Duray quickly followed.

Their attention was further distracted when Spiegel's first missile hit with a loud thunder, followed by the others in quick succession. When they looked back at the other three, they had inverted toward their "painted" targets and roared downward.

Both skydivers redirected their chutes back to the glide path they needed. The roof of the mansion was clearly visible to them now with the added light from the explosions pointing the way.

The barracks should go next, Spiegel thought. He knew that was Jon's responsibility and it would also be a welcome sign that all was going well on the ground. Both Spiegel and Duray noticed the lack of personnel moving around. They had expected more.

~

The guard just inside the compound spun and crouched low as the first missiles struck. He turned his head and watched as the three towers behind him exploded one after the other. As he straightened up the towers on the other side met the same fate and his gaze turned directly to them. By the time he turned back to the gate, Silas was on him. Their face to face was intense but minimal.

Reaching out with his powered right arm, Silas grabbed the man's neck, twisted it, and tossed him to one side. With sparks and flames from sections of the towers dancing all around him, the man in the black suit walked deliberately toward the main house. He pointed the rocket launcher at the barracks building as it began to light up with activity.

The 75mm Javelin rocket went in the building's front door seeming to disappear. There was a second of calm before the building joined in with the surrounding chaos.

Exterior walls stretched then bulged out emitting a short lived but eerie creaking sound. As the structure transformed, it became a mass of swirling red flames followed by black smoke. Before the first ball of fire had reached its crescendo, the armory within erupted.

Flames now soared, mainly skyward, but angrily consuming all remnants of what had been. Small pieces bounced from Silas' suit as he continued his walk to the mansion's front entrance. No other guards confronted him. He walked with a steady even pace checking the surroundings carefully as he moved forward.

Up and onto the porch, Silas kicked in the front doors of the mansion.

As Murray sat asleep in the chair, the explosions, first to his right and then his left, rocked the room violently. Through the thick glass window the bright reds and orange flumes bellowed and reflected in the water of the bay. His small room lit as though a bright, red sunrise was over it. Then the room was dark again. Smoke had taken over, obscuring all light. But the rumble and noise were relentless.

"They're here," he screamed, more in his head than out loud.

Half falling from his perch, Murray immediately grabbed the wooden chair and raised it high above his head.

"About time," he muttered, slamming the chair against the floor. The impact of the chair against the floor created bits and pieces,

224

shattering the object into varying shapes and sizes of what it had been.

One back rail section broke off into a tapered wedge. Murray knew that Palmero would come to kill him if any attack occurred. He shoved the angled end under the door and hammered it home the best he could, hoping that would slow the drug dealer from getting to him.

Another explosion sounded to his right.

"Damn guys," he cried out. "Git some!"

Beside the wedge in the door, he picked out a large section to use as a club and others of throwing size were piled in front of his position. He now stood in the far right corner and waited.

~

A groggy Geraldo Palmero had jumped to his feet at the first blast. Though shaken from his sleep twice in less than an hour, most of his faculties were still with him.

He grabbed a sawed off shotgun from a closet and three specially made shells. Running to the stairs, he pointed to guards on the first floor.

"Check the side entrances," he screamed and the three men dispersed.

Palmero hurled himself down the staircase, his back bouncing off the curved wall and his eyes constantly on the front entrance. As he reached the first floor another large blast from his left rocked the mansion and nearly threw him to the floor.

The startled and shaken man stumbled toward a door and stairs near the entranceway. The stairs led to the basement.

Throwing the door open, Palmero lunged down those steps with a vengeful mission in his heart and a growl on his face.

~

Spiegel and Duray steered their chutes to pin point landings on the mansion's rooftop. They quickly stripped off the jump suits and activated their black combat outfits. A flare set fire to the chutes and jump suits. Little would remain but black soot on a darkened spot.

Spiegel pulled one of his loose missiles, provided by Ben, from his bag and ran to the edge of the roofline near the artillery. He painted the center gun with his laser and fired the mini-missile. The blast took out all of the cannons.

Duray had found a short jump down to the patio off the rear. That patio was part of Palermo's bedroom suite. Rappelling down, with Spiegel right behind him, he found the room lit, but empty. *If Palermo had been there, he was gone now*, he thought.

They heard two short bursts of gunfire followed by another single shot coming from inside. Spiegel slapped the bottom of the magazine on his MP-5 and shot out the glass doors to the room. They stormed in and through the room, finding a short hall and a staircase just to the left.

~

The little resistance he confronted in his stroll to the main house surprised Silas. Still, he kept his assault rifle at ready while stepping into the mansion's main foyer.

Deep inside, two armed men approached from either side beyond the entrance hallway. They stopped suddenly and raised weapons at the intruder. Silas fired three shots in each man's direction. As the gunmen fell, Silas continued his move forward.

A third assailant ran into the hallway. He saw the others lying dead and turned to take cover. Before he could clear the area, Silas fired again. The single shot found its mark.

More gunfire and breaking glass came from the upper floor.

"They're here," he muttered with a smile. "Good."

He was drawn to the open door and stairs leading down into darkness.

He's gone after Murray, Silas said to himself and charged into the pit.

~

The lower hall was dimly lit and Palermo was more intent on the keys for the door than looking at the floor under it. The wedge of wood stuck out four inches into the hall, but the drug lord unlocked the door and pushed as he always had.

It didn't move so he leaned into it with his shoulder. The top half bowed in but the bottom would not budge. He looked down finally and kicked at the piece of chair coming under the door. Murray stood inside the room, to one side of the door with club in hand. Geraldo pushed heavily against the door again and noticed a shadowy figure appear at the bottom of the steps. He was only ten feet away.

"Crane?" Palmero called out in his best English. "Is that you?"

Standing in the shadows at the base of the stairs, Silas spoke. "You wanted to see me," he answered. "Here I am."

Geraldo spun, the 12-gauge shotgun leveled at Silas. The special shotgun shells contained fewer pellets and more gunpowder. They had been loaded for him for this use, against Jon's armored suit.

The recoil of the gun knocked Palmero back three steps. The impact to Silas was even more extreme. Though none penetrated

227

the material, the five lead balls that struck carried enough impact to take Silas off his feet. He landed on the stairs behind him, dazed and stung from the shot.

The MP-5 had fallen to his left, so he reached for it with that hand. Silas felt Palmero's boot on his forearm and looked up to see the killer standing over him, reloading his lethal weapon.

"So...Mr. Tough Guy," he taunted the man in the black suit. "You like my new toy, no?"

Silas didn't respond, but as Palmero slammed the breech closed with another shell in place, his expression suddenly changed and the weapon fell from his grip.

The drug lord's eyes locked into a wide stare, his mouth fell open with no sound. Geraldo Palmero arced forward, his body rigid as though locked in position.

Feeling the splatter of liquid land on him, Silas glanced down through the poor light. He could see a large stick of wood protruding from Palmero's chest. After what seemed an eternity, the man's body fell away to one side and there stood Murray Bilstock.

"You were supposed to rescue me, remember?" Murray jested.

"Good to see you too, old friend," Jon's voice came through as he sat up.

"Yeah... good to see ...wait a minute...what took you so long?"

"Customs was a bitch," Silas grinned and threw the bag at his friend. "Your suit is in there. You'll probably need it," he said climbing to his feet. "We're not out of here yet."

As he stood, Murray stared at him. Through the dim light in that hallway, he had noticed the scar on Jon's face.

"What did you do?" the cowboy asked in genuine concern. "Bite a tree in half?"

"Several, I'm afraid," Silas answered and returned the stare. "I can't say that I recommend it."

Murray shook his head. "You could have told me," he lectured. "You could have trusted me."

Jon took over inside Silas' black suit. "Murray, it had nothing to do with trust. Come on, man... I trust you with my life." His stare became a glare. "I felt I had to do it, for all of you. Just to take the heat off... for a while. Put yourself in my place, will ya?"

Murray picked up the bag and pulled his black suit from it. He looked back at Jon and nodded. "I knew you had to be alright," he said.

"We'll talk more later," Jon assured him. "You, me, and Ben." With that he smiled.

Murray caught the meaning and smiled back. "I need to change," he quipped.

They heard voices getting louder from up the stairs. Spiegel finally shouted down, "One prisoner up here. Are you clear?"

"Clear," Silas called back. "Murray's good." He stepped up three stairs and shouted again, "What's with the prisoner? We don't have time for that."

"You'll see," Spiegel answered. "Let's get going... how 'bout it?"

42

"Whoa!" Ben exclaimed at his satellite monitor. "Did you see that?"

"Is that good?" Cheryl asked.

"Oh, gosh yes," he answered. "Those first blasts were from Tim. The second group was your Dad's work."

The third and loudest explosion filled the screen with images of flames.

"That had to be the 80mm," he turned to Cheryl grinning wildly. "They're all in the fight now."

The girl stepped back and sat in a rolling chair. "When will we know?"

"About Murray?"

"About all of them," she emphasized.

"Should be soon...very soon."

~

Silas took several pictures of Palmero's body and found the other shotgun shell in his pocket.

"These things are something else," he bounced it in his hand as if measuring the weight.

"I heard it go off," Murray commented while finishing up his suit. "I thought it had misfired and blew his butt up."

"It's not the gun...it's these shells," Silas broke open the gun and extracted the unfired other shell. Look...you can see where it was reloaded. And not very well either." He threw both back on the floor and started up the steps.

"You don't want to study those?" Murray asked.

"Naw, I see what he did. Those two are just plain dangerous like they are."

"Who's upstairs?" the cowboy asked.

"Tim...and another guy you'll get a kick out of. I'll explain about him in a bit. He's a good man."

"Hey," Murray cracked. "He came down here to help get me...He's better than good!!!"

~

Pilfoy was awake, though the hour was early, when a cell phone rang across his office. It was "the" cell phone. The one only used by Franz. He slowly walked to it, shaking his head in disgust.

"Yeah?" he answered.

"Yeah, hell," the garbled voice was obviously upset.

"What do you want me to say? It was short notice for that kind of work, damn it." The Chicago heavy was angry himself. "My reputation is on the line now because you got in a hurry all of a sudden."

"You're supposed to be professional," Franz's chastisement came through the garble.

"I am," Pilfoy nearly screamed at him. "And what was with pulling my men off that bunch up in Michigan? We had them cold."

"That family is too close to the girl's incident. They are part of that case and I didn't want any ties to those hits. Can't you understand that?" The masked enunciations somehow made the message even clearer.

"Sure," Pilfoy acknowledged in a calmer tone. "But all we got was Kinkaid and I haven't heard confirmation on that yet."

"Reino got away?"

"That's what I'm told."

"He could be dangerous now."

"I've got three men looking for him."

The cryptic voice sighed with frustration. "Petteri is the priority now."

"I hear someone made a run at Greer, too. That wasn't us."

"I know. I handled that one myself."

Taken aback, Pilfoy paused for a moment. "Never known you to be so 'hands-on' with dirty stuff," he teased.

"Like you said...I'd already put enough pressure on your resources."

"Did you get him?" Pilfoy asked.

"Doesn't look like it."

"Well, don't feel too bad, boss. As you can tell...it even happens to us professionals." Pilfoy laughed.

"I learned something though," the voice retorted.

"Yeah?" he challenged the voice. "What's that?"

"The job goes smoother when you verify the target is in place."

Pilfoy's mind had started to unravel that riddle when the sound of breaking glass made him turn towards a window. If he was aware of it will never be known. The bomb went off as it hit the floor.

~

Ben waited, eyes glued to the monitor in front of him. Cheryl heard a buzz coming from a machine to her right.

"What is that, now?" she asked.

Ben slid down and pulled up the info coming in. "That's interesting," he mumbled under his breath. "That phone...the one that went 'out' suddenly. Well, this is one of the numbers he had talked to. In fact, it was the last call made to the one in Arkansas."

Cheryl just looked at him.

Ben ran a diagnostic on the number. "It's coming out of Venezuela as point of origin," he said. "Caracas to be exact."

"You sound puzzled, what's wrong?"

"That was way too easy." Ben said still looking at the screen.

"What?"

"The trace...that was very quick... and too easy."

"It's gone now," Cheryl said pointing to the screen.

"What?"

"The call...it's gone."

43

The generator powering the Palm Cartel mansion started to sputter. Fading and flickering lights added to the already strange effects the flames outside were causing. Silas and Murray topped the stairs to the entrance hall where Spiegel and Duray were waiting with the "prisoner."

"Who's this?" Silas asked even before greeting the skydiving daredevils.

"Nice to see you, too," Spiegel snapped. "She was just standing here when we came down from upstairs."

Murray looked at Duray and nodded respectfully.

Silas glared at the woman this time. "I asked who you are," he repeated.

"Maria," she said in a calm voice. "I am Maria Charvero."

Silas turned from her, looking out the open, front door and challenged her. "So what am I to do with you, Maria Charvero?"

"Is Jerry dead?" she asked, her voice more meek this time.

"Jerry?" Silas barked.

"That's what they called Palmero," Murray threw in. "Yeah, sweetheart," he looked directly at the woman and she at him. "Even if he's a vampire...He's dead now."

Maria lowered her head, but only for a moment. "Then you either kill me now...or take me with you," she demanded.

The four men traded glances at each other, none knowing quite what to say next. Duray stuck a hand out toward Murray. "Weston Duray," he offered.

"Murray Bilstock...my pleasure and my thanks to you, man."

"You have good friends, Mr. Bilstock," Duray added.

"Weston Duray? Is that your real name?" Murray teased.

"Absolutely."

"Damn... I'd nearly kill to have a name like that," Murray grinned.

"Thanks. Oh yeah, that's right," Duray laughed. "You're the cowboy, huh?"

"You will take me with you..." Maria interrupted with confidence. "I know this."

"Lady, you don't know any of us," Murray turned and corrected her.

"You are a good man," she looked right at him. "Stephan said you were a Samaritan," she was referring to the gang lord's brother. "Your friends must be as well."

Agent Spiegel smiled at that comment, "Yeah...that's us alright, The Four Samaritans. Now can we get the heck out of here?"

They surrounded Maria and headed out onto the porch. There was no resistance within the compound, none at all. It was quiet.

"Where is everybody?" Duray asked. "Surely we didn't kill 'em all in the first hit."

Silas suddenly threw his hand up, signaling everyone to stop. He turned to Maria, "Just how many men did Palmero have here tonight?"

She paused a second to think. "Twenty-five," she offered, "maybe thirty."

From their left, the sharp piercing sound of a small motorcycle engine interrupted the discussion. A bike screamed around the corner and one man slid the machine sideways going through the gate. Duray raised his rifle but a small crowd of townspeople had begun to grow outside the gate. He didn't shoot for fear of hitting one of them.

Silas grabbed Maria and turned her to him. "Why only so few here?" he demanded of the girl.

"Many are out guarding the bridges and the roads," Maria told him. "Jerry thought your attack would come through Mexico City. He has every bridge between here and there heavily guarded."

"How far to the nearest bridge?" Spiegel threw in.

"Maybe four miles," she answered.

Silas turned and looked to the mansion's roofline. "Can you get back up there?" he asked Tim. "To get a look around and see what's coming?"

"Sure," he responded and headed back into the house.

"I'll go too," Duray shouted and followed him.

Murray grabbed Silas by the arm. "How are we getting out of here, anyway?"

"Diaz is coming," he answered. "He's going to pick us up at the golf course about three clicks from here."

"Diaz?"

"Yeah, I'll explain later..." Silas started to say when Maria put her hands on him to get his attention.

"You haven't seen the golf course...have you?" she asked.

"Why? What's wrong with it?"

"How is your friend coming to get you?"

"Helicopter," he said. "He's going to land on an open fairway. The big one with the flat surface, number fourteen."

Maria's face showed her concern. "Your friend cannot land on any fairway, now."

Remembering the heavy equipment he saw from the hotel, Silas grabbed her shoulders. "Why do you say that?"

"Jerry has a bad temper. After your friend hurt his brother, he tried to play golf to ease his mind. He did not do so well," She replied. "He got mad at the course."

Silas' head turned without saying anything. Maria went on.

"He ordered it destroyed. They've been working on that for two days."

"Where can my friend land?" Silas demanded. "Quick."

She stared out, seemingly into space and then looked back at the group's leader.

"There's an oil refinery just up that road," she declared excitedly and pointed to dirt road across from the compound. "Pemex Tad. It has a large parking lot."

"Phone lines? Trees? What all is in the way there?"

"I think it's clear," Maria assured them while thinking hard herself. "It is off to its self, sitting on a plateau. I believe it is clear there."

Silas punched up a phone. "Ben," he nearly yelled. "Get hold of Diaz. Tell him the golf course is no good. Have him watch for my signal at a parking lot near an oil refinery."

"Okay," Ben answered.

Silas looked up to the roofline. No sign of them yet.

"How long till he's here?" he asked Ben.

"Hang on a sec," Ben answered back.

The conversation paused for him to contact the helicopter.

"He says he'll be there in five."

We needed more time, Silas thought. "Ask if he can swing around, give us ten to fifteen," he appealed.

Another short pause and the answer came back, "Can do. He wants to know what signal are you going to use?"

"The only one I've got. My laser pen."

44

Luke Diaz kept the Blackhawk out over the water since entering Mexican airspace. The Army CWO was well out of his normal training area. He had with him a co-pilot and one gunner, half the normal crew of six. They needed to fly as light as they could, knowing they would be picking up four additional men for the trip back to Guatemala.

The crew could see the fires from the compound, but had missed the initial explosions. Diaz turned his UH-60 Blackhawk helicopter inland, toward Parotillas, before approaching the Acapulco airport's airspace. Though the traffic was sparse over that area, it could mean trouble, so he chose to avoid it.

Ben's call came as they turned back toward Acapulco. To give Jon and his men the time they asked for, Diaz swung north, making a full 180-degree turn.

"Johnson," he radioed back to the gunner. "What's the fuel in that auxiliary tank looking like?"

"We're good, Chief," the sergeant replied. "Even with a thousand extra pounds, we can make it back to the fuel dump and have spare change." The reference was to the added weight of Jon, his men and equipment.

"You'd best be right, Sergeant. I've got a reputation at stake here."

The double loop took twelve minutes. Diaz, satisfied that should be enough, made his heading directly into the south east of Acapulco.

~

Spiegel had climbed up on a short chimney coming from the kitchen. It stood about four feet above the roof and from there he could see a line of headlights coming in their direction.

He tapped his intercom to raise Jon, "There's a convoy coming this way. Twelve, maybe fifteen vehicles, they're about three clicks out and moving slow."

There was no answer. Jon had not put on his intercom headphone.

"See if you can get Jon's attention from the edge," he yelled to Duray. "Have him get his intercom on."

Duray ran to the roof's edge and waved his arms. The heavy discussion going on below was preoccupying those there. Duray picked up a handful of pebbles and threw them. The shower of bouncing rocks did their job.

Silas turned and looked up. Duray was poking himself in the ear in a very animated way.

"Crap," Silas yelled at himself. He reached into his bag and pulled out the headset. As he did this, some of the money he was carrying fell out.

"Yeah," Silas spoke into the headset. "Sorry...my bad."

"We've got company coming," Spiegel shouted back at him. "We need to go."

"How many?"

"More than a dozen vehicles...can't tell how many personnel."

"We've got an idea," Silas told him. "Can you see the road just across the street?"

Spiegel strained to see as far as he could. "Yeah, it looks clear."

"Do you see where it goes?"

"No...too many trees and vines...wait, I think there's a clear spot up high. Looks like the hill flattens out up there."

"Good, that's where we're going," Silas informed him. "Get down here, fast."

"One more thing," Spiegel added. "This town is waking up. There are civilian curiosity seekers coming from all directions. Cars, trucks... but most are walking."

Silas looked down at what he had spilled from the bag. Murray was picking up the money and stuffing it back in. "What's this all about," the cowboy asked.

"It just may come in handy," Silas told him. "Tim," he hollered back into the radio. "You guys get back here. We're gonna head for that road. If we get separated, that's where we're headed."

"Roger, that."

~

"Chief," the co-pilot was pointing through the Blackhawk's front windscreen. "You see those fires? Is that where we're landing?"

"Negative. Watch for a thin laser beam. I believe it will be within a click north of that compound."

"Nothing like that yet, sir. What do we do?"

"Go around...give 'em more time."

The tail gunner spoke up, "Chief...there's a convoy heading towards town from the northwest. Looks like military vehicles."

Diaz grimaced as he processed the information. "Guys," he told his crew. "I'd love nothing more than to go in closer," he lamented, "to check those trucks out and even light 'em up if they're bad guys. But we don't need the attention."

The co-pilot nodded and Johnson, the gunner waited a few seconds before he responded.

"Next time, Chief," he said, "next time."

~

Silas and Murray, with Maria in tow, waded into the crowd that was gathering outside the gate. The townspeople pushed back at the sight of the weapons the guys waved in their direction.

"Grab a handful of these," Silas opened his bag and held it out to Murray. "The coins first...watch me."

Murray extracted a double handful of the silver coins and watched as Silas took his and threw and rolled them toward the crowd on his side. He then charged into the mass of people and tossed paper money into the air. It swirled in the wind and dispersed high before falling back to the ground. The throng went absolutely wild, scrambling for the money.

People in their cars and trucks stopped, left the vehicles and joined into the mad dash. Murray turned to his right and copied what Silas had done. Soon, the entire area was awash with bodies fighting over coin and paper, some still lofting through the air.

When the bag was empty, Silas raised his arm and signaled to leave. He, Murray, and the woman ducked through and around the people. They ran up the dirt road and into the tall brushy trees.

45

Spiegel and Duray got to the gate within a minute of the others' departure. The mob scene in the street was in full fury. Their route completely blocked off by bodies, walking, rolling, and crawling in the search for money, Spiegel looked at his partner and raised his assault rifle high above his head. He fired several volleys off into the air. Duray followed suit.

The crowd parted like the Red Sea. Not overly wide, but enough. They elbowed their way across and to the dirt road. Duray turned to look back up the main highway.

"The convoy is stuck in this mess," he yelled into the intercom.

"That's good...but it won't hold them for long," Spiegel answered.

They ran up the dirt path. It was more that than a road, but after a couple hundred yards they found the clearing. There stood the others, waiting. Silas held his laser pen in hand.

Murray waved for them to hurry and Silas turned the beam on. Its red stream cut through the smoke and the night, turning blue after a few seconds.

"We heard the Blackhawk go over once," Murray told Spiegel excitedly. "They're here."

~

CWO Diaz saw the light beam as his co-pilot calmly informed him of it through the radio. "Two o'clock," he announced.

Diaz dove through the smoke toward the signal. The crew strained their eyes, looking for the open area, but all they could see were trees.

He leveled off at sixty feet and slowed his forward air speed. The origin point for the beam was not visible so he swung around to starboard and refocused on it.

The clearing was there. About forty feet by eighty feet and Silas and the others came into view as he floated in. The side doors of the Blackhawk flew open as the struts touched the pavement of the parking lot.

The five ran to the chopper, but Weston Duray stopped and turned around. He had noticed the lights of a vehicle coming up the dirt road. Instincts kicked in and the old man ran back to the edge of the dirt road. Dropping to one knee and resting his rump on the heel of his boot, he assumed the classic sniper position. Duray then hoisted his weapon's muzzle into the air, checking the magazine and the side launcher. Both were loaded and ready.

"What are you doing?" Spiegel yelled. "Let's go!"

Silas grabbed Spiegel's shoulder. "Leave him be," he exclaimed loudly, "I see what he's doing."

Duray held firm in his position. When the leading truck got to within fifty yards of him, the old soldier tensed up. Holding up one finger for his team to see, he then leveled his XM8 assault rifle and opened fire.

Both front tires on the lead truck exploded and its metal rims dug into the dirt, the impact with the soft ground turning them sharply left. Using his weapon's side mounted rocket launcher, Duray propelled a missile into the dirt and gravel directly in the truck's path.

The explosion threw dust, smoke, and rock high into the air, leaving a gaping hole in the road.

Duray continued to fire from the 5.56mm magazine, pelting the truck's cab area as one of the vehicle's steel wheels dropped into the hole. The truck leaned heavily into the crevasse. Metal screamed as parts of the vehicle came into contact with other pieces they were never meant to touch. Forward momentum pushed on the cab from behind and the thing rolled over, blocking the road's entire dirt path.

Three gunmen rolled out from the dust cloud and stood near the rear of the downed carrier. They began firing toward Duray who calmly took them out with his steady aim. He waited a second for more to appear and then stood, pivoting back toward the chopper.

"Get your ass in gear!" Spiegel shouted and lobbed another grenade into the prone vehicle. The gas tank went up causing Duray to stumble as he ran.

While the old man retreated to the Blackhawk, Silas, Murray, and Spiegel rained down covering fire around and behind the flaming truck. With Duray safely aboard, the Blackhawk lifted and swung around, allowing the rear gunner to engage with his mounted fifty-caliber weapon. The loud, "thump, thump, thump" of its recoil rang through the chopper.

Luke Diaz lifted his bird to just above treetop level and roared away.

~

In the Dalton workshop, Ben and Cheryl waited for word. When the phone rang, Ben nearly dropped it trying to answer.

"Hey!" he said apprehensively.

245

"Mission good," Silas reported officially. "All hands fine... plus one. Will explain later."

"Thank goodness," Ben exclaimed. Cheryl sat down and buried her head in her hands quietly.

"Is Harold in position with the plane?" Silas asked.

"Yes. He's there now. Should I advise about the extra passenger?"

"We're still a ways out from there," Silas looked at Maria while thinking. "Let me get back to you on that."

"Excellent," the boy sighed, his relief clearly echoed in his voice.

Slowly, Silas closed his phone and continued to stare at the woman. She seemed to understand what the next question would be, so she asked first.

"Where are you going now?"

"Georgia. That's our final destination today," Silas told her.

"This machine can go that far?" she asked skeptically.

"No...no," he smiled back. "This bird is going home...to Panama."

Maria rocked back on her bench seat. "Panama?" she said. He could see in her eyes that thought brought new possibilities. "I have a cousin there, in Corozal," she said.

"That area sounds familiar," he reached for the copter's intercom microphone. "Would you rather go there?" he asked her one last time.

Maria nodded. "I think it would be safer there...for a while anyway. Jerry had many enemies...and many friends." Her expression became sorrowful as she went on. "They would all want me dead now."

"In the states?" Silas asked.

"They are all over your states," she countered. "Besides...I would run the risk of being deported and that would expose me."

Silas rubbed his forehead with two fingers. He had no argument for her, the logic made sense. Keying the microphone, he asked Diaz, "Can you handle a spare passenger into your base?"

"Who?" Diaz replied, "The woman?"

"Roger that. She thinks she has family there."

The pause filled the speaker with static as the CWO considered all that was involved. "If I can get her off the base without anyone knowing...she's on her own from there."

Maria heard the response as clearly as Silas had. She nodded in agreement.

"She understands," Silas told him. "And that's good with her."

"We'll work it out, then," Diaz quipped. "It might be touchy, but I've done worse," he laughed.

"Okay, Luke. You've got a new crew member."

46

Harold Foster heard the approach of the Blackhawk through his nap. He sat in the cockpit of the G5, feet stretched across the center console, trying to rest as he waited. The plane was parked off to the side of the main runway and was fueled and ready to go.

Foster pulled his feet back and sat straight in his left side seat. He fired up the interior and exterior lights and brought the jet's engines back to life.

The helicopter softly touched down near the fuel depot and the G5 pivoted, pointing its nose back onto the runway. Within minutes, Foster could see his cargo walking towards him, four silhouettes in black, carrying their bags and weapons.

Jon stuck his head into the cockpit area while the others settled down.

"Good to see you, sir," Foster greeted him.

"Good to see you, my friend. Do you have something for me?"

"It's in the cargo bin next to the parachute. Ben said he'll know when you turn it on."

"Good...thanks." Silas' persona took over as he leaned back out of the pilot's control room. "How long till we're home?" he asked.

"Right at three hours."

Silas checked his watch. That would put them in Dalton around 8:30am. He nodded and closed the cockpit door.

The others were having an animated conversation as he walked by. Murray had been briefed on the Duray's situation and his reaction was as expected. Silas sat down near the rear of the cabin and opened the laptop computer he had retrieved from the cargo bin. The machine booted up quickly and the screen went straight to a question, "Download now? Y or N." He punched "Y" and files began to stream into the device.

Silas noticed Tim Spiegel get up and walk back toward him.

"Jon," the man started. "I've been listening to what happened to Weston's daughter. It's a clear miracle that she got away."

"Absolutely," Silas answered, his head nodding fiercely. "She's quite a girl."

"She didn't fall far from the tree, ya' know?"

Silas looked up and smiled. "Yeah, I see your point."

"Westy is a good man... a solider...a real fighter."

"I couldn't agree more, Tim."

"This kind of stuff gives me the creeps," Spiegel went on. "Ever since that girl from Alabama," anger flashed in his eyes. "Hell, we really don't know what happened with her." The NCIS agent took a long, hard breath. "She could still be alive...somewhere."

Silas remained quiet, but he leaned back and looked directly at his friend.

"I know you're going after them..." Tim said, "The ones responsible." Spiegel waited for a response to that...but none was offered so he continued. "I've seen a lot in my life...I'm a pretty hardened guy to most things."

Silas nodded very slightly in agreement. "Same here, but I really dislike people who hurt kids."

"I want in on this," Spiegel spit out with a grin. "I need to go back to New Orleans for a day, but I've got personal time coming to me. I want to help get these guys."

The smallest of smiles registered on Silas' face. "I was hoping you'd say that," he responded. "I'll see if Harold can run you home later today. It'll take a day or two for us to get ready."

Spiegel nodded that time. As he turned to go back up front Silas asked, "How's Phil doing?" Phillip Stone was a retired Police Captain from Shreveport. He had worked with Jon and Spiegel before.

"Talked to him a week or so ago," Tim smiled. "He's doing too much fishing he claims."

"There's no such thing," Silas laughed, but his grin turned serious, quickly. "I'd like him to sit in on the planning session." he added. "Would you reach out to him?"

"Sure... Does he need to come back with me?"

"If he can, yeah... If not, I'll arrange a conference call thing through Ben."

"We'll get 'em, Jon." Tim Spiegel assured his friend.

"I know," the sullen reply lacked any emotion. "I know."

Spiegel went back to the others and Silas returned to the downloaded information Ben had supplied for him. All the players were listed indexed by cross contact with each other. The latest news was there, including Borton's death, the attacks on the other suspects and one very significant detail. The last listing showed that the other phone, which had been traced to the Arkansas cabin and connected to Kinkaid, was on the move.

47

The sun coming up and reflecting off the car's hood awakened Clyde Kinkaid. It took him a minute to realize they weren't moving. Glancing to his left, confusion set in. His driver was nowhere in sight. Pushing himself upright to look around more thoroughly didn't help. There were trees, a blacktop road and the glaring sun, but that was it.

Where's Acree, his mind nearly screamed.

Trying to control his panic, Kinkaid opened the door and jumped from the SUV.

Acree stood from behind the car, "Are you alright?" he asked.

"What the hell are you doing?"

"Changing the tag."

Kinkaid stepped to the back of the vehicle and saw his friend was finishing replacing the Arkansas tag with one from Mississippi. "Where are we?" he asked.

"Just off Hwy. 61, above Clarksdale."

Kinkaid was impressed but still asked, "You really think that's necessary?"

"Look," Acree told him. "People are trying to kill us. We don't even know for sure who." He closed the box that held multiple tags for different states and then the back of the SUV. "I took back roads to here," he continued. "Once we get to Memphis, I'll do this again... and then we'll use the interstate."

"They think we're dead, remember?"

"I won't rely on that." Acree was getting agitated now. "I just don't want to stand out while we're on the road," he admonished his boss.

Kinkaid shrugged off any further questions about the tag. "You want me to drive for a while?" he asked instead.

"Actually...yeah. I could use some sleep. Just keep going north. It's about fifty miles to Memphis. Wake me up when we get there."

"Sure," Kinkaid told him while in his mind he thought, *better safe than sorry, I guess.*

~

Petteri had also fallen asleep at his post. Watching his business from across the street, he had lost track somewhere around four in the morning. The sound of the door opening stirred him.

"Mr. Reino," the man asked. "What are you doing here?"

Jumping to his feet, Petteri shook his head and looked hard at his building through the window. Everything seemed fine, but he wasn't supposed to get caught here. He rubbed his eyes and tried to gather himself.

"I'm sorry," he explained. "I thought there might be a break-in at my place last night."

"A break-in?" the storeowner became startled, "What made you think that?"

His made-up excuse now needed further deception. "Something I heard at the bar down by the docks," Petteri fabricated.

Lights began to come on at the Pest Control business and both men stopped to take notice. Petteri checked his watch. "That's my assistant," he said. "I'd better get over there. Hope you don't mind my using your shop as a vantage point."

"No...no problem. You are fine," the man responded. "Anything I can do?"

After taking two steps out the door, Petteri turned back. "I may be going out of town for several days. Keep an eye on things for me will you?"

"Si, of course I will."

Petteri pulled a business card from his pocket and scribbled a number on it.

"Here's a number where you can reach me," he explained, giving the man the card. "If anything weird happens...call me, ok?"

The dry cleaners owner nodded and took the card. Concern came over him and showed on his face. *I thought I had gotten away from this mess*, he thought silently in his native language.

The man watched his neighboring business owner walk away. Something didn't add up. They shared the fact they were from other lands, but past that they were not alike at all. Petteri was always strong and sure, a demonstrative leader in the community.

This behavior is not like him, the man thought. *There is more to this and I don't like it.*

He hung up his coat, turned his equipment on to warm-up, and then put on a pot of coffee. He looked again across the street. Everything was normal at the RP Pest Control Company.

It must be nothing, he smiled and consoled himself. Perhaps his own past was making him more paranoid than need be. Taking his keys from his pocket, he nodded confidently, and then got on with opening his own store.

~

George Vincent arrived at his office in Dalton at his usual time. The message light flashing on his desk wasn't usual. The office manager would normally take all calls and pass them on, in her own selected order of importance. It was still very early, and she wasn't in yet.

The recording was from the mayor. Not the mayor's office...the mayor himself.

"Call me as soon as you get in, George." Short, terse and sweet.

The Whitfield County District Attorney had been ambushed before, he stepped to his coffee machine and inserted a mini-cup and closed the unit. Three minutes later, he was at his desk, the strong aroma clearing his thoughts as he wondered what this call could be about.

He took a sip and looked out his window. It was daylight but still early. A few employees were arriving. That was normal too. Still unable to imagine what politically charged nonsense the mayor wanted to talk about, he picked up his phone.

"Good morning, sir," he addressed the man on the other end.

"So...it's banker's hours for you now, huh, George?"

"When I can get away with it, Mr. Mayor," he tried in vain to jest. "What can I do for you?"

"What do you know about the Durays?"

"Who?" the DA asked.

"The Duray family...from Michigan. You know, that kidnapped girl that got away last week."

"Yeah...yeah," George played the question the best he could. "I read about that."

"I had a call from the Chicago mayor's office this morning."

"You do start early, don't you?" George attempted to break the man's concentration.

"So do they, George," the mayor offered with no humor. "They want to know if your friend might be harboring them down here."

254

"My friend?"

"Crane," the mayor wasn't pleased with George's pretense. "Jonathan Crane."

"Sorry you didn't hear, sir. Jon Crane was killed a few months back."

"Let's not dance around this, ok? Chicago thinks that may not be the case at all."

"Who called you, mayor?"

"He's an authorized representative of the mayor."

"Authorized?" George wasn't moved. "Who the hell called you?"

"The associate Police Commissioner," the man snapped back. "Greer, I think he said his name was."

"You're not sure what his name is? Come on..."

"Look George, they're not sure Crane is really dead, ok?"

"Well...whatever they think," the DA got testy right back. "What does this have to do with the Durays?"

"They escaped protective custody in Chicago."

"Escaped? Protective custody?" his sarcasm was thick, nearly laughing.

"Don't give me a hard time, George. The mayor up there swings a big stick. You know that, as well as I do. He wants our cooperation... and we're gonna give it, am I clear on that?"

"Mr. Mayor, the best I can tell you is this...Jon Crane couldn't have had anything to do with that business," George was mad now himself. "You cooperate all you want, with whomever you want. When a crime has been committed...give me a call back and I'll deal with it. But I don't have to be part of your political hand-holding."

"I want to search that mansion, George," the politician suddenly demanded.

"Then get the judge to issue you a warrant." the DA became very official and very firm. "That's not my property. It belongs to the estate and the corporation Crane started. Then George issued his own warning. "You may want to have your ducks in a row before you go up against them, Mr. Mayor."

48

Lawrence Gibbons sat in his condo outside of Philadelphia waiting for a call. He was a contractor in what he referred to as "the transportation business." Though the job paid well, he had not heard from his client in over a week. Larry didn't know why.

News reports of the escaped girl and the bust at the huge farm in Mississippi didn't register with Larry. The name Clyde Kinkaid meant nothing to him. He knew only one name, Franz.

Franz was Larry's only customer. The jobs would come on a fairly regular basis. He had been notified to be ready over a week ago, but the details never came. Nervously, he checked his gear in the closet. Long flowing white jalabiya robes with colorful headscarves. Gold trimmed ties with tassels and ornate sandals made of leather and silk. He had three in all. The main difference between them would be the headscarf. Varying colors of different tribes allowed him to appear to TSA agents as his fraudulent passports would claim.

Gibbons' natural dark coloring, the thick black moustache and beard and the heavy tan helped with his portrayals. His job was indeed to travel, but not alone. He would pick up his cargo and then accompany her on a long journey that normally included several separate flights. Larry would do all the talking, as was customary in his supposed native land, as he escorted the new bride to her husband.

He closed the closet doors and walked back into his living room. Staring at the silent phone, his thoughts became confused. *Has he dropped me? Did I do something wrong? Why hasn't he called?* There were too many possible reasons he hadn't heard from Franz. None registered as good.

Fear began to build in his mind. *If I did screw up*, he panicked and jumped to the side of a front window, peering out. *Is he going to have me killed?*

There were other reasons for his concern. This was Larry's only job. The money was good, but it was running low. It had been months since his last transport.

~

Jordan Sterns talked with his brother-in–law for over an hour by phone. The story of how Waylon Steggers had helped Westy Duray leave Michigan all began to add up.

"The thing that doesn't make sense to me," Waylon told him. "Is why did they just give up and leave like that? Those guys had the upper hand. I'm not sure what I could have done to stop 'em."

"How many guests do you have there now?" Jordan asked as he turned away from the rising sun now blasting through his office window.

"After yesterday, not many...maybe two."

"You need to shut it down and get away from there for a while."

"This is my livelihood, Jordan. I can't just up and go."

"If those men come back...and you lose guests in the process...what does that do to your livelihood?"

The quiet from the other end meant Jordan had won that round. Steggers rubbed his head in frustration as he tried to think.

"I've got friends over on Mackinac Island," he finally said in a weak voice. "We could fly over there for a few days, I suppose."

"Do it this afternoon, ok?" Sterns implored him. "I'll have the state police keep an eye on your property. Just remember...all that stuff can be replaced."

The beleaguered brother-in-law took a minute then agreed. "I'll call you from the island later today," he promised.

Jordan Sterns closed his cell phone and looked over at his anxious wife. He simply nodded his head and she smiled slightly.

~

Ben received a strange call early that morning from George Vincent.

"Hey," the DA began. "I was wondering if you ever moved all that stuff into the new garage area Jon built for you?"

The garage from the Shaw's old house had been reassembled for Ben on the second sub-basement level of the new mansion. George had helped with the move, so the question seemed out of place.

"I've been so busy lately, George." Ben answered still trying to figure out what the man meant. He knew his soon to be stepfather was being cryptic, but he didn't know why. "I thought I had done all that already," he played along.

"Naw...I saw some come in the other day. You got enthralled by that one item and probably haven't thought much about the rest. You should get it all moved pretty quick, okay?"

What had come in the other day was the Duray family. Ben realized he was being warned. Someone would be coming to look for them.

"Thanks, George, I remember it now. You're right. It shouldn't be left out in the open. I'll get it handled right away."

"Good, your mom keeps asking me if I'd said anything. So now that's done, right?"

"Will do," Ben answered and hung up.

He called upstairs to Marsha. "Have the Durays pack up and come down here, quickly. George says we're gonna have company soon."

~

The "ghost" crew from the preempted hit in upper Michigan arrived back in Chicago unaware of what had happened overnight. After no answer from Pilfoy's phone, the group's leader contacted another team's headman.

"Where's the boss?" he demanded to know. "What the hell is going on?"

"You don't know?" the other man asked indignantly.

"Know what?"

"Pilfoy got waxed last night...in his office."

The first man was a bit stunned by the news. "This is just too weird," he proclaimed. "We get called off a job...I am wondering now if it even was the boss...and now this?"

"It was the boss who called you, all right," the other man assured him. "He had us on stand-by to go help you clean up. He'd called here, too."

"What else do I need to know...except where I can get my money that's owed me?"

"Can't help you there, Mac. Did you hear someone made a run at Kinkaid over in Arkansas?"

"I take it they missed?"

"Well, we don't know."

"What team did that?"

"Wasn't any of us. I talked to the other guys earlier, to tell 'em about the boss. It wasn't any of us, man."

There was a break in the discussion that lasted nearly two minutes.

"You still there, Mac?"

"Yeah...look." He warned. "Somebody is wiping the slate clean. You do what you want, but I'm going to ground for a while."

"I'd already thought about that," came the reply. "It might be time for me to retire anyways."

"I hear ya," was followed quickly by a "click" of the phone going dead.

49

The Jeep turned down Hwy 71 and as they passed the house Silas noticed the two city vehicles in the main driveway.

"Guys," he told the others, "I'm going to have to use an entrance I try to keep secret. Silly as this sounds, would y'all duck down for me?"

The three men looked at each other quizzically, then Murray spoke up, "Do it, okay?" The others shrugged and complied. They were in the third sub-level within two minutes and Silas spoke as the doors to that level closed behind them.

"Thanks, we're good," he said and everyone sat upright. Looking around, the scene was a new one to the guests. Jon's vehicles were all lined up in their stalls, the door to the elevator just beyond them and a large safe within a chain link cage to the left.

They climbed from the Jeep and Silas noticed a note Ben had left for him. It explained what was going on upstairs. Everything was in a short hand form except the last line. "You're still dead," it read, "City here... with warrant."

Duray took a few steps forward, looking around. "This isn't where we planned the trip," he directed his comment at Spiegel.

"Sure isn't," the agent added. "What is this?" he looked at Murray and teased. "He had to go one better than you, huh?"

"One better... and before," Murray grinned.

"Where is this?" Spiegel asked.

Murray acknowledged that he knew about it. "But I've never been down here before."

"Down?" Duray questioned.

"Oh, yeah," Silas spoke up. "This is the third level below the main floor. These last two levels are my little secret," he laughed a rare laugh. "Or so I thought they would be."

"Can I ask where my family is?" Duray piped in.

"That's what this is all about," Silas explained bluntly. "Ben has them hid out one floor above us. Those cars in the main driveway are Dalton police, here looking for you guys."

"I thought the Dalton police worked with you?"

"Some do, Murray," Silas walked to a monitor and scrolled through to where the officials were, "But not all. Ben will explain what the deal is after they leave...till then, we all sit tight."

On the master bedroom level, Ben was following the searchers.

"What's this?" one asked while pointing to the tube-shaped elevator.

"Elevator," Ben responded with calm. He had pushed a button on the main door casing that slid a panel over on the elevator's control buttons. The regular choices were now covered, exposing three new selections..."Second, Main, and Basement."

"What's in the basement?" a man with a badge clipped to his overcoat challenged.

"Basement stuff," Ben offered and reached out his arm to the elevator. "Pull the door closed and go down there if you want."

"Are there stairs?"

"Of course...on the main level... off the kitchen."

"We'll use those," the cop scoffed and puffed out his chest.

"Suit yourself, sir." Ben smiled.

~

Clyde Kinkaid had turned the SUV, with the Mississippi plates, onto Interstate 40 at Memphis. He headed east and checked Marvin Acree, who was sound asleep. It had been a long night. Acree had wanted to be awakened at Memphis to change the tags once again. Kinkaid decided to show his dominance and kept going.

An hour outside of Memphis he looked over at his partner and confidant again.

You're a good man, Marv, he thought with a smile. *But this is still my show.*

~

Reino Petteri had begun packing up his office. He called in his assistant.

"Look, I don't want you to worry, your job is fine. In fact, I'm going to pay you for two weeks in advance before I leave."

"Leave?" her face turned ashen. "What's wrong, sir?"

"Just personal business that's come up. I need to go see about it, and I think it's only fair to simply close down till I get back."

"There are service calls scheduled already..."

"Call and ask for a delay. I can't explain all this right now," he stopped and looked straight at her. "Go make the calls while I do what I need to do, please. We need to be out of here in an hour."

Nearly tearing up, the assistant turned and went back to her desk to begin the calls. Petteri closed his office door, which he hardly ever did, and went back to work.

He contacted his last crew member and shared what he was planning. "If I get back, I'll call you."

"If?" the startled man repeated.

"This is going to be a major play. If it works, we'll be in charge from now on."

"And if it doesn't?"

"If I'm not back here in one week, make your way home...it will all be over here."

Petteri hung up and continued with his packing.

The assistant sat at her desk and opened the appointment book. She began the task of calling customers to postpone their service. Looking up, she noticed the owner of the dry cleaning shop across the street. He was standing at his window staring back at her.

50

George Vincent arrived at the mansion as the official search party was loading up. Their efforts were unsuccessful and attitudes showed that.

"We may be back," the lead officer warned. He looked at the black and white car rolling up the driveway and did his best to ignore it. Ben Shaw grabbed the man's door, intent on getting in the last word. Yet another dirty look from the frustrated official made that even more fun.

"You're welcome here... anytime," Ben smirked at him. "Give me a bit of warning and I'll have mom bake some cookies."

George stepped forward from Gil Gartner's patrol car.

"Everything all right here?" he directed the question at Ben.

"Yeah...they were just leaving."

The unwanted visitors backed up around Gil's car to get to the turn-around area.

Gil stared down the officers in the vehicles, making mental notes of who they were. Offering a stern nod to those in each car, he opened his cell phone before they headed down the driveway. The pictures he took would have more mental effects on those in the party than anything else.

The Dalton search team drove away and Ben looked at George.

"How did you know they were coming?"

"The mayor called me this morning," George began. "Seems he has his nose buried in a powerful posterior. At least he thinks it is."

They walked back to the house while Gil stepped beyond the Elm tree and watch the cars go out of sight.

266

"He got wind that the Durays might be here," the DA went on, "Then demanded access to the mansion. I told him to get a warrant and figured he would...looks like I was right."

"How did he know that?"

"The rear end he was snuggling belongs to the Mayor of Chicago...or a surrogate of his."

Ben didn't seem too surprised. "A lot appears to be tied to Chicago," he admitted.

"I was afraid you would say that," George shook his head.

"Jon and the guys are here," Ben turned to go inside. "I saw the light on the microwave when we went through the kitchen."

That light was a silent signal that someone was on the third sub-level. Ben ran up the stairs to the master bedroom. He reset the elevator controls and asked George, "You coming?"

The DA squeezed in and they made their way down. The doors opened and there stood Silas.

"I should have known you would be involved," he directed at George. "Thank you, again."

"This case is taking on a strange tone," George answered.

"You're right about that, too." Silas walked back into the area and pointed to Murray. He spoke again to the DA. "Look what we found."

As George and the cowboy shook hands heartily, Silas asked Ben, "Did you run a scan yet? To see if they left anything?"

The boy's eyes lit up. "Give me two minutes," and he jumped back into the elevator to go up one floor. He was met there by Rita and Cheryl Duray.

"Is my daddy, ok?" the girl asked anxiously.

The smiling boy answered her, "He's better than ok. Let me do this and we'll all get together, ok?"

He pulled up a program on one computer and initiated a search for any electronic bugs that might have been installed. The system found one stuck under a table in the living room.

"I'm going upstairs to deal with the one present they left us," he said into an intercom. "Give me three minutes and you can all come on up."

~

Driving into the sun with little sleep the night before took its toll on Kinkaid. The SUV had been weaving from lane to lane for several miles when the blue lights and siren got his attention. Marvin Acree awoke, startled and angry.

"What the...where are we?" he jumped from his deep sleep and looked behind them.

The groggy Kinkaid mumbled something and pulled over.

The Tennessee highway patrolman stopped a car length back and issued his orders through a speaker system.

"Driver...turn off the truck and exit the vehicle...do it now."

Kinkaid complied and climbed out.

"Walk backwards to the sound of my voice," the trooper continued. "Do it now."

As Kinkaid got near the rear of the SUV, the officer stepped toward him. It was then that Acree pushed his door open and slid out, a gun in his right hand.

"Passenger...stay in the vehicle!" The trooper barked, but Acree raised his left hand and kept moving toward the rear. He stayed against the car with his right hand hidden.

268

"I have a question, officer...that's all," he pleaded with a weak voice.

"Stop there," the trooper commanded and reached for his revolver. Acree jumped forward and leveled his handgun, firing twice.

The officer spun to his left and fell.

"Now what?" Kinkaid was spitting mad. "You've killed a state trooper."

Looking around, there was no traffic on that part of the interstate at the moment. Acree grabbed the downed policeman and issued his own orders. "Shut up and help me get him in his car, quick."

Using the seat belts and a laptop computer to hold the body in place, they set the officer up in his front seat. Then propping his arm up and placing the microphone in his hand, the dead officer looked to be making a radio call.

"Let's go," Acree yelled and jumped into the driver's seat of the SUV. "Before somebody comes along."

Kinkaid asked him if they were going to change license plates.

"Not here," he replied with a glare. "We're on borrowed time here already."

They exited the interstate at Poplar Springs and turned under the overpass.

"We'll need to find a small country store or gas station with just one customer," Acree explained as he stopped in the shade under the expressway. He opened his door and climbed out, but looked back in at his boss. "I'm going to change the plate, but that won't help for long. We need to change vehicles."

51

Ben knocked on the door of the master bedroom where Silas tried to rest. Marsha was there with him, sitting in a large chair and watching him. It was almost four in the afternoon and the house had been quiet for hours. She opened the door quietly.

"What is it, Ben?"

"I hate to bother him," his look showed yet more concern. "But there's info he needs to know about."

She turned around to see Silas sitting upright, one arm supporting his weight, the other rubbing his face. "What is it, Ben?" he muttered.

"Remember Colonel Swanson told us the pest control guy had gone to Kentucky a few days ago?"

"Yeah," he sat straighter to listen.

"I've picked up a signal from the other phone that was in Arkansas. It's moving on I-40 toward Nashville. If he goes north from there, and I believe he will, he'll be heading for the same location below Lexington."

Silas lowered his head to think a minute. Looking back at Ben and still blinking heavily, he said, "See if Harold can take Tim to New Orleans this evening... and wait for him and possibly Phil Stone to come back tomorrow night."

Ben nodded and made notes on a pad, "I'll bet Murray wants to go home, too.

"You're right..." he muttered. " Oh yeah, then call Colonel Swanson," Silas rattled off. "See if you two can sync up a few lipstick cameras around the road leading into that farm. We need to keep an eye on that with her."

"Okay," Ben knew there had to be more.

"Get me on a flight to Duluth later this evening." Silas continued. "I need to see what and who this pest control guy really is."

"Is that it?"

"No..." he yawned as he rolled over. "Wake me up at 5:30 pm."

Ben looked over at Marsha who was shaking her head, but smiling.

"I'll pack him a bag," she offered.

"No gun," Silas said from beneath a pillow. "I'll be flying commercial."

~

Phil Stone was also packing that afternoon. He had been talking to Tim Spiegel who had brought him up to date on Jon, Murray and the current case.

"I knew he had to be alright," the retired cop rejoiced to his wife. Sara Stone wasn't as comfortable with this trip, but Phil assured her, "he just wants my opinion of the tactics and plan, that's all."

They had been following the case of Cheryl Duray since she escaped. The idea of now being part of solving it was a kick to Phil. Sara was pleased with that aspect, but her concerns still showed.

"I can see if they have room for you there, while we work." Phil suggested.

"No...I don't want to be any bother," she fawned, but actually liked the idea.

Within ten minutes, Marsha was on the line asking for Sara.

271

"I would love for you to come," she exclaimed. "Jon should have thought of that right away."

So it was all set. Agent Spiegel would stop by northern Louisiana and pick up the Stones on his way back to Dalton.

"I am looking forward to seeing that house," Sara grinned at Phil.

~

A local private pilot was on his approach to a small airfield near Lexington, Tennessee. His glide path took him and his Cessna Skycatcher over Beech Lake.

"Memphis control," he called excitedly into his radio as he pulled the craft up for another pass over the water. "This is November 451 Charlie Echo, my position is six miles south of Interstate 40 over Beech Lake. That's near the west side of the lake off Route 104. There is the reflection of a vehicle in the water, completely submerged...over."

"Roger, November 451 Charlie Echo, Memphis control will dispatch search units who are in the area."

The dead trooper had been found several hours earlier. The discovery set off a statewide hunt for the SUV shown on the dash camera of his patrol car. But until now, it had been nowhere in sight.

"Can you see any signs of life?" the Memphis controller asked.

"Negative, Memphis. I've just gone back again, lower, and slower. The car is red in color. There is no sign of anything around it other than a slight oil slick."

Within the hour, authorities had arrived with a crane and removed the SUV. The tags were gone, all of them including the one that had been on the rear. There was one naked body in the vehicle. No identification was found but it was clearly not either of the men in the video.

"Colonel," a man standing by a patrol car hollered to the leader of the recovery team. "They've ID'd the men from the tape. You ain't gonna believe this, sir."

"What is it Corporal?"

"The shooter is Marvin Acree."

The colonel's face lit up. "Acree? No shit?"

"Absolutely, it's him. And the other guy is Clyde Kinkaid."

"Find out who this body is...fast. They've got his car...truck or whatever the poor fool was driving." The captain looked at his watch. "It has been five hours since the shooting. This is only fifty minutes from where it took place." He rubbed his face in disgust. "They could be anywhere in four hours."

52

Jordan Sterns knocked as he barged into his Captain's office in Muskegon.

"Sir, this report on the internal com-line," he started, "about that police officer killed in his office in Chicago."

"Yeah?"

"It was Frank Borton."

"So?" the senior officer asked. "You know this Borton?"

"Three or four of the confidential informants from that area told me about him. There was never any proof, but they said he was dirty."

"Dirty... how?"

"These guys were all ex-ghosts, Pilfoy's former team members. They claimed Borton was a scheduler."

"You're going on the word of a few ex-thugs?" the captain scoffed.

"The ones who survived at my house each had a card with Borton's number on it in their wallets."

"Have you heard what all else has gone down in that rat hole city?" The senior man had stood up and walked to a side table in his office.

"Some bombing...and I don't remember who."

"It was an associate police commissioner's office that got completely taken out, and in the same building as the mayor."

"You think they are connected to Pilfoy?" Sterns asked.

"That's the other thing," his captain answered. "Pilfoy is dead too."

"How big is this?"

"I don't know, detective. But there's a manhunt going on in Tennessee right now for a cop killer. I'd bet my pension that's connected to this as well."

"What can we do, sir?"

"Get a hold of the boys who investigated your family's cabin up in the Upper Peninsula. See if we can have a copy of the fingerprints they took from the house."

"On it," Sterns said as he almost ran out the door.

~

Tension was getting thick at the Kentucky farm. News, orders, and updates were what Deacon Harkness was accustomed to. This silence was nerve racking. His knowledge of events was also limited. Having heard of the bombing in Chicago's City office building, he did know that the man named Walter Greer was unhurt. But he knew only through news reports.

"Boss," a worker opened the farmhouse front door and stuck his head in. "These girls are getting gamey." Stepping inside timidly the man tried to hide his grin. "The boys think we might should hose 'em down," he looked straight at his boss in childish anticipation.

Wilbur Harkness flashed red and bowed his chest out at the man. His anger came from knowing what that would lead to, and he had strict orders.

"You men leave them be," he yelled. "Not one hair on their heads...do you hear me?"

The man nodded and backed away. Harkness wasn't through with him. "Take the hose in there for 'em...but then close the door and get out. If they want to clean up, they get privacy to do it." He stared holes in the man, letting his frustration with the whole situation boil over and relieve itself.

"Yes, sir," the thoroughly chastised assistant backed away. His head bobbed profusely this time as he pulled the door closed.

Harkness was so wound up that the sound of his phone ringing nearly drew him out of his skin. It was the phone whose number only his superiors knew. He grabbed it and answered, his voice still tight with rage.

"Yeah," he half spit into the phone. "This is Deacon."

The voice on the other end was not one Harkness had actually heard before. He had heard of it, but the messages from this voice were usually relayed to him.

"Harkness," the harsh, garbled tones inquired. "Is this Wilbur Harkness?"

The farm overseer didn't know quite how to speak to this voice, or worse yet, what did the call coming straight to him mean? He delayed his response as long as he could, finally answering, "Yes, sir. I'm Harkness."

"I will need you to prepare a shipment... to be ready to leave in two days." The voice paused as though expecting a response at that point. "Is that clear to you, Mr. Harkness?" it demanded.

"Yes, sir," the Deacon told him. "Which one?"

"First in...first out," the harsh answer came fast. "Do you have coverings for the merchandise?"

Harkness had to think about that for a second. *Coverings meant burkas. Did he have a burka for her?*

"Yeah...yeah," he finally acknowledged. "I've got three or four still here."

"You will deliver the merchandise to the carrier at the main highway entrance to your facility in two days... at four in the afternoon." The voice paused again.

Harkness was getting the hang of this communication, "Right...sure," he stammered. "That would be Saturday at four pm, got it."

"Do not be late. The carrier will not wait for you."

"Right, I've been through that part before...Say," he asked the voice. "What the hell is going on? Where's my usual contact?"

"Things change, Mr. Harkness. You need to work with me, don't question me."

"Yeah I know, sir...but Petteri was here a few days ago and..."

"Don't listen to Reino any longer," the voice interrupted him and warned. "Should he call again, hang up. Understood?"

"Who's still in charge then...besides you?"

"Right now, just worry about me...if you like staying alive that is." The voice was now even more sinister. "That's all you need to know, Mr. Harkness."

That last part somehow took the edge off the fear this voice had initially struck. Even with underlings, some respect should be shown and this guy wasn't even trying.

"Sure," Harkness told him. He could feel himself churning inside as he spoke. *Who the hell does this jerk think he is?* He thought while maintaining the respect to his superior. "Is that all?"

"For now, yes," the voice now reeked of arrogance more than terror, but it did not realize the line it had crossed. The phone line went silent, then buzzed.

Harkness laid down his phone and stood, breathing calmly yet deeply. He walked to a closet and opened the door. Taking a long flowing set of robes from inside the space, he removed them from the hanger and folded them neatly.

I need to get this pressed, he said to himself.

~

Ben sat at a computer terminal on the second sub-level. He had gone there to check a program he'd set up several days ago. Hacking into the Lexington, Kentucky, airport's security cameras, he had his machine search for anything unusual or repetitive. The parameters he set were targeted on people coming or going who seemed out of place.

He watched it run for several minutes, as it had for days with no real hits. It was after 7 pm. Jon, Murray, and Tim were on their way, Cheryl was spending time with her family upstairs, and it was quiet. He rocked forward onto the table. The position was one he was used to. Ben was asleep within a few seconds and didn't hear the machine "ding" as it hit a strange occurrence. It copied and tagged the footage, then moved on with its job.

What the computer had found was a man in white robes leading a burka-covered woman from the entrance to the airport to a gate. They boarded the flight and were gone. What made this a remarkable event was that it was now the third time in three weeks this had happened.

Ben slept on as the computer continued to work.

53

It wasn't quite winter yet, but the air that struck Silas as he stepped down from the plane to the tarmac burned his lungs. Duluth-Superior Airport was white and grey under the lights from and around the terminal building. The change of planes in Chicago was all indoors, *but still...this was cold*, he thought, hustling to the building.

His cell phone buzzed in his pocket, but he didn't notice until standing at the rental car counter. It was a simple text from Ben reading, "The voice is coming from Chicago."

So, he told himself. *This Franz guy may not be what he appears*. Just how Ben had managed to trace him would have to wait. It was after 9:20pm central time and he needed to get into town and look around.

They didn't have a Mercury. The clerk even looked at him funny when he asked for one. So settling for a mid-size Chrysler, Silas was soon on his way.

He drove past the address for RP Pest Control, which was dark and obviously closed. Everything in sight was closed, even the coffee shop at the end of the block. He drove toward the docks, the lights there were the brightest, and he found a bar that was open.

Inside, the place was fairly lively with dockworkers and men speaking in all languages. There were four cargo ships being loaded, three scheduled to depart later that evening so the crews were getting in some last minute good times.

Silas found a table near the door yet facing the main area. He sat down and ordered dinner and coffee. Somehow the thought of a beer sent a shiver down his back. As the server brought his food and stepped away, Silas noticed a man who had begun to leave. In the shadows, this man stood perfectly still. After nearly a full minute, the man walked towards him and sat down across the table.

"Ah, Diablo," he said in broken English and then smiled. "I knew you must be alive somehow."

Silas stared back in wonder. The face speaking to him was an old friend. One he had never expected to actually see again.

"Juan?" he smiled back.

They both sat, staring in silence until Juan Castrono reached out his hand. Silas shook it fiercely. "I'll be damned. What are you doing here?" he asked.

"I live here," Juan shot back with his arms wide. "Your turn!"

Silas laughed and began to explain his presence. He didn't use any names at first. They discussed Murray and Ben, Silas left out the latest adventure involving the cowboy, but he told him about the kidnapped girl and the cartel he was after.

"What brings that to Duluth?"

"I need to check on a pest control business. I think it may be part of the group."

Juan suddenly looked pale. "Pest control?" he asked. "What name is this company?"

"RP Pest Control," Silas shared with him and Juan began to shake his head. "What's wrong?" Silas leaned forward.

"I was afraid of this," his friend told him. "I've known Reino since I've been here. His pest control business is across the street from mine and my sister's cleaners."

"You know him?"

"Si," Juan admitted. "I thought I knew him well." He went into some detail about the last couple of days and owner's actions. "He's gone from here, now. I don't know if he's coming back."

"I need to get into that shop to look around," Silas said flatly.

Juan leaned back and took in a huge, deep breath. "I can get you in there with no problem," he replied pulling some keys from his pocket.

"You've got his keys?"

"And the alarm code."

"Can I buy you dinner, Juan?" Silas smiled and began to eat.

"I've already had mine," the old friend told him. "But I'll take a beer...or three."

"How 'bout some coffee till we get done with this?"

Juan nodded meekly. "Si," he agreed. "But maybe a shot in the first one, no?"

~

Colonel Stansfield Gruen of the Tennessee State Patrol waited in his office for word on the identity. The body found in the red Ford Explorer was not mutilated or disfigured in any way. He just wasn't anyone recognizable. What was worse than that, no one had an idea what type of vehicle this man had been driving, so they didn't know what to look for.

Gruen checked his watch. It was now over twelve hours since his trooper had been murdered. He wanted action, some direction to move in, anything.

His phone rang and two Lieutenants charged in through separate doors at the sound.

281

"Gruen here," he answered sternly. "Yeah...right, okay. We're sure about this?"

The colonel hung up and looked at his junior officers, "Put out a BOLO for a late model sedan, silver in color. It's a lease car...a Toyota with West Virginia plates." He started to call out the numbers but stopped and looked up.

"Discount the plates," he ordered. "Don't even worry about plates, there's no telling what tags are on it now anyway. Stop every silver Toyota you find."

"Who was this guy?" one of the officers asked.

"A traveling salesman from West Virginia," the colonel responded. "Forty-seven years old. No family, thank God. I hate those notifications."

The colonel sat down and picked up his phone. "I'll call Alabama and Georgia," he started. "You guys see that all the other surrounding states have this information, too."

The Lieutenants exited through the doors they'd come in from. The search was back on.

~

The Toyota sedan was traveling west on Kentucky highway 92 with Clyde Kinkaid at the wheel. Behind him, in a thirty-year-old Buick he had bought from a man in Caryville, Tennessee, was Marvin Acree. The old car had been sitting on a vacant lot with a sign on the windshield. Acree called the number on the sign and paid $350.00 cash on the spot.

Far as the seller knew, Acree was Stephen Wilson and he was alone.

At Hollyhill, Kentucky, a winter skiing community, the Toyota was allowed to roll off a steep ridge and disappear into the trees below. Kinkaid joined Acree in the Buick and the pair backtracked to Interstate 75 north where they continued toward the Kentucky farm.

"You mentioned a 'backdoor' to the farm," Acree asked his companion. "That farm sits against the mountains, doesn't it?"

"We go above Berea to an old logging road just below the Army Depot," Kinkaid answered without even looking at him. "It winds back down close enough."

"Close enough? What does that mean?"

"It means we walk a couple of miles," the former congressman explained with no apology. "I found the route back when we were setting this place up. They'll never know we're coming."

54

It was late, but that was his norm. Virgil "Mac" McElroy tried to be quiet coming in, but his wife was waiting for him.

"You had a call, tonight," she advised him without emotion.

McElroy responded with a glare and reached out to take the note from her hand. "Who was it?" he asked, seeing the note was only a number he wasn't familiar with.

"He didn't say. But he wants you to call, whatever the time is."

The man grunted and walked over to a desk where he pulled two items from the main drawer, a list with phone numbers and a new, pre-paid cell phone. None of the listed numbers matched the one on the note. His first instinct was to ignore it, but with everything going on he was almost afraid to do that.

"Leave me," he ordered his wife. She huffed and turned in a snit, going back to her bedroom. McElroy sat down and slowly dialed the number. It answered on the fourth ring.

"Mac," the voice asked. "Is that you?"

The accent was unforgettable. McElroy knew right away who it had to be. "Mr. Petteri?" he responded in a half question. "How did you get my home number?"

"Pilfoy gave it to me some time back," Reino told him. "I've got all your numbers."

"Pilfoy's dead." McElroy spit out.

"I heard. They took a run at me, too."

"Who did? It wasn't my people."

"Oh, believe me, I know that," Petteri acknowledged, his tone more than serious. "If it had been you...I'd be dead."

"Then who's doing this?" McElroy was almost pleading for information.

"I figure it must be Franz. I would have said Greer, but they blew his office up too."

"Greer's dead?"

"No...they missed him as well. I heard a few minutes ago that Kinkaid has surfaced and is on the run through Tennessee."

"Could it have been him?"

"Naw...I don't think so. He's with Acree, do you know Marv?"

"I've heard of him."

"They were hiding out at Acree's place in Arkansas. It got blown to hell last night, too."

McElroy was getting more confused.

"You know this how?" he demanded.

"The news, man," Petteri's frustration came through. "It's been all over the T.V. and the papers!"

"I don't understand...why is this happening?"

The Finlander got hold of himself. He inhaled and kept it in for several seconds, then tried to explain what he knew.

"Franz got spooked, I guess," he started. "He must have figured he needed to start over with a new team."

There was quiet on the line, so Petteri added, "we're all expendable. That includes you."

The silence was longer this time. The old hit man rocked back in his wooden desk chair till it squeaked and the hard top rail hurt his spine. His voice became weak and muffled.

"I'm retired," McElroy tried to say. "I'm out of it...for good."

"That won't fly, Mac," Petteri was quick and loud. "You know it. He'll come for everyone...you and all your guys, too."

"So," the hit-team leader sat forward in near resignation. "You have a plan, I suppose."

"Look...I don't like this any more than you do. But I don't want to die right now, okay?" Petteri chose his words with care. "The only way I can think to turn this around is to take over the operation. Starve Franz out."

McElroy rubbed his forehead. He knew much of what he was hearing was risky, but had to be true. This could be his only hope. "So...what do we do?" the man asked from a newly found calm.

"There are three girls in Kentucky... live merchandise waiting to be shipped. They are worth over $750,000.00 each." Letting that thought have time to be absorbed was a bit obvious. He hoped the money would help his next, weaker statement, sound better.

"All we have to do," he pushed forward, "is take over the farm and get them to the buyers."

"Oh...is that all?" now McElroy nearly laughed in his sarcasm.

"Stay with me, Mac." Relived that the man had not hung up already, Petteri went on with more confidence. "We can do this. There are only a few guys at the farm and they're bumpkins, locals with little skill or experience. Harkness can't handle this."

He then listened to the man on the other end breathing as he considered the plan.

"Ok..." McElroy finally answered, "Maybe."

"There's one thing you need to know." Petteri added with caution. The other man began shaking his head before even hearing.

"We know Kinkaid and Acree were in Tennessee," Petteri told him. "I think they have the same idea and are headed to the farm."

McElroy thought quietly, *Duh? Of course they are.* He could feel himself relaxing. *That's the only catch? That's nothing.*

What he said to Petteri was quite different.

"Maybe I might want to work with them, instead of you."

"No doubt some of your guys may have already heard from them," the Finlander admitted. "I understand that. But you need to hear me. Kinkaid is convinced that vigilante guy is after him."

"What?" McElroy was lost.

"That 'Son' fella. The one who goes after politicians."

McElroy thought for a minute. "I don't see how that would affect me."

"You want to risk working with a paranoid leader who may be marked for death already...or for me?"

There was yet another lengthy pause in the conversation. Petteri had more to offer. "Don't forget...Kinkaid got busted in Washington. He couldn't get to his files. I've got mine. I know how to reach the contacts in the Caribbean. I know how to get more inventory and how we process them. The three in Kentucky are just seed money."

"Let me make a few calls," McElroy finally told him. "Is this where I can reach you?"

Petteri gave him yet another number. "I'll be there in the morning. Call me either way."

He hung up leaving McElroy sitting and stewing in the dark. He looked up to see his wife standing in the doorway.

"Are we okay?" she asked.

"Go to bed," he said dismissively, "I've got work to do."

55

Murray got to Caddo Mills after 10:30 that night. The G5 had dropped him in Shreveport where a night duty copter pilot for the police volunteered a ride for him.

The cop had heard about Murray's new fling-wing, a Sikorski X2 modified to the newer S-97 standards. "Can I get a look at her?" he asked.

"Sure," Murray beamed. "I was working on her when I got called away."

The Lucy Too was as he had left her. They walked into the hanger and the lights came on automatically.

"Oh, man," the officer smiled. "What a beauty."

The original X2s were all blue over white and much smaller. The hybrid was larger like the S-97 models that wore an Army standard green paint job. Lucy Too sported her custom Midnight Blue paint and she was something to look at.

"What's her specs?" the other pilot wanted to know.

"220 knots, ceiling 10,000," Murray started. As its new admirer walked around the craft, the man noticed bulges from the rear fuselage.

"What's with these?" he asked.

"Auxiliary fuel tanks. Takes the range to over 1000 miles if I don't push the speed too hard."

"A jet copter going 1000 miles? Damn!"

"Range can be a limitation," Murray told him as he walked over to a tarp-covered mound. Pulling the cover back exposed a military grade, 50 cal. with five rotating barrels. "As can firepower. I was setting up the mounting bracket for this, but got interrupted."

~

Juan turned the key and stepped inside the building. He went straight to the alarm panel and keyed in the numbers telling the system to "stand down." Silas found the light switch.

"Everything looks pretty normal in here," he said.

Pointing to a closed door across the room, Juan explained, "That's Reino's office. I've never seen that door closed before."

He reached for the knob but Silas jumped in front of him.

"Easy..." he held his friend back. "You've not seen it closed before...let's go slow, okay?"

They stood on either side of the door while Silas gently turned the knob and pushed. Nothing really happened.

Reaching in with one hand, Silas felt for and found the light switch. There was no booby-trap...but the room looked like it had been stripped down.

"He's not coming back," Juan lamented. He gazed on the nearly bare walls. Many pictures were gone. The open drawers on the big desk and file cabinets stood as they'd been left. Many of those were empty. "He cleaned out."

"Something had him spooked," Silas said half under his breath.

The sheer volume of what appeared to be missing struck Silas as odd. "Is there a dumpster out back," he asked Juan.

Walking to a rear door, Juan turned on an exterior light and unlocked that door. The large metal box sat several feet away at the edge of a parking area.

Most of the contents were loose papers, nothing that looked important to the case, but there were also many of the pictures from the walls.

"He had a bunch of pictures, huh?" Silas smiled.

"The walls were coated with 'em, yeah."

Silas picked one up that interested him. He stared at the picture of Petteri with another man, apparently in that man's office. What caught Silas' eye was the part of another wall hanging shown in that picture.

"Do you know who this is?" he asked Juan.

"Not really, why?"

"See that," Silas pointed to a spot on the photograph. A five-pronged star, made of numbers, was hanging in a frame on the man's wall. "Ever see that anywhere else?"

"Yeah, Reino had one here." Juan looked confused. "What is it?"

"I don't know," Silas leaned into the corner of the container. "It just keeps turning up... and usually with bad people." He suddenly looked up as he remembered something. "I need to call Ben," he said. "Is he going to be surprised to hear from you!"

~

"Just leave that here," Kinkaid told his companion. Marvin Acree had brought a large cache of weapons from his cabin. The duffle bag was cumbersome and heavy. He was trying to balance it around his back for the remaining hike to the farm.

"Just get a couple of AKs and some grenades," Kinkaid suggested.

"You want me to just leave this stuff here?" Acree complained.

"It's not that far to the farm," the boss explained. "After we get established, you can bring some of the others back here to carry it for you."

Marvin mumbled under his breath, but went along with the idea. They walked through the dark for several hundred yards to where they could smell smoke from a fireplace. Over a slight ridge covered in trees, they saw the lights of the three buildings that made up the farm.

"Okay," Kinkaid whispered. "Now we split up. There should only be two or three guys in the bunkhouse. The other little shed over there...that's where they keep the inventory."

"Who's in the house?" Acree asked.

"Usually just Harkness." He thought for a second and added, "Maybe one of the guys will be with him...probably not."

"How do you want to do this?"

"I'm going to call him."

"Call who?"

"Harkness," he smiled. "I'm going to call him like I'm back home or something, then you come in through the back. When he hears you, I'll come through the front door and we've got him."

"You want to kill him?"

"No...no," Kinkaid squinted at his friend. "He'll work with us. Once he realizes we're in control."

Kinkaid got into position behind a stump a few yards back from the front of the house. He waited for Acree to go around back and dialed Harkness' number.

The man answered his phone and heard a voice he didn't expect to hear again.

"Hello, Harkness. This is Clyde. How are you?"

56

Ben was awake and waiting. He would have called Jon, but the rules were very clear on that. When his phone finally rang he jumped on it.

"Jon, I'm glad you called, man."

"Hey," Silas started. "I'm in the RP Pest Control guy's office and will be sending you some pictures in a minute."

"Great...but Jon I need to..."

"Before that," Silas cut him off. "There's someone here you'll be surprised to hear from."

"Yeah, but..."

"Okay," he cut him off again. "Here he is."

Juan took the phone, "Hello, Ben?"

The voice was unforgettable. Ben Shaw froze a second as his mind absorbed what he'd just heard.

"Juan...are you kidding me?" he finally answered.

"Si, Mr. Ben," the voice was now toying with Ben, playing up on his natural accent. "How are you?"

"What? So...you live up there? How did Jon find you?"

"Providence, my friend, Ben," he told him. "Some things just are what they are."

"Look..." Ben begged for understanding. "I don't mean to be rude, but there's some stuff Jon needs to know about...right now."

"Okay...sure. But he really seems to be hung up on the Silas thing right now."

"That's an understatement," Ben agreed. "Can I speak to him?"

Silas took the phone from Juan's outstretched arm. "Ben, this guy had a star on his wall," he started. "He's one of 'em...whatever 'they' are."

That threw Ben slightly but he quickly gathered his thoughts. "Jon...they're on the move for sure and I think I know how the group moves the girls."

Letting the urge to correct him on the name used slide by, Silas picked up on his first point. "You got their phone tagged again?" he asked.

"No...it's on TV. They killed a cop in Tennessee. It's all over the news."

"Did they get 'em?"

"No," Ben reported. "They've disappeared again."

Silas thought in silence about that news and calmly asked for details on Ben's other find.

"Back a couple of months ago," Ben started. "There were three cases of a Sheik taking a woman through the airport at Lexington."

"A what?"

"You know...a Sheik, Lawrence of Arabia stuff."

Knowing Ben had to have some, Silas asked for the details.

"It's the same guy every time. His robe and stuff is a bit different each time, but it's the same guy. All the occasions were before Cheryl escaped and there hasn't been one since."

"Go on," Silas leaned on the table he was standing next to. "I'm listening."

"You can't tell who the girls are at all. They're wearing full burkas with face shields and the whole bit. Close study of the films show they are different heights. It's three different girls going with him."

"Have you identified this guy, yet?"

"Facial Recognition is working on it. He must not be anybody important cause it hasn't found him so far."

"Did they fly in from somewhere else?" Silas asked.

"The surveillance tapes show this guy coming in through the parking decks each time, a girl in tow. We found two of the cars...they both appear to have been rentals. I'm working on finding out... by whom."

"Okay...great work, Ben."

"There's more."

"This whole group has been spooked big time," the boy surmised. "When you add up all the news going on it's a mess."

Silas didn't question Ben's statement or disagree. He simply listened.

"Shootings and bombings are all over the country," Ben continued. "The ties are kinda loose I know, but that cop in Chicago you mentioned once... Frank Borton. Well, he's dead. Shot in his office in broad daylight."

Silas was now sitting at the desk in Petteri's office, still listening.

"That Walter Greer guy you found...somebody blew up his whole office, but missed him by a few minutes."

"Anything else?" Silas almost sounded amused. "This case is handling itself so far."

"There was a home invasion up in Michigan. The family runs a lake cabin getaway. Anyhow...the head of that family had helped Mr. Duray get out of Michigan, back when he went to Chicago."

Silas perked up at that news.

"You sure about that?" he challenged.

"Absolutely," Ben assured him. "How these people found them...we don't know."

"What's their condition?"

"Oh...that's another weird part...they're fine. The bad guys had 'em, could have killed them all, but got a phone call and left."

Ben took a breath and went on. "All this stuff happened in the last thirty-six hours. I'm just finding out about it."

Silas sat still with the phone to his ear. He glanced over at Juan who had an expression of growing concern. Instinctively, he nodded at Juan as though silently telling him all was okay, and then put his concentration back on the phone.

"Ben," he was firm and calm. "Can you isolate that Sheik guy's face into a photo and get it to Colonel Swanson? I'd like her people to watch for him at the farm road, if they can."

Silas glanced back at Juan while still talking to Ben. "If you're right...and I believe you are... he's picking the girls up at that farm."

"Right away," Ben acknowledged and slid across the room to another computer. "What else?"

"I was going to send you some stuff from here...but in reality it doesn't look like much." He tossed the papers he'd been going through to the floor. "You said last time that Franz voice was coming from somewhere in the states?"

"Yes...Chicago actually."

"How did you figure that out?"

"The last time he used that phone, I assumed it would go to Caracas first, so I started there." Ben voice swelled with pride as he went on, "that gave me time to run it down. Point of origin is definitely Chicago."

"Well, that makes sense," Silas grinned. "With all this...that makes perfect sense." He stood from the desk as an inspiration hit him. "Ben, get the guys outfitted and have them meet me in Kentucky. You know, near that college where the Colonel's people are."

"They should be back tomorrow. Murray is going to bring his new copter."

Looking at Juan again, Silas smiled a broad smile, "It could come in handy."

"Where are you going now?"

"I'd like to talk with this Petteri fellow, but I guess he'll come to us soon enough. I'm headed back to Chicago... to see if I can speak with this Walter Greer in person."

"You're going all the way to Chicago to see him?"

Silas' stared down at the picture with Petteri and the other man. The picture with the unknown, star shaped object hanging on the wall.

"Follow the yellow brick road, Ben," he said in a cryptic tone.

"What?"

"Ask Harold to meet me at Midway Airport tomorrow," Silas changed the subject. "And bring my stuff, please."

"The suit?"

"Yeah...all of it."

57

Packing began early. He didn't need to leave until the next day, but Larry Gibbons had read the message five times.

That was a bit unusual, he thought at first. *Franz had always called before.* But the courier message was good enough for him. *It had to be authentic, who else would sign a note as 'Franz?'*

The robes were clean and pressed. His headdress was picked out and carefully laid in the case. He would have driven to Kentucky as he normally did, but Franz must have realized how low on cash he was getting.

The message included a ticket from Philly to Lexington and a rental car, besides the normal flight out with his cargo.

As he grabbed his normal supplies from a dresser drawer, he realized he could not take his Smith & Wesson handgun this time. He liked to feel protected on the road, especially out around the farm.

Those guys are strange down there, he remembered. But there was no way to carry it, not on the plane.

Adrenalin kept him going. He checked and rechecked like a kid going to camp for the first time. When he finally finished, it was three in the morning on Friday. The flight out of Philadelphia left at 10:15 AM Saturday.

"I need to get some sleep," he said out loud.

Gibbons didn't take any chances. He swallowed two Lunestas and a Motrin PM with a shot of scotch whiskey. A strong and potentially dangerous mix to some, but nothing like the contents of the small plastic box he had packed earlier.

~

The phone call itself made Wilbur "Deacon" Harkness rise to his feet. Then the sound of a rear door opening nearly rattled the hardened criminal.

"Kinkaid?" he said into the phone. "Hang on a second...I've got something going on here." He stepped into the kitchen area as the lights came on. There stood Marvin Acree with a shotgun leveled at him.

"What is this?" Harkness demanded. "Do you have any idea where you are, fool?"

Kinkaid had also entered the farmhouse and now stood behind Deacon. "Yeah, I know where we are," he said.

Harkness spun around and looked down at his phone in confusion.

"You can hang that up now," Kinkaid smirked.

The other man threw his cell phone to the side and it crashed against the wall. "So now, you're busting in on me," he complained. "What the hell is going on with this job?"

"Management changes, Deacon," the former congressman came up to him and checked him for weapons. "Just a management change."

"So, you took care of Petteri?" Harkness asked him.

"I heard he was here. How did that go?"

"Well...he didn't draw down on me, I'll tell you that."

"Maybe he wasn't serious." Kinkaid got right in the man's face. "I am though."

Harkness backed away, but maintained what composure he still had. "You're welcome to it, Clyde. I was thinking of retiring anyways."

"Can't have that just yet, Deacon," he responded with his head tilted and eyes squinting. "Marvin there, he's holding your retirement plan, if you're intent on that."

Harkness looked back as Acree directed the shotgun at his middle.

"You see... I still need your help... For a while anyway." Kinkaid's tone changed like a crazy man. "We're going to process the merchandise and regroup. Then you can go."

Harkness stayed quiet.

"How many men do you have here?" Kinkaid asked.

"Three in the bunkhouse and two out on the road, supposed to be guarding it."

"First thing in the morning, I want a meeting with everybody. We'll establish a schedule going forward."

"Gibbons is already coming tomorrow," the Deacon informed him. "Or Saturday, I mean."

"Gibbons?"

"You know...Larry the Sheik."

"Oh yeah," Kinkaid laughed. "So they're all still alive, huh?'

"We don't do the other thing here, Clyde. Never have."

"Well..." Kinkaid scoffed at him. "I'll evaluate what's here and see. We might need to fill some parts orders that are pressing by now."

Harkness' eyes grew wide. "Hold on, man," he bowed up. "That's over the line for me."

Kinkaid turned and walked away. After three steps he looked back. "That's what new lines are for," he muttered cynically. "You can be part of the plan...or part of the inventory." He smiled at the now frightened man. "Think about it."

~

About the only other thing of value Silas could find in Petteri's office was the fact that everything of value was gone.

"No phone numbers, no list of names, nothing," he told Juan. "All that stuff was here, it had to have been, and he thought to take it with him."

"So he's covering his tracks, huh? Doesn't want to be found out," Juan thought he was agreeing.

Silas shook his head and looked at Juan slowly. "He wants to start over somewhere else."

"You really think so?"

"Yeah...he's got all his tools, his information and organization charts. There's no money here...he took all that as well." Silas stepped forward and kicked at a pile of papers out of minor frustration. "He'll be in Kentucky...if he's not already there."

"Can I help?" Juan asked sincerely.

"You kidding me?" Silas grinned at him. "You've already been great."

They locked up the doors and stepped back out into the cold.

"How do you stand it here?" Silas asked him.

"You get...." Juan started to say and then he laughed at himself. "Naw, you don't get used to it. It's freaking cold, man." They hurried towards the cars, "But my sister already had her business set up here." Juan pointed cross the street. "It's work, but at least I don't have the worries I used to."

"You sound like you're happy," Silas told him.

300

"Yeah...I am, Mr. Jon," he smiled. "And I 'thank you' for this being possible."

Silas slid behind the wheel of his rental car and Juan stood back to tease him, "No Mercury?"

"They didn't have one," it was Jon's cheerful voice that somehow came through that time and Juan noticed the difference. "I asked for one though."

Pushing the door closed, Juan could read Jon's lips as he said, "Come see us," and drove away.

58

The cold morning wind slipped down through the Kentucky foothills. Harkness had not turned up the furnace in the farmhouse and the internal temperature was fifty-four degrees when Kinkaid opened his eyes.

"Damn," he shuttered and wrapped himself in an old blanket to make his way to the kitchen. Marvin Acree stood by the counter watching the coffee maker slowly drip as he came in.

"Where's the Deacon?" he asked Acree and grabbed a cup from the cabinet.

"I tied him up with his boys out in the bunkhouse," Acree answered. "Couldn't be sure about him in here," the explanation went on. "They're alright. I tied 'em all up good." He looked at the now empty cabinet with raised eyebrows. Kinkaid had taken the last clean cup.

"Have you seen the girls yet?" He asked as he rinsed out a dirty one with his fingers and tap water.

The boss had poured a hot cup for himself and answered while walking back into the main room.

"No," he said and then wiggled his shoulders. A shiver went down Kinkaid's back and he adjusted his blanket wrapper. "I'll go down there in a few minutes. You bring those boys and Harkness up here... and keep 'em calm."

"Yeah, I can handle that," Acree muttered. Then he seemed to perk up a bit. "You know," he chirped. "This is kinda making me feel young again. It's been a while since I played the heavy myself." He sipped on the coffee and shook his head at its bitterness. "I used to be pretty damned good at this shit."

Kinkaid stared at him like he had gone crazy. "Just don't forget how old you are... and try something you can't do, Marv."

Acree shrugged his shoulders and walked to a corner of the room. "Do you think Petteri will come here?"

"Oh, yeah," Kinkaid was quick and confident, "maybe even today."

The ex-congressman sat deep in a worn out stuffed chair. As he adjusted his blanket yet again, another thought on Petteri came to him. He spoke it as it had come to him.

"He'll try to get some help, though," he declared and then paused a second, considering his own statement. "I don't think he ever did any dirty work himself." After a slow sip of his coffee, he finally added, "Course, I don't know anything about before he came over here...Finland, I mean," he shrugged and looked up at Acree. "Wonder what that's like over there?"

"We can't stay here long..." Acree announced, changing the subject like he had had an epiphany. "You know that, right?"

"Marv, don't screw up the time we do have here... worrying about it. There's work to be done. We've got to process those girls and get some seed money."

"Then what? Where can we go, seriously?"

"I may not have my lists, that's true," Kinkaid scowled at him over his cup. "My numbers and contacts were all in my office and I couldn't get back to it. But I know we can go to the Caribbean. We'll just start over there."

Acree didn't really believe they could pull that off, but what else could they do? *He's not even considering that assassin who's after him*, he pondered in silence. *This whole deal is messed up.*

Marvin Acree finished his coffee and went back towards the kitchen. "I'm going to rinse my face... then I'll go get those guys," he walked past his boss without really looking at him.

Kinkaid buried his face in his cup and said nothing.

~

The Hampton Majestic hotel was just over a quarter mile from City Hall in downtown Chicago. Ben had arranged a room for the marketing manager of Rayfall Bearings, a subsidiary of Crane Industries, while Silas was on his late night flight from Duluth. A waiting taxi took him to the hotel.

Ben also studied the entrance protocols for the floor where Greer's temporary office was located and found two other businesses Silas wanted in the area.

Silas awoke around 8:30 that morning and took his time getting ready. He even had breakfast.

Walking this trip, he first went south, away from City Hall along South State Street. The first shop Ben had located was on West Adams. They were open and busy. Their biggest time of the year was just a month away and the workers were stocking the current inventory of costumes. Silas found the items he sought, including an old briefcase and paid with a corporate card. He then set out for his other stop, an electronics store.

Along the way, he found a busy UPS shop and went inside. The clerk was trying to help four customers at once so when asked about receiving a Fax, he handed Silas a note with the incoming number. A quick text message to Ben contained only that number.

The second of three pages that came in contained a perfect copy of the City Hall security badge, complete with gold seal and a fuzzy picture that showed Silas made up as he planned to appear. They had discussed it the night before.

The clerk grabbed the pages without looking at them and said, "$4.27."

Silas gave the clerk a five. "Keep the change," he told him and moved on to the last stop. He found the electronic "bugs" he wanted and again sent serial numbers to Ben via text messages.

From the entrance of the electronics store he could clearly see the massive City Hall building and the blue tarps draping the upper floors. Scaffolding was being erected which blocked off the main front entrance.

A construction van stood open near the side of the building. A set of coveralls and a hard hat hung just inside the rear doors.

~

McElroy had six men agree they wanted to keep working. They were to meet at McKinley Park around noon. Mac spent several minutes considering his decision before he dialed the number for Petteri. The man answered on the first ring.

"I got a crew," McElroy spit out. "Now what?"

"We need transportation and we leave for Kentucky...today."

"McKinley Park...noon," McElroy asserted. "Look for a tan van and a red one parked next to each other."

"Good," Petteri was impressed and it came through in his voice. "I'll see you there."

~

"Okay," Kinkaid started. "Is this everybody?" He looked at the group of misfits sitting in front of him with obvious disdain.

"You ain't got no guards out there right now," one of them spoke up meekly. "Nobody's on lookout."

"Yeah, I know that. This won't take but a minute."

"Who are you...sir?" another man asked.

"I'm your new boss. That's all you need to know."

"Maybe we don't want to work for you," a third offered with his chest puffed out.

The blast from Acree's shotgun sounded more like a cannon in the little house. The spread of buckshot cut through a lamp and ripped the drapes on a window behind the man who spoke. He hadn't moved, but that was more from pure fear than defiance.

"Now," Kinkaid asked smugly. "Anybody want to quit?"

The room remained quiet, so Kinkaid went on. "I expect...we will have company here any time. Could be today," he emphasized. "Marv here needs two of you men to go with him to bring back our weapons...so we can defend ourselves."

No volunteers surfaced so he pointed out two. "You go," he told them.

"What about the girls?" Harkness stretched his neck upward, staring directly at Kinkaid.

"They look pretty good," he responded. "I assume Franz had customers for all three. I need to get the word out that they deal with us now."

"How the hell are you going to do that?" Harkness barked. "You don't even know who they are."

Kinkaid smiled with confidence. He walked closer to Harkness before telling him, "Not right now I don't...but I believe our approaching guests will have that information."

"Petteri?"

"I think so...yeah."

Harkness looked away for a moment and shook his head. "He won't be alone, of course you know that. And he scares me. I've met him. He drove right in here, unafraid."

"He drove in?" Kinkaid asked. "Through the main road?"

"Yeah...that's the only way in here." Harkness disclosed.

Kinkaid liked what he heard. Limited access to property, or the belief in that, played well into his plans. His knowledge of the back road path was not widespread, even to the current manager of the place.

59

The worker strolled in through the front doors carrying a stack of drop cloths. Guards milling about were armed and plentiful, at least six he could see and be sure of. Pausing at the desk, he could see a printed copy of the guard's work schedule taped to the top of it. Times were still tough and the budget for this service reflected that.

Normal business hours were heavily guarded, but mainly for show as it appeared. After hours and weekends were blank, no one scheduled at all. The building would be locked, but that was about it.

Still carrying the drop cloths, he moved on down the main hallway. Looking at the surroundings, he found a storage closet and then a service elevator.

Riding the elevator to the bomb damaged floor, he looked for and found a corresponding closet on that level. The dust on the door's surface and the knob showed it had not been opened for a while. It was locked, but that was short work. Silas was inside within a minute.

Hidden inside the pile of drop cloths were his case and the items he'd bought at the costume store. He pulled off the coveralls and transformed himself into a city employee, badge and all. He now had heavy black-rimmed glasses and thick eyebrows. The reversible sport coat was turned to a brown corduroy side and he wore a tan tie.

Stepping from the closet, he walked around the corner into another worker.

"What are you doing here?" the man stared at his badge. "Swartz?"

"They asked me to see how it was coming."

"Well...we're nowhere near that yet. Use the elevator and get out of here, this is a hard hat area."

"Yes, sir," Silas assured him and stepped into the elevator.

On the secured floor, he was immediately checked by a guard, who looked at his badge and waved him on. This floor also had the same closet in the same location. Again he picked the lock and was in.

This one was obviously used more frequently. *Shouldn't be here that long*, he convinced himself as he turned the coat around and changed the glasses. He placed a tiny earpiece over the arm of the glasses and tapped on the front pocket of his coat.

"You got me?" he asked softly.

"Yeah," Ben's voice came through the earpiece. "Could you turn the camera button about forty-five degrees?"

Silas turned the unit but Ben interrupted.

"The other way," he corrected him.

"How's that?" Silas was putting on a small moustache as he asked again.

"Good, I'm all set."

"Are their cameras in the hall working?"

"No," Ben answered. "The construction wiring is a big mess. The cameras are up, but they're not on... I should have said something."

Silas nodded and finished getting ready. He left the I.D. badge off this time. It was just a few feet to Greer's temporary office and he wanted to save the I.D. for his escape.

"Here we go," he told Ben and with a quick look around, Silas turned the knob on the office door and walked in.

Greer lifted his head dismissively from his work... then looked down again.

"You're in the wrong office, Bud," he said tersely. "Check down the hall."

"I want to talk to Greer." Silas said in a calm, strong voice.

The man at the desk stopped what he was doing. His head rose slowly as he asked, "Who the hell are you?"

"You're Greer, right?" Silas' glare now caught the man in the eyes. He sat up straighter, his stiff expression weakened and his eyes flickered in time with his thoughts.

"I don't have any appointments today," he told the intruder. "There's some mistake...you need to leave now."

"The folks at home said you'd know about it," Silas moved closer as he spoke.

"What?" Greer now was becoming agitated. "Know about what?"

"Folks back home...the newspapers. They said you had information about what happened to her." Silas reached out, leaning on the man's desk. With his right hand, he secured a tiny microphone to the lip of the overhang. He glanced about the sparsely decorated room. There were no pictures, no star made of numbers.

But this is not his regular office, he told himself. *This is temporary.*

Leaning back now, but still keeping eye contact, Greer began to tremble slightly.

"Who are you, I asked?" he spit out. "What are you talking about?"

"She was kidnapped on vacation." Silas matched the man's retreat. With hands still resting on the edge of the desk, he bent forward at the waist. His neck stretched out across the desk as he continued, "We never saw her again."

310

Greer pushed his chair back and stumbled to his feet behind the desk. Silas kept a close watch on the man's hands as a memory flashed over him, *Colorado...Walden...the old gun.* The thoughts were fast and disjointed, but made perfect sense to him. *Lamar Jakes.*

The power of his guest's building rage frightened Greer even more. He reached for the phone on his desk.

"Don't do that," Silas warned him without moving.

Greer froze. "Look man, I don't know who you are, but this isn't funny one bit."

So far, Silas had not evoked the response he'd expected from this man. Fear was clearly present, but guilt was not coming through.

The intruder's expression eased to a calm resolve while still staring directly into Greer's eyes. "I want Franz," he uttered in a low, serious tone.

There it was.

Greer's face flinched and it wasn't simply fear any more. That name registered and the momentary reaction was beyond his control. He reached again for the phone, but this time Silas grabbed his hand.

"I told you ...don't touch that." He considered killing him right there and then. Even without the suit or his powered arm, he knew he could handle it quickly. But this was larger than just one man. Lives were at stake and Silas wasn't sure if this was actually the head of the operation or simply another pawn.

Releasing the man's arm, he warned him, "Touch that phone and I'll snap your neck. Reach for it again before I'm out that door and I'll come back." He stood back a step as though inviting Greer to try. "Am I understood?"

Walter Greer nodded and sat down.

"You ready to tell me what I need to know?" Silas asked him.

There was no response from the man at the desk. His color had left him and he breathed short, labored breaths.

"Then let me tell you what's going to happen," Silas growled. "Those girls will be released by noon tomorrow. All three of them, and they'd better be unharmed."

Greer remained silent but more signs of guilt began to come through. A sweat broke out on his forehead and his lower lip shook erratically.

"I know about Kentucky." Silas went on. "I know about Minnesota and I know Kinkaid is on the move."

Greer's eyes widened uncontrollably as Silas stepped toward the door, then paused and looked back at the phone.

"No matter where you go..." he threatened. " I can find you."

Pulling the door open, he looked both directions and the hall was clear. He took one last glare at Greer and was gone.

The man at his desk sat in a stupor for over a minute. So racked with fear, he found it hard to think. His hand reached for the phone but pulled back. He looked to the door apprehensively and forced his legs to lift him.

With one hand supporting his weight on the desk and the other rubbing his forehead, Greer finally got hold of his breathing. His mind began to clear slightly.

How could this be? He thought. *Who is this man?*

Another minute went by before Greer finally moved to his door and cautiously opened it.

Silas had quickly entered the service closet and changed back into the employee with the heavy glasses and thick eyebrows. His badge prominently affixed to his coat, he cracked open the door and looked around. To the left, he saw Greer headed down the hallway. The man opened the main door to the Mayor's suite and disappeared inside.

"Your trace of those phone calls," Silas spoke to Ben as he moved toward the elevators. "Did you narrow it down to a specific location here?"

"I see what you're asking...but no. Just to the building itself."

"Can you refine it on the next call?"

"I can try, but there's no telling where he'll call from next time."

"You're right," Silas agreed. "Be ready just in case."

"You thinking there could be another layer to this?"

"I don't know yet."

His brow wrinkled in thought, Silas found some papers on a cart that was left unattended in the hall. He grabbed a stack and stepped into the elevator. Back on the bomb-damaged floor, he made it to the service closet with no interference.

Didn't need these, he thought and dropped the papers in the sink.

The worker with the drop cloths soon left the way he had come in. There was no alarm sounding and there were no approaching police cars.

Am I wrong about this? He thought walking back to the hotel. *Why wouldn't he report my visit?*

~

"Colonel Gruen, Sir?" the voice came over the intercom on his desk. It was one of his Lieutenants.

Pushing the button to respond, he answered, "Yeah...what is it?"

"A Colonel Swanson of the Kentucky State Police is on line one, sir."

Gruen released the button and picked up his phone's receiver.

"Hello, Colonel. How are you doing these days?" he started.

"Not too bad Stan," she said. "I hear you're in charge of this detail... hunting that Kinkaid fella."

"Yes, Sharon, I am," he confided. "And without much luck, I must add."

"Any trail at all, anything that leads them my way?"

"We completely lost them after they killed the salesman and took his car, a Toyota sedan."

"I've got reason to think they're coming up here. There's a farm below Lexington we're watching...has to do with a much larger case, but still involving Kinkaid."

"How can we help each other?" he asked.

"Well, your report that they're in a Toyota sedan...that helps. We're watching for that thing up here."

"So you don't believe these two are still in my state?"

"Nope," Swanson told him. "Don't put your guard down on what I say, but my contact about this has a damned good record of knowing what's what."

"Same guy who helped with those Russians?"

"Now Stan," she became coy all of a sudden. "I can't confirm or deny on that."

Gruen laughed into the phone. "We don't think he's dead down here, either."

"I gotta go, Colonel," Swanson laughed back. "You be careful down there."

314

60

Greer was still pale when he got in to see the mayor.

"You don't look good, Walter," the man smirked. "Seen a ghost?"

Greer made sure the door was closed and sat as close as he could.

"That guy you were telling me about. The one Kinkaid thinks is after him?" he leaned in and nearly whispered.

The mayor's face grew flushed and he spun his chair around toward his guest. "What are you talking about?"

"He just came to see me."

The mayor stared at Greer without saying a word. Easing himself out of his large leather chair, the man went to his door and looked out.

"Hold everything for a few minutes, Sally," he ordered. "I'm in a private meeting with the associate commissioner." He closed the door while she tried to respond and slowly went back to his perch.

Greer sat like a child in the principal's office, head down, perfectly still.

"Here?" the mayor whispered as he sat behind his desk. "He was here?"

Greer nodded.

"What did this man say to you?" the mayor asked calmly.

"He knows about everything," Greer spoke without looking up. "Kentucky... Petteri... and Kinkaid."

The mayor cocked his head and looked at Greer through narrowly squinted eyes.

315

"That's not everything," he said provocatively.

"He came into my office, Reggie," Greer explained while trying to maintain some composure. "What else is there?"

"He's still fishing. If he thought he knew it all...you'd be dead for one thing."

"Yeah...well, that's not settled yet. He gave me an ultimatum. I have to have the girls released by noon tomorrow...or he said he's coming back."

The mayor rocked back and half smiled, "That's pretty damn bold."

"What do I do?" Greer pleaded for advice.

"You've got your gun in that office, don't you?"

His mouth fell open before the word reached his lips, "Yeah."

The mayor still seemed amused by the threat. He sat back with both arms on the desktop and looked sullenly, straight at Greer.

"Then...shoot the bastard when he comes back."

Murray landed at the Dalton airport and refueled. He called the house but declined Ben's offer to send a car.

"I'll park across the road," he informed Ben. "I scouted a spot out a few weeks back. Have you heard from the others?"

"Yeah...they're about thirty minutes behind you."

"I'll just wait for them and save the car fare."

Okay...I've been wanting to see this new ride of yours myself."

"I'll let you know as we leave here. You can meet us."

"Good," Ben smiled at the idea.

"Say..." Murray didn't let him hang up. "Heard from Jon?"

"Looks like he wants all you guys to meet him in Kentucky later today."

"So...he's found the girls."

"We hope so."

~

Silas gathered his things and checked out of the midtown hotel. In the taxi taking him to Midway airport, he called Ben again.

"Have you heard anything from the office bug I left?"

"No," Ben told him. "Greer came back, I could hear him enter the room, but he didn't stay long and didn't say a word."

In Silas' mind, that could have been anyone. Not necessarily Greer, but he didn't say that to Ben.

"Are the guys there yet?" he asked instead.

"Yeah, they're on the way from Dalton Airport. Murray is flying them over in the Lucy Too."

Smiling at that thought, Silas asked about Harold and the G5.

"He's already in the air," Ben assured him. "Should be there in a couple hours."

~

"Colonel Swanson," the officer tapped hard on the window of her command post van. "There's a report of an old car on a logging trail north of the farm."

"What's unusual about that?" she asked.

"It was still giving off a heat signature when the pilot flew over."

Night surveillance, light aircraft carried thermo sensing radar units capable of locating human beings on the ground by their body heat. Their flights were restricted to well away from the farm itself for fear of spooking the occupants. The old trail was just inside the search parameters.

"It's nearly noon," Swanson looked at her watch and even pointed at it for emphasis. "Why am I just hearing this now?"

"It's off the tapes, Colonel," the officer explained. "The pilot didn't see anything himself. The tapes picked it up...they were just being reviewed."

"So, they have guests...or reinforcements of some kind."

The officer was a bit ahead of her. "A car like that could carry four...maybe five passengers. We know they had six men there already, so the total couldn't be more than twelve," he calculated as he spoke. "Probably a few less."

"What if they plan to use that path as an escape?" she asked.

"We're watching it, Colonel. The car is still there." He checked his phone for any more text messages. "Nothing new as of a few minutes ago."

"Find the start of that logging trail," Swanson ordered. "Set up a blockade there, just to be sure."

"Yes, Ma'am."

61

The reaction of Phil and Sara Stone to the mansion was as expected by Marsha. They had heard about it, but seeing was another thing.

"I should have known," the retired cop grinned. "But I never really thought..."

"It's beautiful," Sara threw in as she reached out to hug Marsha. "Hi...I'm Sara," she said."

"So nice to meet you...I've heard much about you from Jon."

"So... those dreadful stories weren't true," she asked.

"Most were all too true...but his 'death' is a cover. It was supposed to protect all of us. I think it did allow the heat to die down some."

Phil nodded and reached out to shake Weston Duray's hand. "I have heard a lot of good things about you, sir!" he smiled. "Good to see other maturity around this bunch."

Duray laughed and returned the handshake. "It's a tough group to keep up with, I'll tell you that much," he said laughing.

Ben stepped up from behind and said, "Captain Stone, sir."

Phil turned, "I'd know that voice anywhere...Hello, Ben!"

Greetings wrapped up and Marsha announced that she, Rita and Cheryl had lunch ready.

"You three need to pack and get suited-up pretty quickly," Ben looked at Murray, Tim, and Weston. "Jon will be in Kentucky by 5:00 PM. He'd like you guys to meet him there."

~

Marvin Acree knew to stay off the main trail, even if it was obscure to start with. He and his two helpers trekked along the path, but fifty yards to its right, in the heavy brush and low trees.

When they got to the car, he knelt down and studied the area for several minutes before he was satisfied.

"You see that bag?" he asked one of the men. It stood against the rear quarter panel on the driver's side.

"The duffle?"

"Yeah...crawl out there and drag it back here."

"Crawl," the man seemed confused. "Why?"

In no mood to explain his tactics, Marv pointed his shotgun at the man and tilted his head slightly with a blank stare. The man got down and began to crawl.

Acree continued to look around as the man went out towards the car. *Would there be any motion or sound...anything,* he thought silently. Nothing was apparent to him.

From his observation spot, a hundred yards to the east and halfway up a ridge, a state trooper watched the man pull his body to the car. He started to use his binoculars, but the sun, just reaching its high point above him, posed a potential glare that might give him away.

He keyed his radio microphone and whispered, "Sentry four bravo... I've got movement around the car, over."

He quickly turned the receiver volume down even lower than it was. The response was barely audible, but he could make it out.

"How many?" it asked.

"One visible...could be more. He's dragging a large bag away from the car."

"Large enough for weapons?"

"Oh, yeah..." his voice rose with that answer. " Plenty big."

The control position then called to a spotter across from the reporting officer, "Do you see anything?"

"Negative." the officer said.

"Check the tree line on the far side of the car."

It didn't take more than a minute.

"Roger, control. One moving in the trees. Possibly more. Can't use glasses to confirm."

"That's understood, four alpha. Keep an eye on that area."

When the man and the bag got back to Acree's position, the experienced hoodlum led them deeper away from the trail. His senses were peaked. *Something's not right*, he thought as they slowly plowed further into the brush.

The second spotter reported in again. "Two confirmed now," he said. "One towing a large bag."

"Are they going toward the farm?"

"Negative, control. They've gone east from the car and are now out of sight."

~

Petteri was there early. The park wasn't crowded and he could see from his vantage point most of the cars coming and going. There were no vans yet.

At ten minutes past the hour a red van pulled in and parked. One man climbed out. It wasn't Mac...Petteri had met Mac before. This man was thinner and younger than McElroy.

321

Petteri pulled a stainless steel, Smith & Wesson 45 from under his seat. He checked the magazine and slapped it back into place. In the time it took to look down at his weapon, the tan van had arrived. Virgil McElroy climbed from the driver's seat and greeted the other man.

Reino Petteri unconsciously took a long deep breath and cranked up his car. He drove over to the area where the vans were and stopped. Mac turned his head with a hard look and stepped up to Petteri's window. Rolling it down, Reino slid his weapon under his leg and asked McElroy, "Are we ready?"

"Kentucky you say?" McElroy grunted and Petteri nodded "yes."

"Lead the way...boss," the hit man offered and climbed back into his van. It would be nearly seven hours of interstate highway to Lexington. He figured they'd eat there and decide how to approach the farm, either that night or fresh in the morning.

Petteri headed for I-57 South and turned up his paper cup. The last swallow of coffee was cold, but that didn't matter. He was on his way to take over the business, or die trying.

62

The G5 touched down at Lexington airport just after 4:15 PM. Harold Foster rolled the craft to a secluded section of the taxiway where a Kentucky State Patrol SUV was waiting.

Sharon Swanson stepped from the vehicle and stood almost like a statue. Silas climbed down the short stairs and Jon's smile broke out on his face.

"Good to see you again, Colonel," he beamed.

"You sure look a lot better than the last time I saw you," she responded.

"Did I ever thank you for that?" Jon asked meekly.

"You know..." she said without hesitation. " I believe I still owe you, if we're keeping score."

With his bag over his shoulder, Silas turned to wave at Harold who remotely pulled the exit ramp up. He would return to Georgia that night.

"I suppose you have a plan?" Swanson teased.

"Yes...kind of."

"Well, you know I'm chomping at the bit to take these dirt bags down."

"I know, and I appreciate your patience. But I want to shut the whole operation down...everybody."

"Figured as much," she admitted and told him there was a restaurant in Berea where they would meet the others.

"My friends know about it?"

"I told Ben as they were leaving Georgia."

~

Marvin Acree had spent most of the afternoon cleaning the cache of weapons from his bag. Kinkaid sat alone in the farmhouse, staring out the front door at the main driveway. It was clear he expected the attack from Petteri to come down that path.

Before the sun began to go down, he stood and walked out onto the porch.

"Where's Deacon?" he called out.

Harkness came from the bunkhouse and stood in earshot without speaking.

"Where can you get eighty pounds of ice and some coolers?" Kinkaid asked.

Harkness looked to the ground as he thought. "Over in Berea, I suppose," he answered.

"You and Marv go get it and keep it in the coolers overnight. I'll need it in the morning."

"You'd be better off if we went in the morning," Harkness suggested boldly. "There won't be that much left in town tonight. There'll be a fresh batch brought in...in the morning."

Kinkaid glared at the man for several minutes. He stepped down off the porch in a threatening manner but spoke in agreement with Harkness.

"Just have it all here by noon tomorrow," he said calmly. "When I get the information off Petteri's dead body, I'll need that stuff to ready a shipment."

"You really think he's coming, don't you?" Acree challenged.

324

"I don't think it, Marv. I know it." Kinkaid turned and started back toward the house. Marvin Acree walked, double time, to get where only Kinkaid would hear him.

"Clyde," he spoke low, but the other man stopped and looked at him as he continued, "You said you decided not to kill any of them."

"I did," Kinkaid said. "You're right."

The former congressman whirled and made three more steps, but Acree was still with him. Kinkaid stopped sharply and turned into the man's face.

"I've been thinking about the time, Marv," he again redirected his gaze and moved further toward the house, still speaking.

"Gibbons will be here to take one bride for delivery," he declared and stopped in his tracks. Without looking up, he added, "Petteri has the lists of contacts, the organ brokers."

Marvin's face went pale, but Kinkaid didn't have to look at him to know. Putting a foot on the porch's first step, he muttered, "I'll get that list from him."

Acree reached out and grabbed the man's arm. "Clyde..." he started.

"I changed my mind, Marv."

"There are other ways...."

"We don't have time for any other bride deliveries," Kinkaid cut him off, leaning back into his face. "We'll save the parts... and get out of here."

Acree was stunned and showed it, but Kinkaid was not swayed. He pulled away from his friend's grip. Finishing the stairs, he spoke once again as he walked inside the house.

"We'll need to process the other two."

~

Petteri's caravan reached Lexington at 7:35 PM. Having stopped only for fuel, everyone was hungry...and tired. They found a Cracker Barrel near a Sheraton motel that was just off the main expressway. Dinner was short on conversation, except for Mac and Reino.

"How much do you know about the layout?" McElroy asked him.

"I know where you're going with that," Petteri looked the man straight in the eye. "I've seen it in daylight, but there's only one way in that I could tell. And in the dark, we'd be sitting ducks."

"How many lookouts?"

"Two that I saw, maybe more."

"I've heard of Deacon for years," Mac realized as he spoke. "I don't think I've ever met the man."

"He ran a good operation 'til everything fell on him." Petteri kept his eyes on his plate, "He couldn't handle it all."

McElroy drank some coffee and rocked back in his wooden captain's chair. He looked around the table as though quietly sizing up his own men.

"You think he suspects you're coming back?" he asked Petteri.

"That's not really the point," came the Finlander's odd answer. He sat up, gesturing with his hands to sell his theory. "He looks at everybody the same. This place is so off the path, he'll challenge anyone who tries to come in."

"Off the path enough... that we can make some noise?" McElroy slouched and asked with a smile. "If need be, of course."

Petteri raised his open palm toward the man. This was going too far. "Don't forget," he cautioned. "I want to reorganize this operation, not tear it down. We need to keep everybody alive if we can."

Mac sat back up and leaned closer to the new "boss."

"Then we go in daylight," he declared. "One vehicle, two guys to get their attention... The rest of us go on foot, from either side of that road in."

Reino nodded that he understood.

"Dinner and the rooms are on me," he said.

"You bet they are...boss." Mac smiled.

Guests at The Dinner Bell were subject to a rare sight that night. A large portion of the ample parking lot had been cordoned off by the Kentucky State Police. Within the space sat a dark blue helicopter proclaiming herself to be "Lucy Too."

As Colonel Swanson's SUV pulled into the lot she saw Jon's face light up and she smiled herself.

"Ah..." she said and slapped her knee, "they're here, I see."

The dinner meeting was in a separate party room with the Colonel, her main Lieutenants and Jon's team at the table. On the phone from Georgia were Ben, Phil Stone, and Cheryl Duray.

"This car you found," Silas asked the minute he was told about it. "Can you get me near there, quietly?"

"Way ahead of you, Sparky," Swanson laughed. The nickname caught Jon by surprise. He never heard that before. He sat and waited for her to continue.

"You ride bikes, right?" she asked him. "Motorcycles."

327

"I have," Jon responded. "Mainly dirt bikes...but aren't those kinda loud?"

"Not what I have coming in for you." She took a large gulp from her iced tea and looked back at her friend. "You remember that Volt thing? That car the government tried to push on everyone?"

Silas' eyes grew wide as he tried to figure out where she was going with this.

"Yeah..." he said. " I remember."

"Turns out...that motor did have a good use after all," her grin now lit up the room. "It makes for one hell of a quiet ATV. A three wheel land rover that makes no noise what so ever."

"You've got one?" Silas asked.

"I've got three," she cracked. "One's on its way here. Be here early in the morning."

The rest of this plan centered on one basic element, surprise, which was now on their side.

As the meeting was about to wind up, one of Swanson's Lieutenants received a text message. He got up and moved closer to her, but spoke in a normal tone.

"A patrolman off Newtown Pike, northeast of Lexington, found three vehicles that appear to be traveling together." He looked up at her with a grin which Swanson did not return. Quickly, the Lieutenant continued to read the text. "All Illinois plates," he said, "All males, approximately in their forties or fifties. They stopped for dinner and are now at a local motel in that area."

"Is the patrolman still there?"

"Yes ma'am. He's sitting on them."

"Send him some back-up... but give them room."

Silas spoke up, "Should they come this way...let 'em. Let's see what they're up to."

Swanson nodded her agreement to the Lieutenant who stepped back and dialed his phone.

"This is getting interesting, huh?" she said with no emotion.

~

As the dinner meeting broke up, Silas asked Ben and Phil to stay on the line. Walking to his room, he then asked them to check on someone, using all contacts and connections they had.

"The Mayor of Chicago, huh?" Phil reacted. "That's almost a cliché."

"Yeah...I understand." Silas told him. "But there's a piece of this still missing."

63

That Saturday morning was cold in Kentucky. The black suit worked well against the chill. Still he wondered how the fifty-five below zero must have felt.

Silas was standing near Lucy Too when Murray, Tim, and Weston came out from their motel rooms.

"You guys ready?" he asked. Nobody really answered.

Pointing to a flatbed truck that had come in overnight, Silas told the others, "I'll be driven around to an old logging road. I'll use that ATV to get close as I can and then go in from the rear. I'd like you two," he gestured at Tim and Weston, "to go wide of the entrance road and approach the farm from north and south."

They nodded.

"Murray," he looked at his friend. "Be ready to swoop in and pick up the girls when we get them freed."

"Alright."

"I'll be in radio contact with all you guys, but there will be times I'll have to be silent."

"Understood," Tim acknowledged. "Just cut loose with some noise if you need us."

"In a heartbeat," Silas smiled. "Let's go."

The truck driver was in the cab waiting for him and Colonel Swanson stood near the door. She keyed her radio and spoke.

"Check, check."

Silas responded, "Five by five, Colonel." He climbed aboard the truck and the plan was officially in motion.

~

Lawrence Gibbons left his condo in a hurry. He had everything except his phone...the phone. Realizing the error as he arrived at the Philadelphia airport he paused for a moment and then went on.

I know what I'm doing, he told himself. *They've never called in the middle of a delivery anyway.* He satisfied his own mind with the rationalization.

Gate D-12 was nearly empty as he waited. His flight was on time and they would be boarding in twenty minutes.

A slight smile came over him. It was good to be working again.

~

At her command post off US 421, Colonel Swanson got a cell phone call from HQ in Lexington.

"That small convoy is headed your way. Two vans and a car now on I-75 south, request instructions."

"Follow but fall back," she told them. "Let's assume they're coming this way. I'll have units waiting at the exit off seventy-five."

"Roger that."

"One more thing," Swanson added. "Should they not take the Berea turn off, stop 'em and check them out."

Her phone call was then interrupted by a radio call.

"Swanson here, over."

"Small vehicle from the farm... just entered the road toward town," the report said. "Two occupants. Both males. Over."

What is this now? She wondered in silence. "Stay back, see where they go and report."

Turning the radio to tactical channel four, she called for Jon.

"We've got movement all over the place up here. Where are you?"

"I can smell the fire from the farmhouse," Silas answered. "I'm close. This thing is weird. It's so quiet and these soft tires go over anything."

"I'll sell you one when we're through here," she laughed.

"I might just take you up on that," he said. Then he pulled up and climbed off the electric ATV. "I'm here," he whispered that time. "Tim...Wes, in position?"

Both men acknowledged that they were.

"Hold tight, I'm gonna slip in and look around."

~

Phil Stone punched Ben on the arm. "What's this?" he asked, pointing to a flashing light on another screen.

"That's Franz's phone. He's calling somebody."

Ben pulled up the sound from the mini-microphone Jon had stuck under Greer's desk. There was nothing but ambient noise coming through. Going back to the cell phone, it rang nearly twenty times and then quit.

"No answer," Ben said looking at Phil.

The light started flashing again. "Wait, there it goes...he's trying somebody else."

Both of them stared mutely at the captivating beacon.

"Maybe this one will answer," Phil muttered.

~

Kinkaid walked over to the table and stared at the ringing cell phone. It was Harkness' that had been left in the house. Kinkaid picked it up and answered, "Yeah?"

"What do you mean, yeah?" The garbled voice didn't appreciate the disrespect. Kinkaid didn't speak back. His eyes grew wide as dinner plates as he waited for the voice to speak again.

"Harkness?" it demanded. "Is that you?"

"No, you son of a bitch, this isn't Harkness." Kinkaid felt his blood heating up. "He's not in charge around here anymore."

The garbled voice was slow to respond, but finally asked, "Who is this?"

"You tried to kill me twice... and you don't know who I am, you freakin' creep."

"Kinkaid?" the voice cracked a bit that time. "What...what are you doing?"

"I'm dealing with this order here," he cracked with a smirk. "We've got to get it out today, Franz. Larry is on his way... right?"

"Look, Clyde...don't screw this up. We can work things out."

"Yeah...well, I think I've worked things out pretty well myself." The self-satisfied criminal stiffened his back and stared around the farm house like a royal. The line was still open, but there was no sound from the other side. Kinkaid leaned into the phone, menacingly.

"Oh, and you'd better hope I can't find your sorry ass, Franz," he threatened. "South America ain't all that big, you know."

With that the line went dead, but Ben was all smiles.

"What?" Phil looked confused.

"We got him...Walter Greer. Franz is Walter Greer."

64

Silas crawled up to the back of the middle building. The old, split pine siding was cracked and warped. Its blackish veneer was more from exposure than any coating. The foundation was a poured concrete pad with a formed, curved drain dipping under the structural plate at one end. Silas noticed an abnormal growth of moss and other small vegetation on the ground below the drain.

Some kind of rich fertilizer had once flowed from that drain, he thought and then realized, *blood.*

The sound of movement drew him to the other end of the building. He could hear female voices inside. The building appeared to have two main rooms. One where the girls were kept and where the cracks and splits in the siding were somewhat covered over. The other room beside it, sat over the odd drain.

Studying the exterior framework from this spot, he could see a small trap door with hinges at the top. Simply cut into the siding, it blended in, nearly unnoticeable.

Silas eased his way back to that area and pulled the small door up and open. He peered around before carefully crawling inside that room.

It was dark. There was one window that had been painted black and one other door at the front. There were two heavy wood columns, holding a large cross beam and separated by a rail over a trough. The trough was carved out of the floor and had a small metal post at one end, not far from the heavy structural column.

His eyes naturally followed the trough to where it disappeared under the exterior wall.

The drain, he realized. *That's what fed the drain.*

Silas could hear a vehicle arriving. He walked to the front door where a sizable crack offered a look outside, then froze in place as he saw a small truck drive up.

~

Marvin Acree and the farm hand arrived back with the ice and several large chests. Clyde Kinkaid came out onto the porch and stood, hands on hips.

"I got everything they had at the general store," Acree reported.

Harkness stepped out from the bunkhouse and looked their way.

"Come here," Kinkaid gestured and yelled at him.

Harkness walked toward the house and Kinkaid came down to meet him.

"Get one of 'em ready," he told Harkness. "We need to have a 'bride' up to the main road by noon."

Harkness gave him a blank stare before asking, "Which one?"

"Hell, I don't care...pick one. Just get moving."

The man slowly went to the building housing the girls and entered the room holding them.

Kinkaid shifted closer to Acree and began explaining to him, "There's a slaughter room next to where they are," he started. "This place used to raise hogs," he grinned.

Acree turned his head and glared at him.

"I found a bolt gun in the table drawer in there," Kinkaid added. "It still works. That'll be quiet...you won't spook the other one."

Acree started towards the building, but Kinkaid grabbed him.

"Let him get the one out of there first."

335

~

Reino Petteri, followed by his two vanloads of thugs, turned off the interstate, and drove through the small college town of Berea, Kentucky. Without hesitation, he led them to an obscure road that had only one destination, the farm.

Swanson didn't even check with Jon.

"Take 'em," she ordered. "Maximum forces...try not to kill them."

From nowhere and everywhere, police units swarmed on the small convoy. McElroy's red van tried to turn around as he fired from the passenger side window. With little room for the maneuver, the van driver floored the vehicle in reverse. The tan colored van also roared toward the main road going backward.

McElroy continued to fire at any and everything in his path. A trooper, who had been aiming at the vehicles tire, felt a round go through his calf. Instinctively, he raised his aim and caught the criminal in the forehead.

The side door now slid back and more gunfire poured from the red van. As it reached the paved road a large volley of fire from the troopers took out three of the tires. His foot still to the floorboard, the driver struggled to control the vehicle until a rear wheel got too close to the ditch. Falling hard on its right side, the red van landed on two gunmen who were thrown out a mere second before.

The tan colored van's driver displayed more experience in handling his mechanical beast. At forty-five miles per hour, in reverse, he locked the brakes and spun on the dirt in a near perfect 180 degree spin. With little loss of motion he plowed forward, slicing through heavy gunfire and around other obstacles.

The Kentucky troopers continued to fire on the van from all angles. Several rounds punctured the large gas tank and others sent sparks flying onto hot oil that coated the undercarriage. Smoke soon became fire.

The driver lowered his head and turned left, heading south down the paved highway. He was almost clear of the ambush area when a blue helicopter swooped low in front of him, blades angled down nearly touching the road.

The driver slid sideways and to the edge of the pavement coming to a stop. Gas from the riddled tank sloshed onto the small fires under the van and the whole thing erupted in a ball of red. There was no escape from it.

Murray pulled back hard on Lucy Too's stick and the craft climbed high and to its left. The downdraft from her blades whipped the flames even higher.

The driver of the red van did not climb out. His window was clear but no movement came from it. Officers approached carefully to find him dead, lying atop the body of McElroy. A handgun, still in McElroy's grip, had discharged when the driver fell on him.

Pilfoy's ghosts were now just that. Lutz had lead Petteri's men to their doom against Kinkaid and now Petteri had done the same for Pilfoy's.

Petteri had not moved his vehicle since the shooting started. Still sitting in there, he was attempting to destroy some papers as they dragged him from his car.

"Welcome to Kentucky, Mr. Peetree," the colonel greeted him with her customary smile and a put-on mispronunciation. "We've been expecting you."

She walked over to a Lieutenant and whispered, "Get him in a room ...no calls, no contact with anyone." She waited for his acknowledgement, which came as a nod. "Have all that paper gathered up," she added. "Don't miss a piece. Bring it to my car."

Again, the junior officer nodded and the colonel walked away. She wanted to call Jon, but a sixth sense made her pause.

Things could be heating up at the farm, her mind told her.

~

Walter Greer was in full panic. Dialing a number he knew he should never use, he sat at his desk on the otherwise empty floor of City Hall in Chicago.

"What is it?" the aggravated voice answered.

"We got real problems," Greer trembled.

"You don't call me here."

"But Kinkaid is at the farm."

The phone stayed quiet for nearly a full minute. Then the still calm voice was firm and short.

"Not now...not over this phone." And he hung up.

Greer began gathering up what he thought he needed when his door opened. The man entering flashed a badge.

"Mr. Greer," he said. "I'm Detective Jordan Sterns from Muskegon. I wanted to talk with you about a recent attack on my family."

~

Phil Stone was searching through files on the Chicago mayor when the light blinked again.

"Hey, Ben," he yelled. "He's calling someone else."

They heard the new call but didn't understand. Ben traced the dialed number before it hung up.

"Unlisted and coded," he explained. "It was in Chicago, but I can't get anything else on it."

By then the sound of Greer's visitor was coming through the hidden microphone.

"Who is this guy?" Ben asked rhetorically.

"A cop named Sterns," Phil answered as he turned the sound off. "Probably just some police business."

Ben leaned back, "Why does that name mean something to me?" he asked out loud.

"You want to hear more?" Phil reached back for the switch.

Naw, you're probably right. We've got too much to do now."

~

Tim Spiegel lay behind a pile of brush. His non-glare binoculars gave him a full view of the main yard in front of the farmhouse. He dialed a frequency on his radio to isolate himself and Duray.

"Are you there?"

"Roger, man. I'm here," Duray replied. "Can't see much around the buildings though."

"I can," Tim told him. "We need to get closer...I feel like this is coming to a head, real quick."

"Moving now," came the response. Duray slid forward, staying low, but moving quickly, considering his position and the terrain. Spiegel rolled to one side of the brush and crept forward.

Both men low crawled, from separate directions, towards the farmhouse.

65

Harkness pulled one girl from the building and dragged her by the arm to the house.

"Now," Kinkaid motioned to Acree. The man had a look of determination as he stomped toward the room holding the other two women. Silas looked around. There was nowhere to go. He stood back in the corner near the hinge side of the door and activated the power arm of his suit.

Acree kicked the door to the dark room open and dragging a girl held by her hair, he entered. Standing the blond headed woman against a metal pole at the rear of the room, he tied her to it with a zip tie around the neck. The table Kinkaid had told him about was to his left. The bolt gun was there. This object was a lethal killing device.

Within its six inch long barrel, a half-inch diameter bolt would compress a heavy spring. When the trigger was depressed, a charge of compressed air would release the spring and fire the bolt forward exposing three inches of it beyond the barrel. Nothing short of a heavy steel plate could stop it.

When placed on the head of a cow or pig, the bolt gun would quickly render the animal unconscious or kill it. There was little noise to disturb the other animals in line. It was cheap and efficient.

Use on a human's head would mean full penetration of the bolt into the softer, thinner skull. Death would be instantaneous.

Laying the lethal tool down, Acree shook out a plastic, floor length coverall and pulled it over his head. As he picked up and readied his weapon, the girl caught a glimpse of the dark figure standing in the corner.

Her eyes widened and Silas stepped forward one quiet pace. He raised his left hand, placing his forefinger in front of his lips and made direct eye contact with her. His right hand held a six inch custom Bowie knife.

Silas slowly raised the blade, one of several choices the Navy Seals could pick from, to shoulder height.

Acree's attention turned back to the girl and he grabbed her mouth with his left hand. She attempted to squirm but he overwhelmed her. His right hand, holding the bolt gun, rose towards her head.

Silas stepped forward again and in one continuous motion launched the knife.

He had not thrown a knife with the powered arm before. It just never came up. He had not calculated the effects of its added power on the velocity of the throw. The results were catastrophic and quick.

As his bolt gun approached the girl's head, the large knife cut through Acree's plastic covering, his jacket, and shirt and into his side. Entering three inches below the right armpit, it traveled on, through the right lung, clipping the rear wall of his heart and ripping it open. Without any loss of momentum, the turning blade continued on through the other lung and out the man's opposite side.

The bolt fired, but while it was still six inches from her head. Its lethal projectile sprang harmlessly into the air as Acree's mouth fell open with no sound. Blood immediately gushed over his lips, barely missing the girl. His eyes locked and in them she saw the stare of death. He was gone before he moved.

The gangster collapsed in a pile at the girl's feet and Silas maintained his "quiet" signal as he ran to her. Cutting the plastic tie with a smaller knife, he looked to see where the Bowie had ended up.

Four of its overall six-inches of blade were buried in the hardened wood of a six by six post. It took the strength of Silas' powered right arm to retrieve it.

The traumatized girl gasped and began to scream as the first of two gunshots rang out and hit Silas' back. One glanced upward and to the left, submerging itself in a rafter. The other projectile had completely flattened against the suit and fell to the floor.

~

Walter Greer was using all his self-control to stay calm. This newest visitor was the second in so many days to drop in.

"How can I help you with that?" he asked the man now sitting across from him.

"I had some thugs from down here break into my house," Sterns began. "Then a few days later, more attacked my wife's family up in the U.P."

"I'm sorry for all that..." Greer started to realize this guy knew nothing. He leaned toward him with his best sincerity. "What does that have to do with this office?"

Jordan Sterns looked slightly uncomfortable. He twisted in his chair trying to find the right phrase to use. "I understand...that you were almost killed... around the time all this was going on."

Greer nodded and again his emotions turned. *Maybe he does know*, he thought.

"I found links to the Pilfoy gang on the guys that came into my house. You know...the Ghosts?"

"I know of that group, yes." Greer felt his stomach tighten.

343

"Well...they tried to get to me, because of an odd link to this Duray family." Sterns paused to see if the assistant commissioner was paying attention. "Then," he added, "They went after our family upstate over the same connection."

Greer's eyes danced about, but he had no comment.

"Next," Sterns went on, "you're attacked. Shortly after that, everything goes bad and Pilfoy is taken out."

Greer still stared at the man in silence.

"You see my idea here, right?" Sterns asked him. "This Pilfoy had to be involved in the Duray case...and he screwed up, somehow."

"So you think whoever is behind the Duray situation...probably Clyde Kinkaid and his people, are responsible for all this other stuff?"

"Yeah," Sterns agreed. "I just don't know where you fit in."

Greer's mind searched for something...anything to say.

"We've been investigating him... on gambling charges," he offered, "For a few months now."

"Who?" Sterns qualified, "Pilfoy or Kinkaid?"

"Pilfoy...that's the only tie in I can think of, Detective."

Jordon Sterns stood and shook his head gently. "Not what I was hoping for," he muttered. "I really thought there was something more concrete...more..." He raised his hands into an open round, shape as though he was holding a hot volleyball. Then he continued, "Sorry I bothered you."

Moving toward the office door, Sterns looked over his shoulder. "I'll be in town a few days, checking a few more details. I'd appreciate any professional courtesy you can offer."

"Sure...sure," Greer smiled. "Just tell any officer you've met with me and I expect their cooperation, okay?"

"Thank you, Commissioner," Sterns stepped out of the office. "Nice talking with you."

66

Clyde Kinkaid stood in the doorway of the killing shed. Curiosity had brought him to see how Acree was doing. What he found confused and frightened him. The fear pulsed through him so deeply that it took his breath.

Acree lay in a pile that didn't appear human, with blood rushing from it in several directions. Standing over his partner's corpse was a figure entirely in black. The girl, tied to the post seemed unimportant at first. There was another figure in the room. Instincts reacted and he raised his weapon to fire at the unknown intruder.

When his bullets had no effect on the man, a shudder rocked him violently. Complete terror vibrated his arm as he attempted to take aim at the girl. Silas stepped in front of her, shielding her and reaching for his own gun.

Kinkaid's next shots again bounced from the suit. Before the ex-congressman could react or adjust, his eyes bulged as another gun sounded from the left, low and behind where Silas stood.

The first round struck Kinkaid in the gut, folding him forward. The second hit high and between his eyes. That impact launched his body back and out the main door. The former congressman landed face up, spread eagled in the dirt.

Silas turned to his left to see Weston Duray lying half-way through the small trap door, his Glock still pointed and ready.

Duray glanced up at Silas and then down to a river of blood approaching his position from Acree's body. He looked back at Silas and eased out of the small opening. His expression remained blank.

Silas nodded approval that went unnoticed and grabbed his radio.

"Murray," he almost screamed from the pumping adrenalin. "Are you in the area?" He looked at the nearly unconscious girl and undid her wrist bindings as he waited for the response.

"Roger that, Jon." Murray answered. "How we doing?"

The other captive girl cautiously stuck her head into the dark room. Silas paused and smiled to himself. *With the one in the farmhouse, they were all accounted for*, he celebrated to himself quietly.

Leading the girls outside, he sat them down then pushed his radio button again.

"Come get these girls out of here..." he called to his friend in the helicopter. "Fast!"

~

Walter Greer tried a third time to call "the groom." But Larry Gibbons had left his phone back home and it rang without notice in his Philadelphia apartment.

"Damn all of this," Greer screamed as he slammed a fist down on his desk. He closed the phone with one hand and rubbed his forehead, hard, with the other. Kinkaid controlled the farm and the girls. One customer was already pissed and this wouldn't help anything.

How will Gibbons react, or will he even notice the change? He worried and threw himself back into his chair.

I've got to get a grip, he told himself. Then spinning around in his chair, he stared out the window and tried to think.

~

Lucy Two dropped in as though from nowhere. The men in the bunkhouse ran out at the noise and right into Tim Spiegel. Without saying a word, his stance and appearance convinced them to lie on the ground, face down.

The third girl, dressed in the burka, emerged from the farmhouse and ran to meet the others Silas had brought out.

Within minutes, the three young women were loaded up to go. Murray looked toward Silas for clearance, but his friend was obviously searching for something.

"Where's Harkness?" Silas asked the girl in the burka.

"He ran out the back," she stammered through her fear. "When the first shots were fired... he left."

Silas stepped back and motioned for Murray to go. Lucy Too lifted and kicked up a dirt cloud. As Silas turned from the swirling dust there stood Weston Duray.

"I heard her," he said standing stiff against the prop-wash.

"Yeah," Silas acknowledged and took a step. "I'll be back shortly."

"No," Duray reached out and stopped him. He glanced at Tim and then back to Silas with a stern stare.

"I'll get him," he proclaimed. "I want this."

Silas thought for a second and waved his arm in the direction of the farmhouse. "It is your right, I suppose," he told Duray. "Do what you need to."

Duray holstered his Glock and jogged through the settling dust. He disappeared into the hills behind the farmhouse.

~

The mansion in Chicago belonged to him, though the city would have supplied him with one, his ego preferred his own. Either way, it was still cold this time of year and the high ceilings in his den didn't help. A blanket over his lap, he read the latest on the reports coming from Mexico.

The first accounts had been little more than speculation. Hindered by the infighting that broke out among the gang's factions, all that had been known for the first several days was that Geraldo Palmero was dead. Now, a piece at a time, other facts began to leak in the press. He laid them out to study.

The discovery of the charred material from the jumpsuits and parachutes on the roof of the main house presented more questions than answers. Additional evidence found in the basement led to talk of a possible captive having been rescued from there. Palmero was found in the basement, in a dark hallway. He was only feet from the damaged door to a prison-like room, the body impaled by a section from a broken chair. The remainder of that chair was still in the room.

The name, Murray Bilstock, appeared as the possible captive. As the man under the blanket read the accounts, it didn't take much paranoia to lead his thinking to the assassin called The Son. Many believed he was dead. This man did not.

Whoever did this wasn't ordinary, he thought as a shiver ran through him. *But neither was the man who came to see Greer.*

Greer was spooked and on edge. *He could soon be a liability*, the man thought and rubbed his chin. *But I still need him. I can't operate without his cover.*

349

He folded the paper in his lap and stretched back to think. *If I can't get rid of one side of this problem...then I'll deal with the other,* he finally decided.

~

Tim Spiegel tied up the four farm hands and sat them on the dirt. He then went inside the "killing room" to help Jon with the two bodies.

"Whoa," he remarked as he rolled Acree's body into its back. "What did you do to this guy?"

Silas grunted and mumbled, "It was probably real quick for him."

"I'll say...wow," Spiegel closed the dead man's eyes and added, "a bit too easy for the likes of him."

They covered the dead thugs in blankets. Acree had all but bled out completely, so there wasn't much mess left. Silas noticed the trough had done its job.

"Not what he had in mind," he quipped to himself.

"Say what?" Tim asked.

"Naw...nothing. Let's get this trash out of here."

They loaded everything into the farm's truck and Tim drove, the bodies and the prisoners, out to the main road. Silas stayed to wait for Duray.

Sitting on the porch's steps, he called in to check with Swanson. He gave her his report and then she shared her news about Petteri.

"Can we keep all this quiet for a few days?" Silas asked her.

"Days?" she repeated..."I don't know about days, maybe a day or two."

350

"Long as you can...I want to wrap this whole thing up before the leaders know what's going on."

"I understand that, and I'll do all that I can...oh, wait a second, will ya?"

Colonel Swanson was getting a radio message of more activity along the road. Silas could hear her reaction before she spoke.

"We've got more company out at the road site," the Colonel tried to keep a straight face. "From the picture Ben sent me, it's that Sheik fella you were looking for."

"I can't believe this is all happening so fast," Silas laughed.

"Real nice of 'em to be so cooperative, huh?" Swanson cracked.

"Yeah, I guess," he added. "As soon as Duray gets back with Harkness, we'll be along. I want to talk with the Sheik and Mr. Petteri...alone."

"You sure Duray can catch this Harkness guy?"

Silas thought about that for a second.

"I'd bet money on it," he assured her. "And I don't gamble."

~

The man in the Chicago mansion had put down his newspaper and threw his blanket to the floor. Reaching for the phone on the desk, he dialed a number from memory.

"Jane?" he started. "Get me the superior court judge on duty down in Dalton, Georgia, will ya?"

The woman protested that that might be a tall order for the day.

"I realize it's Saturday," he answered her concern. "You can find 'em. I have faith in you."

She agreed to do what she could and the man followed up with, "And get me that mayor down there while you're working on this. Okay?"

~

Silas also called home, to let Ben and the others know things went well and to ask about the background check he'd requested.

"There's nothing on him...at all." Ben reported and looked at Phil Stone.

"Jon," the retired police captain joined in, "I tried every contact I have, same story as Ben got. The guy's squeaky clean. I know...the mayor of Chicago... should be a cliché, right? Oh...I said that before."

Silas didn't respond.

"He's clean," Phil amended his statement, "Nothing on him. We even had Daniel check him out through his contacts. The man covers himself at every turn." Phil waited for a response that didn't come so he went on. "Daniel says the guy is so paranoid over you he hardly does anything himself."

"Me?" Silas injected. "What makes him say that?"

"Daniel heard the man has a secret file on you. He acts like a guilty man yet there's nothing on him. Go figure, huh?"

"I'm going to speak with a couple of new guests we have here," Silas went straight into a different subject. "That'll keep me here the rest of today, at least."

"What do we do, here?"

"Stay alert. I don't think you've seen the last of those clowns from town. Somebody's pulling some strings. I have my suspicions. I need to go get my proof."

352

"Go... where?" Ben asked.

"Back to Chicago...but keep that under your hats, please."

Cheryl Duray leaned over to get nearer the phone. "Is my Daddy ok?" she asked.

"Young lady," Silas beamed as he spoke. "What do you think? He's better than ok."

"Can I speak to him?"

"He's gone to pick up something for me," he told her. "I expect him back any minute and I'll have him call you, alright?"

"Thank you, sir," Cheryl said meekly.

"Hey!" Silas hollered. "I'm very proud he's with me on this."

She nodded and stepped back, wiping a tear from her eye.

The phone line went dead but Ben was already sliding across the room on his chair.

"Where are you going?" Phil chased after him.

"I'm still bothered by that name, the cop who went to see Greer," he explained. "There's a recording here I need to check, that conversation from earlier in Greer's office."

Ben dialed up the recorded discussion between Jordan Sterns and Walter Greer. A few minutes into it, Sterns mentions the Durays.

"Did you hear that?" Ben turned to Cheryl. "He said your name. Do you know this guy?"

She shook her head in bewilderment, "No...I've never heard of him."

"Muskegon," Ben repeated what he'd heard. "Let's find out who this Detective Sterns is."

67

Silas heard the commotion from behind the farmhouse. He pulled his Glock and eased around toward the noise. Its cause was quickly apparent.

"Is this our guy?" Weston Duray asked, holding a man by the coat collar.

"I believe it is," Silas grinned and walked up to the disgruntled man. "Mr. Harkness, isn't it?"

Receiving less than a word from the man, Silas told him to, "sit," in a firm voice. Harkness found a spot on the front steps to do just that.

"Call your daughter," Silas said looking at the reinvigorated pathfinder. "I told her you'd call." He tossed a phone to him and Duray walked toward some privacy.

"So," Silas now directed his questions to Harkness, "What do you want to share with me?"

The man scoffed at him. "You kiddin' me?" he spit. "I'm not saying a word."

Nodding very heavily, Silas looked at him. "Oh...I see." He sat down next to the man and grabbed at the wooden stair between them. His right hand crushed it into powder and Harkness' eyes all but jumped from his head.

"You see that man over there?" Silas pointed at Duray. "His suit is just like this one. And... I bet you don't know who he is."

"Doesn't make no matter to me," Harkness bluffed.

"Oh...I think it might. You see, his name is Weston Duray. His daughter was kidnapped by your gang a few months back." He smiled a sinister smile at the man. "We've been looking for you guys."

Harkness stayed quiet but began to lose some of his bluster.

"Remember," Silas began again, "nobody knows you came back down after you ran away." He stood and walked toward Duray. "I'm sure Westy would love to take you back up there...deep into those woods."

"Now you hold on..." Harkness barked.

"Hold on to what?" Silas glared at him then continued walking away. "You haven't given me anything to hold on to."

"Alright...alright." Harkness raised his hands, "I don't know that much."

Turning slowly, Silas returned to stand over him. "I'm listening," he said.

"I run this farm, that's all I do. Girls come in and we hold 'em till time for them to go."

"Hold them?" Silas pushed him. "How many were killed here?"

"No...Now, you just wait," the man got animated and pushed himself up a step. "We never did that here. That was all Kinkaid and he just came in couple of nights ago."

"What does the star picture mean?" Silas threw that in, hoping to catch him off guard.

"What?"

"The star picture...hanging in the offices."

Harkness' eyes scoured the ground, searching for an idea of what the man in black was asking him. "I don't know...I never heard of anything like that."

"A logo for the group, maybe?" Silas offered.

"They don't have a logo...it's all secret stuff, man." Then Harkness had a realization. He wanted to keep it in, but his face betrayed him.

"What?" Silas leaned in, "What are you thinking?"

Putting his hand to his forehead, Harkness exhaled a labored breath. "I heard the big shots talking from time to time," he started and then looked down.

"Go on," Silas urged him.

"They talked about going to see some new guy or another... and to be careful. ' Make sure the welcome mat is out before you say anything,' they would always caution each other."

"Welcome mat?"

"Never saw it myself...but there's something they hang in plain view... that lets the others know they are among friends."

I'll be damned, Silas thought as he stepped back in silence. *That's it...that's what it is.*

He looked back at the man sitting there and said something quite the opposite of what his thoughts were. "Naw...we know about the welcome mat. That's not it."

"But there is one, right?" Harkness begged to know. "Like I said...I never saw it, I just heard there was one."

"We've been on that thing for a while now. It's how we got to you."

"I don't have one." the man was getting confused.

"No... but you're listed on it, everywhere else."

"Huh?" he leaned back. "They never told me that."

"I have to warn you," Silas went on. "We had three guys tell us about it already. Each one was killed in his jail cell right after telling us."

"Well...you said I wasn't right about it," Harkness climbed to his feet in fear. "You're not gonna tell I said anything, are you?"

Silas looked at him for a few seconds before shaking his head. "I see no reason to get you killed over a wrong guess. We just won't mention 'welcome mat.' If you do, hell... that's your own funeral. Be my guest."

Weston Duray returned having talked with his daughter. "There's more news for you, Jon," he said. "A friend of yours has just been arrested back your way."

"Arrested?" Silas squinted his eyes unconsciously. "Who? Do you know?"

"The man that met us when we got there..." Duray recalled. "George...George Vincent."

~

It was now past noon in Chicago. Walter Greer had gathered what he needed from the temporary office and was leaving. He looked in the credenza drawer, next to his window. His Smith& Wesson 9mm was there. Greer simply stared at it.

Noon here is after one in Kentucky, he told himself. *Shoot him when he comes back...Ha! That's a laugh.*

Leaving the gun where it was, he closed the drawer, picked up what he was taking and left the office. His fear wasn't finished with him yet.

He pushed the elevator button and then hid around the corner till the doors opened. *Can't reach Gibbons...can't reach Harkness because of Kinkaid...what the hell is going on?*

Greer wanted to call the mayor but again, that wouldn't work. He was on his own.

Survival of the fittest, went through his mind. *Oh, God! I sure hope not,* he finished the thought with a bit of a laugh at himself.

The entire organization was coming apart. His mid-level leaders were gone or being picked off one by one. His own position was protected or he believed it was. Covered by the fake voice and the calls bounced from Venezuela. But what he didn't know was that he sat in the highest verifiable position in the gang. Past him didn't exist. No links, no connection whatever.

For all intents and purposes, he was the man in charge.

~

Colonel Swanson's men unloaded the prisoners and pulled the tarp back from the two bodies.

"Somebody get the Colonel over here, quick," he ordered.

Swanson took one look and reached for her cell phone. The call was answered within three rings. "Gruen here," the voice said.

"Stan, this is Sharon. I need a favor."

"What would that be?" he asked sarcastically.

"You wanted those two guys that killed your officer, right?"

"Kinkaid and Acree? Hell yeah." The Tennessee State patrol officer knew this meant she had them.

"An old pick-up truck will be in Jellico in about two hours," she told him cryptically.

"Okay."

"Keep 'em on ice for a day or two if you will. They won't be much trouble. All I ask is that you explain it, however you choose."

Gruen laughed, "Nice doing business with ya, Sharon."

68

Silas called Ben while Duray drove. They had Harkness trussed up in the back though he offered little resistance.

"What the heck is all this about George?" he asked the boy back home.

"They came and got him a few minutes ago...from his office in town. Mom was there, thank God, or we wouldn't have known for several hours."

"I don't understand," Silas prodded him for more. "What's the charge?"

"Criminal obstruction," Ben spelled out. "They say he's covering for you."

Silas put the phone in his lap for a second, grappling with his anger and frustration. *It's never over*, played in his mind, but rational, more useful words finally came from him

"They'll be coming for you and Marsha next," he calculated.

Ben sighed, "They're already here."

"You haven't let them in, have you?"

"No...but there are more state troopers out on the road than I thought we had."

"Lock the place down and set security to D-4."

Ben knew the system as well as Jon did, "That's not very strong," he argued.

"We don't want to hurt any of them, Ben. Just keep them out for now."

"Alright," the boy responded as he turned the dial back from D-15. "Done."

"Who's watching over George at the jail?" Silas asked.

"Gil is there. He's already called."

Changing gears out of necessity, Silas informed Ben about the "star" pictures. "But we have to keep this quiet. If they know we've figured it out, they'll take 'em all down," he explained.

"So...we're going after all of 'em, huh?"

"I don't even know how deep that is right now, Ben. But after we take care of this faction...the kidnappers, we'll see if we can help expose the rest of them."

"The rest of them?" Ben didn't understand. "If we get this group...we've got 'em."

"No...remember Shanahan," he said. "And Cheryl saw one in her Governor's office. Not all of the larger entities are involved in this case. I'm afraid they have separate agendas. If I can find the connection, you can reach out to the authorities one at a time."

"Ok." Ben's mind tried to wrap itself around all of the possibilities.

"One other thing that just came to me," Silas added. "Is Harold at Dalton?"

"I think so. I'm not sure."

"Well, have him go to Shreveport and wait there. If they tie him to us they'll grab him up as well."

"What are you doing now?" Ben asked him.

"Getting ready to interview two of our bad guys," he told him. "We may need Daniel and Matt Turlock to help us with some cover stories. See how many news departments they can trust to help."

~

The Mayor of Chicago called his administrative assistant from his home.

"Cal, I'm going to that conference after all," he informed the man.

"Kansas City?" his assistant didn't understand. "That's midwestern mayors, sir. Mostly small towns and their problems."

"One can learn from the smallest of things, Cal."

The assistant was perplexed, but knew not to argue. "How long will you be staying there, sir?"

"What is it...a week?" the mayor asked.

"Yes, sir... Through next Saturday."

"Cancel everything I had for this week, but do it quietly. No press release, ok?"

"Yes, sir. You want to fly out tomorrow?"

"No, Cal. Get me a flight out this afternoon. I haven't had any good ribs in years."

Jordan Sterns spent his time in Chicago searching for signs of the "ghosts." Many of his tactics would be considered foolhardy, but his intensity only grew with each attempt. Pool halls and dive bars where the name Pilfoy was known quite well. Most even knew the man was dead. But mention of his associates, the ghosts, would bring blank stares.

He was walking back toward the city hall building on that Saturday when he noticed the figure emerge and half run into the parking deck. *That's Greer*, he remembered from their short meeting earlier. *Where's he off to, all loaded down?*

Torn between following the man or taking the opportunity to snoop around his office, Sterns chose the latter. Weekends were a quieter time at the building and security not as tight. He took a somewhat evasive route back to the man's office, which was locked, but a trained and experienced detective gained access within a minute.

The sparsely adorned office he remembered from this morning was even more vacant now. Sitting at the desk, he pulled on the drawers, finding a simple toggle to unlock them. Again, everything was surprisingly empty.

There was a note taped beneath a side drawer. The numerals 4-8396 and nothing more appeared on the note. It was hand written and obviously meant something.

Letting his police intuition run free, an idea came to him. The Chicago phone book listed more than half-dozen prefixes for phone numbers. Only one of those ended with the digit, 4.

He picked up the desk phone and hit 9 for an outside line. Then dialing the area code, prefix that ended in 4 and the rest of the number from the note, he sat back.

The other end began to ring.

In his limo driving him to the airport, the mayor pulled his ringing phone and looked at caller's number information. "Assoc. Com. Greer" it said. The mayor grimaced and punched "ignore," then put the phone away.

I'm going to have to come up with another form of cover and fast, he scolded himself. *This is getting out of hand.*

~

The noise in Greer's office got Phil's attention and he realized he had not followed up on looking into Detective Jordon Sterns of Muskegon.

A screen soon filled with vitals on this man and Phil spoke out loud for Ben and Cheryl to hear.

"Fourteen year veteran of the department in Muskegon... unblemished record... four commendations and a citation for bravery." Phil turned and looked at the others, "Not a bad guy," he surmised. "Married, no kids...in-laws live up state, brother-in-law is Waylon Steggers..."

"Wait," Cheryl interrupted him. "Who did you say?"

"Waylon Steggers," Phil spun his chair in her direction and repeated.

"He's a good friend of Daddy's," she told them with her eyes wide as saucers.

"Small world, huh?" Phil laughed. "This is all circling the bowl now."

69

Colonel Swanson showed Silas to the room they held Petteri in. Before entering, he asked her, "We really need to keep all this under wraps. The leaders need to think their farm is still operational."

"One big problem is your Sheik fella," she pointed out.

"Did he have plane tickets on him?"

"Yeah."

"Maybe one of your officers could pretend to be him...and another wear the burka."

Swanson smiled and shook her head. "What the hell," she exclaimed with acrimony. "I've already shipped two dead bodies to Tennessee. What's another subterfuge, right? We're neck deep now."

With his hand on the doorknob, Silas smiled at her and waited.

"Okay," she said, staring straight at him. "It might just work. It could give us a few more hours if nothing else."

Silas's smile became a grin and he opened the door, stepping into the room.

"Mr. Petteri, is it?" he asked politely.

"Who are you?" the man demanded.

"You can call me Silas."

"Well, Silas...you don't look like a cop to me."

"Good for me," he grinned again. "I wouldn't want to."

"You think?" Petteri was sharp and abrupt. "I want to talk to my lawyer...now."

Silas walked to the window. Poking his finger through the plastic blinds, he pretended to be looking for something.

"No lawyers around right now," he snapped the blinds withdrawing his finger. "It's just not that kind of situation." Turning back to glare at Petteri, he added, "This is between me...and you."

The first, ever so slight, sign of fear flashed across the mobster.

"I don't have to talk to you, you're not a cop."

"Oh...but I believe you will," Silas assured him.

"Am I supposed to be afraid of you now?" Petteri tried to mock him with his own glare. "Your funny suit doesn't affect me...at all."

"Oh...I assure you, sir. It's not just a funny suit." Silas had the beginnings of a grin show on his face. "It's my persuader suit."

"Look...you boorish clown." The man strained to stand from the chair he was tied to. "Go persuade someone else. I'm not interested."

Silas walked up to him and looked down into the man's eyes. "I love a challenge, Mr. Petteri," he nearly whispered to him. "Tell me...are you ticklish, at all?"

Silas reached down and grabbed the man's elbow. Using the powered right hand, his thumb felt around inside the joint applying a slight amount of pressure.

Petteri suddenly winced and shook. "You can't do this," he protested.

"Found your funny bone, huh?" Silas glared.

"This is torture, it's not legal."

"I'm not a cop, remember?" Squeezing a bit harder this time, he leaned down to asked Petteri, "What laws protected those girls from you?"

Petteri did not respond except to take a deep breath. Silas moved to the other arm and went after him again.

"Maybe we'll just use your rules...what do you think?" he leaned into the man's face. "Tell me more about your idea of legal."

Petteri's screams grew and could be heard outside, even down at the street level.

There were other pressure points, but the elbows seemed to work best on the Finlander. It went on for just over thirty minutes.

~

Ben heard the conversation and nearly jumped from his chair.

"That's it," he nearly yelled. "I knew that name meant something. The rental car...the name Sterns was on the rental car."

"So... he helped Daddy." Cheryl surmised.

"Or...he could have been helping his brother-in-law." Phil had pulled up information on the Steggers name. "That's the family that was under siege in upper Michigan."

"This guy is in Chicago trying to figure out why that happened," Ben added.

"We've got an extra player," Phil leaned back and looked at the other two. "And he has no idea what he's in the middle of."

~

When Silas came out of the room Swanson was waiting for him.

"Get what you wanted?" she asked with a strained tone.

"Oh no... Not yet. We just needed to come to an understanding," he offered.

It took him a second, but he realized his friend was not amused or consoled by his quip. Looking more directly at her he could see red streaks growing from behind her ears and running down her neck.

"We're there now," he added with exuberance, but found her strangely difficult to look directly in the eyes. He tried speaking again, "I'll let him think about it a bit...then I'll ask my questions."

His words fell off her, not making an impact. Swanson stared at the floor, her attitude changing more with each second.

"I could go to jail for what you did in there," she spoke calmly, but her words scolded him.

"Possibly," he nearly muttered. Measuring his response, Silas gave her plenty of latitude. "Yes ma'am...you could."

He looked unrepentant but inside he knew he owed her an explanation of some kind.

"I don't respond well to people who hurt children," he shook his head as he spoke. "Call it a weakness...or maybe a lack of discipline. It's how I am." He remained calm, but very firm. "And I don't have time for all the niceties your laws give people like that."

"Do you think you're God or something?" she lashed at him.

The question cut him deeply. Jon surfaced to reply.

"You've decided to judge me now?" he struck back.

"What you do..." she struggled to explain her conflicted thoughts, "whatever you feel, the law protects those cretins from that." The Colonel stared him right in the eye. "I can't do that stuff...no matter what, and I shouldn't stand here and let you."

"They get the same protection they offered their victims." His voice began to show the slightest signs of emotional stress. Then he stiffened his neck and spoke with forced composure.

"Seems fair to me," he snapped.

An awkward silence followed. Swanson searched for words, and then Silas sluggishly moved past his friend down the hallway.

"As for God," he said looking straight ahead as he moved. "I'll accept his judgment when that time comes. But when I see the things these guys are doing...and these are 'the guys,' there is no doubt of that... I have to stop it and them."

Pausing, he looked at the door he was now standing in front of before completing the thought, "and stop it fast," he added reaching for the doorknob.

"Is this where you have the Sheik?"

Swanson stepped closer. She wasn't finished.

"So now you're gonna torture him?"

Silas stared at the door and spoke as though to it.

"Ma'am, I respect you more than you know. If you want to stop this, we have to be sure we get to the top. That's the only way. The snake has to be killed at its head. These low level guys are replaceable, and too easily. But they can show me where I need to go."

He then stepped back from the door and turned toward the Colonel with a softer voice. "This guy won't need coaxing like Petteri," he assured her. "I just want to know about his drug mixture and where he gets it."

With concern still in her eyes Sharon Swanson stepped beside him. She opened the door and announced for the occupant to hear, "Silas, this is Mr. Lawrence Gibbons."

"How are you, Larry?" Silas asked as he walked in and closed the door behind him.

~

The megaphone bellowed its warning and command.

"Open your doors and come out," echoed through the area.

Marsha called down to Ben, "Have you talked to Jon about this, yet?"

"Yes, ma'am...he said to sit tight. To me...that means we ignore them."

She walked to a front window and stared out with her phone still in her hand. "I'm worried about George," she declared firmly.

"Gil has gathered up all the local officers and surrounded the jail. If anything goes bad it'll be a big mess." Ben rubbed his forehead, realizing that might not have come out the way he meant. "What I mean is they won't let anything happen to George."

"How long will they do this?" she wondered out loud.

"Jon thinks it's all for show. They're trying to prove a point...make him come forward." He pulled a printed piece from one of the printers. "The story in Chicago is that the authorities suspect Jon was involved in the bombing at city hall there."

"How do they figure that?"

"It's a stretch, sure. But somebody in this deal is afraid Jon is still around. That points to a politician in my book."

Marsha thought the theory through. "It's beyond Kinkaid then," she surmised.

"Oh yeah," Ben agreed wholeheartedly. "We have an idea but can't prove it."

Marsha didn't ask. She knew it wouldn't do any good. As she started to turn away from the window a muted "thud" sounded. A shot struck the glass where she stood, leaving little more than a scratch.

The Colonel in charge of the siege jumped up waving his arms. He grabbed a megaphone from an officer standing near him and screamed in a high pitch order, "Stand down...everyone. Stand down." There were no more shots fired.

"What was that?" Ben asked fervently.

"Nothing," she told him calmly. "It was nothing."

Knowledge of that silly attempt would only detract those in the basement from their jobs. If word got to Jon, it could affect his thinking. In that flash of a second, Marsha had reminded herself of the value of isolated information.

She pulled the drapes closed and walked away.

70

Silas picked up the small box of powder Swanson's people had found on the Sheik. He opened the box and tasted a small bit, finger to his tongue.

"Do you know what this is?" he asked the bound man.

Gibbons looked at him for a second and then turned away defiantly.

Still rubbing his tongue on his lower lip, Silas moved in front of the man. "I'm tasting catnip...huh. Is that right?"

Gibbons had heard enough from whoever was down the hall. He didn't really want to find out if all that was real or staged. "I just give it to 'em as they tell me," he disclosed. "Keeps 'em docile, that's all I care about."

Silas now spread the mixture around on his palm. His old training came back as he recognized granules and colors.

"Diazepam, and there's some Seconal." He knelt down and got in the man's face, "Good gracious...triazolam," he stirred it a bit more and added, "Chloridiazepoxide. You can kill people with less than this."

Gibbons was now clearly afraid for his life. "I don't know anything except what they told me to give 'em," he repeated as though that would absolve him.

"How did you give it to them, little man?" Silas was now trying to dig under his frightened skin.

"I mixed a half a teaspoon in with a syringe of that stuff...there."

Silas picked up the small medical syringe marked, "immunoglobulin G."

"That's nice of them...concerned about infections, are they?" Silas words were heavy with sarcasm and anger.

Instinctively, the man responded, "It mixed really well."

"What's the set up drug?"

Gibbons was confused, "I don't know what that is....what?"

"They give them something to start with," Silas insisted.

"Man...I have no idea," he pleaded. "GHB, I would guess."

Silas tossed the powder toward Gibbon's face, causing the tied up man to squeal and push his chair over backwards.

Swanson came in at the noise. She found Silas walking toward her, dusting off his hands. "He's fine," he scoffed. "The creep will live to do his forty years."

She followed Silas back into the hall where he turned and took a very deep breath before speaking.

"Look, Colonel...I apologize for snapping at you back there."

Swanson looked at him without comment.

"When I first came on this case...it was just another set of bad guys." His tone suddenly changed, "But I've met one of their victims, got to know her family... and I've dug up what these creatures were doing to the girls."

He leaned against the exterior wall for support and continued. "I can understand murder out of anger or vengeance, even for power. That has emotion to it...humanity of some sort. This stuff is inhumane and for nothing more than money. Cold...." he searched his mind looking for more words to use, "I mean...the drug business is cold, but this is way below that."

"Don't even try," Swanson said with compassion. "I do understand. I know what you do...I always have. I just never saw or heard it before."

It was Silas' turn to listen.

"The information you get has saved my life..." she began very thoughtfully, "and a bunch of my people's lives. I knew how you had to be getting it out of them...I just allowed myself not to think about it."

"I'm not always this worked up over a case," he tried. "I need to stay calm...at all times, but this thing got to me." His face pointed to the floor, but his eyes angled up to check her reaction. "I got carried away on Petteri," he said.

Swanson looked to be at a loss for words. She wasn't.

"I wish my way...the system I work for, was right every time," she said. "But I know it's not always successful. It should be, and maybe someday we'll get back on top of this mess and it will be again."

"I'm sorry this upset you," Silas' sincerity was thick. "I believe I know who is responsible for all this...but I can't prove it yet. Not even to myself." He stood away from the wall and headed back down the hall. "That's the frustration...I only need to prove it to myself, but this guy is good. He's got himself covered from every angle."

"Nobody's perfect, Jon," the Colonel assured him. "You'll find his error...his misstep. It's there and you'll find it."

"Thanks my friend," he told her. "I'll work harder to control myself. I know I have to do that."

Colonel Swanson smiled just a tiny bit. "I'm glad that stuff with Petteri was not your norm," she said.

"Do you have those papers you took off of him?" Silas asked suddenly.

"Yeah...they're right here," she turned around to a table and gathered a stack.

Silas stared at the back of her head with a blank look. His eyes reflectively blinked as he heard his ego tell itself, *she bought it.*

He didn't like deceiving her, not even this little bit. But it was better than her knowing he was capable of the fury she had witnessed, at any given time. Some of what he shared was absolutely correct. His target was elusive and good at it, but Silas' tactics were born of expedience...not frustration.

The colonel turned to hand him the stack of papers and notes. She caught a glimpse of his dispassionate expression though he managed to smile and nod at her. Swanson cast off her uneasiness. "This is what we found in his car," she explained.

"It's time to find out what these mean," Silas said as he took the papers from her.

71

Colonel Swanson's faux Sheik and "bride" drove to Lexington and went through the motions of boarding the flight to New York without actually doing so. With the assistance of the airline's ground crew, any film of their departure would appear legitimate.

Police at New York's Kennedy airport were preparing look-a-likes to be presumed to be changing planes there. The final destination was to be Damascus, Syria. Interpol agents were planning their observance of whomever might meet the flight there, though that would not be until early Monday. It would take a full day before the flight arrived.

With the cooperation of authorities in their home states, parents of the rescued girls were notified and quietly taken to Kentucky to be with their daughters. All this kept carefully under wraps from everyone, especially from the press.

Murray, Tim, and Weston drank coffee until it was time for beer and basically waited to hear what Jon had plans for next. To them, that Saturday was a long day.

~

Detective Sterns made a copy of the number he had deciphered from the note found in Greer's desk. He had very little to go on, but his gut told him that Greer was somehow involved in the attacks on his family.

Deciding that Saturday, though quiet, was a risky day to look deeper into the city hall office, he slipped out to do more checking around town. He would return to the office on Sunday, when things should be completely dormant.

~

Renio Petteri was still pale and he struggled to get a full breath. Over thirty minutes had passed since Silas left him, but his muscles ached deeply from tensing up and his nerves had not recovered. The ulnar nerve, particularly, is quick to react and slow to recover. Petteri was trying to straighten his arms as the door opened again.

Silas stepped into the room, and looked at Petteri's hands. They were drawn into knots from the muscles to the lower fingers being wracked by the nerve. His forefingers and thumbs pointed straight outward, but the rest pulled in uncontrollably.

Silas glanced down at the papers held in his own hand.

"Let's see," he started. "What do I need from you?"

Paging through the notes as though he were completely familiar with everything on them, Silas finally asked a question.

"Who's this Jurgon? I know who Greer is, and Pilfoy," he looked up at Petteri and added, "I've met with Mr. Kinkaid earlier." He sternly looked back to his papers and continued, "Harkness...know him...humm. Who is Jurgon?"

The question and the listing of the names nearly caught Petteri off guard. He jerked his upper body, but the bindings were still firm. "I don't know," he protested.

"Oh...sure you do," Silas leaned over him and pointed to the name written in Petteri's own hand. "This guy...right here."

The tied-up man defiantly turned away. Silas started to reach for his elbow, but paused for a few seconds. He pulled his hand back and leaned further into Petteri's face.

Without making a sound, Silas suddenly took one knee beside the hoodlum's chair. He checked the glove on his right hand with deliberate care, adjusting each finger and then flexing them altogether. Tilting his head up to meet Petteri's eyes once again, Silas simply stared at him, for over two solid minutes. Then, slowly standing, the man in the black suit spoke again.

"You screamed pretty loud a while ago," he taunted him, "Real ear piercing stuff." Reaching slowly back toward the man's elbow he went on, "Some out there don't think you could get any louder."

Petteri began to shake. Twisting his head to face the tormentor, he found Silas staring into his eyes as though looking through him.

"I told 'em you could be much louder," Silas whispered, "With enough motivation."

Renio spit and rocked his head back, "It's Walcovitz," he pleaded, "Jurgon Walcovitz, Captain of the Cordova Queen."

"A boat?"

"A freighter," Petteri clarified. "A Great Lakes freighter."

"So these other two," Silas ran a finger down the page and verbally pushed Petteri harder. "Castenoff and Biswienki, they are ship captains, too...huh?"

"Yes," the man wailed in a broken, trembling tone.

"They didn't carry live girls, did they?" the question was more sinister than the tone used to ask it.

Petteri eyes grew larger. He lowered his head and shook it slowly before speaking. "No."

"Who did the killing?" Silas demanded without any let up.

"There is an old goat farm and processing plant," Renio struggled to speak, "Near Russellville, Alabama." Suddenly a slight calm came over him and information was now flowing like water, "The man's name is Smyden, Kurt Smyden."

Silas ran his finger down through the papers. "Oh...yeah, Smyden. Here he is."

The tormentor took a small step back from his prey, but continued to throw questions at him.

"Whose trucks were used?"

"Kinkaid handled all the trucks." The man's answers came quicker now.

Silas nodded, made a note, and turned to another page.

"Okay..." he sighed heavily and then pointed to a name listed as "Frank." "Who is this guy?"

"Frank is in the Caribbean," there was another case of hesitation in Petteri's voice. Silas leaned down again, looking sternly into the man's face.

"We're not done till I say we are..." he hissed. "You understand that, right?"

"Frank grabbed the girls and flew them out of there for us."

Writing furiously, Silas grimaced and said, "Frank is someone I really want to meet. What's his real name?"

"Franklin Fogerty...he's a tour guide out of Montserrat. He covers the entire area down there."

"How does he get them to the states?"

"There's a small freighter that makes a regular run from The Virgin Islands to Miami."

"Whose boat is it?"

"It's the 'Island Mercy'...I don't know who owns it...really."

Something in the way he said that made Silas believe him.

"Okay then...who would bring them from Miami?"

"That was Kinkaid's people...his trucks."

Silas looked at yet another page. This name wasn't there, but he pretended it was and asked about it anyway.

"Who is Franz?"

That name caused Petteri to lose even more color from his face.

"The boss...," he shuddered almost uncontrollably. "Never met him myself...he's down in South America." Petteri sucked down two deep breaths and added a tidbit, "That bastard tried to kill me."

Silas' chin dropped and his eyes tightened. He didn't know about that. Reshuffling the papers, he walked to the door.

"That's it, I guess," Silas said as a dismissal. "You know you're done, right?"

"Done how?" Petteri asked sheepishly. "Done... here?"

"Oh..." Silas turned back to laugh at the man. "You're done everywhere, friend. This stuff," he raised the papers and wrinkled them in his hand. "It's over. You're done... totally done."

72

Cheryl Duray put her hand on Ben's shoulder, "What have you been doing so long...and so quietly?"

He sat up and thought about just how to explain it all.

"Somebody made a call from Greer's office a while ago. I enhanced the audio tones given off by the dialing phone to identify the number called."

"You can do that?"

"Oh yeah, each number on a keypad has a distinct tone...anyway, I've been tracking down the location of the number dialed. Luckily, it's a cell phone and the GPS led me right to it."

Cheryl waited for the payoff to this story by tilting her head.

"The phone is in Kansas," Ben said with no small amount of pride, "In or near Kansas City."

"Whose is it?" she asked.

"That...I'm working on. I'm running a search for things happening in that area."

"And that will tell you whose phone it is?" Cheryl didn't understand this part.

"Not directly...but it could point us in the right direction."

The computer stopped and a red light lit up. Ben zoomed in on the findings and rocked back with a huge grin.

"Jon's gonna love this," he said. "It's what he's been looking for."

"What is it?" she shook him with her hand.

"A connection to the Mayor of Chicago," he beamed. "There's a conference of mid-western mayors in Kansas City starting tomorrow.

380

If he ain't in Chicago...I'll bet he's there and this is his private cell phone."

~

The blinds were closed. Even though it was early afternoon, the motel dining room was dimly lit. The customers who would normally be there had been displaced by officers and guests of the State of Kentucky. Silas found the guys at a table near the rear. Empty brown bottles showcased their mood. They were men of action...with nothing to do.

"A bit early for that isn't it?" he asked them.

Murray looked up at his friend. "We're open for suggestions, Jon. You can't do it all yourself...or can you?"

Silas pulled the fourth chair out and sat down. He went immediately into a slump, letting his handful of papers scrape the floor.

"We're all in this one with you, you know?" that chastising tone came from Tim Spiegel. "It's the Four Samaritans...remember?" he chided.

Looking around the table, Silas tried to apologize. "I wasn't leaving you guys out," he explained. That drew little or no reaction from anyone. "There's just some stuff I needed to do...some information I had to get and I've always done that by myself."

Westy sat up straighter and glanced down at the papers Silas held.

"You ready to share that stuff with us?" he asked politely. "And..." looking around in an exaggerated fashion he asked, "Where's the Colonel? Isn't she a part of this, too?"

"She's a huge part," Silas assured them. "Some of the parents are here... and the other set is on the way. Swanson is handling the meetings." Though that was clearly accepted, it didn't change the mood in the room.

He lifted his arm and placed the papers on the table. "Here's the cast of characters running this operation," he told them, "All underlings."

They sat up and pushed the beer bottles to the side. Each man took a few papers and swapped them around as they studied their contents.

"So..." Tim looked at Silas. "What do we do with these guys?"

"We could kill 'em all..." Silas said flatly. "That would be fine with me, but it wouldn't end anything. These jerks are all replaceable."

"Some easier than others," Murray disagreed as he pointed to the name of the man in the Caribbean. "Franklin, here," he declared emphatically, "Has to go."

"Normally I would agree," Silas nodded and continued, "This goat farmer in Alabama, too. Several of them have earned the dirt nap, no question. But I need to find the boss of this deal. That's the only thing that will stop it. We start leaving a trail of dead bodies and they go underground." Under his breath he added, "And that's just this group, who knows how many others are out there?"

"Is that this 'Franz' fella you wrote down here?" Weston asked him. "Is he the boss?"

"We're supposed to believe he is."

The other three were taken aback slightly by that answer.

"So...you suspect somebody else?" Murray figured.

"No proof, but yeah," Silas sighed and leaned back. "I just need one firm link to him, but this damned guy is good. He has himself covered from all angles."

"What about your house?" Weston threw in without looking up. "I know it's a fortress, but my family is in there. What are we gonna do about the siege?"

Before he could answer, Silas' cell phone rang. It was Ben. Offering a quick "excuse me" look at Weston, he grabbed the phone and listened intently. The news about the Chicago mayor was welcome.

"That's great work, Ben. So he's out of the office for a few days?"

"Looks that way," Ben told him. "Here's that number."

Silas made note of the phone number and quickly told Ben help was on the way.

"We'll be there Monday, okay?"

"We're fine...and Gil still has George protected."

"This mayor of ours... turned into a real piece of work, didn't he?"

"Oh, yeah..." Ben's voice was full of disappointment. "I just wish I knew what he thinks he's going to gain from this?"

"He's simply afraid to go against the grain of power," Silas muttered. "His fear will be his ruin."

As Ben hung up, Silas closed his phone and looked at the other guys.

"Here's what I'd like us to do," he said leaning forward. "I'm going to check on my suspicions of this Chicago mayor tomorrow. I'd like you guys to pick a few of the more important players on these lists..." he pounded the papers with his finger. "And deal with 'em."

Everyone was sitting upright and fully attentive. Silas looked to Weston Duray, "We'll all go to Dalton on Monday. They're good and safe, but we need to end that mess as well."

"Deal with 'em?" Murray slid back against his chair and added, "That's pretty open ended, isn't it?" He wasn't afraid to do what was necessary, but Jon's suggestion appeared contrary to his prior sermon. "How far do we go?"

"Just get 'em out of the loop," Silas squinted, realizing what Murray meant. "You know I don't want you going too far, but time is short on this. If we don't close it down before they're on to us, they'll be gone."

"And they'd set up and start all over again, wouldn't they?" Weston's question wasn't really a question. The others understood.

"Okay then," Murray wanted to know. "Who do we pick?"

"You guys decide," Silas grinned. "Heck...do I have to do everything myself?" he teased Murray with his own words.

~

That afternoon, Murray placed a call to Ben.

"I assume you have this list Jon put together," he started.

"Yes... sir."

"Do you have a phone number for this Franklin Fogerty?"

"I have his business number," Ben told him. "But if I think I know where you're going with this, I can figure out what cell phones he uses in a few minutes."

"Yeah...you've got me," Murray smiled. "I also bet you've got a voice distorter or two lying around, right?"

"Yep."

"See if you can find out which Island has a group of young girls visiting this weekend. Then call our friend, Frank and...pretending to be this 'Franz" guy, tell him you need a girl shipped up right away."

"Isn't that risky?"

"I've got an idea...just make sure we know as much as we can... about where he might do the grab." Murray's voice filled with urgency, "be quick, it's already Saturday. We need this in place by tonight."

"Get back to you, shortly," Ben said as he hung up. *He's thinking more like Jon every day,* he thought.

73

Sunday morning poured in over the clouds as the G5 reached 27,000 feet quickly. Silas knocked and opened the cockpit door.

"Hey..." he asked. " Is this door airtight?"

"Close as you can get, I suppose," Harold told him. "Why?" His voice went up a few octaves as he asked.

"Just keep it closed tight until I knock again," Silas shut the door and went to the rear of the plane.

He pulled out his black bag and dug down into the bottom. A wooden box, wrapped in plastic and thoroughly sealed, was withdrawn carefully. The safety gauge, inside the wrapper, was fine. So he began the process of opening the box. With his mask in place he mixed up a vial of compound and added the aerosol blaster.

If this trip is successful, I'll need to act quickly, he told himself. *There won't be time to go home, plan, and come back.*

The vials all had special transport containers that were sealed. He placed his weapon into one vial and started replacing everything else. The entire process took nearly an hour, the longest hour Harold Foster could ever remember.

The Lucy Too was airborne that morning with Duray and Spiegel on board. The trip to Minnesota took just over four hours and used one and a half of Murray's auxiliary fuel tanks.

Binoculars at the ready, the men flew over the harbor looking for three boats, the Cordova Queen, the Joseph P. Harnell, and the

Mesibian Major. Amazingly, two of those were present and being loaded with iron ore. The aerial lift bridge was swung wide and the harbor filled with activity. Ten huge ships were in port between Duluth Harbor and Wisconsin Point.

"Mesibian Major, that's Zeno Castenoff's ship," Westy called out. The boat rode low in the water and still sat under the big crane. "Looks like it might be ready to go later tonight."

"Hey," Spiegel pointed to another large freighter. "Doesn't that say Joseph P. Harnell on the bow?" It appeared to stand some forty feet taller than some of the others, but the reasons were soon to be clear.

"Roger that," Murray jumped in. "Now all we need is the Cordova."

That wasn't to be. Two out of three was lucky enough. The Joseph P. Harnell had been in port since Saturday afternoon and was being unloaded to make room for the cargo that would be added. Thus she rode high like an empty soda can on the frigid waters.

Murray found a spot to set Lucy Too down. Sky Harbor airport welcomed all comers. They took a taxi into town from there.

The dry cleaner's was there, as Jon had described it, but closed on Sunday. Murray found an "in case of emergency" number on the glass front door and dialed.

"Juan," he said to the man who answered. "This won't be as surprising as it would have two weeks ago, but how are you doing?"

"Mr. Cowboy?" Juan was excited to hear his other old friend's voice. "Is that you?"

Murray explained what Jon had told him. That Juan would know the hangouts for the boat captains. He knew Castenoff. He had met him in town more than once, but not Biswienki.

"I've heard Wolfgang talked about, he's a pretty tough hombre, but I've never met him." he told Murray.

Do these guys know each other?" Murray hoped. "They might be in town together."

"That I don't know for sure," Juan thought for a minute. "But if they work together as Jon thinks they do...they know each other. Those boats make regular runs into Duluth."

"Good point." Murray agreed.

Juan told of the bar and restaurant where the ship captains would most likely stay while their boats were being attended.

"Can I help?" he asked Murray.

"You've done plenty, my friend," Murray told him. "Sorry we can't stay to see you in person this trip. But we have someone to see in Alabama later today."

As they entered the bar, a news report came on the TV about two bodies found in Tennessee. "Both males, one shot to death and the cause of death for the other was not yet determined," the news reader told. He finished his report with, "There was no identification on either body."

Tim Spiegel looked at his friends and muttered under his breath, "Colonel Swanson gets things handled...doesn't she?"

~

Silas entered the Chicago city hall building dressed as a housekeeping worker. He found a cart in the storage closet on the fourth floor and slowly pushing it, checked the area. The main door to the mayor's suite was, of course, locked. He picked it with ease and slipped inside. Leaving those lights off, he moved to the private office doors and worked his way in there.

388

His first thought was a negative one, *no star picture*. That would have been too easy. The desk was huge with two side by side center drawers and four cabinet style drawers on each side of the chair well.

The normal search turned up nothing, no secret compartments, no notes taped to a drawer bottom, nothing. But Silas came prepared for the tough search.

The evidence he sought, *must be here*, he told himself again. It would be too important to risk moving around.

He pulled a sonic resonator from his inside pocket. Tracing the walls, it searched for any void in the construction. A tedious process, but his patience kept him focused.

After no luck with the walls, he attached the unit to an expanding pole. Moving the resonator slowly into a high corner, he heard the door behind him open.

"What the hell are you doing?" the security guard asked.

Silas glanced back over his shoulder.

"Cobwebs," he declared.

The guard looked up at the small, rectangular thing atop the pole. He grunted and nodded his acceptance while pulling the door to.

Silas turned back and stared into the corner for a second. His mind reset itself as he felt the air expelling from his lungs. He directed his gaze up to the resonator and continued his work, scouring the ceiling and then the floor. Nothing was indicated as out of the ordinary.

Standing in the middle of the space, he slowly scanned the room, thinking. The huge desk again caught his attention.

After tapping on the solid wood top, he ran the detector unit all along the sides and started pulling out the drawers again.

Then...*there it is,* he beamed quietly. The hidden compartment he knew had to exist. Not in the bottom of a drawer, but in the side wall of the right hand center drawer.

Silas felt around and found the latch, a spring trigger that reacted to touch. The slot opened and out fell a small flash drive for a computer. With the back of his hand, Silas slid the flash drive out of the way. He knew what that had to be. What he wanted to know more about was the hidden compartment.

He spent time studying the spring action of the slot.

"This could work for me," he muttered softly.

The niche was so well hidden it had to be a very private cubbyhole. Known only to the mayor himself, this was the perfect way to strike at him... and him alone.

Silas measured and calculated the space and the release mechanism. He figured out how to adapt his vial to that opening and then turned his attention to the contents.

The zip drive appeared to be a standard off the shelf data storage module. Slightly more than two and half inches long, the plastic housing held a sliding USB connector, a tiny chip for the memory and a miniature LED bulb.

He took the memory drive to the outer office. A desk top computer sat with its screensaver flashing. Silas hit a couple of keys and nothing happened. He tapped a button on his chest and spoke low but audibly.

"Ben," he called. "Can you see this thing?"

Within a minute Ben was on-line.

"Where are you?" he asked.

"I'm at a computer that's locked with a password or something. Can you get into it?"

Ben didn't even try his question about Silas' location again.

"Stick your keychain into the SD/MMC slot for me."

Silas searched for the opening but couldn't find it.

"Ben, where is the thing?" he asked.

"It must be under a sliding panel on the front."

Silas rubbed his hand over the front cover and sure enough, a piece of plastic moved down revealing several slots. One was marked as Ben had requested. His keychain had a metal looking fob with a FORD logo stamped on it. He stuck it into the slot and with a few keystrokes from Georgia, Ben brought the computer to life.

"You in?" Ben asked.

"Yep...thanks," he responded and tapped the button on his shirt again, disconnecting the communication.

The key fob was removed and the flash drive inserted into the USB slot. He touched "enter" on the keyboard and the screen danced with the information from the secret drive. Names, numbers, and listings by groups were all there. This one piece of plastic contained all the information the mayor had on his organization, plus more.

Silas had his proof. He pulled the zip drive and put it in his pocket. Then, returning to the private office, he began the process of connecting the breakable vial to the compartment's sliding door.

But something stopped him.

Leaning back in the man's huge chair, a thought played over in his head. It was what Phil had told him. The original words came from Daniel and that always meant they were worth considering.

"This guy is obsessed with the 'Son'," he had said. "He has survived this long by being that careful."

Silas stared at the flash drive.

There must be another way to do this, he told himself.

~

Jordan Sterns had spent his Sunday touring the bars on Chicago's south side. No one had seen any of Pilfoy's men in several days. The fact that they admitted to the "ghosts" existence gave the stories some credibility.

"I heard they were going into business on their own." One man told him. "I think they left town with a guy from out of state, but I have no idea who."

Sterns checked his watch. It was past the middle of the afternoon and he had not eaten since early that morning. He grabbed a cab, deciding to ride back toward city hall, get a meal, and then look around that area a bit more.

Leaving the bar, he noticed the TV was showing a dark blue helicopter had landed in the middle of some road. He watched, like everyone else, for a couple of minutes. Then hunger overrode his curiosity and he stepped outside to hail a cab.

~

"Have you heard about all the excitement, sir?" the limo driver asked. They were enroute from his hotel to a banquet in Kansas City.

"No," Mayor Rigby told him. "What's going on?"

"They think they've got that 'Son' fella cornered down in Georgia."

"Really," Rigby sat forward and leaned over the seat. "Have you got a news feed in this thing?"

"No, sir. Just my radio."

The mayor shrugged and relaxed in his seat. "Okay," he said. "Thanks for letting me know about it. How far to the hall?"

"Ten minutes...tops," the driver replied.

Rigby nodded. *Well, that little hick mayor may have accomplished something*, he smiled to himself.

74

Jon had suggested they fly to Chatsworth, Georgia, to meet. The area around Dalton's airport could be under surveillance, watching for the G5. They lacked the time for such interference.

The jet came into Chatsworth a half an hour ahead of the Lucy Too. Everyone, including Harold Foster, then flew west in the jet helicopter, making a cautious pass over Dalton's airport before landing there.

Lucy Too was on the ground long enough for one man to exit.

Airborne again for only minutes, she buzzed and then circled the mansion. With everyone's attention now on the blue machine, she then made a spectacular landing in the middle of the highway just above the house.

Ben and the others watched from inside on both closed circuit monitors and national television.

"What are they doing?" Cheryl spoke up through the tension.

"I don't have a clue," Ben answered. "I really don't."

Phil searched the console. "You are recording this, right?" he asked.

"Oh yeah," Ben told them, "From our private feed."

Lucy Too sat still, allowing her rotors to slowly stop as the state police moved in around the craft. Officers lined up and leveled their weapons at the helicopter as its doors opened wide on both sides.

"Look what they've done," Sue Stone pointed out.

The national television feeds were now on a seven second delay.

"That's in case something happens that they don't want to go out on the air," Phil advised. "Let's hope it isn't needed."

No one else had anything to add.

With nearly all eyes on the helicopter, no one noticed the Jeep approaching the old gas station from the south, no one except Marsha.

The one monitor of the south facing camera was away from the others, but Marsha's intuition caused her to keep a watchful eye on it.

In less than four seconds the Jeep had appeared and then turned into the station, vanishing from sight. Marsha smiled slightly but didn't say a word. She looked back toward the others. All were staring at Ben's other monitors.

~

The mayor's car pulled up at the Bartle's Convention Center and Mayor Rigby stepped out. He waved at the photographers and hurriedly made his way inside.

An unplanned reception preceded the dinner and the organizers hustled him into the waiting throng. Rigby ignored initial advances while he scoured the big room for a television. None were in that area so he finally succumbed to media pressures.

For over thirty minutes he would field questions about his being at this conference and other impertinent requests. He desperately wanted to know what was happening in Georgia, but couldn't afford to ask.

With his broad smile he tried to cover the anxiety building in him.

"What the heck is all this fuss about?" he laughed at the four deep ring of reporters. "I'm just here like everyone else for the food."

~

The coaxial rotors of the copter had stopped and now thrust out in angles that seemed improbable. Dust from the roadside settled around the machine leaving a stark visual for the cameras.

Georgia State Patrolmen lined the sides of the street and the front side of the helicopter. Their commander stood before the aircraft waiting patiently. He stared into the blackout glass saying or doing little else. The entire scene took on the eerie look of a painting, everything standing completely still.

~

It was raining in Chicago. Not hard, just a steady rain.

Jordan Sterns had finished his dinner while watching the coverage of the Georgia billionaire and the State Police. He had heard of Crane, and he knew about the theories of the assassin. The story interested him as long as it lasted. But his thoughts were back on Greer and his possible connection to the threats on his family.

He finished his coffee and checked the time. It was still four and a half hours till the flight back to Muskegon. His cop sense kept pulling his mind to the mayor's office.

"There's a connection if I can just find it," he said out loud.

The young waitress appeared stunned at the outburst as she stood with his check.

"Sorry," Sterns smiled at her. "Just thinking about something."

He paid the bill and walked out into the rain. Hailing a cab, Sterns robotically asked about a coffee shop near the LaSalle Street building.

I've got to wait anyway, he told himself quietly this time, *Might as well keep an eye out while I do.*

~

Four men in black suits and helmets climbed from the helicopter and lined up in front of it. They began walking down the road, unhurriedly and side by side. The state troopers slide-stepped closer, weapons at ready, to cut them off. When the four had reached about thirty feet from the copter, a voice rang out in front of them.

"Hold it right there," the commander of the unit ordered.

The four stopped and stood in silence.

"I want Jonathan Crane," the officer added to his command.

An uneasy quiet settled in for several minutes. Everyone in the mansion swapped stares as Marsha covered her mouth with her hand. She was trying to hide her smile.

The man in black to the far left stepped forward proclaiming "I'm Jonathan Crane."

Then, as though making a repeat of the movie "Spartacus," the man next to him stepped forward shouting the same line, "I'm Jonathan Crane."

The commander of the state police tilted his head in disgust. "I don't have time for games, gentlemen," he shouted. "Which of you is Crane?"

The third in line stepped forward and proclaimed he was Crane. Then the last man also stepped up with the same line.

The commander and six of his men walked up to them. Bent forward at his waist, he spoke in a voice for only them to hear.

"Very funny, guys."

He pulled the helmet from the first man and Weston Duray was standing there.

"Who are you?" the commander demanded.

"I already told you," Duray glared at him defiantly.

The officer grimaced and said, "Okay...we'll do this your way."

The second helmet exposed Tim Spiegel. The commander quickly checked his photo of Jonathan Crane and went to the next man.

Lifting that helmet exposed a smiling Murray Bilstock.

"Nice to meet ya," the cowboy quipped but the officer did not respond. Instead he pointed to the last helmeted man and two guards grabbed him and started to pull him away.

"Aren't you gonna check under that helmet, sir?" Murray challenged him.

The commander's face fell as a realization came to him. He quickly undid the chin strap and pulled the helmet from the man's head. There stood Harold Foster.

"What is this?" the commander demanded, throwing the last helmet to the ground. "Some sick joke?"

"Not at all," Spiegel stepped to him, speaking in a calm voice. "You see, you guys came for Jon Crane. You guys are the ones so sure he's really alive." Spiegel looked to the cameras that were filming everything. "Jon Crane is alive in all of us," he yelled.

"Give me a break," the commander whispered. "This is nonsense, where is he?" the red faced man demanded.

"You tell me, Commander," Weston Duray asked him. "His spirit saved my daughter...through these men and others. I wish I could meet this man, Crane. But I'm told I'm too late for that."

398

The trooper in charge pointed to the helicopter and five men quickly searched it completely. They returned shaking their heads.

A reporter on camera turned to point at the four men surrounded by state police while giving his live account of the scene.

"Forcing the issue, local and state authorities did their best to expose a perceived plot today. Is billionaire industrialist, Jonathan Crane, really dead? Or is he avoiding the eyes of the law?"

Sticking his head back before the lens again, the smiling reporter went on. "As you can see, these efforts have proved only the man's legacy to be alive and well, in the hearts of those who knew him. As for the man himself, his mysterious sacrifice to save the President earlier this year still appears to have been his last great act."

The commander on scene turned toward his men and motioned for them to stand down. He started to walk away, but looked back at the men in the black suits.

"Get that thing off my road," he ordered, pointing at Lucy Too.

Murray nodded and assured him, "Right away, sir."

The group on the second level sub-basement quietly hugged each other, still not totally sure what had just happened.

Marsha, Ben, and the Durays squeezed into the elevator to go upstairs.

One level below them, Silas gathered his bag from the Jeep and walked to the elevator. The light panel indicated "busy."

75

Mayor Reginald Rigby settled into his seat at the banquet. The meal was catered by The Hitchin Post restaurant. Aromas filled the hall that made him check his mouth with his napkin.

The mayor of Chicago shouldn't be caught drooling, he laughed at himself.

The television sets in the hall were all turned off. His curiosity and concern pushed him to lean over to the man sitting next to him.

"Any word on that thing down in Georgia?" he asked.

The man smiled sarcastically. "They blew it," he whispered.

"Blew it?" Rigby was confused. "What does that mean?"

"The guy they were after wasn't even there." The man turned toward Mayor Rigby, recognizing him now. "Sorry, Mr. Mayor. I didn't see you come in," he stammered.

"Yeah, yeah...what do mean...he wasn't there?"

"It was a mess!" the man proclaimed. "They had the whole place surrounded. Four guys climbed out of this helicopter, huge drama...I mean, it was wild."

"Crane wasn't there?" Rigby pressed.

"No...After all that they say he really is dead. The head cop down there had egg on his face, big time."

Rigby sat back, staring straight ahead.

"Say," the other man leaned toward him this time. "Could I get a picture with you before this is over?"

"Huh? What?" Rigby tilted his head at the man.

"A picture. Could I get...?"

"Yeah...sure," Rigby cut him off. He noticed the staff bringing salads to the table. Trying to organize his thoughts so he could enjoy the meal, the Chicago mayor rearranged his silverware as he waited.

~

Jordan Sterns' cab pulled in front of Intelligentsia Coffee, just off LaSalle Street. He tipped the cabbie for the great location and pulled his coat collar up to keep the rain from going down his back.

The shop was not busy and he found a seat near the large window facing the building he was interested in. He could see the side and most of the front. Everything was clearly lit by street lamps and large fixtures hanging from the building itself.

"This will do nicely," he said to himself.

Settling in, he waited for the server and brushed water drops from his head.

~

After several minutes, the troopers outside gave up. A call from the Dalton mayor, embarrassed by his involvement in this, had ordered them to withdraw.

"I figured that much out myself, Mr. Mayor," the commander responded. "You can expect to hear from the governor after I make my report." He hung up as the Dalton mayor attempted an explanation.

Within minutes, the task force was gone.

Tim Spiegel, Foster, and Duray walked up the long driveway to the mansion while Murray lifted the Lucy Too from the road. They were met at the door by the Duray women and Ben.

Marsha had stopped to retrieve a phone message from a private line.

"That was great!" Ben all but yelled as the ladies hugged Weston Duray. "But where is Jon?"

~

Silas stepped off the elevator onto the second sub-basement. Doris Shaw was the first to see him.

"Jon..." she grinned, walking to him. " There you are."

He glanced around as the others came to greet him.

"Marsha and Ben?" he meekly asked.

"Upstairs," Phil spoke up. "The guys are coming in up there. Man that was another one for my book."

Shaking his friends hand, Jon nodded at Sue Stone, "Have they been taking good care of you here?" he asked her.

Her grin became a huge smile. "Better than I deserve," she told him.

Silas noticed the monitors.

"It's all over then?" he moved toward the computers as he asked.

"Yeah..." Phil assured him. "Murray took the chopper up to the hilltop. He'll be along in a minute. The others are upstairs."

Silas moved closer to the table with the monitors, "What's the status with George?" he asked.

"Gil has him under guard," Doris assured him. "We haven't heard anything new since all this started." She waved her arm at the TVs.

The elevator doors opened with Marsha, Tim, and Harold Foster. The pilot's eyes grew wide in wonder.

"Where are we now," he asked.

"Two levels below the main floor," Marsha answered. She looked to Jon and smiled as he came closer. Her smile dropped a bit as she grabbed Jon's arm to chastise him.

"You put Harold in danger," she barked. "You said you'd never do that."

"It was his idea," Jon responded and transformed her 'grab' into a hug. "He said they'd be expecting four guys, something about the news coming from Mexico."

"That's right," Foster stepped in. "It was about time I got in on the action anyway."

Tim Spiegel spoke up. "They didn't know what was going on up there," he laughed. "To the world, you're still a dead man."

The elevator opened again as the rest of the party arrived.

Silas took on a stern expression as Ben approached.

"What's this about news from Mexico?" he asked.

"Oh yeah," Ben responded. "It was slow to get going, but the reports are all about how four guys took down an entire cartel."

"This is news everywhere?" Jon asked.

"Yeah," Ben told him. "It was a big deal...still is really."

Jon motioned for Ben to follow him and they stepped to a dark corner.

"I've still got one task we needed to complete," Jon told him.

Then asking Ben to get a fresh cell phone and a voice distortion device, he added, "Set caller ID to read 'Franz' on the other end."

Silas thought about just what to say while Ben got the equipment. *I need him to react, but not panic,* he told himself.

Ben walked up and handed him the phone with the added box attached. Dialing the number Ben had retrieved from the unknown caller in Greer's office; Silas leaned back and waited as the phone began to ring.

A man's shaky voice answered on the tenth ring. "What the hell is this?" it swore.

"I have your stuff," is all Silas said to him before hanging up. He looked at Ben without emotion.

"I hope that'll do it," he muttered.

At the jail George Vincent also received a call as he was being released.

"George," the mortified mayor of Dalton said. "I was just honoring a request from a powerful colleague," the man begged for understanding. "He was certain Crane was alive... and involved in the bombing at his building last week."

George could feel everything he wanted to say backing up inside him, but instead he simply offered this notice, "We'll see you at the polls...next election, Mr. Mayor."

With that he hung up and followed the smiling Gil Gartner out of the jailhouse.

George went by his office for a few minutes, gathered some papers, and then was driven to the mansion by Gartner.

The area was clear when they arrived. One local Dalton police unit passed them as it was leaving the area.

The blade tips of the Lucy Too stuck out over the ridge high on their right. George smiled and nodded as Gil turned up the driveway.

~

In a banquet room in Kansas City, a large man closed his phone and felt his color go flush with anger.

"Everything alright, Mr. Mayor?" his neighbor at the table asked.

"Yeah," he answered tersely. "Something's come up, that's all." He stood, looking around the room for his aide. The man came running.

"What do you need, sir?" the man implored him.

"Call the airport and have my plane ready," he ordered. "I need to get home...now."

Walking out through a side door, Rigby dialed a number on his cell phone.

"Charles," he said when it was answered. "Pick me up at O'Hare in about an hour and a half. Keep this quiet...just you and the car, got it?"

"Yes, sir," the voice on the other end responded.

76

In North Georgia, the sunset brought only a fall chill to the air. Silas cornered Tim and Murray away from the others and asked them about their trip.

"We haven't had a chance to catch up," he said. "How did it go in Duluth?"

Tim and Murray looked at each other and Spiegel smiled, turned to Jon, and answered, "Good as could be expected, I suppose."

"What does that mean?"

Murray spoke up, "Juan says 'Hi'", he added but nothing more.

"What... happened?" Silas tried again.

The next silence was interrupted by a news monitor across the room. The report was a local news station from Duluth, Minnesota. Ben was monitoring all locations of interest to the team.

"Two merchant marine captains were found shot and frozen to death in a snow bank outside a Duluth bar this evening." the first report said. "The men were missing from their ships for the full day until search dogs finally dug into the snow. They were bound and appeared to have been robbed."

Silas stared at Murray as he moved closer to the screen.

"What did you guys do?" he insisted.

"It all happened really quick," Murray began. Then Tim Spiegel broke in.

"These weren't easy-going, regular, law-abiding fellas, Jon," he explained.

"Why didn't you say something before now?" Silas demanded.

"Like you said, we didn't exactly have the opportunity to talk about it, Jon."

Murray followed Silas and stood next to his friend. "The ride down here, you weren't with us... and then in the copter...hell, we were all busy with those plans."

"What happened?" The question from Silas was now more an order than a request.

"We saw them coming out of that bar," Murray told. "Tim flashed his NCIS badge and tried to arrest them... They weren't having it."

Silas stayed quiet, waiting for the rest of the story.

"One of them pulled a gun and shot at Westy who was only a couple of feet from him," Tim had picked up the tale. "The round bounced off the suit and hit the other captain in the throat."

"I didn't even feel it," Duray added casually.

"Murray grabbed the gun...they struggled and it went off again." Tim then rubbed his chin indicating he was finished.

"You buried them in the snow?" Silas followed up. "Why not just tell the authorities?"

"We didn't have time for all that, Jon," Murray explained. "They were dead and we had to get to Alabama."

Rain continued to fall in Chicago as the sun eased its way west. Jordan Sterns sat in the small café near the mayor's office. His view of the surrounding area was well lit and expansive. It was still over three hours till his flight left for home, so he pushed back in the padded chair and slowly scanned the streets.

"More coffee, sir," the young server asked.

"Sure," he responded. "And could I get a fresh cup?" The one he'd been using the last hour showed signs of sediments building up.

The girl nodded and stepped away. Looking back toward LaSalle Street, Sterns noticed a small car pull up. A man in chauffer's attire climbed from it and walked quickly to a limo that was parked in front. The large vehicle roared to life and sped away.

Now what could that be all about? Sterns wondered.

~

Alabama meant the goat farm. Silas didn't really want to talk about the goat farm in front of everyone...especially Cheryl.

"That went better, right?" he asked hopefully.

There was no response for nearly a full minute. Weston Duray walked over and spoke up.

"You ever been attacked with an axe?" he asked.

Silas said nothing. He did rub his forehead with his fingertips, waiting for more.

The room remained silent so Duray continued, "Well, it changes everything real fast, I'll tell you that much."

Trying to keep the conversation limited, Silas looked up and asked softly, "So...he's dead, too?" His three brothers-in-arms stood in total silence which amounted to the answer.

Duray took Jon by the arm and led him away from the group. Murray and Spiegel followed.

"Listen to me," Duray said sternly. "I wanted to talk to that guy, that damned butcher. I really wanted to talk to him."

Murray leaned in, "We crawled into that slaughter room to check the blood on the slabs and the saw blades." He glanced at the others, but they let him finish that part of the story. "It tested positive as 'human' in several areas," he disclosed.

Tim reached for his pocket camera and offered, "I found a storage building full of Igloo coolers." The look on his face indicated everyone should know what that meant. "And a collection of various types of dry ice making equipment," he added and opened his camera and showed Jon the pictures. "We had the evidence we came for, but then everything went crazy when Smyden rushed at us with an axe."

It became quiet again and Silas turned his glare toward the floor. They could tell he understood their predicament.

"It was a freakish accident," Duray picked up the story, "I just ducked a swing of the axe, and Tim pushed the jerk away..."

"Smyden tripped," Murray interrupted. "And fell onto this large saw table."

Tim jumped back into the conversation, "His axe went flying across the room. It hit the wall and a "start" button for the blade." He paused to see if anyone else wanted to tell the last part, but they left it to him. "The damned blade swung down and caught Symden diagonally...right across his chest."

"It was a real mess," Murray added. "We just left it like it was."

Silas looked around the room and caught the disapproving glare Marsha was giving him. He could read her mind, but still knew he would hear it, first hand, later.

The evening continued though the mood was somewhat tempered by the realities of what had happened. The news reports continued to come in, some did not.

What was not reported was that Captain Jurden Walcovitz, of the Cordova Queen, heard the report and the names of his friends. The coincidence so frightened him that he dove from the deck of his ship into Lake Erie. Several of his crew saw him go over, the body was not found.

An obscure local headline from Alabama showed up on one of the screens.

"A local goat farmer, Kurt Smyden of Russellville," the reporter read, "died sometime yesterday in an industrial accident at his farm. Equipment used to dismember slaughtered goats apparently malfunctioned and Smyden was pulled into a cutter with no one else nearby. He was fifty-eight years old."

Silas looked over at Murray who simply shrugged his shoulders.

77

Walter Greer had spent the day in his apartment in Cicero, an urban community south of the city. His mind had gone through every level of fear, leaving paranoia in its wake of emotions. His terror now all but paralyzed him.

That man said he would kill me...in my own office, he thought. *An assassin, the one even Rigby is scared to death of.*

Isolated from the outside world, he wasn't aware of the unfolding events in Georgia. He had no TV or radio on. Greer didn't want any news. He wanted everything to go away. Then his cascading thoughts would turn to the boss, his mayor, and how the man needed him. That would lift his spirits, if only for a minute.

Walter Greer stood at his window looking at the rain.

"We'll rebuild it all," he muttered under his breathe. "He'll need me to do that. There's no way he'll risk exposing himself. The mayor needs what I do."

His rationalization worked to pull him together. For the first time that afternoon, Greer smiled.

Then the ringing sound began from behind him. At first he didn't realize what it was. He turned from the window and stared into the room. The chimes echoed again.

"My phone," he snapped back into sanity. "It's Rigby."

~

The celebratory mood in Dalton was muted by the unknown. Silas was clearly holding back, expecting news of some sort, but he wouldn't discuss it. He and the men stayed downstairs, the ladies and Cheryl had gone to see about some food.

"Don't leave the house yet, please," Silas had warned.

One of the monitors came on with a local report from Richmond, Virginia. Silas and the guys perked up and moved closer to hear.

"Authorities in Berea announced the arrest tonight of Wilbur Harkness of Sandgap, Kentucky, and four employees of his small farm located in the foothills outside the quiet college town.

Details of the charges against these men have not been released but appear to have a possible connection to the arrest of a Duluth, Minnesota, man, Renio Petteri, following a car chase on Highway 421 this afternoon."

The reporter looked over his copy as though something was missing and then stared into the camera. "That's all we have at the moment, folks. If anything more comes of this will let you know...back to you, Peter."

Murray was the first to speak after the report.

"Swanson really has a lid on that," he half-laughed. "Two vans shot all to pieces and no mention of it...wow!"

"She knows this has to stay under wraps for a few more hours, anyway," Silas commented and looked toward Ben.

"No mention of Kinkaid and his pal?" Duray asked.

"She shipped them down to Tennessee," Silas told him. "I don't know how they plan to release that."

"All this," Murray commented, "just to try and trip up Franz."

"Tell me," Silas asked Ben, "was that strictly local news in Kentucky?"

Ben checked the feed and replied, "Yeah, Richmond, Kentucky, local station."

~

Climbing from his private jet, Mayor Reginald Rigby waited for his call to be answered.

Walter Greer did so with one quivering word, "Yes?"

"Meet me at the office in thirty minutes." Rigby ordered.

"The office?" Greer nearly froze at the suggestion. "I can't go there... not now. He said he'd kill me...and that time has run out."

"Don't argue. I don't have time for your silliness. Park in the back lot and use the rear elevator. Be there in thirty minutes."

With that the mayor hung up and closed the door on his limo.

"The office, quickly," he told the driver. "Take me to the rear entrance of the building."

~

The elevator on the second floor sub-level opened and Marsha stepped out.

"We've got pizza upstairs," she hollered.

Everyone except Silas and Ben headed toward the elevator.

"You're not hungry?" she asked, walking over and putting her hand on Jon's shoulder.

"I want to monitor these things for a while yet," he pointed at the screens. "You go ahead."

Marsha looked at Ben and without words requested some privacy for her and Jon. Ben stood and moved to the far side of the room.

"You had a call earlier," she told Jon, "From Doctor Adams."

Silas didn't react. But she knew he understood.

"He says it's time to do that surgery on your scar," she said leaning down into his face. "He thinks he can make it much better."

"I'm busy right now, Marsha."

"I know you better than that," she challenged him. "You're not saying it, but this mess is done with...or it isn't gonna be."

With still no reaction from him, she moved herself directly in line with his face. Nearly nose to nose she went on, "I know you...I can tell by the way you're acting."

Tilting into her gaze, Silas smiled.

"Okay..." he said reluctantly. "We'll talk about it in the morning."

"He can do it next week down at Emory in Atlanta. You'll be checked in as Fredrick Hanson of Decatur, Georgia.

"Sounds like you've already told him 'yes' then"

"You need to get it done," she smiled. As she walked away with her victory, Marsha looked back at him.

"I know it hurts you like it is," she told him.

78

Jordan Sterns noticed the limo as it turned the corner and proceeded to drive to the back of the building.

"That's odd," he thought out loud and waved for the server to bring his check.

He opened the door of the coffee shop as another car, stopped by the red light, caught his eye. Inside, tapping nervously on the steering wheel, was Walter Greer.

Sterns stood still in the doorway and watched the man drive behind the large building and disappear.

Walking into the rear parking lot, Sterns looked for a door into the building. The only one he found was locked.

~

He paused as the doors opened. Walter Greer did not like elevators, but from this level he had no choice. He stepped out at the fourth floor and turned the corner. There was no sign of the mayor, but his office lights were clearly on.

He passed his own office at first, but he could not help taking a moment to check it just to be sure. He unlocked the door and reached in, flipping the light switch on. Then he heard the voice down the hall.

"You've led him to us, you fool!" the mayor screamed at him.

Pulling his door closed, Walter Greer nearly ran to his mentor.

"What the hell do you mean?" he begged.

"He may well have my files, damn it."

"Whaaa...what files?" Greer asked in a trembling voice, "who?"

415

Reginald Rigby glared at him in return. "Shut-up and be quiet," he said dismissively and turned back into his office suite.

Everything in the outer area appeared to be in order, so he proceeded to his private office door. As he turned the knob, he turned back to Greer.

"You go in first," the mayor pushed the door open and stepped away.

A pale Walter Greer followed his instruction. He found the light switch and shed light on the private office. Greer looked back to the door as Rigby first stuck his head in and then straightened up to stride inside.

"Go to the elevator," he ordered the shaking man. "Let me know if anyone comes this way."

Greer nodded with meek obedience and went up the hallway. He passed his own office and did not notice the lights were still on. At the elevators, Greer leaned against the opposite wall for support and kept his eyes glued to the floor indicator above the doors.

Back in his office, Mayor Rigby sat at the huge desk and immediately pulled the center drawers open. Everything appeared as he had left it. He started to reach for the secret release, but stopped short. His eyes squinted and he leaned back into the big chair.

All the studies he had read of "the Son" indicated the assassin used booby-traps. Rigby's eyes now grew wide and then wider.

He stared at the drawer, looking for any mark or smudge. There was nothing visible.

It could be rigged with something, he thought. His now shaking fingers unconsciously went to his lips as he considered what to do next.

~

Ben hurried back across the second level workshop to the monitors near Jon and Marsha.

"You need to see this," he said excitedly.

After adjusting the setting, the screen showed a report from a Knoxville station that was being carried nationally.

"The cause of death has not been released for either man," the reporter said in progress, "but local authorities in La Follett tell Eyewitness News that the hunt for former Mississippi congressman, Clyde Kinkaid and his longtime aide Marvin Acree is over. The bodies of the men, accused of the murder of a Tennessee Highway Patrolman, have been found near the Cumberland Mountains town."

Silas looked at his watch.

"That was a good twelve hours she bought us," he said speaking of Colonel Swanson. "I just hope it was enough."

Marsha again caught the slightest look of apprehension on his face.

"What are you waiting for?" she asked softly.

"We have to be patient," he told her.

The elevator opened and Murray and Tim Spiegel rushed out. Noticing that those there were watching the report, Murray slowed his pace and shouted out, "Swanson knew what she was doing, huh?"

"And that Colonel Gruen is a stand-up guy," Tim added with a big smile.

Calmly turning his chair to them, Silas smiled.

"Yeah. So far...so good." he nodded his approval.

~

Jordan Sterns walked the exterior of the building looking for a way in. On the far side, near a mounted fire-escape, he made out an upper window sash, pulled down about three inches.

That's not locked, he told himself excitedly.

The fire escape's lower ladder was drawn up, just out of reach. He found a wooden pallet laying several feet away. Sterns dragged it to the brick wall below the fire escape and leaned it against the bricks.

A foothold in the pallet, about half-way up, gave him enough height and leverage to reach the spring loaded ladder.

Five minutes later, Sterns was in the building.

~

Mayor Rigby pushed back his chair, stood and began pacing the room. His head moved rapidly looking at each piece of furniture, every item in the office, anything that might offer an idea of what to do. Then he stopped, staring at his easel with the three foot by four foot paper pad.

"That's it," he said out loud and launched himself toward a credenza.

From a top drawer, he pulled a long, expandable pointer used in meetings and presentations. Pulling it to its full three foot length, he paused again. Across the room, a fluffy pillow lay on the sofa. Rigby grabbed it and returned to the area behind his desk.

With the pillow over his face, he paused for a second and then reached out to the release button with his pointer. The sliding drawer popped open. Rigby winced as the plastic flash drive fell out, but nothing else happened. He nudged the flash drive with the pointer, still nothing. His immediate thought was to almost laugh.

"He's pulling my leg," the man said out loud and then realized the need to stay quiet.

The jerk knows nothing, his mind rejoiced. *He was bluffing.*

He picked up the device and studied it carefully. His joy became overcome by paranoia.

What if he swapped it for a different one?

On its back side, Rigby had made three small scratches in the plastic housing. Markings he could use at times like this. They were there, but his guilty mind wasn't finished with him yet.

What if it has been tampered with? Maybe he erased it.

Rigby jumped up and went to the nearest computer, in the outer office.

79

Silas sat in the midst of his friends, yet his mind was in its own world. He played over and over the events of earlier that afternoon.

Sitting at the mayor of Chicago's desk he remembered what Daniel had said. From those thoughts, a new plan came to him. He took the flash drive back into the outer office.

Looking through the desk there, he found a box with several new flash drives, still wrapped in their packaging. Silas made a copy of the files and quickly realized there was more there than just the kidnapping operation. The syndicate this man was involved with was vast and far-reaching. The list of those who extend, and looked for, the "welcome mat" was long and international.

If the law starts going after these people because of this information, most will get away, he thought and pondered a solution.

After making the total copy for himself, Silas erased all but the kidnapping files from the original flash drive. He then sat down at a nearby table, to study the drive's housing.

Looking at his watch again, Silas' thoughts returned to the present time. Murray and Spiegel were toasting each other with lite beers while Phil, Weston, and Harold appeared caught up in their own conversation. His team had done well...and his secret was secure.

They're proud of what they've accomplished, he reminded himself. *I just hope that accomplishment is complete.*

Silas rubbed a hand over his pants pocket. The flash drive copy was there. *It's been three hours since I called him. If this is gonna work... it should be any time now.*

~

Jordan Sterns was at first disoriented by the layout of the second floor. The walls were in different locations and he appeared to be in a private office of some type.

Finding an "exit" sign at the end of a hall, he took those stairs down to the main lobby.

The interior lights illuminated the empty space and he could see the elevators on the far side. Not wanting to risk being noticed, he slid along the wall to a spot in the shadows. There he crossed and pushed the elevator "up" button.

The signal above the doors showed the unit was on "four" and had started coming down.

~

The elevator's floor indicator came on and Walter Greer stopped breathing. As the indicator moved down, he pictured the man who had threatened him. The lights stopped on "One" for a minute, then began tracking upward again. Greer's eyes began to blink uncontrollably. He heard his own mind screaming at him,

GO!

Greer ran toward the door of the mayor's office, but noticed his own office's lights on. Hurriedly, he keyed the already unlocked door to get inside. Slapping the switch, he turned the lights off.

Then he heard the elevator opening.

Panicked, he closed his door and stood silently behind it. Through the frosted glass, Greer watched a figure pause at his door and then move on to the office with the lights on, the mayor's office.

421

~

As he stepped off the elevator on the fourth floor, Jordan Sterns looked around and then turned the corner to the main hall. Light from the mayor's office caught his eye. He stopped for a second in front of Greer's office, but decided to check out the lights further down.

He twisted the knob on the door to the mayor's suite and pushed it. As it swung open a slight bitter smell exhausted passed him. Sterns shook his head and waved a hand in front of his face until the smell seemed to dissipate.

From where he stood, he could see a man slumped in a chair. Sterns cautiously stepped inside. Taking a pulse wasn't necessary, the man was clearly dead. The body was lying sideways in the chair and draped across a table in front of a computer terminal. The computer was running.

Sterns' police instincts kicked in and he backed out of the office, touching nothing but leaving the door open. His presence would be difficult to explain if even possible. He had to leave but could not do so without reporting what he'd found.

Remembering a guard station, further toward the front end of the building, Sterns quickly walked further down the hall and around the corner. The guard desk was unoccupied.

He took out his handkerchief and picked up the desk phone there. Dialing 911, Sterns spoke through his fingers to muffle his voice. Reporting a man's body in an office on the fourth floor, he offered no other details.

Sterns wiped the phone and laid it down. He then headed back the way he had come, toward the elevators.

~

Ben was waving his arms, trying to get everyone's attention, "There's more yet," he said pointing to the TV. "This is national news," he added.

The report was in progress...

"Larry Gibbons, of Philadelphia, was arrested this afternoon on kidnapping charges and violations of the 'Mann Act.'"

"What was the beginning of the story, Ben?" Westy asked.

"They tied him to the farm and Harkness. Nothing about the girls directly, but it's clear they know about the kidnapping ring."

Murray rubbed his forehead and laughed to cover his disgust. "I can't believe these people existed," he said loudly. "And that Franz guy...the leader, goes Scott free."

Jon again checked his watch. Phil Stone caught him that time.

~

Greer's mind and body were in complete lock-down for several minutes after the figure passed his door. He had reflexively stepped backwards to the edge of his desk. The warm feeling that ran down his leg brought some of his senses back to him. His fear had caused a total loss of bladder control.

Shaking the offending leg, Greer stepped toward the door leaving a small puddle on the floor. There was no time for embarrassment. He put that out of his mind before cautiously opening the door and glancing down the hall. No one was in sight, but he could tell the door to the mayor's main area was standing open.

Walter Greer stuck his head into the mayor's office area and saw the man lying dead in the chair. He looked around the room and saw nothing out of the way. His body now quaking in fear, he hit the light switch and stepped back into the hallway, pulling the door closed.

Two steps back toward his own office, a shadow from behind raced down the wall and caught his eye. He looked over his left shoulder as a figure turned the corner and came his way.

"It's him!" he screamed more mentally than verbally and raced toward his own office. Sterns froze initially, watching the man run.

My gun, Greer thought. *I have to get to my gun.*

He kept a handgun in his credenza drawer next to the window. Racing to it in the dark, the frightened man tripped on a throw rug, bounced off the edge of his desk and slipping on the wet spot, went headlong into the lower sash of the window.

As his body slid down, a broken pane took out his jugular. Death was messy, but quick.

80

Sandhills Community College of Pinehurst, North Carolina, was on an extended break. Renovations to the main dining hall had broken a water line that went undiscovered for several days. The water eroded foundation areas and created sinkholes in too many sites on the campus. Students were on "break" and a fortunate few had chosen to go to the Caribbean. The group split between Aruba and Curacao.

Joyce Elsworth had found the Hook Huttery on Curacao to be her hangout of choice. This Sunday evening she sat alone at the bar, nursing one Goombay Smash rum tallboy after the other. It was her first night there but the second night of the stakeout.

The hour grew late and Joyce had just ordered a fresh drink when she jumped down from her seat and strolled to the rest room. Her napkin lay over the top of the glass, indicating she would be back.

A man glanced around from his perch across the bar and suddenly moved toward her drink. The napkin was slid away and a handful of powder went in. A quick stir, while again looking around the room, and the napkin went back into position.

~

In Chicago, Jordan Sterns got to Greer's now open door and could see nothing in the dark. He knew the man had gone in there and he'd heard the noise, yet the room was now totally quiet.

He found a switch and turned on the lights. The scene before him was surreal. Greer's body hung through the broken glass, blood running down both sides of the window. There was nothing Sterns could do other than get out of there. "And fast," he reminded himself.

425

He had already reported the other body. The local cops would be there any minute. He had to move quickly.

He carefully wiped down the door knobs in both offices and any other areas he remembered touching. He then opened the elevator, wiped the internal buttons and let it go to the main floor. He found the stair case door and used that exit to reach the second floor. From there he left the building as he had come in.

Sterns walked several blocks trying to make sense of what had happened. There would be no answers to his questions now. All he could do was go home.

Sterns hailed a cab to take him to the airport. He still had two hours and twenty minutes before his flight.

I'll just wait at the terminal, he thought, shaking his head.

As he started to move from the stool at the Hook Huttery bar, the man who had "bothered" Joyce Elsworth's drink was bumped into, rather hard, by another man. The collision knocked over the drink, spilling its entire contents.

"Oh, excuse me, mate," the intruder told him. "Looks like I messed up your plan, hey?"

The jostled man gave him a harsh glare, a shove and tried to walk away.

"Oh now...hold on," the intruder told him. "Was that your drink there?"

"What's it to you?" the man demanded and again tried to pull away.

"Oh, it's plenty to me, Frank," he answered and watched the man now grow panicky. "I've got a few pictures here, showing you messing with that drink...it must be yours right?"

"How do you know my name?" Fogerty spit as he spoke. "Who are you?"

"Me? Oh, I'm Luke Diaz, my friend. I know all about you and the men you work for. I've got some people who want to talk to you."

With that Fogerty dropped to the floor trying to get away and came up swinging.

Luke caught the man's arm and twisted it around, flattening him on the bar. Local authorities came up and took custody of Frank Fogerty.

"Here's your kidnapper, gentlemen. He's been working this region for years."

"Where did you learn about this?" the officer challenged.

"Friends in high places," Luke told him. "That's all I can tell you. You can verify it," he said handing the officer his pocket camera. "These pictures should help."

"High places, huh?"

"Very," Luke smiled. "Keep an eye on the news for the next few days. You're now part of it."

The officer pointed for his men to escort Fogerty out.

"Do me one favor will you?" Luke asked him.

The leader of the group stopped and asked what that would be.

"Keep this quiet for twenty-four hours... please. Those friends I mentioned are cleaning up the other end of this mess. They need about that much time... if you would."

The officer nodded and tossed the small camera Luke had given him in his hand. "This better pan out," he warned.

"Oh...it will. There's one other thing, Officer," Diaz added. "You might want your guys to check out a small ship, the 'Island Mercy' out of the Virgin Islands. It's part of this mess."

They escorted Franklin Fogerty out as Joyce returned looking totally confused. Diaz laid a five dollar bill on the bar and told her, "Your drink got spilled, missy. Have another on me."

~

By leaving the lights on in Greer's office, the responders to his 911 call went to that office. They processed the grisly scene and loaded the body. Local news outlets were informed.

It would be nearly an hour later that Mayor Rigby was found.

It would be even longer, weeks as it turned out, until Sterns would learn just what all had happened that night.

81

Still looking as anxious as anyone had ever seen him, Silas remained almost sullen as those around him celebrated.

The report was national, but barely so. It made the big time news because of the bombing at the building earlier. Ben cranked it up on all the monitors and held his hands up for quiet.

"This just in..." the bright banner and loud voice proclaimed. "An Associate Police Commissioner, whose office was bombed in an attack on him earlier this month was found dead in city hall this evening."

Everyone in the second level sub-basement looked around at each other.

"Walter Greer," the report went on, "apparently fell through the fourth floor window of his temporary office in that building. No details were given, but witnesses on the scene say the body was partially out the window. Broken glass, cutting Greer's neck, appears to be the cause of death. How this happened is completely unknown at this time."

Silas sat as though stunned. He said not a word, but his eyebrows furrowed and his hand went to his chin. This wasn't what he expected at all. But in their celebration, no one there seemed to notice.

"Well...that takes care of 'Franz'," Murray declared. "Greer was him... we all know it."

The Durays hugged in silence.

Phil Stone grabbed Sara's hand and squeezed gently.

Ben stared at Cheryl as she stood with her parents. His heart filled with relief for her... and something more.

Harold Foster and George Vincent tapped beer mugs.

Tim Spiegel slapped his hands together. "What's that they say about 'Karma'?" he yelled out loud.

Silas stood deliberately and spoke slowly. All eyes turned to him. He was not smiling.

"Greer was the man behind the curtain, that's for sure," he said convincingly. Then continued with authority, "But the curtain only hid the voice." He moved closer to them and the group encompassed him to listen.

"That voice wasn't from the wizard," he declared. "It was only a puppet, given words from a silent, more sinister master."

He paused and looked around, but no one interrupted

"This master," he went on, "the real wizard, is much more sophisticated, more concealed."

Tim Spiegel saw where Jon was going with his speech.

"Oh, come on, Jon." he half laughed. "It was Greer for sure."

"Pay no attention to the man behind the curtain, Tim." Silas smiled coldly and chided him. "Time will tell."

"I know...you think the Chicago mayor is involved," Spiegel joked back. "Where is he anyway?"

"They say he's at some conference in Kansas City, Kansas," Ben muttered while glancing at Jon.

The TV news subsided and the room grew almost quiet. Everyone settled down into smaller conversations except for Jon. He stood, staring at the TV set as though it had let him down.

Rita Duray's voice broke the silence as she talked of plans to go home.

"It should be safe, now," Westy surmised. He smiled and nodded towards her in agreement.

"There'll be a truck load of questions when you get there," Murray advised him. "Been there...done that."

"Our friends are pretty good about offering shelter from that kind of stuff," Rita Duray said confidently. Her husband nodded once again.

Cheryl looked down and then mumbled she wanted Ben to come visit.

"I'm needed here," he told her meekly, "as you've seen."

Silas didn't plan to get into that discussion, but couldn't help himself.

"I think some time away might do you good," he told Ben putting an arm around his neck. "You should go. We'll see if Harold can take you guys."

Raising his glass, the G5 pilot grinned and nodded affirmatively.

82

Murray's cell phone rang. He stepped to a quieter corner of the area to hear it better. The call only lasted two minutes, but it put a huge grin on the cowboy's face.

"Luke did it," he yelled, holding his phone high. "That was him. They caught Fogerty red-handed and the local cops down there are seizing the boat."

"When did you call Luke?" Spiegel asked.

"Saturday morning, before we left for Duluth," he answered beaming.

Silas nodded approval and managed a smile.

"Good job," he said to his friend. "Great thinking."

Then Ben hollered from across the room, "Hey, there's another report coming on."

A national TV reporter had broken in with a major headline. "Breaking news...Reginald Rigby, the Mayor of Chicago, seen earlier this evening at the Mayor's Conference in Kansas City, has been found dead in his private offices in downtown Chicago."

The report showed scenes of the building, with construction scaffolding now surrounded by police and emergency vehicles.

"This is quite the mystery," the news reader continued, his voice thick with fake concern, "with it being the second major death in that building tonight and the fact that the mayor was just seen in another state only a few hours ago."

The report went on but didn't seem to connect the two stories. "The earlier death of Associate Police Commissioner Walter Greer is what led investigators to the building and is oddly responsible for the discovery of the mayor's body."

Everyone in the second sub-level basement turned and stared at Silas. His eyes were locked on the television.

The report continued, "The Mayor was found at a computer terminal in the outer office of his suite. The initial cause of death is reportedly a heart attack, but that is not confirmed."

The reporter suddenly appeared stunned. He looked up at the camera with a calculated pause before he continued reading.

"The computer screen is said to... again by witness accounts..." he looked up at the camera cautioning the audience, "this is not confirmed."

The reporter again tried his best to fain shock and remorse. "These files... from a flash drive appear to implicate the Mayor, Reginald Rigby himself, in a massive plot to kidnap young women."

Pretending to be reading from papers in his hands, the reporter looked again at the teleprompter and continued.

"Names and locations found on the files are already being investigated by the FBI and," the TV newsman stopped and looked to his left. "Is this right?" he asked someone off camera. His reaction to the unheard response was not understated in the least.

Staring back at his audience, the newsreader laid his papers down and added, "Interpol."

With a stern look now, he pretended to be adlibbing, "Yes, ladies and gentlemen, this appears to be an International, white slavery ring, broken up tonight...in our fair city." Another extended pause was followed with, "Back to you, Carl."

When the report was over, the silence in the second floor work area was intense. Dalton mansion had the feel of a vacuum.

Slowly, each one there turned again to look at Jon.

"So... the Feds have everything?" Tim half-way asked.

Without looking up, Silas answered him. "Not quite everything."

~

After making a complete copy, Silas had managed to pry open the housing of the flash drive and found the interior to be quite roomy. The top of the housing had a small window which allowed light from an LED to shine through vapor thin material. This had no use other than to tell the user, his device was "thinking."

Cutting tiny slots into the shear, light covering plastic was delicate work, but left no readily visible signs.

The USB male plug was exposed by pushing the housing onto the computer's female connector. Silas positioned his vile next to the sheer LED window and in the way of the sliding retractable USB cover. When pushed into the computer's USB slot, the vial would rupture and spray its deadly mist.

Silas carefully wiped the flash drive and the unit was then replaced where he had found it. The copy was in Silas' pocket.

~

"What do you mean...not everything?" Tim asked Jon.

Silas acted as though he was ignoring them. He did return a smile from Marsha and finally stood from his chair. Silas walked toward the elevator as the others followed.

"Whoa now," Murray exclaimed. "What did you find on him?" The cowboy's look became a wry smile. "And heck... he's been in Kansas for three days."

"Yeah...you went to Chicago, but he was in Kansas." Phil Stone had a quizzical look about him. "That's another story you owe me, Jon."

Silas laughed slightly at that. They couldn't see it as he walked away, but they heard his reaction.

"Yeah...How about all that, Jon?" Murray grinned, challenging him. "You in Chicago and that mayor down in Kansas...and then you're here and he's in Chicago. What's up with that?"

The others followed Silas with their eyes until he turned and stared right at Ben, tossing a flash drive to him.

"You know what to do with this," he said.

Then Jon paused and looked at each one there... with the respect he felt for them warming his heart. He said nothing, only smiling at the group he proudly thought of as his friends.

"Come on, Jon," Murray tried again. "You've got to tell us about the mayor. How...what did you do?"

"I don't recall saying, 'I did' anything," Silas said flatly.

As the door to his elevator opened, Jon smiled ever so slightly. He turned to step inside the lift and Marsha joined him. The question of the mayor still hung in the air. Tim Spiegel tried... one more time.

"Come on...," he pleaded. "How 'bout a hint...at least?"

Marsha tapped Jon's chest with her fist, prodding him to give them something. Smiling directly into her eyes, he said loud enough for all to hear, "Well... the wizard's not in Kansas anymore."

"The public cannot be too curious concerning the characters of public men."

Samuel Adams - 1775

Coming soon......

Eight of Six

Silas' toughest challenge

Now available...

by Doug Dahlgren

The SON Series

The SON Silas Rising

The Only Constant

The Basics of Fundamentals

And...

The Story of a Tragedy that Should Never happen

It Was Thursday

www.dougdahlgren.com